PRAISE FOR ANGIE HOCKMAN'S
"SPARKLING DEBUT"
(*ENTERTAINMENT WEEKLY*)

Shipped

"A divine enemies-to-lovers tale set against the backdrop of snorkeling with sea lions and hikes ending in breathtaking ocean vistas. . . . It's as sunny and inviting as its tropical vacation setting, one of those books that makes the heart swell with joy. If readers crave an escape, it certainly offers one, but it also feels poignantly real. *Shipped* is a literary vacation I never wanted to end. Grade: A."

—*Entertainment Weekly*

"Newcomer Hockman creates a paradise in the sunny and distinct Galápagos setting, educating readers on the wildlife of the islands and the conservation efforts that become a powerful part of the story. For fans of Helen Hoang and Sophie Kinsella, this charming romp at sea will make readers wish to stay with the characters well after the story's end."

—*Library Journal*

"An extraordinary debut. Witty, romantic, and completely addictive."
—Lauren Layne, *New York Times* bestselling
author of *Made in Manhattan*

"A healthy dose of competition powers Hockman's laugh-out-loud debut about love on the high seas. . . . With flawed but lovable characters and exotic locales, this quirky, thoughtful love story will whisk readers away."

—*Publishers Weekly*

"Close quarters, high seas, and dreamy destinations provide the backdrop for this battle of the sexes. . . . Like a tropical cocktail . . . [it] goes down easy."

—*Kirkus Reviews*

"A classic enemies-to-lovers tale . . . smart, swoony."

—*USA Today*

"A funny, smart, and easygoing story, this book was a fresh breath of air and a must-read for all romance lovers. Beautiful settings, a mix between *The Unhoneymooners* and any other recent office romance stories, this book will keep you invested from the beginning to the end."

—*BookBub*

"Witty, charming as hell, and layered with real passion for ecotourism, *Shipped* is a sparkling debut. The perfect slice of vacation in book form."

—Rosie Danan, author of *The Intimacy Experiment*

"[An] utterly charming, perfect-for-warm-weather romance novel."
—*Real Simple*

"Hilarious and sexy."

—*PopSugar*

"Angie Hockman's *Shipped* is the rom-com beach read you've been waiting for."

—*Insider*

"Hockman's debut is smart, witty, and charming, with steamy on-page chemistry that will make you want to take a dip even in winter."
—*Vulture*

ALSO BY ANGIE HOCKMAN

Shipped

DREAM ON

A NOVEL

ANGIE HOCKMAN

G

GALLERY BOOKS

NEW YORK   LONDON   TORONTO
SYDNEY   NEW DELHI

G

Gallery Books
An Imprint of Simon & Schuster, Inc.
1230 Avenue of the Americas
New York, NY 10020

First Gallery Books trade paperback edition July 2022

GALLERY BOOKS and colophon are registered trademarks of Simon & Schuster, Inc.

For information about special discounts for bulk purchases, please contact Simon & Schuster Special Sales at 1-866-506-1949 or business@simonandschuster.com.

The Simon & Schuster Speakers Bureau can bring authors to your live event. For more information or to book an event, contact the Simon & Schuster Speakers Bureau at 1-866-248-3049 or visit our website at www.simonspeakers.com.

Interior design by Michelle Marchese

Manufactured in the United States of America

10 9 8 7 6 5 4 3 2 1

Library of Congress Cataloging-in-Publication Data

Names: Hockman, Angie, author.
Title: Dream on : a novel / Angie Hockman.
Description: First Gallery Books trade paperback edition. | New York : Gallery Books, 2022.
Identifiers: LCCN 2021055103 (print) | LCCN 2021055104 (ebook) | ISBN 9781982177577 (trade paperback) | ISBN 9781982177584 (ebook)
Subjects: GSAFD: Love stories.
Classification: LCC PS3608.O33 D74 2022 (print) | LCC PS3608.O33 (ebook) | DDC 813/.6—dc23
LC record available at https://lccn.loc.gov/2021055103
LC ebook record available at https://lccn.loc.gov/2021055104

ISBN 978-1-9821-7757-7
ISBN 978-1-9821-7758-4 (ebook)

For my two loves, Cooper and Jimmy.
And for Mom, whose lifelong love and support
has given me courage to try.

PROLOGUE

"Care for breakfast?" Devin's deep voice caresses my body, rumbling through the dark like the intoxicating purr of an engine.

I blink open my eyes and stretch my arms above my head until my knuckles brush the smooth headboard. Devin's smiling at me from beside the bed, dressed in the same fitted jeans and navy polo from last night. Soft morning light creeps through the hotel room's translucent curtains, casting his normally coal-brown hair in a mahogany glow.

"Are you referring to food or yourself?" I say. Curling onto my side to face him, I pull the crisp white sheet up to my chest.

The mattress dips as he sits next to me, dark eyes twinkling. "Take your pick." Brushing a lock of hair from my face, he presses his lips against mine in a lingering kiss. My chest expands, filling with joy until I'm sure it will crack.

After years of putting love on the back burner to focus on school and career, I can't believe I've *finally* found someone. We've only been together a few months—three, I think—but this is the real deal. I can sense our soul-deep connection in my marrow. I have that overwhelming *you-complete-me* feeling I'd only hoped I'd find with someone someday. And guess what? He feels the same way about me.

How in the world did I get so lucky?

Devin graces me with a heart-melting smile. "I brought your favorite." He reaches behind him, and from out of nowhere proffers a piece of strawberry-covered cheesecake on a gleaming white plate.

I grin as he hands it to me. "Dessert for breakfast? How decadent." I take a bite, and immediately wrinkle my nose. The taste is off. Rather than creamy, tart deliciousness, something stale and plasticky fills my mouth. I take another bite, just to be sure, and somehow manage to shove the fork down my throat. Pain sears my esophagus and the urge to gag overwhelms me. A burst of dazzling light fills the room, blurring Devin's edges like watercolors.

My heart beats faster. Something's not right.

Gripping the sheet, I tug it to my chin as I shrink against the pillows. Above me, the ceiling recedes into an endlessly blue sky. And it's filled with *flying kittens*. Tiny, feathered wings flap as they dip here and there, playing oversized violins like furry, fluffy cherubs. One of them, a tabby with green-golden eyes, winks at me as he draws his bow across the strings, causing a shower of effervescent sparks to rain down on Devin and me.

Welp . . . guess I'm dreaming. At least Devin's in my dream too, which means it's a Very Good Dream.

I realize now that my body feels like it's floating in the ocean; I'm in that twilight space between awake and asleep—aware that this is a dream, but still not quite conscious. This hotel room, the cheesecake: they're from the weekend trip to the lake that Devin surprised me with last month. Maybe if I don't think too hard about waking up, I'll stay asleep. Maybe I can make the dream change . . . call up another favorite memory . . .

A thick blanket of clouds passes overhead, but the sky is as bright as ever and I squint. A pair of strong arms snakes beneath me, lifting me against a firm, familiar chest. *Devin* . . .

"*Cassidy* . . ." A faint voice echoes from far away, no louder than a reverberation from a church bell. It's easy to ignore, so I do.

The dream shifts. I'm no longer lying in bed, but standing in the center of a dimly lit restaurant, clothed in a knee-length burgundy silk dress. Devin's wearing a white button-down with a red scarf, and we're dancing—just like on our first date. Soft music curls around us. I'm vaguely aware that people are staring, but I don't care. I cling to Devin so tightly my body melds with his and our souls tangle together. We're complete.

"*Cass, come back to us,*" a distant voice echoes, louder this time.

"Time to go." Devin's deep voice rumbles in his chest.

I sigh into his neck and grasp him tighter. "I want to stay here with you."

Gently disentangling himself from me, he steps back until he's an arm's length away. I smooth my dress over my stomach. Rather than lush, soft fabric, my gown is oddly thin and scratchy. I frown. A truck beeps somewhere in the distance, a steady, rhythmic sound. Devin takes my hand, but his palm is no longer rough. It's small and smooth, and long nails prick my skin.

"Cass . . ." he whispers, his form blurring.

"*Cass . . . can . . . hear me?*" says a higher-pitched voice.

The dream turns fuzzy. *No, not yet. I don't want to wake up.* But Devin's form swirls and dissolves like smoke.

I surface to consciousness like a creature emerging from the deep. I'm vaguely aware that I'm lying in a bed that's not mine, and something's beeping. An alarm clock? I open my eyes. A fluorescent light blinds me and I blink sluggishly. My eyelids are heavier than dumbbells. Someone squeezes my hand so hard it aches, and the blurry but familiar form of my best friend fills my vision. Her blond hair is pinned in a messy bun, her face a mask of concern. "Brie?" My voice is a raspy whisper and I cough.

"Oh my God, Cass! You're awake!" She squeezes my hand again. Behind her delicate, round gold glasses, her honey-brown eyes are as wide as hubcaps.

"Where am I?" I ask.

"In the hospital. You had an accident."

My vision clears, and I realize that I am, in fact, lying in a hospital bed, wearing a thin patterned gown with a stiff white blanket pulled up to my waist. A heart monitor beeps steadily from the corner. Brie's here, but where's Devin? He must have stepped out.

"Where—"

"Hold on. Mel . . . Melanie!" she shouts over her shoulder. Rapid footsteps approach and my mother appears beside Brie. Dark circles ring her eyes, and her normally shiny hair is limp. She's only forty-two—she had me at seventeen—but she looks at least fifty today. My stomach tightens as she smooths a lock of damp hair from my forehead. "Cass, is that you? Can you hear me?"

I clear my throat. "Yeah, Mom, I hear you. You're shouting." I attempt to scoot higher in bed, but pain blasts through every cell of my body and I wince.

"Shhh, don't try to move. You were in a car accident, honey. You've been in a coma. We weren't sure if you . . ." Mom's chest heaves and a sob rips through her. Oh God, Mom never cries. Brie curls an arm around her shoulder while she struggles to regain her normally unflappable composure.

Wait, a *coma*? The heart rate monitor beeps faster. "How long was I—"

"Out?" Brie finishes. Gnawing her lip, she takes a deep breath. "I don't know how to break it to you, but . . . the year is 2041, and the robots have taken over. I'm sorry. I hope you're ready for the apocalypse." Her lips twist in an obvious attempt to suppress a smile. I blink.

Mom slaps Brie's arm. "*Brielle Owens.*"

"What? The opportunity was too good to pass up. I couldn't help myself."

Warmth fills my chest. Brie's always known how to make me smile.

Mom shakes her head. "It's August 4. You've been out for six days."

I glance around the hospital room, at the blue vinyl chair pulled out into a bed in the corner, the open bag sitting on top of the twisted sheet, the lunch tray of half-eaten food on the rolling table. It looks like Mom, or Brie, or both, have been staying with me. Maybe they've been taking turns with Devin to visit. "Hey, can you—"

"Someone's up, I see." A rosy-faced nurse bustles into the room, and a swell of activity ensues. The nurse calls in a doctor, who examines me and asks what feels like a million questions. *Do you know your name? What year is it? Who's the president?* Half an hour later, a specialist arrives and introduces herself as Dr. Holloway, a neurologist. She studies my chart as the nurse inclines my bed.

"I could use some caffeine," announces Brie. "Can I get you a coffee, Mel?"

"Yes please. Two creams, one sugar. Thanks, Brie," says Mom.

"You got it. I'll be right back." She flashes me a reassuring smile as she leaves the room.

Adjusting her laptop, the doctor peers at me over her tortoise-shell glasses. "Tell me, Cass, what's the last thing you remember before waking up today?"

"I—" I cough, and Mom hands me a paper cup of ice chips. I slurp one into my mouth. The chilled liquid feels good against my abraded throat. Apparently I was on a ventilator until two days ago, when I began demonstrating bouts of wakefulness—of which I remember nothing—but my throat still feels like someone shoved a red-hot poker down there. "I remember taking the bar exam."

"Mmm-hmm. And what about after that?" the doctor asks.

I think back. I recall the last day of the two-day, soul-sucking exam, how I felt elated and exhausted when I left the test center in Columbus, and then . . . "Nothing."

She types for several long seconds before shutting the lid of the laptop. "The good news is it looks like there's no brain damage."

Across the room, my mother slumps in relief. "Oh, thank God."

"But she has a long road of recovery ahead. We were able to relieve the swelling on her brain with an emergency craniotomy, but it's possible she may experience lingering adverse effects."

I automatically finger the thick bandage behind my ear.

"What kind of adverse effects?" asks Mom.

"Possible trouble with coordination, short-term memory loss. We won't know until we run further tests. And with two cracked ribs and a fractured tibia, I'm recommending she be moved to a rehabilitation center . . ."

I close my eyes while the doctor explains my recovery plan. The back of my neck tingles, and a memory lumbers to the surface. "Wait," I say, opening my eyes. "I do remember something. Before driving home after the bar exam, I had dinner with Devin."

Mom frowns at me. "Who's Devin, honey?"

I blink. "You know, Devin Bloom. The guy I've been seeing."

"You didn't tell me you were seeing someone."

"I did, you've just been working too hard," I mumble. "So wait, he hasn't come to visit me?" Disappointment swells in my chest like a cresting wave.

"No one's been here except me, your stepdad, and your brothers. They came by yesterday after you were moved out of the ICU. And Brie, of course. She jumped in the car and drove up as soon as she heard about your accident."

Maybe the hospital only allowed family to visit? No, that couldn't be, because Brie's here and she's not family. *Wait.* Maybe Devin didn't even know I was in an accident. Panic constricts my lungs. I look around automatically for my phone, but it's not on the nightstand. "Where's my phone? I need to call Devin and tell him I'm okay. He must be worried sick."

Mom frowns. "Your phone was destroyed in the accident."

The door opens and Brie returns, holding two cups of coffee. She passes one to my mom and takes a sip from the other.

"Brie, can I borrow your phone? I need to call Devin."

She splutters. "Huh? Who now?"

I let out an exasperated huff. What the hell is wrong with everyone? "Come on, Brie. Devin, my boyfriend. We talk every week, so I know I've told you all about him." At her blank stare, I continue. "We met at a bar in April, hit it off, and we've been dating ever since? He grew up in Cleveland and he helps run his family's business? You haven't met him yet, but I'm sure you've seen pictures. He's six two, dark brown hair, brown eyes. You know—Devin Bloom."

Brie's cheeks pale as she slowly sets her coffee on the nightstand. The doctor looks between me, Brie, and my mother, opens her laptop, and begins typing. Dread slithers into the pit of my stomach, coalescing into a writhing ball.

Brie stares at me with wide, confused eyes. "Who the hell is Devin Bloom?"

1

Life with a head injury is nothing like the movies.

A bandit gets conked on the forehead with an iron and, minutes later, shakes it off and continues his scheme to burglarize a young boy's booby-trapped home. *No, fool, you should be in the hospital with a blow to the head like that!* Or a woman runs into a metal pole only to wake up in a world where every gorgeous man wants her. *Ha, I wish.* Film characters fall off subway platforms, step on rakes, and absorb knockout punches, banging their skulls so often you could stitch the scenes together and make the concussion noises play "The Star-Spangled Banner." Then they simply pick themselves up and continue with their lives like nothing happened. In reality, a head injury is a hell of a lot more life-altering— and in my case—strange.

Crawling across the crumb-strewn back seat of my mom's minivan, I scoop out the cardboard box I've carefully stashed on the floor. Cassidy Closet is printed neatly in big, innocent letters. As I wiggle back through the open door, I glance out the window and catch sight of a trash can sitting on the curb.

Guilt needles my stomach. I should have thrown away what's inside this box months ago. Not the various knickknacks or get-well cards from my law school classmates—I mean the *other* thing. But I haven't been able to bring myself to do it for reasons I don't want to explore.

Rolling my neck, I stand and lift the box out of the car.

"Where do you want this?" one of the movers calls from the double-parked moving truck. Broad-shouldered and bald, he's pulling my dresser on a red dolly behind him. I blink at his T-shirt, which features an eight-bit kitten riding a rainbow and the words Call me Mr. Cat Daddy scrawled beneath it.

"In the—" I begin, but a familiar song blares from the radio on the porch and the back of my neck tingles. *Oh no.* It's happening again. There's nothing about Sonny and Cher's "I Got You, Babe" that should inspire this level of dread-soaked anticipation (unless you're Bill Murray in *Groundhog Day*), but I'm not exactly normal. The opening lyrics drill into my brain, and I squeeze my eyes shut as an unwanted memory flickers to life.

No, not *a memory.*

In my mind's eye, I'm no longer standing on a tree-lined street in Cleveland on a cool June day. I'm swaying on a dim stage in a beer-soaked karaoke bar, microphone in hand. And *he's* there—Devin Bloom. He's smiling at me, cheekbones illuminated by a spotlight, dark eyes crinkling as he changes the lyrics so the chorus includes my name: "I got you, *Cass.*" I clutch the cardboard box so tightly its contents threaten to rattle.

Most people wake up from a coma with memory loss. I woke up with memory surplus—specifically, countless memories of a man named Devin Bloom.

Except Devin isn't real. He's a figment of my coma-rattled imagination.

At first, I didn't believe it. But the cloud revealed the truth: I didn't have any photos of Devin, any text history, or even a contact labeled Devin. There was absolutely, positively no evidence that Devin Bloom, my supposed boyfriend of three months, was a real person. No one in my life had met him, knew him, or heard of him. Googling and obsessively searching social media revealed nada as well.

There have been cases before of coma patients waking up with false or conflated memories, but waking up with a full-on imaginary boyfriend? The doctors called it a "medical anomaly." I call it a heart transplant without the heart and an unnecessary distraction from getting my life back on track.

Not that I feel sorry for myself or anything. In fact, I have a lot to be grateful for: I'm thinking, walking, talking, and back to my normal self—mostly. I could have died in that car accident. Or never recovered at all from the coma. If an imaginary boyfriend is the worst thing I have to deal with, I'm lucky. Shutting my eyes, I take a deep, reassuring breath.

"I'm here. I'm real. He's not real," I mutter my therapist's mantra to myself.

"Oh, I'm real, honey," says a deep voice.

My eyes pop open. The mover, Mr. Cat Daddy, is still staring at me, bushy eyebrows raised. "Dresser?" he asks.

My cheeks flame. "Upstairs bedroom. First door on the right."

"Want me to take that up too?" He nods at my box.

I hug it tighter to my chest. "No, thanks."

Shrugging one massive shoulder, Mr. Cat Daddy pulls the dolly up the cracked stone stairs leading to the century-old Ohio City Victorian that's officially my new home. Just before he reaches the porch, he steals a wary glance at me over his shoulder. Irritation bursts through my nostalgia, burning away the last fragments of imagined memory like smoke.

"I'm not crazy," I call after him.

"Whatever you say, lady." He disappears through the front door.

With a huff, I march up the steps toward the house. The soles of my white Adidas thud against the porch as I stride over to the radio. Balancing the box on my hip, I switch the station. "I Got

You, Babe" cuts out and a jaunty, bass-heavy pop song takes its place. I nod.

Much better. This is a day for new beginnings.

The cobalt-painted front door is already propped open and I step inside. But before I can climb the stairs to deposit the box in my bedroom, Brie strides into the foyer. My heart lightens automatically. Ever since I met Brie on the first day of seventh grade and we swapped lunches—her nanny-prepared ham and Gruyère for my generic PB and J—we've been best friends. Now we're twenty-six, and we're finally, *finally* moving in together now that I've more-or-less fully recovered from the accident and her last roommate moved out.

Her gold glasses sparkle, highlighting her light brown eyes. "Cass, there you are! Can you *please* tell your mother to chill out? Marcus stopped by a few minutes ago to drop off your key, and she's been haranguing him ever since. For a landlord, he has the patience of a saint, but I can practically see him contemplating tearing up our lease."

An ear-splitting squawk steals my attention, and I register the African gray parrot perched on Brie's shoulder. I take a hasty step back out of habit. "I didn't know Xerxes was here. I thought you said he was living with your parents."

Xerxes rustles his gray wings and edges sideways along Brie's shoulder, long red tail feathers twitching. "*Squawk!* Damn it, Char. Damn it, Char. Screw you, Bill. Screw you. Screw you. *Squaaaawk!*"

She winces. "He was." Reaching into the front pocket of her vintage overalls, she pulls out a sunflower seed. Xerxes nibbles it gently. "I liberated him last month. I told you, remember?"

"I—" I swallow hard. Did she tell me? I *can't* remember. Before the accident, my memory was airtight. I could rattle off case law like LexisNexis and recite my grocery list by heart. Now, if I don't write something down—tasks, appointments, reminders, names— it *poofs* out of my head like a cloud of steam wafting from a hot shower. I blame Devin. Maybe if he wasn't taking up space where he doesn't belong, my brain could function normally again.

I shove my short-term memory issues out of my mind before my stomach twists itself into knots.

"You know what?" Brie smacks her forehead, her voice overly bright. "I didn't tell you. I was going to, then some work stuff came up and it slipped my mind. I'm so sorry, that's my bad." She shifts her weight from one sneakered foot to the other.

I sigh. "You definitely told me, didn't you?"

She opens her mouth then freezes, her eyes flicking left and right. Brie's never been a good liar.

"Pi," I invoke.

When we were twelve, we made a pinky promise to always tell each other the truth. "*But how do I know if you* really *want to know the truth?*" Brie had asked. "*Like sometimes my mom asks my dad how she looks, and even if she looks 'meh' she wants him to tell her she looks good.*"

"*What about a code word?*" I had suggested.

"*Yes! How about 'pi'?*"

"*Like, apple or blueberry? Oooh I love blueberry pie. Or is it short for 'pinky promise?'*"

"*I was thinking more like the circumference of a circle divided by its diameter. Pi is always 3.14. It's constant. You can't change it— just like you can't change the truth.*" Brie's always been brilliant, with a head for math. No wonder she grew up to be a literal rocket scientist.

"*That's perfect,*" I'd said. "*So if one of us says 'pi,' the other one has to tell the truth, no matter what?*"

No matter what.

Brie's shoulders slump and Xerxes flaps his wings in indignation at being jostled. "I told you about Xerxes."

"More than once?"

Grimacing, she nods.

"Most recently?"

"Last week."

I blow out a long breath. "Damn it."

"If you're not okay with Xerxes being here, I can take him back. I know you two have had your . . . differences."

I snort. "Pi."

"Okay. He hates your guts and would love to peck out your liver while you sleep."

"Damn, Brie. I didn't know he hated me that much!"

"Oh, it's bad."

We both laugh, but the mirth quickly fades from her face. "Seriously though, he doesn't have to stay. I can give him back to Charlotte. He's technically hers, after all."

Anchoring the box on my hip, I squeeze her forearm, careful to stay a healthy distance away from Xerxes's beady glare and razor-sharp beak. "He stays." Brie's always loved that bird with her whole heart. I would never send him packing, let alone back to Brie's toxic parents. I make a mental note to stock up on Band-Aids the next time I'm at the drugstore. Which means I'll probably forget. I suppress a groan.

Too bad I can't text Devin and ask him to remind me. Nope, nope, not going there, no way. I shove any thoughts of Devin down deep until they're out of sight. Behind us, the movers' heavy footsteps thud up the stairs as they carry my full-sized mattress to my bedroom.

"Cassidy!" my mom calls from the living room.

"Yeah, Mom?" I shout back.

"Can you come here and look at this?"

"See? This is what I'm talking about. Rampage," says Brie.

Brie and I weave through the front dining room. My arms are beginning to ache, so I set the box on the edge of the table. Inside the living room, light filters through the bay widows, illuminating a cascade of dust motes. Mom is standing in front of the hand-carved fireplace, arms crossed over an open wool blazer while my twin six-year-old half brothers chase each other around the overstuffed couch.

My gut twinges. Part of me wishes my mother weren't here today. She's the top paralegal at one of the most cutthroat law firms in town and she can be *intense*. But she insisted on helping me move. Too bad my stepdad, Robert, isn't here too. He married my mom eight years ago when I was a freshman in college, and he's particularly adept at mellowing her out. But he's a real estate agent, which means he works most weekends, including this one. My brother Liam, ever the instigator, cackles with laughter as he holds a foam football out of Jackson's reach.

"Boys, take it outside, please," Mom says over her shoulder.

I ruffle Jackson's hair as he races past. He blows a raspberry at me. I blow one right back and both boys giggle as they run out of the room. Mom motions me over with an impatient flick of her fingers. Her makeup is impeccable, as usual, and her straight brown hair is cut into a neat bob that highlights her youthful jaw. Her style mirrors her personality: no frills, no nonsense. At least we have that in common—except for the hair. Mine is more chestnut than cinnamon, and decidedly not sleek, thanks to my energetic curls.

Tugging the sleeves of my gray shirt up my forearms, I brace my hands on my hips. "What's up?"

She motions vaguely at the fireplace. "There's a draft."

I shrug. "Fireplaces are drafty."

"And there's mold on the ceiling." She points directly overhead at an ominous brown spot marring the white plaster.

A shadow in the corner shifts, and for the first time I notice our landlord, Marcus, is in the room too. Marcus Belmont graduated from the same high school as Brie and me, but two years before us, so I don't know him that well. Brie knows him better than I do—somewhat. He lives directly above us on the third floor, which he converted into a separate, self-contained apartment, so she's had more occasions to talk to him than me since she moved in nine months ago.

"It's not mold. It's a water stain," he says, expression flinty.

Mom raises one arched eyebrow. "Are you sure? It looks like mold."

This time, when Marcus lifts his chin to the ceiling, he closes his eyes briefly as though praying for patience.

"Don't worry, Melanie." Brie steps forward. "I've been living here for months and I feel fine." As if on cue, Brie sneezes. The sound is as tiny as she is. "That was unrelated."

"I had the property tested last year when I renovated, and I promise there's no mold," says Marcus. "I wouldn't have been able to get the construction permits otherwise."

Mom frowns at the faded hardwood floors and cracked windowsills before settling her gaze on Marcus. "Which rooms have you renovated?"

"The bathrooms. And I installed a new HVAC system and roof. The kitchen is next on my list."

Mom leans to the side to peer around him through the open door into the kitchen with its cramped layout and ancient appliances. She concedes with a shrug. Stepping closer to me, she lowers her voice. "You don't have to do this, you know. I'm sure you could find someone to sublet your room. You can still change your mind."

"Mom—" I place my hands on her shoulders. "We're not doing this."

"Cass—"

"No, we've discussed it already."

With a huff, Mom paces to the opposite side of the living room. When she turns around, her lips are pressed together so tightly they form a thin line. "I simply don't know why you want to move out when you can live rent-free with me, Rob, and the boys for as long as you want."

"Because I can't live in the suburbs anymore, Mom. My job at Smith & Boone starts tomorrow, and I need to be able to walk there."

"If you started driving again you wouldn't have to walk."

My jaw tightens. "You *know* that's not an option."

I still don't remember the car accident. Or the hours leading up to it. All I know—courtesy of police reports—is that, over ten months ago, I lost control of my car and crashed it into the concrete median on I-71 at ten o'clock the night after finishing the bar exam. But something in my subconscious *must* remember, because every time I sit behind the wheel of a car, my heart races and I breathe so fast I nearly pass out.

"Sweetie, I'm just looking out for you. You've been through so much and you're still not your old self. You need all the support you can get."

Brie places her arm around my shoulders and tucks me against her side. "She has me, Mel."

"I know." Mom's smile turns watery as she pats Brie's cheek. "You girls . . . so eager to be out on your own." Shifting her attention to me, she drops her chin to look me in the eye. "But I don't have to remind you what's at stake this summer, do I?"

"Mom." I groan.

"Smith & Boone didn't have to give you another shot. You turned down their offer to start as a first-year associate last fall—"

"Yeah, because I was still recovering from the accident."

Mom shakes her head. "It doesn't matter. Smith & Boone is a prestigious firm with no shortage of talented young lawyers clamoring to join their ranks. They didn't have to consider you again, but they were willing to bring you on temporarily this summer as a trial run—to give you a second chance. If you want them to honor their original offer for a permanent position in the fall, you'll need to show them you're as sharp as you were before the accident. You'll have to wow them."

"I know, I know. I don't plan to mess this up, okay? I'm ready."

Her blue-gray eyes search my face. "Are you?"

"Yes."

Something relaxes in her features, and for the first time, I think she actually believes me.

Crash.

"Liam!" my brother Jackson wails from the other room.

Mom launches toward the commotion. I follow. In the dining room, the twins are squabbling. A cardboard box is on the floor, one side open as though it exploded on impact. All the blood drains from my face. *Oh shit.* It's my "Cassidy Closet" box. "I got it." I stumble forward, but Mom is already kneeling among my scattered belongings.

"What happened?" she asks the boys.

"Jackson didn't catch the football," says Liam.

Jackson punches him in the arm. "Liam didn't throw it good."

"Enough." Mom's voice cuts through the commotion like a gavel. "Timeout. Couch. Now."

Brie bustles into the room as the boys shuffle out. Xerxes is no longer on her shoulder and she's holding a dustpan and broom. Marcus has disappeared; he must have taken the opportunity to gracefully remove himself from our family bickering.

"Shoot," Mom mutters, gathering up a handful of loose greeting cards.

I edge around her, heart thundering. "Don't worry about it. Here, let me—" But before I can even finish, her gaze snags on the edge of a worn green sketchbook peeking out from under a scarf. Recognition registers and her jaw tightens. I close my eyes briefly, and when I open them again, she's flipping through the book while Brie peers over her shoulder. My stomach plummets to the cellar.

Devin's face stares back from every page, rendered in painstaking graphite detail.

After the accident, my hand-eye coordination was shot, so the earliest sketches look like something my brothers would have drawn—loopy, disjointed messes. But as I worked my way through rehabilitation and as more Devin "memories" surfaced, the sketches became more detailed. More vibrant. I hadn't drawn in years, not since my last studio art class sophomore year of college, but I couldn't stop. It was as if the only way I could get him out of my head was to get his likeness on the page. It went on for months. I hate to admit it, but I cried over those sketches. Slept with them under my pillow. And since Christmas, I'd kept them tucked away in a dark, dusty corner of the guest room at my mom's house and tried to forget about them.

Confusion flickers behind Brie's eyes. "I thought you said you got rid of it," she says softly.

"That's . . . I don't even . . . how did . . . ? *Weird*," I stammer.

Mom stands and shuts the sketchbook with a snap. "I knew it. This move was a bad idea. Clearly, you're not ready. Not with your *struggles*."

The word "struggles" hangs in the air like a guilty verdict.

How could I explain that nearly dying in a car accident and being forced to put my life on hold *was* the struggle? It had been almost a year since my law school friends moved on and found jobs and Brie finished her master's at Purdue and started her career at NASA's Glenn Research Center. Meanwhile, I was stuck like a pin in my hamster-wheel life full of hospital rooms, therapy, and an omnipresent, overbearing mother.

I couldn't live like that anymore. I wouldn't.

I step forward. "I *am* ready. More than ready. I can't let the accident make me a prisoner in my own life. You want proof I'm ready to be on my own?" Snatching the sketchbook out of my mom's hands, I march straight through the open front door. I nearly run into Mr. Cat Daddy, but he hastily sidesteps me. Blood pounds in my ears as I walk over to the trash can I spotted earlier. Flipping open the heavy plastic lid, I hesitate for several heartbeats.

Can I really do this?

Throwing the sketchbook into the trash, I slam the lid closed.

It's after one in the morning and my muscles ache from the move, but I can't sleep. The mattress groans as I roll over and stare at the dark ceiling. The house is quiet; Brie went to bed over an hour ago. Light from a streetlamp outside peeks through my slatted blinds, while a car engine revs somewhere in the distance. I try to swallow, but my mouth is full of cotton.

I throw the covers off my bare legs and creep out of bed and down the hall. Inside the bathroom, I grab a small paper cup from the wall shelf and flip on the light. It flickers in and out twice before buzzing to life. I glance at my reflection. The back of my neck tingles. A memory of Devin smiling at me through a mirror while a light winks overhead flashes through my brain. In the next instant, the image fades, and the only person I'm staring at is myself. The cup slips out of my slackening grip and bounces onto the tile floor.

I brace my hands on the porcelain pedestal sink, breathing hard.

Before I quite realize what I'm doing, I'm tiptoeing down the creaking stairs and easing open the front door. Chilly night air washes over the skin exposed by my shorts and T-shirt, but I ignore the cold. Scurrying over to the trash can on the curb, I hesitate for only a second before opening the lid.

I dig through bits of paper and refuse, holding my breath so I don't gag. *Where is it? Is it still here?* My fingertips brush a coil of metal before finding worn, familiar cardboard. Hands trembling, I lift out my sketch pad and wipe it off with the hem of my night shirt. It smells faintly of fried chicken and coffee grounds, but I don't care. Swallowing down a wave of guilt, I close the lid softly and walk back to the house, sketchbook tucked tightly against my pounding heart.

Devin's not real, but I can't let go. Not yet. The memory of finally finding someone after being alone for so long is like a drug: powerful and calming. And, despite my bravado earlier about being ready to restart my life, it's scary as hell. I'm not the same person I was a year ago. So what if I hang on to the memory of what it felt like to be loved, cherished, and supported by someone who made me feel whole? Opening the front door, I close it quietly behind me and pad softly to my bedroom.

Some comfort's better than none. Even if it's as thin as paper.

2

A morning breeze whips tendrils of hair across my cheekbone as I stare at the stainless steel Smith & Boone sign above the building's wide glass doors. Was it really over a year ago that I was standing in this exact spot, about to walk into the interview that would land me the job offer of my dreams? Somehow, it feels like last week. Or maybe several lifetimes ago.

The law offices of Smith & Boone are housed in a modern, three-story glass and steel building along the Cuyahoga River—an odd juxtaposition next to the century-old, converted brick warehouses, rusted train lift, and other emblems of Cleveland's long-gone glory as an industrial powerhouse.

Pulling my phone from the inside pocket of my shoulder bag, I check the time: 8:12 a.m. I'm eighteen minutes early for my first day as a summer associate. My lungs squeeze. I should have been here last September, reporting in as a *first-year* associate, but thanks to the accident that didn't happen. Now I'm back where I started—competing for a postgrad position against a host of hungry law students, each of us hoping to snag one of the precious few offers the firm will extend at the end of the summer.

And one of those positions already has my name on it, which

means I'll be the one to beat. The one the other summer associates will be trying to outdo. I'll have to be on my A-game all day, every day if I want to stay on top.

Hungry gulls screech overhead as I amble past the door and round the corner of the building. Leaning against a railing next to a small visitors' parking lot, I pull up my contacts and hesitate with my finger hovering over the screen. After a quick shake of my head, I tap Brie's face and request to FaceTime.

Her phone rings once before she accepts.

"Hey! Looks like you made it okay," she says thickly, propping up her phone. She's sitting in her oversized pink cotton pajamas at our snug two-person kitchen table with a giant ceramic bowl in front of her. A crunching noise filters through the speaker as she chews. "How was the walk?"

"Not bad. Just a little over half a mile."

She swallows and scoops another bite of what looks like Lucky Charms into her mouth. "I would have driven you."

"Yeah, but that would have required you to get up early, and we both know mornings are not your friend."

"Understatement. Are you nervous?"

"Honestly? A little. It's been over ten months since I took the bar." *And had my accident.* "I've been out of the loop."

"Cass, you got this. You've already landed the job once, now you just have to jump through a few hoops to prove yourself a second time. In three months, you'll have your name on a desk. Permanently."

"Right. But what if I'm not as good as I was? What if I can't remember anyone's name or what if the accident knocked half of law school out of my head?"

"I seriously doubt it. You didn't lose any memories from before the accident, just gained a few new ones, so I'm sure law school is still intact. Plus, you've been reviewing your old bar exam books and that's going well, right?"

"True."

"Okay. So if your noodle starts giving you trouble in the memory department, there's a simple fix: when in doubt, write it down. You'll be fine."

"Thanks, Brie."

"Hold up, turn your head. The other way. Oooo, yes. Rogue Curl at it again."

I crane my neck, and in the tiny image of myself in the corner of the screen I see what she's talking about. Sure enough, the short curl behind my left ear is sticking straight out. Thanks to the emergency craniotomy after the accident, doctors had to shave off a patch of hair the size of a Snapple cap, and it's still in that awkward growing-out stage.

"Damn it," I mumble. "Hold on." Tucking my phone in my armpit, I fish around in my bag and find a bobby pin at the bottom. I secure the curl, then use the phone's camera to check my reflection. Brie takes the opportunity to rinse her bowl in the sink.

"How do I look?" I ask.

"One sec," she calls, flipping the wall switch for the garbage disposal. Nothing happens. She toggles it several more times before cursing under her breath. "Garbage disposal is on the fritz again. I'll see if Marcus can come over later to fix it." Flopping back into her chair with a huff, she squints at her phone. "You look perfect. Every last hair in place."

Yawning, she stretches her arms above her head. "Well, we should both get a move on. I need at least two more cups of coffee and a hot shower before I can face down a Monday. I'd wish you luck on your first day, but I know you don't need it. Text me later?"

I blow her a kiss. "Definitely."

"Bye-ee," she chirps, then ends the call.

Guilt pecks at my spine, but I push the feeling away. I haven't told Brie yet about my late-night trash mission on moving day or how my Devin sketchbook is currently buried in the bowels of my closet instead of on its way to the dump. Pinching my eyebrows together, I shake my head. This is *my* life. And just because I'm not ready to throw away months-worth of Devin sketches doesn't mean I'm not ready to move on, launch my career, and find someone *real*.

I am. I so, totally am.

Standing up straight, I slip my phone into my bag and smooth my navy suit coat over my white blouse. I feel like myself in a way I haven't for a long time in my go-to lawyerly attire of patent leather pumps and a formal suit. Old Cass would have strolled into any job interview with her head held high because she knew she'd crush it. New Cass might still be finding her confidence through the memory fog, but hey—fake it till you make it, right?

Pushing my shoulders back, I open the door to Smith & Boone and step inside.

The lobby is exactly how I remember it from my initial interviews: gleaming black-tile floor, oversized abstract art with bold strokes of crimson and gray hanging on the sleek walls, and a curved desk at the far end of the lobby set against a door that I already know leads to a hive of offices. My heels clack as I approach the desk, but the man behind it doesn't look away from his computer screen.

"Can I help you?" His tone is laced with boredom.

"My name's Cassidy Walker. I'm one of the summer associates starting today."

Peering at me through thick, black-framed glasses, he brushes a lock of hair off his smooth forehead. "Late much?"

Fear ricochets around my chest. "What? No. The email said 8:30. It's"—I check my phone—"not even 8:20. I'm ten minutes early."

"Are you?" he drawls.

What the . . . did I misread the email? I quickly pull up the welcome email with the details for my first day. There it is: start time, 8:30 a.m.

"The email I received says 8:30." I hold up my phone, but the receptionist doesn't even look at the screen.

"You must have missed the follow-up. They changed the time to eight."

My mind splutters, but no words come out.

"Take the elevator to the second floor, down the hall to your right, conference room five. Glenn Boone is about to deliver remarks to the group, so I suggest you hurry." I recognize Glenn Boone as one of the managing partners—he's an attorney of national acclaim and the one who can make or break my future at the firm. I need to impress him if I want to secure my permanent spot this fall. "Oh, and you'll need this." The receptionist extends a mustard yellow visitor's badge. I stare at him, mouth open. He jiggles it. "Chop-chop."

Snapping out of my panic, I grab the badge and power walk to the elevator on my right. I hammer the button, and when the doors open I launch myself inside. Hitting the two button, I clip the badge on to the lapel of my jacket with shaking fingers. As the elevator slowly rises, I take a deep breath in an attempt to calm my racing heart.

Okay, so I'm late on my first day. How can I triage this situation?

When the doors open, I push my shoulders back and step out of the elevator. Three long hallways stretch before me—one left, one center, one right. All the blood rushes from my face. *Shit*. I've already forgotten where to go. This is *not* happening.

Hitching my bag higher on my shoulder, I march down the hall straight in front of me. I think he said conference room five. No, four. Definitely something with an "F." On my left, I pass a wooden door with a brass number three. Farther ahead and to my right, there's a door with the number four. Murmured voices grow louder as I approach. This must be it.

I knock softly before opening the door a crack. Three pairs of stunned eyes land on me and *ohhhh no*. This is definitely not the

right room. A middle-aged man and woman wearing neatly tailored suits swivel to stare at me while an elderly gentleman wob-
bles to his feet on the far side of the oversized conference table.

"I'm so sorry," I say quickly. "I'm in the wrong place." I begin
shutting the door, but a gravelly voice makes me pause.

"Where are you heading to?" the older man asks. His shock of
white hair, deeply lined face, and expensive gray suit are strangely
familiar . . .

"The conference room where the summer associates were asked
to meet."

"You're in luck. I'm on my way there now." He gives me a sly grin.

My stomach nearly bottoms out and I swallow down the panic.
This is Glenn Boone. I recognize him now: he was on the hiring
panel that originally interviewed me last year. And he's caught me
red-handed arriving late on my first day. This is *not* the impression
I wanted to make, but there's nothing I can do. Lifting my chin, I
force myself to stay calm.

"I'll be back in an hour," Glenn adds to the other two people in
the room—presumably attorneys. "Then we'll go over those depositions again." They both nod.

"Now, which summer associate are you?" he asks once he's in
the hallway.

"Cassidy Walker." I surreptitiously brush my sweaty palm against
my thigh and extend my hand. When he takes it, I give him a firm
handshake. His hand feels like fish bones in a leather pouch. "I had
the pleasure of meeting you when I interviewed for a first-year associate position last year."

"Ahhhh, yes. Ms. Walker. The survivor. I was sorry to hear
about your accident, but it looks like you've healed well." His
baggy-eyed gaze drifts down and his thin lips crease into a frown
when he reaches my trousers. Heat climbs up my neck. I know
some old-school judges don't like to see women attorneys wear
pants in a courtroom—they prefer skirt suits only—but I didn't

think Smith & Boone operated under the same sort of antiquated culture. Apparently, they do.

"Thank you. I have, yes."

He lifts his eyes to my face and nods solemnly. "Good. We're delighted you could join us this summer to ease into firm life, especially after all you've been through."

"I'm incredibly grateful for the opportunity, sir. Thank you."

We begin walking down the hall. My feet itch to double-time it to wherever we're going, seeing as I'm already late, but Glenn seems content to saunter along at a stroll, one hand in his vest pocket. When we reach the elevators he turns left—down the hall-way that was originally on my right. I was way off. He pivots toward me as he walks. "So, what did you think of my joke this morning?"

I blink. "Joke?"

He leans in like we're coconspirators in a heist. "I like to razz the summer associates on their first day, so I ask David the receptionist to play a little trick and make you all *think* you're late."

So . . . I'm *not* actually late?

His chuckle sounds more like a wheeze. "Make no mistake. We work hard here, but we have fun too."

Yeah, if your definition of "fun" is giving hapless, type-A twenty-somethings a heart attack. Some of the tension seeps out of my shoulders and I roll them. "Oh, that's, ah . . . a good one." I force a laugh.

We stop, and he motions toward a door marked five. "After you."

"Thank you." I open the door, and *this* is definitely the correct room. Ten people are seated around a conference table and they all sit up a little straighter when they spot Glenn Boone behind me. Most of the other summer associates are roughly my age—mid- to late twenties—and all are wearing their professional finest along with expressions of focused anticipation.

Pounding footsteps approach, and a red-faced man wearing a navy suit bursts into the room. Like the rest of us, he must have fallen for Glenn's joke and probably sprinted up here, judging by the sweat beading on his forehead and the panic oozing from every pore.

"Welcome," says Glenn, sauntering toward the head of the table. "Have a seat."

The guy doesn't need to be told twice. He barrels past me toward the closest empty chair, but veers at the last second and opts for a seat on the far side of the table. *Okay then.* I cross the distance to the chair he snubbed, which is situated between a man wearing a wrinkled khaki suit and a pinched expression and a primly dressed young woman with an air of unflappable intensity.

I pull the nearby rolling chair away from the table, and okay *now* I understand why the other guy didn't sit here. An oversized red shoulder bag is occupying the seat. Clearly, it belongs to the woman on my right. Her silk blouse is the same shade of crimson, and so are her perfectly manicured nails. She flicks her gaze between me and her bag. I clear my throat. With a toss of her sleek strawberry-blond hair, she swivels to face Glenn, who's easing himself into a seat at the head of the table.

My jaw muscles twitch. She doesn't move her bag.

It's a power play. She's subtly attempting to throw off the competition by forcing the last summer associate to arrive to sit at the head of the table across from a managing partner—awkward at best and an office faux pas at worst. I purse my lips. I forgot how cutthroat summer associates can be, especially when it comes to competing for jobs at top firms. Five minutes into the job, and this Gloria Allred wannabe is already trying to establish herself as the one in control—the one to beat.

Too bad she's never met *me*.

I pick up her bag by its stiff leather handles and place it on the floor next to her chair. Despite my quiet, smooth movement, the woman jerks. Turning her head slowly, she stares at me, icy blue eyes full of sparks. *Wait*, do I know her?

Narrowing my eyes, I study her airbrushed complexion and delicate features. Did we go to law school together? High school? The wash of recognition passes, and I shake my head. No, I don't think we've met before. "Excuse me." I offer her a tight smile as I pull out the chair and assume the now-empty seat.

"No problem." Her voice is light and musical, but her lips curl as she pulls her bag onto her lap, snaps it closed, and sets it on the floor on the opposite side of her—away from me. The other summer associates glance furtively our way. One lanky young associate with a crew cut and a thickly starched shirt scratches his nose, covering a smirk.

Yeah, I've got your number, Allred.

Pulling a legal pad and pen from my bag, I tuck it under the table and cross my legs just as Glenn Boone begins his welcome speech.

Early evening sunshine filters through the glass walls of the lobby as I step out of the elevator. "Have a good night," I call to David, the receptionist. Despite the fact that he was a willing participant in Glenn's joke earlier, I want to get off on the right foot with everyone here. Best to stay on his good side.

David's head snaps up and he adjusts his glasses. "Thanks. You too."

Edging through the doors, I pull out my phone. I already have a text from Brie.

How did your first day go?

Fingers flying across the screen, I respond.

It was . . . a day

Good or bad?

> Mostly good. I met the other summer associates
> and they were all cool (except one, but whatevs).

> Tomorrow we get our practice group assignments.

> So yeah, a good first day, I guess!

Woo-hoo! Let's celebrate tonight! I'm
thinking . . . takeout & champagne?

> YES PLEASE! I'll pick up some
> champers on the way home.

Home. Because I have a home here, in the quaint Ohio City district of downtown Cleveland, with my best friend in the whole wide world.

HERO.

> *bows*

Be home in 30 . . . see you soon!

Tucking my phone into my bag, I grin at the cloud-dappled sky. So *this* is what normal feels like. I'd nearly forgotten. I've started a new job at one of the top firms in town like a normal twentysomething—it might not be the permanent job I'd hoped for but it's a job nonetheless. And nobody stared at me with pity or asked how I'm doing in hushed tones of sympathy. Plus? I haven't had a single Devin episode today. It's official: after a year of painstaking recovery, my luck is *finally* turning around. Heck, maybe I'll even meet someone new this summer—someone real this time.

I snort. Okay, that might be a stretch. "Big law" life, working for a large, high-revenue law firm, doesn't exactly leave a lot of room for socializing. But, hey, you never know what the future has in store, right? And after a day like today, I'm feeling just about ready for anything.

3

I take the long way back to my neighborhood along the Cuyahoga River, soaking in the fresh air and sunshine. A quick Google search reveals that Dave's Markets is the closest purveyor of champagne, so I walk the extra few blocks to the store, splurge on a twenty dollar bottle of champagne and several bags of M&M's—because every good celebration needs chocolate—and stash my purchases in my tote bag. Outside, I take a deep breath through my nose, preparing to head home, but freeze.

I know that scent. I inhale deeply again to confirm the delicately floral yet achingly familiar smell. *Lilies.*

My favorite flower. And not just because I thought make-believe Devin bought me a bouquet of lush white lilies on our first date. I've loved them since I was a kid—their silken, oversized petals and a scent that transports you to sun-soaked gardens full of mystery and beauty.

I glance around automatically for the source and spot a dusky purple Victorian house tucked along the nearest side street, sandwiched between a squat brick building and a historic home, both with Foreclosure signs out front. Blooms & Baubles is printed in large letters above the Victorian's front door and a sign in the window proclaims Open in red block letters. A flower shop. That certainly explains the lilies. Shifting my weight, I run my tongue along the edge of my teeth.

That's it, I'm doing it. I'm going to buy myself some flowers. Because I have another success to celebrate: I did *not* have a Devin episode just now. I thought of him, sure. But I didn't drown in a whirlpool of fake flashbacks. Yesterday might have involved a minor setback, but my "*struggles*," as Mom likes to put it, are well on their way to existing solely in the past. And I'm going to prove it—if not to her, at least to myself.

The crisp scent of flowers grows stronger as I approach the shop and okay, this place is *adorable*. An assortment of bouquets fills the window display along with art prints dangling on wires and a small shelf of colorful ceramic vases. Looped purple script on the bay window proclaims, "Flowers, gifts, and more. Let us brighten your day!"

"Cute," I murmur to myself as I open the door. A bell tinkles and a dog barks from somewhere deeper in the store. I tense at the series of growl-laced woofs, but relax when I spot the dog waddling over from behind the counter. He's long and plump like a corgi with the floppy ears of a beagle, and his short white-and-brown fur is covered with dusty yellow splotches. Not exactly a ferocious Cujo.

"Hi, sweetie," I say, extending a hand to let him sniff me. When he licks my fingers, I give him a good scratch behind the ear. "Who's a good doggie? *Who's a good doggie?*" He wags his tail once at my ridiculous baby voice, then moseys back through the shop, brushing against a row of lilies as he goes. And that must be why he's yellow—from the pollen. Retreating behind the counter, he flops into a worn navy-blue bed strewn with petals and bits of greenery.

"He likes you." I look up to find a man about my age studying me from behind the counter, chin resting on palm, elbow propped next to the cash register. His thick, tawny-brown hair gleams in the light. Straightening, he flashes me a grin. "To be fair, The Colonel likes everyone."

"The Colonel?"

The guy nods at the dog. "Colonel Archibald Buttersworth III. But he prefers The Colonel for short. Don't forget the 'The.'" He winks.

The Colonel heaves a grunting sigh that's halfway between a potbellied pig and a humpback whale, rolls onto his back, and splays out with all four legs in the air. A giggle bursts out of me. "Very dignified."

The man chuckles and edges around the counter, careful not to disturb the snoozing dog. "What can I help you find?" He shoves his hands into the front pockets of his jeans and the lightly corded muscles of his forearms flex. His height is a touch above average, maybe a shade under six feet, and he has a lean build. I wouldn't call him "hot" exactly—a mop of wavy brown hair crowns a pleasant enough face—but there's a crackling energy to him, like he's about to either pull an epic prank or deliver the knockout punch line to a joke. Maybe it's the way his eyebrows tilt upward at the end, giving him an inherently mischievous look.

Tucking my bag closer to my side, I grip the leather strap. "I came in for lilies, but I'd like to browse a bit first."

"Well, in addition to flowers, we offer frames, vases, cards, candles, art, and handcrafts. What's the occasion? Don't tell me. Let me guess." Narrowing his eyes at me, he taps a finger against his Cupid's bow lips. "You had a rough day and need a pick-me-up."

"No, the opposite actually. I started a new job."

"Ah, well. That was going to be my second guess. Congrats."

The phone on the counter rings. "Can you get that?" he shouts over his shoulder. The phone rings again. "If I might make a sugges—" he begins, but the insistent trill of the phone cuts him off.

His smile tightens. "Excuse me." Bounding to the far corner of the store, he sticks his head through a door marked Employees Only. "I'm with a customer. Phone." I can tell from his tone that he's gritting his teeth.

"Okay, okay. I'll get it," a muffled, deep voice responds.

Goose bumps rise along my forearms, and I pull my suit coat tighter around me. The air conditioner must have kicked on. Rubbing my arms, I examine a shelf of hand-dipped candles.

A door clicks shut and the clerk reappears. "Where were we . . . flowers, right? While you browse, how about I make you a specialty bouquet? Say, fifty dollars?"

His open, eager face pulls a smile from me. "Okay, sure."

"Great!" The man is a whirl of movement. Plucking a tall glass vase from one of the many shelves lining the shallow, semiopen area behind the cash register, he fills it with water and places it in front of me on the counter. "Now let's see." His gaze flickers across my face as though he can divine my future from the constellation of freckles on my nose. Heat travels up my neck and into my cheeks at the scrutiny—I can't help it. After several long seconds, he blinks, seeming to rouse himself from whatever trance he was in, and snaps his fingers. "Got it. You need anemones," he says.

I lift my eyebrows. "You sell fish too?"

The man chuckles again, eyes shining with mirth. "Wrong kind of anemone." He plucks several flowers out of a bucket on the floor and holds them up so I can see. The petals are a striking shade of deep, rich violet. "We had a cool spring this year, so we still have some of these beauties left." Twirling one of the thick green stems between his fingers, he strides to the back wall, which is filled with rows of tilted bins holding a multitude of different flowers. "We need blue delphinium, for height. Snap dragons. Limonium." As he says each name, he picks flowers out of bins—a gorgeous array of shades ranging from pale lavender to royal purple. "What else?"

"Hydrangeas?" I say, drawn in despite myself.

He makes a sound in his throat halfway between a snort and a laugh. "No."

"Why not? I like hydrangeas."

"Of course, you do, and there's nothing wrong with that. Everyone likes hydrangeas because they're everywhere. But I have a feeling . . .

your occasion is too special for hydrangeas." When our eyes meet, he offers me a shy smile.

This guy is *flirting* with me. When's the last time a man actually flirted with me? Maybe law school? There was Ben, my ex. But after we broke up third year I got so buried in school and job hunting I didn't go to a single party or law school get-together until graduation. And postaccident I was a literal wreck. I'm so out of practice it's pathetic. Should I smile back? Wink? Toss my hair and say, "Why, thank you," in a throaty purr? Do I even *want* to flirt with him?

A little voice says yes. How long has it been since I've been in an actual relationship—one that wasn't a tepid train wreck or straight-up imaginary? My lungs squeeze at the realization that I can't remember the last time someone made me feel *seen*.

Before I can do anything besides close my mouth, the man clears his throat. "I know, we need contrast. Light green. Bells of Ireland." He picks out more flowers. "And then some filler greenery, and finally—" He holds out a stem with dark green leaves. "Smell it."

I take the stem from him and inhale deeply while he arranges the flowers he's selected in the vase on the counter. "Mint?"

"Close. Eucalyptus. For fragrance. Go ahead." He nods at the bouquet. I wiggle the eucalyptus into the vase, nestling it among the blooms. The man adds two more sprigs, then steps back and examines his handiwork. Reaching under the counter, he pulls out a thick piece of twine, loops it around the vase, layers it with a jaunty green ribbon, and expertly ties it into a bow.

"There you go," he says, pushing the vase toward me. "One hooray-I-got-a-job bouquet."

I rotate the vase, appreciating the flowers from every angle. The arrangement is magnificent—a stunning mixture of shades, textures, and scents. Nothing I would have thought to pick for myself, but somehow, it feels perfect for this day, this moment. Leaning in, I close my eyes and inhale deeply. A symphony of scents greets me, and I resist the urge to smoosh my face into the blooms.

Opening my eyes, I run my fingertips along an anemone's silken petals. "Why'd you pick purple?" I ask, tearing my gaze away from the flowers.

The florist shrugs. "Because it brings out the color of your eyes."

"My eyes are brown."

"They are. But you have a little green around the pupils. And if you look at a color wheel, purple and green are—"

"Contrasting colors," I finish.

He blinks in surprise. "Exactly. So purple highlights your eyes."

Our gazes lock. His eyes are the opposite of mine, I realize. While mine are mostly brown with a hint of green, his are emerald green with a splash of brown ringing the irises. It should be illegal for men to have eyes that pretty. Heat fills my cheeks and I'm the first to look away. "You're very talented."

He runs a hand over his smooth chin. "Thank you. And you know about color theory—I'm impressed. Are you an artist?"

I snort. "Hardly. I'm a lawyer." At his raised eyebrows, I clarify. "I was a studio art major for a semester before I switched to public administration."

He folds his arms across his chest but almost immediately unfolds them. "I bet there's an interesting story there."

I shrug. "Not as interesting as you think."

"Maybe you can tell me about it sometime . . . perhaps over drinks?"

My lips part but no sound comes out. Did he just ask me out? Am I ready to date?

An image of Devin flashes through my mind before I can stop myself, and I attempt to shake off a flash of guilt. *I am not cheating on my imaginary boyfriend because: He's. Not. Real.* This guy—this cute florist with the mischievous eyebrows and the soulful stare? He's real. And he's clearly interested in getting to know me.

So why can't I answer?

I'm saved from coming up with a response when a door clicks

open on the other side of the shop. "Hey, Perry? I'm heading out," says the same deep male voice from before. The back of my neck tingles. I jerk my head toward the sound, but the numerous store displays obscure my view.

"Where to?" the man behind the counter—Perry, according to the newcomer—says.

"Dropping off the Schmidt order. You're welcome."

There's *something* about that voice. Licking my lips, I lean back to peer around the nearest display. The profile of a man catches the light, his features too bright to make out. But then he turns, giving me a full view of his face.

I gasp and my heart thunders so loud it echoes in my ears.

The man has dark eyes and thick, nearly black hair that tumbles over his forehead and sweeps across his brows. A long, straight nose. Bold, sensuous lips. Cheekbones so high they would make a supermodel weep. My knees buckle and I catch myself on the shelf behind me. Something rattles and topples over, but I don't care.

A tsunami of memory fragments and bits of conversation coalesce into the achingly familiar form of the man standing on the opposite side of the shop. I know his features so well I could draw them. Because I have drawn them. Hundreds of times.

It's Devin. My Devin. Devin Bloom.

My heartbeat accelerates like an out-of-control freight train. With a final wave to Perry, Devin tucks an oversized bouquet of roses against his chest, crosses the room, and walks out of the store. He doesn't spare me a single glance. The thud of the door closing behind him reverberates through my skull like the gong of a church bell.

Devin. He's here. He's real. He's—

My head goes fuzzy. The room spins. And the floor rushes up to greet me.

4

"Hey. Hey! Are you okay?" A hazy form hovers above me.

Hope leaps in my chest. "Devin?" I blink several times, and the man's features solidify. It's not Devin—it's the florist, the one who made me the flower arrangement. Beyond his pale cheeks and pinched frown, a white ceiling fan drifts in lazy circles above him.

A grunt snorts in my ear before a wet tongue licks my chin. I look over to find myself at eye level with a dog's snuffling snout.

Wait, I'm on the floor. *How did I get on the floor?*

"You fainted," says the florist.

I scrunch my nose. I must have said that last part out loud. A dull ringing fills my ears, and my head throbs as I push myself into a sitting position. At least a nearby display of chunky-knit blankets cushioned my fall. The last thing my Swiss cheese brain needs is a concussion. The dog wags its tail as he nudges my hand. I pat him absently.

"I—what? Where's Devin?" I whip my head to look around the shop and immediately regret it. The pain intensifies, and I rub my aching skull. Maybe I hit my head harder than I thought.

The man's eyes narrow. "You know my brother?"

"*Brother?* Your brother is Devin Bloom?"

"No, he's Devin Szymanski. I'm Perry Szymanski, and you're in Blooms & Baubles," he says slowly.

"Devin Szymanski. Blooms & Baubles. Devin Bloom," I mutter under my breath. Fantasy and reality come crashing together into an incomprehensible tangle. My vision turns blurry as I stare sightlessly at the floor. "I dreamed of Devin. But Devin is real. What does it mean?" I whisper.

"It means you hit your head pretty hard. I'm calling an ambulance." Standing, the florist—what did he say his name was, Gary? No, *Perry*—strides toward the counter.

"Wait!" I shove roughly to my feet. Gravity is not my friend today though, and I lurch to the side.

Perry lunges for my forearm, steadying me before I topple over like a domino. "Whoa, there. Take it slow."

I wave him away. "No more doctors. I need to find Devin."

His expression clouds as he studies me, suspicion crowding out concern. "You need to sit."

A heady mixture of panic and desperation wells up inside me, and I snatch two fistfuls of Perry' T-shirt at his collar and jerk him toward me until we're nose to nose. His eyes widen and he sucks in a shocked breath.

"You don't understand," I enunciate. "I *need* to talk to Devin. When will he be back?" I fight the urge to shake him like a rag doll.

Nostrils flaring, Perry peels my fingers off his shirt one by one. Once he lets go, he backs up, putting a good five feet of space between us. "I don't know."

My knees threaten to buckle at the loss of contact, or maybe because my head feels like pudding and I can't quite grasp this new reality—the one where my imaginary boyfriend actually exists. I shuffle toward the counter, intending to lean against it for support, but before I can reach it, Perry procures a stool from God knows where and shoves it underneath me. I slump onto the circular seat, the panic leaking out of me as quickly as it came and confusion taking its place. Burying my head in my hands, I dig my fingers roughly through my hair.

Perry's jaw tenses as he studies me. "He did it again, didn't he?" Cursing, he rubs his temples like he can scrub away a memory. "Look, I'm sorry if my brother gave you a fake name at a bar or something, but just so you know, he recently got out of a bad relationship and isn't looking for anything serious right now."

"What? No, that's not it at all. Wait—was he in a relationship with a woman named Cassidy?"

"No."

"So you've never seen me before?"

"Not before you walked into my shop and started freaking me out with the fainting and the psychokiller stare."

I ignore the dig. "But that *was* Devin Bl—Szymanski." I try the name out, and it tastes foreign on my tongue.

"Yes."

"I'm going crazy."

"If you say so."

I scramble off the stool. "I have to go."

He straightens. "What?"

Stooping down, I gather up my shoulder bag from where I dropped it on the floor. My wallet, phone, and several bags of M&M's have spilled out, and I shove everything back inside.

When I stand, I find Perry holding the bottle of champagne I bought at the store. It must have slipped out of my bag and rolled away when I fainted. He looks pointedly between me and the booze, a look of understanding spreading across his features before I snatch the bottle from him.

Heat sears my cheeks. "I'm not drunk," I snap.

"Uh-huh."

"You don't understand."

"I think I do." He folds his arms across his chest. "You came in here and pretended to flirt with me so you could creep on my younger brother. Admit it."

My cheeks warm. "I wasn't flirting with you. And even if I was, do you think I would have *fainted*?"

"Honestly? I have no idea." He scrubs a hand through his hair so vigorously it stands on end like he stuck his finger in a socket. "This is weird. *You're* weird. And my brother has dealt with too much shit over the past year to handle whatever this"—he motions toward all of me—"is."

My mouth turns dry and it takes me three tries to successfully swallow.

Drawing himself up, he folds his arms across his chest. "Look, if you don't want an ambulance and you don't want me to call anyone for you, I'm afraid I'm going to have to ask you to leave."

My chest tightens. "Fine. You wouldn't believe me if I told you the truth anyway. I barely believe it myself," I mumble under my breath. I'll just have to figure out another way to find Devin. At the door, I toss one last look at the flowers on the counter. My gut twitches with regret at the gorgeous blooms that were supposed to be symbolic of today's fresh start at life. Perry is watching me, expression clouded. "Sorry for the trouble," I say quickly. Turning, I yank open the door and march down the steps. My gait is shaky and I have to pause to steady myself against the wrought iron fence along the sidewalk.

Devin is real.

Except Devin's brother thinks I'm a basket case, so clearly he doesn't know me and has never met me before in his life. But if Devin and I were actually together, his brother should know who I am . . . right? *So what does it all mean?* Does Devin know me or not? Were the memories churned up during my coma real—or not?

My blood pounds as I walk home, anticipation burning off the haziness from my fall. When I round the corner to my street, I kick off my heels, stuff them under my arm, and jog the last block to the duplex barefoot. Taking the front stairs two at a time, I bust through the unlocked front door like the Kool-Aid Man. The door slams against the wall and bounces back, nearly smacking me in the face.

"What the—!" Brie yelps from where she's sitting cross-legged on the couch in the living room, upsetting the bowl of tortilla chips nestled in her lap. A few chips spill out, and Xerxes flaps over from where he was nibbling fruit slices on the coffee table and begins pecking. I drop my shoes onto the floor.

"Oh, Cass, it's you," she says, then stops when she catches sight of my face. The next instant, she's off the couch and striding over to where I'm standing in the foyer. "What's going on? What happened?" Grasping my shoulders, she studies me, concern seeping from every pore.

I grab her forearms and squeeze. "He's real, Brie."

"Who?"

"Devin."

She pales. "*What?*"

"I saw him."

"Cass." The one word is loaded with so much pain, worry, and resignation my heart plummets to my toes. She curls an arm around my shoulders and steers me to the couch. "Come on, sit down. Start from the beginning."

I tell her everything. When I'm finished, she swivels to face me more fully. "I know you think you saw him. There are a lot of guys out there who probably look like how you picture Devin looks. But, sweetie, we all know he's not real," she says quietly.

"But he is. I *saw* him. I met his brother."

Blowing out a long breath, she rubs my back in slow, long circles. "This has been a big change for you. And the argument with your mom yesterday and starting a new job at the firm today . . . you're facing a lot of pressure. Have you been taking your meds?"

"Of course."

She grimaces. "Pi?"

"Yes!" I shove off the couch, and she jolts. "*Brie*. I'm not making this up and I'm not having some kind of anxiety-induced breakdown. He's real. Look, I'll show you."

I run upstairs and retrieve my sketchbook from the closet. Standing opposite from where she's curled on the couch, I place the sketchbook gingerly on the coffee table between us. "Now, don't be mad . . ."

She jerks forward. "You still have it? What, did you dig it out of the trash last night?" The look on her face makes my gut squirm.

"I'm not ready to part with it, okay? I didn't want to get into it with my mom."

"You could have been honest with *me*."

"I know, I'm sorry. But look—"

I try to ignore Brie's thinned lips as I flip open my sketchbook to one of the more recent drawings. Devin peers back at us, his head tipped in laughter.

"Now, where's my phone . . ." Fishing my phone out of my bag, I drag the adjacent armchair up to the sofa and begin googling. "Here. Blooms & Baubles. This is where he works." I tap on their website. Hours, order information, bestselling bouquets, but nothing about personnel besides a few lines about being a third-generation family run business. I tap on their Instagram account. All flowers.

I snap. "Devin's brother works there too. What was his last name again? Not Bloom. Devin Sizeman . . . Seymour?" Blooms & Baubles has more than a thousand followers on Instagram, and I type "Devin" in the search bar. No accounts with Devin in the name are following the store. I try googling several iterations of his first and last name. Nothing.

"Damn it!" I smack my sketchbook. Xerxes lets out an ear-splitting whistle from the arm of the sofa. A single traitorous tear spills onto my cheek, and I dash it away with my fist. "I saw him. I *know* I did."

Silently, Brie slides over until her thigh is inches from mine. Her chest rises and falls heavily, but her hand is steady when she places it gently on my forearm. "Cass, I want to believe you. I really do. But we've been here before, remember? You were so sure when you woke up from your coma that you had a boyfriend named Devin. But we *know* he's not real. Even your doctors agree he's the result of your traumatic brain injury. So, is it more likely that he's somehow been real all along and hiding out—despite the fact your phone and text records show no routine communication with anyone last spring besides me and your family? Or is it more likely that you *think* you saw someone who looks like Devin?"

All the air rushes out of me and I deflate like a balloon. Tipping forward, I dig my fingers through my hair and attempt to ignore the stone settling over my chest. "You're right. It doesn't make sense. It couldn't have been him."

"What's the name of that Cleveland Clinic neurologist you were seeing?"

"Dr. Holloway."

"Why don't we call Dr. Holloway and schedule an appointment for sometime in the next few weeks? I'll take off work and drive you, for moral support."

My eyes burn when I look up at her. "Am I going crazy, Brie?"

She winces, and her shoulders lift in a half shrug before she smooths her expression. "No, sweetie. You've just been through something none of us can possibly understand. Your brain isn't operating exactly the same as it used to, but that doesn't mean it's broken. Or that you're crazy. Which, come on now, isn't a very helpful term. You're experiencing some neurological struggles, that's all. We'll find a solution, I promise."

Toppling sideways, I rest my head on her shoulder. "What would I do without you?"

Wrapping her arms around me, she gives me a squeeze. "You're the most resilient person I know. You'd do just fine."

A doorbell cuts through the heavy silence. "I'll get it," says Brie. She pads through the dining room and disappears around the corner.

"Hey, Brie. Is the garbage disposal still not working?" Marcus's deep voice hums through the house.

"Now's not a great time, Marcus," Brie says.

"It's okay, he can come in." I attempt to inject some pep into my voice, but it comes out as miserable as I feel.

What am I going to do? Can I really continue living on my own and working at the firm if I've already succumbed to Grand Devin Delusions? Mom was right . . . I never should have moved out or tried to reenter the workforce. Clearly, I'm not ready.

Heavy footsteps approach, and Marcus appears in the living room behind Brie. He pulls a double take when he spots me. "Are you okay?"

I give him a weak smile. "Fine."

He nods hesitantly, but ambles closer. "Are you sure? You don't look so good. Is there something I can do? Anything I can get you?"

"Unless you happen to have the world's strongest drink in your back pocket, no. Thank you though."

"Okay. I might be your landlord, but we are neighbors, you know. I'm here if you need anything."

Brie pats him on the shoulder. "You're a peach, Marcus."

The ghost of a smile flits across his lips as a flush creeps up his neck. Turning to follow Brie into the kitchen, his gaze skims over the coffee table . . . and lingers on my sketchbook. Eyebrows furrowing, he thrusts his chin toward the drawing on the open page. "Hey, how do you know Szymanski?"

Wait, did he just say *Szymanski*? My eyes go wide and I stop breathing for several heartbeats. "How do *you* know him?"

"We play in the same softball league."

Brie jogs over to the coffee table from across the room. "You play softball with *him* . . . this guy here?" She jams her finger at the sketch.

"Yeah, that's Devin Szymanski, right? He works with his brother at Blooms & Baubles, the flower shop on Providence and West Twenty-Eighth."

"Flower shop?" I say at the same time Brie squeaks, "You're sure that's really *him*?"

"Um, is it supposed to be someone else? Because damn, that could practically be a photograph." Bending over, Marcus flips through a few pages. "Why do you have all these drawings, anyway? Did you do them?"

Nodding vaguely, I bite the inside of my cheek so hard I taste pennies. Swiveling slowly, I face Brie. I imagine my expression matches her own openmouthed shock.

"Cass. You were right. You do know him, you must. So Devin is . . . real?" she breathes.

"He's real."

"Devin is real." She sinks onto the couch next to me.

"He's real. He's real," Xerxes squawks.

"Will somebody tell me what's going on?" asks Marcus.

I snort. "You're not going to believe this."

In one smooth move, Marcus pulls the coffee table away from the couch and sits on it so he's facing us. Resting his elbows on his knees, he steeples his fingers. "Try me."

5

Marcus's mouth hangs open like screen door in a stiff breeze. "I don't believe it."

Brie shifts beside me so she's sitting cross-legged on the couch. "I didn't until approximately five minutes ago. So, understandable."

I scoot forward until I'm perched on the very edge of the cushion. "I know it sounds nuts, totally impossible. But I'm telling the truth."

Pushing to his feet, Marcus strides over to the fireplace. "So you were in a coma for a week, and when you woke up, you suddenly had all these memories of . . . Devin Szymanski?"

"Memories of him as her boyfriend, yes," Brie says.

I shoot her a *thanks, Brie*, look.

"But you say you've never actually met him before?" Marcus's eyebrows knit.

"Right," I say.

"How do you know?"

I blink. "Because Brie never met nor heard of him."

"And she meets all your boyfriends?"

"Well, yes."

Brie sticks a finger in the air. Her hot pink nail polish shimmers. "I never met Tucker."

"That's because you were at Purdue and I only dated him for two months junior year of college. You didn't miss anything. He was a dud."

Marcus paces the length of the room. "And according to your memories, how long were you with Devin?"

"Three months," I say.

He shrugs. "Three months isn't much longer than two. Maybe you were keeping the relationship a secret?"

I chortle. "No way."

"Why are you so sure?"

"Because I never texted or called anyone named Devin, and I don't have any pictures of him. If we really had dated for three months, I would have at the very least had his number saved in my phone."

"Unless you wanted to keep your relationship a secret." He shrugs. "In which case it's conceivable you wouldn't have his number stored in your contacts. Maybe you communicated with him through an app or DMs and deleted the messages. Or used a burner phone to talk to him."

"A burner phone?" Brie snorts. "You watch too many thrillers."

Flopping back into the sofa cushions, I cross my legs. "That doesn't make any sense. Why would I want to keep a relationship with someone a secret?"

Marcus taps his long fingers against a jean-clad thigh. "When was your accident again?"

"Last July."

"Okay, so eleven months ago . . ." Marcus's narrowed eyes flick back and forth. "Yeah, if I'm remembering it correctly, he was seeing someone back then. What if he had a girlfriend, and you were, like, his side piece?"

"Piece of what, exactly?" Brie demands, folding her arms across her ample chest.

He holds his hands up in surrender. "No disrespect intended. All I meant was, maybe you were casually seeing him on the sly because he was technically with someone else."

Brie scoffs. "No way."

"Absolutely not," I add. I would never get involved with someone who was already in a relationship . . . *Right?* The last year of law school had been the hardest of my life until then—increasingly difficult classes, applying for jobs, and *Law Review* editor duties, with a daily dose of Lexapro for anxiety on top. Not to mention a tough breakup at the beginning of the school year. I was under a mountain of pressure. Was it possible I indulged in a fling with a guy who was already spoken for, just to blow off steam? I shake my head hard. "No. Never in a million years."

Marcus shrugs.

Bracing an elbow on her knee, Brie pinches her lower lip between her thumb and index finger. "There has to be a logical explanation."

"Like the one I just offered?" says Marcus.

Brie flattens him with a glare.

His eyes glint. "Okay, what if it's fate?"

"How so?" I ask.

Marcus shifts his weight. "What if you and Devin are *supposed* to meet? What if your memories of him, your accident, was fate at work?"

Brie sighs. "Fate is the excuse people use to justify when life-altering things happen, when in reality it's the result of the decisions they make—and maybe a dash of pure dumb luck. Good or bad, people's actions determine their future. Cause and effect. Action, reaction. Blaming things on fate only downplays the importance of choice."

"So you don't think there's a guiding hand in the universe nudging people in the right direction—God, karma, kismet, something?"

"No, and in case you're wondering, I don't believe in Santa Claus or the tooth fairy either."

Marcus tilts his head. "But there's so much about the world, the universe, we don't know. Perhaps it's possible a higher power is at play here, guiding Cass and Devin together."

Her lips tilt into a grin. "Marcus, are you a closet romantic?"

"Just playing devil's advocate." The tips of his ears flush.

She pushes her glasses farther up her nose. "Well, I don't believe in woo-woo magical explanations for anything; I believe in provable facts. Science can explain what happened to Cass; we just need to form a hypothesis and test it."

"What do you mean?" I ask.

"Here's my theory: Devin was never your boyfriend, but maybe you *have* met him before. You just don't remember. There's no other explanation."

I sigh. "So how do we test your hypothesis?"

"You talk to Devin, of course. I bet he can crack this mystery wide open and tell us how you know each other."

My thighs tense. "That would have been a good idea, but I kind of burned that bridge already."

"How so?" asks Marcus.

"I went to Blooms & Baubles after work to buy some flowers, and I totally embarrassed myself in front of his brother, Larry."

"You mean Perry?" says Marcus.

"Yeah, him. Guys, I saw Devin for approximately two-point-five seconds and I *fainted*. Like a Victorian damsel."

"Are you okay? You didn't hit your head, did you?" Brie grabs my skull and twists it around, looking for a goose egg. I'd left that detail out in my earlier explanation.

"Not too bad, I'm fine. But yeah, let's just say Perry thinks I'm bonkers. Either that or a stalker. If I show up at the flower shop again, I wouldn't be surprised if he called the cops."

"How about I invite Devin to swing by my bar so you guys can talk?" asks Marcus.

"*Your* bar?" I ask.

"Marcus manages Zelma's Taphouse on West Thirtieth," Brie says.

I had no idea. "Oh, well, then yes. Sure. That'd be great."

Marcus's phone is in his hands before I can object, his thumbs already flying across the screen. After a minute of tense silence, he looks up. "He's free tonight."

"*Tonight?*" I blurt. "What did you say? Did you tell him about me?"

"I asked if he wanted to meet me for a drink and catch up since it's been awhile. I didn't mention you—way too hard to explain your situation in a text. I figured I could introduce you when he arrives and you can take it from there. Is that okay?"

"Yes, that's perfect." Brie pats my knee. "We need to get to the bottom of this," she says to me.

I shrug in surrender despite my stomach pulling backflips. "Okay."

Marcus nods and texts Devin back. After several long moments, he looks up. "We're all set for seven."

I check the time on my phone and swallow hard, trying to shove down the total freak-out I feel coming on. It's already after six, not even an hour before I meet Devin face-to-face. "Yes, good. Seven. Perfect."

"I'll be right by your side the whole time," says Brie. I shoot her a grateful smile.

Marcus slips his phone into his pocket. "Speaking of Zelma's, I need to get back to work. See you guys there?" Marcus looks at me expectantly and Brie nudges me with her elbow.

"Yep." My voice is steady but my stomach is anything but. Doubt, dread, anticipation, fear, and tendrils of hope swirl and collide, sucking me toward a head-spinning vortex that threatens to pull me under.

How the hell do you prepare to meet a man you've only dreamed about?

"I don't think I can do this," I shout over the bar's loud music.

The push-up bra Brie insisted I wear under my low-cut top digs into my ribs, and I tug at the underwire. I'm wearing three-inch heels, but even without them I tower over her. The other kids in school used to call us "the odd couple." Petite five-one Brie with her eye-catching curves, thick blond hair, perfect button nose, and adorable gap-toothed grin. And then there was me: gangly Cass Walker with the too-long legs, twiggy five-nine frame, and long nose always stuck in a book. Kids at school openly wondered why we were friends. Even now we tend to attract looks when we go out.

And attracting looks is the last thing I want at the moment. What if Devin walks into the bar, spots me, and there's nothing there? No recognition. Or worse, disgust. Or even worse . . . recognition *and* disgust. I need to be the one to see him before he sees me. My heartbeat accelerates and I wipe my sweaty palms on my black skinny jeans.

"You can *so* do this." Brie bumps my hip with hers.

"You ladies doing okay? Need anything else?" asks the bartender. She's at least twenty years older than us and moves with the precise efficiency of someone who's spent years tending bar. My mouth is so dry all I can do is shake my head.

"Another round of Miller Lites, please," says Brie.

The bartender nods. With practiced movements, she plucks two bottles out from under the bar and cracks them open before placing them in front of us.

"Thank you," I finally manage to croak, but the bartender has already moved on to a couple seated at the end of the bar.

Brie shoves one of the beers in my hand. I finished the first one in about fifteen minutes flat, but it hasn't done anything to calm my nerves. I take several noisy gulps, then hold the bottle against my neck. The cool condensation feels good against my heated skin.

The door to the kitchen swings open and Marcus appears. He strides over when he spots us. "How are you holding up?" he asks from behind the bar.

"So far so good," Brie calls over the general murmur, giving me an encouraging pat on the shoulder. "Any updates on Devin's ETA?"

Marcus shrugs. "He said seven."

I check my phone for the dozenth time since we arrived at 6:55. It's a quarter after seven. Maybe he's not coming. Relief and disappointment wage war in my intestines. I swallow a burp.

"Hey, Marcus, my man," a deep, silky voice rings out behind us. Every muscle in my body stiffens and I nearly drop my beer. Breathing heavily, I swivel my neck just enough so I locate the source of the familiar voice out of the corner of my eye.

Devin. He's here. And he's standing directly beside Brie—barely five feet away—and my *God*, he looks good. He's wearing a faded gray T-shirt partially tucked into slim jeans, and a cotton blazer with the sleeves rolled up to midforearm. I knew from spotting him today that he was the same Devin I remembered, but I'd questioned whether my memories would continue to live up to reality when I eventually saw him up close and personal.

But this Devin, the *real* Devin? At this distance, I can absorb the subtle tilt to his eyebrows, the soft color in his tanned cheeks, the golden glimmer in his chocolate-brown eyes, and the rise and fall of his broad chest. His features are so sharp and vibrant, they're mesmerizing . . . and even more alluring than I remember.

I dimly register that I'm not the only one looking at him. Several women nearby glance in his direction, whispering together with heads bent over cocktail straws. Even the bartender's eyes widen as she stares several beats too long, and the beer she's pouring momentarily overflows.

Reaching across the bar, Devin slaps then shakes Marcus's hand. Something clatters to the floor beside me. Brie disappears for a second and reappears clutching her phone. Her face is pale and her mouth is a thin line. "Holy shit, that's *him*," she whispers.

"I told you so," I say through gritted teeth.

My head goes fuzzy, and I clamp a hand against the edge of the bar to steady myself. I will *not* faint. Not this time.

Devin slides into an empty stool and leans across the bar. "How've you been?" he asks Marcus.

"Good. Haven't seen you in a while. Thought it'd be good to catch up."

Devin nods and takes a swig of his beer as he scans the room. I hold my breath when he looks my way, but his gaze slips past me. I take a hasty sip of beer to cover my bemusement.

"Go on. Say something," murmurs Brie.

"What the hell am I supposed to say? *'Hi, you probably don't know me, but I imagined we were boyfriend-girlfriend when I was in a coma. Wanna grab a drink?'* " I hiss.

Brie shrugs. "Not bad."

Groaning, I attempt to lift my beer to my lips but my hand is shaking so badly I immediately set the bottle down again. I flatten my palms against the bar's grainy wooden surface. If I can survive law school, a car accident, and a coma, I can do this. I suck in a deep breath through my nose. "Okay, time to woman up," I mutter under my breath.

"Damn straight. You got this," Brie whispers.

Marcus's voice booms across the bar. "So, uh, there's actually someone I want you to meet . . ."

"Oh yeah?" says Devin. He follows Marcus's gaze, his dark eyes bouncing between me and Brie.

Brie nudges me forward so I'm face-to-face with Devin. This is it. Time to see if he knows me . . . and how well.

"Hello," I say.

His focus settles on me and I lift my chin and look him straight in the eye. His irises are a dark, soulful brown—just like I remember. I hold my breath. His gaze flicks over my features then his lips curve into a slow, sensual smile. Is that a sign of recognition? My chest aches so deeply I'm afraid it will snap.

How many times have I seen that smile in my mind? Except now Devin's here, in real life, grinning at me like there's nowhere he'd rather be than right here, looking at *me*.

Was Marcus right? Do we know each other?

His lips draw me in like a homing beacon. Memories of how they feel against mine—their soft fullness teasing, tasting. I only realize I'm leaning precariously toward him when I nearly lose my balance, and I stumble forward half a step. Devin's smile widens, revealing gleaming white teeth. He chuckles, and the low sound washes over me like silk. "Hi there. I'm Devin." He extends his hand.

So . . . he *doesn't* know me?

I stare at his hand, at his long fingers. The tip of the pinkie on his right hand is slightly crooked, exactly how I knew it'd be. Brie gives me a sharp poke in the back. Right, I'm standing here, staring with my mouth hanging open like a guppy. Our palms slide together and my breath catches. His hand engulfs mine, and he squeezes slightly as we shake.

"Hi-nice-to-meet-you." My voice comes out in a single, breathy syllable. I clear my throat. "I'm Cassidy Walker. Cass."

"Nice to meet you, Cass."

Marcus shifts his weight, looking from me to Devin. "I haven't introduced you two before, have I?"

"I don't think so," says Devin, eyes twinkling.

"So we *haven't* met before?" I press.

Devin's laugh is velvety, and one corner of his lips lifts as he settles the full force of his gaze on me. "I think I'd remember you."

Being the subject of his scrutiny is like looking into the sun. He's so attractive his attention is blinding. My lips part, but no sound comes out. His palm slips from mine after several long seconds. I don't know whether to giggle hysterically or burst into sobs.

"So, um, funny story—" I begin, but a male voice cuts me off.

"*You?*" Devin's brother storms toward us from across the bar. He's wearing the same white T-shirt and loose jeans from earlier, but his expression is so tight you could say "boo" and he'd probably jump out of his skin. Any whisper of the fun, flirty florist from earlier is long gone.

I close my eyes and groan.

"Who's that?" Brie whispers.

"Devin's brother, Harry," I whisper back.

"You mean Perry?"

"Right."

"Hey, bro. Glad you could make it. I hope it's okay I invited Perry," Devin says to Marcus.

"Of course." His smile tightens from behind the row of taps. "Good to see you, Perry. We've missed you at softball lately."

"I've been busy. What is *she* doing here?" He jerks his thumb in my direction.

I lift my chin. "Marcus invited me."

"We went to high school together," Marcus says. "Cass is one of my tenants."

"You might want to rethink that," Perry mutters under his breath. Edging between me and Devin, he uses his body as a shield as though I might launch myself at his brother like a rabid cat. "Dev, this is her, the woman I told you about. The one who came into the shop earlier and demanded to see you." His back is to me and his voice is low, but I don't miss his words. Or the way Devin's expression immediately shutters.

"Wait, let me explain." I attempt to talk over Perry's shoulder, but he shifts to block me.

Sliding off his barstool, Devin backs away with his hands raised. "I don't know what you're playing at, Marcus, but I'm—"

I put my long-dormant high school basketball skills to use and step resolutely around Perry, blocking him out. "Look, I know this might sound weird, but I—I think we've met before. In fact, I think we know each other pretty well."

Devin narrows his eyes. "I already told you. We've never met."

"I know, I know. But please, just hear me out. I realize this is strange, but there's something going on I can't explain, and it has to do with you."

"How so?"

"Well . . . ahh . . ." How should I even start?

"She woke up from a coma ten months ago and swore she knew you," Brie blurts. I glare at her. "What? Better to get it out in the open now," she adds with an apologetic shrug. That's Brie for you—about as subtle as a Mack truck.

Perry's jaw goes slack.

"You were in a coma?" The way Devin's eyebrows pinch as he looks me over for signs of obvious damage has my skin itching. I can't stand this sort of reaction—pity mixed with a dose of wariness. Like my head is a melon being eyed for soft spots.

"I was only in a coma for a few days. When I woke up, I had all these memories I never had before, and you were in them. Maybe not *you*, you. More like the idea of you? That's why I had such a strong reaction to seeing you in Blooms & Baubles today."

"You fainted," says Perry.

"Thank you, I'm aware." My voice is stiffer than cardboard.

Devin tilts his head. "So it might not have been *me* you remembered?"

"If not, it's one hell of a coincidence. I mean, you look exactly like how I remembered you. I even knew your pinkie would be crooked—I remember you telling me you broke it falling off a trampoline when you were eight."

Devin rubs his hand, the one with the crooked pinkie, and slowly tilts his head. "What else do you think you know about me?"

"Well, um . . ." I shift my weight. "I know your favorite food is pizza rolls, but you don't like real pizza because it's too greasy. You played soccer in high school. Your favorite color is red—"

"As if you couldn't have learned all that from the Internet." Perry snorts.

"Wait, so I'm right? What I know about you is true?"

Perry shoots me a withering glare before grabbing Devin by the shoulder. "Come on, Dev. Remember what you told me? To warn you if I sense a stage-five clinger headed your way? Well, *warning, warning, arooo-ga.* She's a stalker. Let's go."

Devin stares hard at his brother and some unspoken understanding passes between them. After a long moment, he pulls out his wallet and tosses a ten-dollar bill onto the bar. They turn toward the door.

My heartbeat ticks faster. *No, he can't leave. Not until I have answers.* "Wait," I shout, and they pause. "I'm fully aware how bonkers this sounds, but I swear I'm not a stalker. Please, just give me a chance. I've been living with you in my head for almost a year, and until today I thought I imagined you. But here you are—you're a real person, and I have no idea how or why I know things about you, but I do. Please, help me figure out why."

Devin assesses me, lips pursed. "How do I know you're telling the truth? For all I know, you saw me out at a bar and cooked up this story in some lame attempt to get close to me."

"Yeah." Perry folds his arms across his chest. "I wouldn't be surprised if you have an Internet search history a mile long and a Devin shrine in your bedroom, complete with bits of hair and nail clippings."

Marcus shakes his head. "No, Cass is good people. I've known her and Brie here since high school. I can vouch for her. You should hear her out."

"You want proof Cass is telling the truth?" Brie steps forward. "Here's an article from *The Columbus Dispatch* about her accident." She extends her phone toward Devin. On the screen is a headline, "Case Western Law Student Almost Dies in Crash," accompanied by a photo that still makes my gut wrench every time I see it—my little white Camry crunched like a tin can against Interstate 71's concrete median. Red and blue police lights reflect in the broken, blood-splattered glass.

Gingerly, Devin takes Brie's phone and begins scrolling. Perry reads over his shoulder. Jaw tight, he shifts his gaze to me, then back to the article.

"And there's this . . ." Fingers trembling, I reach into the bag at my hip and pull out my sketchbook. The familiar, worn cover is smooth under my fingertips. "I—I started drawing pictures of you. A few weeks after the accident . . . look." Swiveling, I set my sketchbook on the bar and open it to a page near the front.

In the drawing, Devin is resting his chin in his hand, staring into the middle distance as though he's listening intently. Real Devin shuffles closer; I register his presence as he hands Brie's phone back to her and stands at my side. Heart hammering, I steal a glance at his face. His wide eyes dart across the image, no doubt attempting to process what he's seeing. I swallow hard and flip a few more pages, letting him take it all in.

"What the hell?" Perry breathes from over Devin's shoulder.

"I drew this one seven months ago. And this one"—I thumb through several more sketches until landing on one of Devin lying in the grass with his hands behind his head—"five months ago. They're dated, see?" I tap the date scribbled at the bottom of the page.

"As if you couldn't have faked the dates," scoffs Perry.

I whirl on him, heat rising in my cheeks. "I know it's hard for you to believe, but I have better things to do than cook up an elaborate scheme to trap some guy. I have a life and a law career, you know."

"This is a lot to take in," Devin murmurs. Scrubbing a palm over his mouth, he blows out a long breath. "Okay. Tell me something no one else would know about me. Something you can't learn from the Internet."

Conversations buzz all around us while upbeat music fills the air, but it's like I've stepped into the vacuum of space. Everything seems to go quiet as I narrow my focus to a laser point on Devin's determined features. How can I possibly tell him something so personal? Most of my memories of him are fragments or clips—scraps of conversation and impressions of feelings, sounds, and scenes. I open my mouth, but only a croaking sound comes out.

Perry shakes his head. "I knew it. Come on." Tugging Devin's arm, he ushers him toward the door.

"Wait!" I call. "I—I know that your parents divorced when you were six. You like watching murder-mystery documentaries with your dad. And . . . and . . . I know about your plans for the family business! How you want to . . ." A phrase echoes from the depths of my memory, and I seize it. ". . . deliver it into the future."

I'm not exactly sure what that means, but Devin and Perry must because they both freeze. Perry's eyebrows raise so high they've disappeared underneath his mop of copper-brown hair.

Devin's face pales. "How do you know about that?"

"That's the whole point. I have no idea. And that's what I want to find out." I put every ounce of earnest conviction I can behind my words, willing him to believe me. We stare at each other for several heartbeats. He's standing a mere few feet away, but the space between us feels as cavernous as a football stadium. My gut squeezes and I hold my breath.

Finally, he shifts his weight and looks away. "Well, shit." Tipping his head back, he lets out a peal of deep laughter. The sound pierces my chest and travels all the way to my toes. "So I'm the man of your dreams?"

A breathy laugh escapes me. "Kind of."

"Okay then."

My heart hopscotches. "*Okay then?* Does that mean you'll hear me out?"

"Sure. This is wild. I don't think we've ever met . . ." Devin's voice trails off as he studies my face. Shaking his head, he looks away. "It's a lot to process, but maybe there's something to it. How about we put our heads together over drinks and see if we can solve this mystery? Say, Friday?"

My mind goes blank. "Ahhhh—"

"Friday. She'll be there," Brie chimes in.

I swallow thickly. "It's a date. I mean—not a date," I hastily add when Devin blinks. "It'll be more like . . . an interview. A get-to-know-you sort of thing." Heat pools in my cheeks and I want to dive under the bar to hide. *Why am I so awkward?*

Devin scratches his nose. "So, we'll sit down. Have a couple drinks. Talk. Exchange life stories. See what we have in common or who we both might know besides Marcus who can explain this situation. That kind of thing."

"Right."

"Okay." His tongue sneaks out to wet his lower lip and sparks dance in my belly. Snagging a pen from behind the bar, Devin jots his phone number on a napkin and hands it to me. Clicking the pen closed, he peers at me from underneath a lock of dark hair that's fallen across his forehead. "See you then."

Behind me, someone groans, and I spot Perry staring at the floor shaking his head. My gut tightens. I've been through so much in the last year, but to have my dream man be . . . well, real? And to have a chance to figure out why he's been in my head since the accident? To turn that opportunity down would be like saying no to a giant handout from the universe. If I have any hope of living my best life again, I need to figure out what happened in the imaginary one—Perry's disapproval be damned.

Brie snatches the napkin from Devin and tucks it into my bag, along with my sketchbook. "Well, we should get going. Early day tomorrow. Right, Cass?"

"Right. It was good seeing—er, meeting you."

Chuckling, Devin draws his thumb across his lower lip. "Same. See you Friday, *Cass*."

The sound of my name on his lips nearly buckles my knees again, and I only manage to make it to the door with Brie steering me by the shoulders like she's pushing a boulder up a hill.

I'm having drinks with Devin. Except this time, it's real.

6

How I've made it to Friday without dissolving into a puddle of nerves is a mystery to me.

I tap my toe under my desk and force myself *not* to look at the time on my computer. Still, the tiny numbers in the corner are visible whether I like it or not, so I can't help but absorb them in my peripheral vision.

It's after three o'clock. Only four more hours until drinks with Devin.

At least, I assume we're still having drinks tonight. I texted him on Tuesday with a time and place for us to meet on Friday. Within ten minutes, he'd texted me back. Junction, 7pm. Got it. Looking forward to getting to know you, mystery girl.

And then . . . nothing.

No follow-ups. No how's your week going? Or, what are you up to today? Radio silence.

I can't exactly blame him; I haven't texted him either. But only because I'm not sure I can trust myself to engage in normal, casual chitchat. Even though we only met a few days ago, part of my brain still thinks we're in a relationship, which is just plain weird. The reality is that we've never dated. He might look like Dream Devin, but who's to say Real Devin isn't completely different?

The only way to know for sure is to get to know *him*. Tonight's my chance to understand who he is and why my brain has manufactured memories of us together—a chance I never thought I'd get. I can't screw it up.

My phone's dark screen taunts me from beside my keyboard. Flipping it facedown, I force my attention back to the multiple Westlaw tabs full of research and the memorandum I've been drafting that are crowding my double monitors. The words seem to blur together, and I drag my knuckles up the bridge of my nose to my forehead in an effort to dispel the dull headache that's taken up permanent residence behind my eyes.

I was lucky enough to earn an assignment this summer in the litigation practice group—my top choice—but I forgot how exhausting it is to sit for ten to twelve hours a day, analyzing dense legal documents. Shaking my head, I take a long gulp of water from my Hydro Flask and refocus on the screen.

Someone coughs—a dainty sound that somehow manages to slice through my noise-canceling earbuds. Closing my eyes briefly in a bid for patience, I pluck out an earbud and rotate in my seat, even though I already know the source.

My cubicle-mate, Mercedes Trowbridge, aka summer associate "Allred," flashes me a razor-edged smile. "Do you mind?" She nods at my foot, which I realize I'm mindlessly tapping against the back wall of my desk. Her strawberry-blond hair is as mirror smooth as it was on orientation day, and she's wearing her signature color— red. Except today her blouse is more poppy red than yesterday's port wine red or Monday's crimson. Turns out I was spot-on with the "Allred" nickname.

Her long, delicate fingers hover over her keyboard as she stares at me expectantly, eyebrows raised.

I slow my tapping, and the dull *tunk tunk* quiets. I recross my legs. "Sorry." The smile I flash is as tight-lipped as her own.

Exhaling briskly through her nose, she flicks her hair over her shoulder as she turns to her screen and begins typing. Grumbling, I swivel to face my own desk. Chalk it up to my rotten luck to be assigned to the same two-person workspace as the most unfriendly, daggers-out law student I've ever met.

After her attempt at a chair coup on Monday, I'd desperately hoped I was wrong about her—and not just because we have to share a cubicle. There are few enough women in law as it is, and even fewer who stick it out, rise through the ranks, and make partner. I say let's lift each other up instead of bat each other down. Out of the twelve summer associates at Smith & Boone, there are only two other women besides me and Mercedes—a middle-aged career switcher and an aspiring patent attorney who's quieter than a Pet Rock. I'd hoped that once Mercedes and I got to know one another, we'd find some common ground. Maybe even be—well, probably not friends—at the very least, mutually respected colleagues.

But no. Every single attempt to crack through her icy shell has ricocheted like putty. If she's not actively ignoring my lunchtime small talk, she's passive-aggressively clearing her throat or dramatically sighing every time I so much as sneeze. And when I deigned to make a peace offering yesterday of a blueberry scone I picked up from the coffee shop down the street, she looked at me like I'd offered her arsenic. Her nostrils flared and her mouth twisted when I shrugged and took a bite, like I was the most revolting person on the planet for enjoying carbs and sugar.

At least our desks face away from each other in the snug three-walled cubicle, so I don't have to see her constant expression of haughty disapproval that she reapplies as often as her power lipstick. A small mercy.

My phone vibrates and I sigh. Fifty bucks says it's Brie psyching me up for tonight. Or else it's my mom texting me for the ump-teenth time for an update on my first week at the firm. The name on the screen makes me jolt so hard I nearly knock over my water. My heart leaps like a ballerina. It's Devin.

> Still on for Junction @7?

I can't stop my fingers from trembling when I text him back.

> Absolutely! I have my magnifying glass packed and ready to go!

As soon as I hit send, I cringe. *Oh God.*

> I mean, like, to solve a mystery 😊

Groaning, I bury my face in my palm. Nearly a year of little to no social contact other than family, Brie, and doctors must have zapped any flirtatious texting prowess I previously possessed—weak as it was.

A dull knock reverberates against the wall of my cubicle. Dropping my phone into my lap, I take out my earbuds. Andréa Miller, a senior attorney at the firm and the leader of the litigation group, is standing beside my desk, deep brown eyes crinkled in a smile. Her white button-down is rolled up to her elbows, exposing her dark, toned forearms, and the pleat in her tailored skirt is so sharp it could cut glass.

Warmth fills my chest. Andréa is the reason I landed an offer from Smith & Boone in the first place. She was my mentor at the US Attorney's Office when I clerked there after my first year of law school. We stayed in touch, and when she landed a job at Smith & Boone as a senior litigator two years later and found out I'd applied for a first-year associate position, she put in a good word for me with the hiring committee. And now that I'm a summer-but-hopefully-soon-to-be-first-year associate, she specifically requested *me* for her practice group: litigation, one of the most well-respected—and lucrative—groups in the firm.

"How's the memo for the Beckley appeal going?" she asks.

I flick my gaze to the open Word document on my screen. The rough draft is done but still needs to be properly formatted with citations and a hefty dose of proofreading. Mercedes has stopped typing. She appears to be checking her email, but her back is unusually straight. She's totally eavesdropping.

"Great. I'll have it in your in-box before I leave today."

"Excellent! Do you have an hour? I'm hopping on a conference call with a client to go over some questions before his deposition next week. It'd be good for you to listen in. And if you don't mind, take some notes."

My phone buzzes from where I'm clutching it in my lap. Devin's texted me back. I quickly glance down.

> Roger that, Nancy Drew. See you at 7

I swallow the dry lump rising in my throat. If I sit in on the conference call, it won't leave me much time to finish my memo and get home in time to get ready for tonight's meet-up.

But this is big law life. There's only one answer. "Of cour—"

"I'd be happy to take notes for you, Andréa," Mercedes cuts in.

Every muscle in my body goes tense. I know what Mercedes's doing. And I don't like it. Not one bit.

Andréa blinks. "Thanks, but Cass has it covered . . . Mercedes, isn't it?"

Mercedes pops out of her seat and extends her hand. Her charcoal skirt hugs the voluptuous curve of her hips. "Trowbridge. Ohio State University Law School graduate, magna cum laude."

What the hell? I thought I was the only graduate in the summer associate program. Typically, summer associates are rising second- and third-year law students. My situation was unique. Or so I thought. That would explain her extra helping of competitiveness toward me. We're competing for the same position in real time.

"A fellow Buckeye. Nice to meet you." They shake. "Which practice group are you assigned to?"

"Public law."

"Ah, Frank Carlson's group."

"Yes. But I'd love some exposure to litigation, and I'm always happy to help if you need an extra hand."

From anyone else, I'd consider this a run-of-the-mill, benign request for practical experience in a different area of the law. But from the tone of Mercedes's voice and the way one corner of her lips curl into a split-second smirk, it's clearly an indictment of my perceived skills. An attempt to hip check me out of her way and into my assigned group. Heat pulses through my veins and I ball a hand into a fist on my lap. My nails dig into my palm.

Andréa blinks twice. "I'll talk to Frank and see what we can do. Ready?" She says to me.

With a nod, I stuff my phone into a drawer, unplug my laptop from its docking station, and follow Andréa out.

"She's intense, that one," she says once we're two hallways down and out of earshot.

The temptation to drag Mercedes from here to Timbuktu pounds in my chest, but I shove it down. I prefer to take the high road. It's less crowded up there.

I shrug one shoulder. "She wouldn't be at Smith & Boone if she wasn't."

Andréa chuckles. "True."

We enter her windowed office and she closes the door behind me. I settle into the sleek, upholstered chair across from her desk and send up a silent prayer to whatever god is listening . . . *please, don't let this call take too long.* I have a memo to finish and the meeting of my life to get ready for. No problem, right?

"Brie, I have a problem." My voice comes out a choked whisper even though I'm alone in the women's bathroom at the end of the hall.

"What's up, buttercup? It's almost seven—why aren't you home getting ready for your get-together with Dream Boy?"

"Because I'm still at the office."

"What! Why?"

"I got roped into a client meeting and then I had to finish a memo for my supervisor that took way longer than I thought." At least Mercedes already went home. The last thing I need is for her to walk in on my bout of unbridled panic.

"You know you're supposed to be there in fifteen minutes, right?"

"I know! And now I don't have time to go home and change . . . help! Can you drive over and bring me the dress we talked about? The knee-length periwinkle one that's hanging on the back of my closet? And the white stone necklace and matching sandals?" It's not a date, but I still want to look my best . . . not like I spent the last ten hours hunched over a computer like a gargoyle.

"Oh, honey, I wish I could. Any other night I'd totally be there, but I have a thing."

"What thing?"

"I'm presenting at an engineering conference downtown. They asked me to speak on a panel for Young Leaders in Flight." Her voice takes on a mocking bravado, and I can practically hear her eye roll.

"A: that's awesome, own it. B: Why did you tell Devin I could do Friday when he suggested it at the bar? I wouldn't have missed cheering you on for the world. Devin and I could have met some other night."

"I couldn't let you put off having drinks with him. There will be other conferences. No biggie. Why don't you text Devin and let him know you'll be half an hour late? Then you can go home and change," she says.

"I texted him earlier to give him a heads-up that I might be a bit late, and he was already on his way from Independence."

"Maybe he got stuck in traffic? It is rush hour on a Friday. Maybe you'll get lucky and he's running behind too . . ."

My phone chooses that moment to buzz and I check the notification on the screen. "Shit!" I blurt.

"What?"

I put her on speakerphone and read the text.

I'm here. I got us a table up front by the bar. What do you want to drink? I'll order for you.

Fingers flying across the screen, I respond. Gin and tonic, thanks! Leaving work now . . .

"Aww, that's sweet," croons Brie.

Warmth expands my chest and creeps up my neck. "Agreed. But, Brie, he's already at the restaurant. I can't make him wait another half hour to go home and change. He barely agreed to hear me out in the first place. If I'm not there soon he might think twice about meeting with me and decide to leave."

"Then it's go time. Come on, let's see what we're working with." My phone buzzes again, this time with a FaceTime request from Brie. I accept and prop my phone against the mirror. Her heart-shaped, anxious face fills the screen, peering at me as I take a step back and turn in a circle, holding out my arms.

She pushes her thin gold glasses further up her nose. "Hmmm," she murmurs.

"That's it? *Hmmm*?"

"Not bad 'hmmm.' Thoughtful 'hmmm.' What do you have in your bag?"

"I don't know. Zip ties, kerosene, maybe a stick of dynamite?"

"Knowing you? I believe it. I meant in terms of confidence-boosting doodads."

Pulling my bag over from where I'd dropped it on the counter, I dig through its murky depths and begin pulling out anything and everything that could potentially help me look like I didn't just crawl out of an office-sized ditch. "Concealer, lipstick, mascara, bobby pins . . ." My fingers brush against something small and metal and I grab it. "Ooo, dangly earrings!" I search for the other half of the pair. I eventually find it and marvel at the glittering gold teardrops I thought I'd lost years ago. Thank God I haven't cleaned out this bag since law school. Or probably ever, to be honest. Brie likes to joke that I'm the queen of clutter, and she's not wrong.

"Perfect!" She whoops. "That's all you need. Brighten up your undereye with the concealer, put on a coat of mascara, and use the lipstick on your lips, cheeks, and eyelids. Swap out your studs and you're ready to go."

I swipe on the makeup in record time. I already look like I got at least two more hours of sleep. My face glows with the added color and the earrings shimmer around my jaw. "What about my hair?"

"Can you take it down?"

"I have bun hair."

"Okay, keep it up. Maybe secure Rogue Curl with an extra bobby pin."

"Check." Wetting my fingers under the faucet, I smooth the flyaways around my forehead and slip a bobby pin into my hair behind my ear next to the one that's already there, ensuring my one short lock doesn't escape.

"Gorgeous. With your bone structure, you can rock a high bun like none other. Now, unbutton an extra button on your shirt."

"Why?" I blurt.

"You're meeting your dream man. It's okay to show a little lace."

"I'm wearing a skin-colored T-shirt bra."

"Just see how it looks."

I slip the third button undone from my emerald-green blouse, and it parts, revealing the barest hint of cleavage, but thankfully no grandma bra.

Brie pumps her fist. "Yass, you look *hot*. Have you ordered an Uber yet?"

I pick up my phone. "On it. Thanks a million, Brie. And good luck on your panel. I know you'll rock it."

"Thanks, doll. Can't wait to hear all about your tête-à-tête with Devin when you get home." She waggles her eyebrows. "Later!"

"Love you!" I end the call and pull open my Uber app as I leave the bathroom. It's still searching for a ride when I step out of the elevator on the first floor. I curse under my breath. The closest available Uber is twelve minutes away, and it's already 6:55. It's only a ten-minute walk to the restaurant though. I can make it on foot and show up more or less on time.

When I step outside, a brisk wind whips my collar around my neck. Ominous purple-gray clouds blanket the sky. According to my weather app, it's not supposed to rain for another thirty minutes. I'll be fine. I hitch my bag higher on my shoulder and start walking. My heels clack dully against the uneven sidewalk.

When I'm a block away from the office, a crack of thunder echoes through the darkening sky. "No." I pick up my pace.

Two blocks later, the first raindrop splatters against my nose.

7

Thunder crashes above me as I yank open the door to the restaurant. The soles of my shoes squeak against the wood floor as I edge around the seven or so people waiting for a table. When the hostess catches sight of me, her eyes go wide. "Can I help you?"

Wiping the water from my forehead, I strive for nonplussed. "I'm meeting someone."

"Cass?" Devin's standing not ten feet away at a small, square table tucked behind a glass divider next to the hostess stand.

My lips part. He's even more handsome than I remember, and how that's possible I have no idea. He's wearing fitted gray jeans and a black polo that clings to his broad chest. Reaching down, he picks something up from the chair next to him—a bouquet of white lilies.

Exactly like our imaginary first date. My lips part.

The back of my neck tingles and the scene blurs. I blink, and an image of Devin wearing a casual black sport coat over a white button-down with a crimson scarf wrapped loosely around his neck flashes across my vision. He's holding lilies just like he is now, except they're not wrapped in brown paper; rather, a whisper of crinkling plastic wrap echoes in my ears.

My breath catches and my knees wobble. The scene rights itself, and Real Devin is standing there, looking as devastatingly handsome as ever, lips tilted into a grin, eyebrows raised as his gaze travels over me.

Has this happened before? Or did I coma-dream this moment, or some variation of it, into existence? I lick my rain-splattered lips. Maybe it doesn't matter. Devin's here, and he's waiting for me. My legs carry me toward him like I'm on one of those moving platforms in an airport. Suddenly, pain explodes across my face. I stumble backward, clasping my nose. "Owww!"

Did I . . . ? *Yep.* I just walked straight into the glass wall next to the hostess stand. What a smashing start to the evening.

"Are you okay?" Devin's beside me now, his voice a warm caress as he gently grips my shoulder. He's so close I can smell the ginger on his breath and the bergamot notes of his cologne.

Dropping my hands, I nod. "Yeah." I can't believe I walked into a wall. At least my nose isn't bleeding, although it aches like a mofo. Heat scalds my cheeks and it's all I can do not to bolt out the door and go jump into Lake Erie. He guides me around the flabbergasted hostess, careful to give the glass divider a wide berth, and steers me to his table. Once I'm settled into one of the metal chairs, he slides into the seat opposite me. The dimly lit restaurant is filled with a menagerie of mouthwatering scents. Behind Devin, the sleek, tiled bar is packed with well-dressed people conversing over cocktails.

I shift in my seat, suddenly conscious that I'm thoroughly damp. My silk blouse is sticking to my skin and I'd bet money my mascara has run under my eyes. Plucking at my collar, I push a few tendrils of wet hair off my forehead and spread my arms wide. "Well, this is a good start." I laugh. I can't help it. For all my worrying, prepping, and primping for my meet-up with Devin, I show up looking like a drowned poodle and nearly break my nose within the first thirty seconds of walking through the door. I definitely do not remember *this* ever happening.

Devin's eyes twinkle and I'm relieved when he joins in my laughter. Now that I've started it's hard to stop, and tears gather at the corner of my eyes. Unfolding my napkin, I wipe away the moisture—and any errant mascara—and force myself to take three deep breaths. "I'm sorry. I'm a mess."

He grins at me, tilting his head back. "Nah, you're gorgeous." Warmth spreads out from my chest with every beat of my heart. "Oh, you have a little . . ." He motions to a spot behind my ear.

Any lingering laughter dies on my tongue. "It's my Rogue Curl, isn't it?" With a self-conscious smile, I remove the bobby pins and band securing my bun and shake out my hair. Water is a reset button for curly hair, so I can let it air dry without worrying about a bun line. And when it's down, I can tuck Rogue Curl behind my ear so it's less noticeable.

"Rogue curl?" he asks.

"I have one piece of hair that's shorter than the rest, and it tends to stick out." At his questioning expression, I add, "Doctors had to shave a patch of hair for surgery after the accident, and it's still growing out." Devin's eyebrows knit briefly, but he doesn't ask me to elaborate, which I'm grateful for. "Are those for me?" I ask, pointing to the bouquet of lilies on the table.

"Of course. Can't show up to meet a beautiful woman empty-handed." He extends the bouquet across the table and I take it from him.

"They're lovely, thank you." I inhale deeply. The powerful floral scent fills my nose, tickling my sinuses, and I sneeze.

"Bless you." Devin chuckles.

I set the bouquet on one of the two empty chairs at the table. "Thanks. And thank you for agreeing to this . . . to meeting with me."

"Hey, it's not every day someone shows up at a bar and tells you you're her 'dream man.' What can I say? I'm intrigued." With a smoldering grin that could break hearts the world over, he slides a cocktail across the table toward me—the gin and tonic I asked for.

I take a long sip. A hint of lime soothes the fizzy burst of tonic as it burns a warm path down my throat. "So." I lick my lips. "Where should we start?"

"How is it possible we don't know *any* of the same people?" I spear a piece of calamari on my fork and nearly moan when I chew. It's lightly fried in a spicy ginger sauce, and the savory flavors twine into a symphony of taste on my tongue. Half an hour of sipping cocktails, comparing social media accounts, and hashing out possible acquaintances sure does work up an appetite. I'm grateful Devin showed up hungry and put in an appetizer order before I arrived.

"You tell me, Scully. This is your show." Our waiter arrives with two fresh cocktails, and Devin lifts his Moscow mule in a salute before taking a drink. I'm momentarily distracted by the way a droplet of moisture clings to his full bottom lip before he licks it away.

I clear my throat. "I thought for sure we'd have other mutual friends besides Marcus. I guess Cleveland's east side/west side divide is real."

"You grew up on the east side?"

"Far east. Chagrin Falls."

He whistles low. "Fancy."

"Not where I lived, trust me. My mom moved us there for the school system when I was twelve, into a tiny 1930s bungalow on the edge of town."

"No mansion on the river then?"

I chuckle. "Definitely not." Chagrin Falls is known for its old money, so it wasn't exactly easy blending in with the other kids at school. Thank God for Brie. She was the only one who didn't seem to care that I was raised by a single working mom who could barely afford our meager mortgage, never mind fancy summer camps, music lessons, or extravagant vacations like so many others enjoyed.

Devin leans forward, resting his elbows on the table. "So let me guess . . . you already know where I grew up?"

"Cleveland, right?"

He nods. "Ohio City. Down the street from Blooms & Baubles, actually."

"I *didn't* know that."

"I thought you knew everything about me," he says teasingly.

"Hardly. A lot of what I 'remember' is a blur, like impressions of half-forgotten dreams. It seems I know some things about your life, but there are other things I didn't know at all. Like the fact you have a brother. Honestly, I don't even know how much of what I remember is true."

"A lot of what you said at the bar the other night was. I did indeed break my finger falling off a trampoline when I was eight. I enjoy a good true-crime documentary, and I hate pizza—sacrilege, I know." He drops his voice to a conspiratorial whisper and my lips part at the confirmation. "So, try me. What else do you think you know about me?"

"Well . . ." I take a deep breath. "Do you have a BA from Denison and an MBA from Ohio State?"

"Ding-ding."

"Okay. Were you an all-state soccer player your senior year of high school?"

"And junior year." He clicks his tongue as he winks.

I laugh. "And . . ." I stare into the middle distance, trying to remember. "Do you happen to have a scarf? Dark red with fringe and a pattern of little white circles? I know it's weird, but somehow I think I've seen it before. I even had a feeling you might wear it tonight—if it wasn't so warm out."

He stares at me for so long sweat threatens to gather between my shoulder blades and I shift in my seat.

"Wrong," he finally says.

"Oh well. See? I don't know everything about you."

"It has white *squares*, not circles. It was my grandpa's favorite—the first thing he bought at Higbees after he immigrated from Poland and started selling flowers out of a pushcart downtown. He gave it to me before he died."

"I'm so sorry."

He waves me away. "He passed a long time ago. But it *is* my favorite scarf, and I *did* think about wearing it tonight . . . but you're right. It's too warm." Even though the restaurant's chairs are metal backed and stiff, he sprawls as though he's perfectly at ease. Like we're sitting on a couch in his living room talking about the weather rather than in the middle of a crowded restaurant casually chatting about an inexplicable quirk of fate or the universe or something.

I marvel at his effortless confidence. Apart from his bone structure, which must have been blessed by the gods, he's one of those rare people who draws in everyone around him simply by existing. Maybe it's the way he holds himself—assured, but not aggressive. Or perhaps it's the way he looks you in the eye when you're talking, making you feel like you're the only person in the room. Whatever combination of qualities it is, Devin Szymanski is magnetism personified.

Even now, two tables over, a pair of young women stare at him over their menus. A fair number of passersby—women and men and everyone in between—pull double-takes when they glance his way, and I don't think the hostess has taken her eyes off him since I walked in. But somehow, I'm the one who ended up here, at this table, having a heartfelt conversation with Devin.

I lean back in my chair with a huff. "How are you so sanguine about all this?"

"About what?"

"Me—this whole situation. I can't believe you're giving me the time of day, let alone trust I'm not some psycho spinning lies about 'coma memories' to *Fatal Attraction* you."

Helping himself to another piece of calamari, he shrugs. "I believe in the supernatural. Or at least, the idea that strange things happen that modern science can't explain. Plus, I have a sense about people."

"Your brother doesn't seem to think so. He's quite protective of you." Forking a piece of calamari, I stuff it into my mouth.

"Perry tries. Even though growing up, he was the one who needed protecting."

I finish chewing, then swallow. "Why? Isn't he older than you?"

"Only by a year and a half—I'm twenty-seven and he's twenty-nine. Perry marches to the beat of his own drummer. Always has. Ever since he was little, he's been digging in the dirt and making bouquets. Talking about taking over the family business and becoming a florist like our mom and grandpa. You can imagine how well that went over with the other kids at school, especially the boys."

I wince. Kids can be real assholes sometimes. "And you never wanted to take over the business?"

"Nah. Mom offered to leave it to both of us, but it's not my thing."

"But I saw you the other day in the store . . . you were about to deliver an order. Do you work there?"

"Sort of." At my questioning glance, he elaborates. "Last year our mom was diagnosed with rheumatoid arthritis—probably from the years she spent working herself to the bone trying to keep the business alive. Her doctor recommended a lifestyle change, so last spring she sold the house, moved to a retirement community in Florida, and transferred majority ownership of Blooms & Baubles to Perry. He ran things on his own for a while, but he's never had a head for numbers. I quit my job in Columbus earlier this year and moved back home to help him right the ship."

"Is that how you're helping him 'deliver the business into the future?'" I recount that phrase that stopped Devin and Perry in their tracks.

"You could say that." His expression is relaxed, but a line forms between his eyebrows as he takes a long sip of his drink.

I tap my fingers against my thigh. "So where *do* you work if not at Blooms & Baubles?"

"For my dad. He's a developer on the south side of the city. My hours are flexible, so you can find me at the shop most afternoons helping Perry with the books or dropping off the occasional order when his regular delivery guy is busy."

Putting down his fork, Devin rests his elbows on the table and folds his hands together. "But enough about me. I want to know about *you*. I mean, besides the fact you graduated top of your class from Kent State and summa cum laude from Case Western Reserve University School of Law, where you served as the editor of the *Law Review* and captain of the mock trial team. And now you work for Smith & Boone—great firm, by the way. My dad's business is a client. Did I get all that right?"

Warmth inches up my neck. "It looks like someone's been doing some googling."

"Well, I had to make sure you weren't going to *Fatal Attraction* me. Guys like me can't be too careful with mysterious women like you."

"I guess I am pretty mysterious."

"The situation? Yes. You?" He stares into my eyes. "You're fascinating."

"Fascinating like a science experiment?"

"Like a *person*. Now, don't get mad . . . but I kind of love that you walked into a glass wall ten seconds after you showed up and laughed it off."

"For the record, I was dying of embarrassment on the inside."

"And you obviously ran through the rain just to get here. I don't know many women who would have risked ruining their outfit or whatever. My last girlfriend never stepped foot in the rain because she hated messing up her makeup."

My gut twists. He's edging awfully close to a "you're not like the other girls" compliment, which really isn't a compliment at all. Flexing my jaw, I clasp my hands in my lap. "Taking pride in how you look isn't a bad thing."

"No, it's not." He scrubs his hand through his hair, seeming to sense my tension. "What I mean is . . . you're beautiful and smart—obviously you're smart, you're a lawyer. And you experienced a brush with death, recovered, and you even seem to be thriving. But despite all that, you don't take yourself too seriously. I like that about you."

Maintaining eye contact, he lets the words settle into the space between us. My jaw unclenches and my muscles go lax under the smoldering intensity of his gaze.

"Now it's your turn. What do you like about *me*?" Grinning, he rests his chin on his hand and damn it if it isn't completely adorable.

"Does that line actually work for you?"

"Sometimes. Is it working now?"

"I thought we were talking about *me*," I tease.

"Yes, we were." He sits up straighter. "So, Cassidy . . ."

"Cass."

"So, Cass. Tell me about *you*."

8

"It looks like the rain stopped." Devin holds the door open for me as we finally exit the restaurant. It's nighttime now—way past nine judging by the bruise-purple shade of the sky. We must have been talking for well over two hours. *Huh.* I can't remember the last time I enjoyed myself so thoroughly in someone's company. Not that basking in Devin's attention is a chore.

Stepping onto the brick sidewalk, I avoid the numerous puddles shimmering in the streetlights. I'm surprisingly steady, despite my three gin and tonics. "Thank God. I don't need another shower." I chuckle. My hair is mostly dry, but my shirt still holds a hint of dampness.

Pausing on the sidewalk, I shift my bag higher on my shoulder, careful not to crush my bouquet of lilies sticking out. "Thanks for meeting with me tonight. And for the drinks."

Grinning, he shoves his hands into the front pockets of his jeans. "My pleasure. Too bad we're no closer to cracking the Case of the Mysterious Memories than we were before."

"Right." Too bad, indeed. If anything, I have more questions than ever. Like why do I know certain random details about Devin, but other big, important aspects of his life are a blank?

Maybe the universe gets a kick out of scattering bread crumbs instead of serving up a whole meal.

Devin saunters closer until only a foot of space separates us. "What do you say we keep the investigation going?"

I blink up at him. "What do you mean?"

"Well, the night's still young, and there's still lots to talk about. How about we continue comparing notes somewhere more fun?"

I swallow, but I can't prevent my voice from going hoarse. "What did you have in mind?"

"Hmmm." He taps his chin. "We could take a walk along the river. Check out an art gallery—wait." He snaps. "I got it. Do you like pinball, by chance?"

My ears perked up at "art gallery"—I haven't been to one in ages—but "pinball" has me intrigued. "I've played a time or two."

"I've got the perfect place. It's not far. Only a few blocks away."

I grin. "You're on."

His phone trills from his pocket. "One sec." His eyes flick across the screen and he taps out what I assume is a text before stashing his cell away. "Shall we?" He proffers his elbow and I slip my fingers around the corded muscles of his forearm. His delicious scent fills my nose, and I inhale deeply, reveling in the solid presence at my side.

We stroll at a slow, meandering pace, taking in the sights, smells, and sounds of West Twenty-Fifth Street, the beating heart of Ohio City. We watch as people dip into bars, dine on patios, and laugh as they meander down the street. The scent of hops and pizza floats on the balmy air, and we chat about our favorite Cleveland restaurants. The next block up, we pause to peer through a store window, admiring the diverse knickknacks and wares for sale.

I catch our reflection in the window and my neck tingles. A vision of us walking arm in arm down a different, less crowded, city street flashes in my mind before it dissipates like the mist rising from the sidewalk.

Why can't the life in my memories be my *real* life? I've busted my ass for as long as I can remember. I didn't party in college so I could land a scholarship to law school. Then three years of nose-to-the-grindstone studying while constantly striving to live up to my mother's expectations and become the self-sufficient, successful woman she wants me to be. Maybe Devin showing up is karma . . . the universe throwing me a bone for once.

Maybe it's too much to hope for. But maybe hoping is everything.

"You're frowning." Devin's warm breath tickles my ear and I jolt.

My fingers flex automatically, tightening around his forearm. "I was just thinking."

"About what?"

I inhale deeply. "What if . . . ?" I shake my head. "Never mind."

"What if you're psychic?" he ventures.

I let out a bark of laughter. "You think I'm psychic?"

"It'd be one way to explain what's going on. I'm thinking of a number between zero and one hundred."

"No way."

"Come on, what number am I thinking of?"

"Seventy-three?"

"Close. Twelve."

I giggle.

"Okay, maybe you're not psychic. But what if you have super-powers?"

I roll my eyes. "I do not have superpowers."

"No, hear me out. What if you can manifest your deepest desires?"

"That's ludicrous. And assuming a lot. Who says you're my deepest desire?"

"Hey, *you're* the one who woke up remembering *me*. Come on, just try it."

"Fine." Slipping my arm out of his, I move to the edge of the side-walk. I roll my neck and shimmy my shoulders. "Okay, now what?"

"What is it you most desire? Picture it in your mind."

Grinning, I close my eyes and say the first thing that comes to mind. "Cheesecake." I lift my palms expectantly. After three heartbeats, I peel open one eye. "Did it work?"

"You tell me."

Behind him, a streetlight illuminates a crisp, black-and-white sign: Pullman's Bakery.

I smile so wide my cheeks ache. "No way."

"Way." Gathering my hand, he tugs me to the corner, and we peer through the window. Inside, upturned chairs crown small, circular tables, and the lights are off.

"Closed." I sigh dramatically. "It looks like I can't make my desires come to life after all."

I only realize Devin's still holding my hand when he sweeps his thumb along my knuckles and the sensation burrows straight into my belly. "We'll see," he murmurs.

We continue, hand in hand. My skin tingles against his and my head feels curiously light, like I might float away on a dream. We take a right at the next corner down a less crowded side street.

"So . . . any other ideas for how we can explain what's going on here?" I ask.

He stops walking. So do I. Behind him, neon lettering in the window of a low brick building proclaims Kinetic Kanteen Pinball Parlor. This must be the place. Before I can make a move for the door, he gathers my other hand and squeezes. My heart stutter-steps when he dips his chin to peer into my face.

"What if your memories are a sign that we were supposed to meet? That fate somehow brought us together?" he asks softly.

"Is that really what you think?"

"I have no idea." He chuckles softly. "But I do know I like you. And I'm glad we met."

My heart thunders in my aching chest. "Me too," I whisper.

He's so close I can see every line, every plane of his beautiful face. The straight, sharp angle of his nose. The dim shadows under his cheekbones. A scar above his left eyebrow catches the light. Thin and white, it's roughly an inch long and follows the contour of his arch, fanning out past the tip. I frown. That's strange; I don't remember ever drawing a scar.

"You're staring." His dark eyes twinkle.

"I'm sorry." With an apologetic smile, I slip my hands out of his. "Part of me still has a hard time believing you're real."

Grasping my right hand, he lays my palm flat against his cheek. His skin is as cool and smooth as satin. "I'm real."

The city noises quiet around us and the only thing in the whole world is Devin. His face—the face I know so well—seems to grow larger until it fills my entire field of vision. My limbs are loose and languid from the cocktails, and I teeter closer, drawn by the powerful urge to live the memories I've only imagined. Devin's gaze drops to my lips. My tongue sneaks out to wet my bottom lip, and his eyes grow hooded.

A loud knock reverberates somewhere behind us, and I snatch my hand back and look around automatically. Standing in the window of the pinball parlor is *Devin's brother*—what is he doing here? The glass is tinted so his features are indistinct, but there's no mistaking the smirk on his face. "Fancy seeing you here," he calls, voice muffled.

"Perry?" Devin splutters. "What the fuck?" he mouths at the window before turning to me. "I'm sorry, Cass. Perry texted earlier to ask where I was, and I told him we were headed here. I didn't think he'd show up. We can go somewhere else if you want."

My gut squeezes with disappointment, but I wave it away. "It's okay that Perry's here."

His eyebrows jerk upward. "It is?"

"I mean, maybe he has some ideas we haven't explored yet that might explain why I remember you? We can say hello, chat for a few minutes, and if you want, continue our evening elsewhere." My voice comes out a few notches huskier than I anticipate, and

Devin's dark eyes smolder as he runs his fingertips down the length of my arm. Heat pools in my gut. Maybe it's the booze, or maybe it's the fact that it's been *way* too long since a man touched me like this, but finding a quieter, Perry-less place sounds pretty damn good right about now.

Perry raps on the window again. "You guys coming or what?"

A giggle bursts out of me, and Devin groans even as he tips his head back and smiles at the star-speckled sky. "Be right in," he calls.

A breeze whips my hair around my shoulders as Devin opens the door for me and we step inside. Despite the dim pendant lighting, Kinetic Kanteen is an explosion of colorful nostalgia and pure kitsch. Vintage Christmas decorations line the walls, interspersed with neon skateboards, movie posters, vinyl records, and garage sale decor celebrating Cleveland's pop culture past. In a high corner above the bar between a 1968 Jimi Hendrix concert poster and a Drew Carey bobblehead, there's even a replica of the famous leg lamp from *A Christmas Story*.

Electronic dings from the dozen or so pinball machines lined up in rows punctuate the classic rock music pumping through the speakers and the chatter from the mostly hipster crowd. Perry's moved to a high table near the bar. When he spots us, he lifts his beer in welcome and saunters over. He's wearing faded jeans slung low on his hips and a fitted olive T-shirt that hugs his biceps—very different from his loose, pollen-stained shirt from Monday. I swallow. Judging by his defined muscles, Devin isn't the only one in his family who works out.

"Dev." Perry nods.

"Per. Why are you here?"

"You invited me, remember?"

"No, I told you where I was going. I don't recall extending an invitation."

"It was implied." He slaps Devin on the shoulder. "So! How's the big meet-up going with Mystery Girl? Make any earth-shattering discoveries?"

"Not yet," says Devin.

"We're still trying to figure out how we might know each other," I add. "Any bright ideas?"

"Besides the one I floated earlier about you being an Internet stalker? None whatsoever." His grin is all teeth.

"Lay off her, Perry," Devin warns.

Perry raises his hands in a placating gesture. "No offense. If Devin believes you're telling the truth, who am I to question?" He swigs his beer. "So what made you want to check out Kinetic Kanteen anyway?"

"It was Devin's idea."

"I thought it might be." Devin's jaw tightens, but Perry either doesn't know or doesn't care, and barrels on. "You know I made a bet with myself earlier today: ten bucks says he takes her to Kinetic after drinks. And hey, I won."

"Why?" I blurt.

"Because when you make a bet with yourself, you always win. That's the beauty of it." His mischievous eyebrows bounce.

"No, I mean why did you think we'd be here before Devin told you?"

"Because this is where he takes all of the women he likes. Oh look, he even gave you calla lilies. Typical Devin."

My stomach tightens at the idea that there might be a revolving door of women in Devin's life all receiving lilies and meeting him for quirky pinball rendezvous, but I shove my doubts aside. Everybody has a past. And hey, it's kind of sweet he has a go-to routine of drinks, flowers, and pinball for impressing the ladies.

I shrug. "So what you're saying is he likes me then." I flash an exaggerated wink.

Laughing, Devin slips his arm around my shoulders. "Heck yes, I do."

"Touché." Perry purses his lips. "Excuse me, I'm being rude. Would you care to join me?" He motions toward his table near the bar.

"Only if you promise to leave soon, brother."

"Where's the fun in that?" He pouts.

"Do you want a drink?" Devin asks me.

"Sure. Whatever they have on tap is fine, thanks."

"I'll have anoth— Never mind." Perry lifts his own nearly empty bottle and lowers it when he realizes Devin's already halfway to the bar and purposefully ignoring him. He clears his throat. "My table's over here."

I follow Perry and settle into one of the three empty seats. Drumming my fingers on the table, I scan the crowd. "So, you're here on a Friday night—alone?"

The apples of Perry's cheeks redden. "Of course not. I was catching up with my dude, Sam." Twisting around, he waves at the bartender, a black-clad hipster with a mohawk who looks like they'd rather swallow a jar of pickles than engage in conversation with anyone. "Yo, Sam, how's it going?"

With a grunt, the bartender gives Perry a wordless salute and begins pouring a beer for Devin. "Sam and I go way back."

Uh-huh. I brace my elbows on the table. "Let's cut the crap. Why are you *really* here? Is it because you don't like me?"

"It's not that I don't like you. I don't even know you."

"Precisely."

"Point taken."

"And look, I realize this situation is . . . abnormal . . . but I'm not out to 'get' your brother or whatever. We're talking, that's all. Besides a little inexplicable mystery of the universe to solve, it's an easy-breezy get-to-know you sort of situation."

"It looked like you were getting to know him pretty well outside."

Narrowing my eyes at him, I fold my arms across my chest. "You know, I can't believe I considered for even a second saying yes to going out with you when you asked me at the flower shop the other day."

I'm gratified when Perry snorts into his glass and beer runs down his chin. He scrubs the moisture away with his fist. "I didn't ask you out."

"Yes, you did."

"I was making conversation. Like I do with all my customers."

"Uh-huh. So you're here again . . . why?"

"Ask him about Sadie." He jerks his chin toward Devin, who's handing a credit card to the bartender.

I blink. "Who's Sadie?"

"The worst thing that ever happened to him, and he never saw her coming."

"There's two sides to every story, you know. Maybe she wasn't as bad as you think?"

He shakes his head. "Just ask him, then you'll understand why I'm protective of my brother." His expression darkens, but before I can probe further, Devin returns, hands me a beer, and claps Perry on the shoulder, making him wince. "Well, this has been a hoot, Perry, but I think it's time for you to go."

Peeling Devin's hand off his shoulder, he lets it drop. "I was here first."

"How about this," I interject before the situation gets even more awkward. "Since you like bets, let's make a wager, *Terry*."

"Perry," he corrects.

I smirk. "You. Me. Pinball. If I win, you leave us alone to enjoy our evening. If you win, we'll leave, and you can hang out here in pinball bliss."

Devin groans like I've punched him in the gut. Perry's angular lips split into a grin so wide I can see every one of his white, even teeth. Interlacing his fingers, he stretches his arms above his head and his bicep muscles pop. "You're on. I'll get us some tokens . . . and another round. You're going to need one when I'm through

with you." Hopping off his stool, he strides to the bar with a definite bounce in his step.

"Oh, you sweet summer child, you have no idea what you've
done." Chuckling, Devin scrubs a palm over his jaw.

"What?" I ask.

"Perry is *killer* at pinball."

"Have a little faith." Cupping his face, I plant a quick peck on
his lips and freeze, my mouth mere inches away from his. Devin's
eyes widen.

Holy shit, I kissed him! I didn't mean to, not exactly. What I did
was the sort of casual display of intimacy reserved for people with
actual history between them—several dates under their belt, at
least. We might have had a *moment* outside, but he didn't ask for
this. What if I misread his signals earlier? What if he doesn't want
that kind of relationship with me? The notion of "Cass as stalker"
is probably back on the table because who in their right mind
would do what I just did?

With an apologetic grimace, I give his cheek a *pat pat*, praying a
portal to another universe will appear and swallow me up. It
doesn't. But before I can run out and bury myself in the nearest
ditch, Devin's arms snake around my back, he tugs me closer, and
then he's kissing *me*.

My nerves melt away. His lips are exquisitely soft—exactly how
I remember them. My brain suddenly kicks into overdrive. Devin's
kissing me. *He's kissing me.* And not just in a memory, in real life.
His tongue teases the seam of my lips, coaxing them apart. I close
my eyes and revel in the scent of his bergamot cologne and the way
his tongue dips into my mouth, accelerating, commanding.

Okay, so *not* like how I remember, but I meet his pace and heat
flares low in my belly at the fireworks of sensation. A shiver zings
up my spine, and memories of kissing him over and over, in dozens of settings, flash through my mind like a movie reel on fast-
forward. Dreams blur with reality. My heart thunders.

Just when I think my head might actually explode with sensory and memory overload, Devin slows down. With a final lingering brush of lips, he pulls back and tucks a lock of hair behind my ear. "Wow," he whispers, his deep voice rumbling as his eyes search my face.

"Yeah." I exhale through a giggle.

Taking my hand, he guides me onto the nearest stool. Good timing, because I'm not sure my trembling legs are capable of holding me upright much longer.

"I'm back." Perry shouts above the music. He plunks a pitcher of beer and three shot glasses full of amber liquid on the table, followed by three plastic cups he has tucked under his arm.

"What's this?" I motion to the shot glasses.

"A peace offering to show my goodwill." Perry slides a shot across the table toward Devin and hands another to me. I bring the glass to my nose and sniff. A burst of cinnamon fills my sinuses, and I cough. "No, but what *is* this?"

"Fireball."

"No-ho. None for me, thanks." I'd had one too many bad experiences with Fireball over the years. Better to stick with beer, especially after the gin and tonics. I push the glass away from me with one finger.

"Suit yourself. Devin?"

"No, thanks."

With a shrug, Perry picks up the nearest shot glass, tips its contents into his mouth, and slams the glass on the table. He immediately takes my unwanted shot and drains it in a single gulp.

He's reaching for the third when Devin slides it out of his reach. "Whoa there, Drunky. You should slow down."

"What? I think a handicap for our game is in order, don't you?"

Resting my chin in my hand, I tilt my head. "You're really that confident you'll win?"

"You've never seen me play."

My lips peel into a grin. "Same here." To hell with it. I might be mixing, but at least I've eaten; I can handle it. I snatch the last shot and toss it back. Cinnamon whisky burns a fiery path down my throat. Licking my lips, I set the empty glass on the table. "An even playing field is only fair. Ready to lose?"

Perry snorts. "Are *you*?" Grabbing the pitcher of beer and cups, he saunters across the room toward a vintage *Twilight Zone* machine. Fitting.

I slide off my stool to follow, but Devin snares me around the waist. His hand is like a brand through my shirt where he grips my side. "You are one of the most surprising women I've ever met," he says softly, his warm breath caressing my ear. The light catches his jawline and *damn* he's beautiful—like a Romantic-era painting. His full, glistening lips, immaculate jawline, and dark, perfectly formed eyebrows cap soulful, deep brown eyes. Like Orest Kiprensky's piercing self-portrait mixed with the bright, breathtaking energy of a Gauguin.

Heart fluttering against my ribs, I feign a bravado I'm not sure I feel. "Stick around. You ain't seen nothin' yet."

"Promise?" The flicker of heat in his eyes is so potent I nearly self-combust.

Part of me wants to haul him out of here and say to hell with Perry and our bet. And by the way Devin's looking at me, I'm pretty sure he'd be into the idea. But a deal's a deal. I promised Perry a pinball game, and I never back down from a challenge—especially where pinball is concerned. "You'll have to wait and see." With a little shrug, I slip out of his embrace and head toward the *Twilight Zone* machine where Perry is watching us intently, waiting.

I let my hips sway more than I usually do, knowing Devin's watching me too.

Chuckling, he quickly catches up and falls into step beside me. "Count me in, Mystery Girl."

9

"Looks like you've finally met your match, Perry." Devin's tone of surprise is nearly drowned out by the electronic dings and flashing red and orange lights of the vintage nineties pinball machine.

I admit, I was initially worried when I watched Perry play. His game lasted nearly forty-five minutes and ended with an impressive score of 1.9 billion points. My score's now at 1.4 billion; I still have some catching up to do. Devin shifts beside me to stand closer, but I can't let his nearness distract me. It's my second-to-last ball, so if I want to win, I need to focus. And that shot of Fireball isn't doing me any favors. My head feels like cotton and I have to squint at the ball to keep it in focus. I aim for a corner where I know I can score extra points if I land the ball just so, and it ricochets into place. I blow out a relieved breath. Lights flash and another ten million points are added to my score.

"How are you so good?" Perry asks me, voice full of awe.

"I lived above an arcade in Euclid until I was twelve—before I moved to Chagrin Falls," I add to Devin. "The owner used to give me free tokens if I helped him sweep up after school."

"That's kind of shady. Child labor and all that," says Devin.

I don't take my eyes off the whizzing ball. "He was the best, actually. A gem. My mom worked long hours, so I was a latchkey kid—alone a lot, you know? I think letting me sweep for tokens was his way of looking out for me without making me feel like a charity case."

Mr. Fitzpatrick, the owner of Euclid's Gametime Arcade, will forever hold a soft spot in my heart. A grizzled vet in his late sixties, he was always kind to the quiet, mousy girl who lived upstairs. He even let me draw on his chalkboard behind the counter whenever I stopped by. He'd scrounge up a few half-broken pieces of colored chalk, toss them onto the counter, and say, "Make it pretty," in his gruff, croaky voice.

At first, I didn't know what to draw, so I tried drawing what I saw in the arcade. The prizes from the prize case—stuffed animals, small toys, temporary tattoos with dragon and butterfly designs. Then video game characters and, eventually, people. But no matter how cartoonish or terrible my drawings were, he'd nod and say, "Nice work." And the next day I'd come back and the chalkboard would be blank again—a canvas waiting to be brought to life by my imagination.

I spent countless after-school hours rotating between playing pinball, sweeping up trash, and drawing on Mr. Fitzpatrick's chalkboard. That is, until my mom found out. She put a stop to my "time-wasting" real quick.

With a shake of my head, I refocus on the game. "Anyway, I haven't played in a long time."

"Could have fooled me," Perry mutters.

I let myself sink into the game—timing when I deploy the flippers so the ball rolls up a ramp and hits a target. I'm dimly aware that a crowd has gathered behind us—I can tell from the shuffle of shoes and the invisible press of bodies. Whispers and the occasional cheer rise up when I hit a target. I lose a ball down the drain and another loads—my last ball. Ten minutes later, I'm within range of Perry's score . . . if only I can . . .

"Ooo, watch out for the—" someone says.

Devin's elbow brushes mine and I'm a split-second too late. My ball disappears into the drain.

Perry cheers and the crowd groans. My heart sinks until a mechanical *plink* steals my attention—I have a free ball! It deploys from the top of the machine. I focus on it as it barrels down, and send it flying back up. It pings against several bumpers in succession before landing against a target. The final door lights up, shortly followed by the doorknob with a question mark—this is it. This is my chance. The ball rolls toward the secondary left flipper. I hit the button, and the ball flies to the correct target. The machine rings out and the lights flash.

"Lost in the Zone!" Someone whoops from the crowd.

Six balls quickly release. I have thirty seconds to hit as many targets as I can and rack up points. I hammer the buttons. Targets light up one after another. When a ball drains, another releases. Finally, the flippers go dead, allowing all the balls to drain.

My score flashes: 2,051,619,580. It's higher than Perry's.

"I won!" I shout.

The group of five or so people behind me cheers and claps.

Devin picks me up and twirls me around in the air. "Team Devin wins!" he shouts.

Sheer mirth fills me, and I'm still laughing when he sets me on my feet. Our gazes connect, and his eyes blaze with triumph.

On an impulse, I throw my arms around his neck and mash my mouth against his. He returns this kiss with enthusiasm, and a smattering of laughter floats from the dispersing crowd. I don't care if we have an audience or that we're kissing in the middle of a pinball arcade. His teeth scrape against my bottom lip. I suck in a surprised breath, and his palm descends, pressing against the dip in my lower back.

A throat clears behind us, and I pull away, breathing hard. Running my fingers through my hair, I turn and find myself face to face with Perry.

His rueful smile can't hide his disappointment. "Team Devin wins . . . as usual," he says so quietly I nearly miss it. A band twists around my heart. Tipping his beer to his lips, he drains it in several long gulps. "Well, I'm true to my word. I'll be going now. That was one hell of a game, Cass. Rematch sometime?"

"Sure."

Pushing away from the pinball machine, he takes two steps and stumbles. Devin catches him by the shoulder, eyebrows furrowing. "You okay?" he asks.

Perry waves him off. "*Pshh.* Fine." His green eyes are glassy and unfocused and there's a raspiness to his voice that wasn't there before.

"I don't think Perry's fine. He drank most of the pitcher on top of those shots," I whisper to Devin.

"I think you're right. Damn it, Perry. Sit down." Devin steers Perry into an empty seat at the bar over his protestations. "Drink some water. Don't argue."

"Aren't you the bossy one," Perry mumbles, but slurps the water Sam the bartender pushes toward him.

Taking me gently by the elbow, Devin leads me a few paces away. "I'm sorry. Perry's not usually a big drinker. I should probably make sure he gets home okay . . ."

"Of course, don't worry about it."

"Want me to give you a ride? I haven't had anything to drink for a couple hours. I can get my car and—"

Perry slumps over the bar and only avoids tipping out of his chair thanks to Sam, who practically dives across the bar to steady him. Devin winces.

"Why don't we split an Uber?" I say, grabbing my bag from the floor next to the pinball machine.

"Good idea."

"No, it's a great idea. Allow me. It's the least I can do," Perry calls. After a few seconds of fruitless fumbling for his phone, Devin strides over and plucks it out of his pocket. He holds it up to Perry's face to unlock it, then taps the screen several times.

"The closest Uber's three minutes away. Let's go." We scoop Perry up from the bar and haul him toward the door. He's about as steady as a Weeble Wobble, so I loop his arm around my shoulders while Devin flanks his other side. Outside the bar, bass-heavy music echoes in the distance, bouncing off the historic brick buildings.

Perry sways between us. "Sorry I got schnockered."

"It happens," I say.

"It didn't have to happen tonight though," Devin mutters under his breath.

Perry swings his head to look at Devin, then at me. "You know what? I think you're okay, Cass. I'm officially 92 percent sure you're not a stalker."

I snort. "A glowing endorsement."

"Sure is." His green eyes are unfocused as they bounce around my face. "But I'm warning you, you better treat my brother right. Or I'll sic The Colonel on you." Squinting one eye, he unloops his arm from Devin and jams his finger in my general direction. The jerky motion throws him off balance, and we careen sideways. I flail, and somehow end up with my face smooshed against Perry's chest. The scent of freshly cut grass, cinnamon, and whisky overwhelms me, and my stomach somersaults.

Devin grabs Perry's arm before we topple over, yanking him back—me along with him. "Jesus, Perry. Get it together."

He holds up a hand. "Sorry, sorry."

The Uber finally arrives, and loading Perry into the little Ford Fusion without him landing in the gutter is a whole other adventure. After several maneuvering attempts, we manage to get all his limbs into the back seat and clamber in after him. My place is only a few blocks away, so the Uber driver suggests dropping me off first. Perry's passed out by the time we get to my house, head tipped back against the headrest, snoring softly.

"Is he okay?" I ask Devin.

"Oh yeah, he's fine. He'll sleep it off."

When I step out of the car, Devin follows and walks with me up the sidewalk. We pause on my porch, standing in the pool of light cast by the outdoor sconce.

"Sorry again about Perry," he says.

"It's okay. I had a nice time tonight."

"Me too." Sauntering closer, he offers me a shy smile. "Look, I know we only met up to try to solve your mystery, but I'd like to take you out. For real."

Joy flutters like a tiny bird inside my chest. "I'd like that."

"Good." A smile tugs at the corner of Devin's lips as he drops his eyes to my mouth. He leans in, intent unmistakable, and our lips connect.

Mint lingers on his lips as he presses them against mine. Out of our three kisses tonight, this is certainly the most chaste—probably because the Uber driver is waiting with Perry passed out in the back seat—only a swift meeting of breath and bodies. An acknowledgment of more to come. A heartbeat later he steps back with a dazzling smile.

"What are you doing after work on Tuesday?" he asks.

I rack my brain and nothing comes to mind, but I've learned I can't trust my memory at the best of times, let alone after several cocktails and a shot of whisky. I take out my phone and check my calendar app. "Nothing."

"I'm planning to see my favorite eighties cover band perform on the East Bank of the Flats. Want to come?"

"It's a date."

"Great. I'll text you." Waving, Devin backs down the stairs and climbs into the waiting Uber.

I watch the car pull away, then unlock the front entrance and step inside. After closing the door, I lean against it and grin up at the ceiling. Tonight was better than I ever could have imagined.

In the living room, I find Brie asleep on the couch. The Netflix home screen shines from the television in the corner, illuminating Xerxes perched above her on the sofa like a bodyguard. Brie must have fallen asleep waiting for me to come home. My gut twists. I should have texted her an update and told her not to wait up. Clicking off the TV, I tug the scrunched blanket at her feet up to her shoulders. Xerxes clicks in warning.

"Oh hush, I'm not hurting her," I whisper.

In the kitchen, I open and close each cabinet as quietly as I can, searching for a vase for my lilies. The best I can find is a large glass pitcher, so I drop in the stems and fill it with water. I trudge upstairs with my flowers, head pounding with every step. After a quick stop in the bathroom to wash my face and brush my teeth, I arrange the pitcher of lilies on my desk, peel off my rumpled clothes, yank on my pajamas, and flop onto my bed. My mattress groans in protest.

My door creaks open, and Brie pokes her head inside my room. Her glasses sit lopsided on her nose, and her blond hair is as wild as a lion's mane. "Hey, how did drinks with Devin go?"

"Good. Really good, actually."

"Did you guys figure out where you met before?"

I shake my head.

"Bummer." Leaning against the door frame, she yawns.

I hug my knees to my chest. "I'm seeing him again on Tuesday though."

She snaps her mouth closed and her eyes go wide. "Like a date?"

"Well . . . yeah."

"Holy shit, Cass." Shuffling into my room, she stretches out on her side along the foot of my bed, propping her head up with her hand. "You know I don't buy into the spiritual stuff, but maybe you and Devin really are meant to be."

My gut squeezes, and I pick at a loose thread on the hem of my pajama pants. "It's way too soon to tell."

"Do you like him—the *real* him?"

"I think so. He's funny, charming, and a really good kisser. Like, textbook good."

"Hold up. You kissed him?" She slaps my shin. "Way to bury the lead!"

"I know. I still can't believe it." My stomach flutters at the memory of kissing him . . . *for real*. "What about you? What did you do tonight?"

"I had that panel, remember?"

I smack my forehead. "Duh. How did it go?"

"*Ugh*." She flops her head onto my mattress before propping herself into a sitting position. "It was a testosterone-filled cluster. I was the only woman on the panel, and the men would *not* shut up. Even when the moderator asked *me* a question, they felt the need to chime in and talk over me. If it wasn't for Marcus being there, I would have screamed."

"Hold up, *Marcus* was there?"

"Yeah. He showed up halfway through."

"Oh really?" I shimmy my shoulders.

"It's not like that. We're just friends. I told him about the conference the other day, and he swung by after his shift."

"I see." Looks like I'm not the only one with an admirer. "Well, I'm sorry I missed it."

Yawning so wide her jaw cracks, she glides off the bed and ambles to the door. "You can make it up to me with brunch tomorrow."

"For sure. Then I want a play-by-play of the entire panel."

"Only if I get a play-by-play of your smooch with Devin." She makes kissy noises as she backs out of my room. I toss a throw pillow at her, but she blocks it with my door. "Good night," she calls, eyes twinkling.

"Night."

Once my door is closed, I burrow under the covers. Rolling over, I reach for my bedside lamp, but pause. My sketchbook glimmers in a pool of light on my nightstand. Scooting higher in bed, I open it on my lap. Page after page of familiar Devin drawings stare back at me.

I study the detailed curve of his eyebrow in one of the close-up portraits. No scar. I flip through more pages. None of my drawings of Devin show him with a scar. Shoving the sketchbook into the drawer of my nightstand, I click off the light and snuggle deeper into bed.

How could I know things about Devin like where he went to college, his favorite food, and the sports he plays, but not remember him having a *scar* on his face? What else about him don't I know?

And how much about him do I have wrong?

I guess I'll just have to spend more time with him to find out.

10

The following Monday begins with a flurry of work emails and a brand-new assignment from Andréa: drafting a letter for a corporate client summarizing our legal advice for averting a potential class action lawsuit. I'm so busy I barely notice when my office phone rings around eleven.

I pick up the receiver. "Cass Walker."

"Hey, Cass. It's David from reception. You have a delivery at the front desk whenever you have a sec." He pauses. "Hot tip? You'll want to pick this one up immediately . . . *before it wilts*," he adds meaningfully.

My cheeks flush. "Oh! Okay, thanks. I'll be right there."

I hang up the phone and stare at it for several seconds. *"Before it wilts . . ."* Did someone send me flowers? Could they be from Devin?

Standing so quickly my chair spins, I double-time it to the elevator. Devin and I texted for over an hour yesterday, talking about our weekends, favorite Netflix shows—his, *Making a Murderer*; mine, *Jane the Virgin*—among other generally cutesy, getting-to-know-you chitchat. I never would have guessed he was planning to send me flowers as a preamble to our first official date tomorrow.

By the time the elevator deposits me in the lobby, my smile is so big my cheeks ache. But then I catch sight of the person standing in front of the reception desk, and I freeze. It's not Devin.

Perry is in the lobby, and he's holding a small vase of purple irises.

He looks a lot better than he did in the Uber on Friday, I'll give him that. His hair is neatly combed, and his expression is clear and no longer glassy-eyed. This Perry, the one standing before me, is the Perry from the first day we met: worn jeans, shy smile, and pollen-streaked T-shirt. He waves when he sees me.

On the corner of David's desk is an enormous bouquet of long-stemmed red roses. I swallow hard. Are those for *me*?

"Perry, hi," I say when I reach David's desk. "What are you doing here?"

"Dropping off a delivery." He nods at the massive bouquet of roses. "Apparently, one of your coworkers is celebrating her thirtieth wedding anniversary today."

My stomach constricts. Oh, so they're not for me then. David peeks up at us from behind his black-rimmed glasses, not even trying to hide that he's listening intently to our conversation. Stepping away from his desk, I lead Perry toward the opposite side of the lobby. I like David, but I also don't want to become the subject of office gossip.

"What about the shop? Who's covering for you?" I ask Perry.

"The store doesn't open until noon, and our regular delivery driver, Chuck, doesn't start until three. Devin mentioned you work at Smith & Boone, so when the order for roses came in this morning, I figured I'd make the delivery myself. Plus one more."

I nod at the vase of irises he's holding. "Are those for me?"

"Yes indeed."

Our fingers brush when I take the vase from him. The curled petals of the deep violet irises are punctuated by narrow stalks of lavender and airy greenery. "These are beautiful," I say, taking a deep breath in of their glorious scent. "And so thoughtful of Devin. I'll be sure to thank him straight away."

Perry's cheeks flush. "Actually, they're from me."

My jaw goes slack and my eyes widen. They're from . . . *Perry?*

"To say sorry for getting drunk and ruining your date with Devin the other night," he quickly adds. "Honestly, I've been unfair to you since the beginning, and I'm sorry. This is my way of making amends."

Holy shit. That's really nice. I mean, it would have been nicer if Devin had sent the flowers, but I appreciate that Perry's willing to own up to his mistakes and apologize. And he chose purple for my bouquet—again, just like he did the day we met at Blooms & Baubles. Because purple brings out the green in my eyes. My neck warms at the memory of our first exchange.

"Apology accepted. Although it wasn't technically a date, so no harm, no foul."

"I was wrong about you, Cass. And for what it's worth, I'm glad you're seeing my brother."

"Thanks, Perry. That means a lot. And for what it's worth, I think I might have been wrong about you too. You're a good egg."

We stare at each other for a long moment.

Perry clears his throat and looks away. "Well, I should probably go. I need to open the shop soon."

"Thanks again for the flowers."

"No problem. See you later." With a cheery salute, he walks toward the door.

Across the lobby, the elevator opens, and a man wearing a delivery uniform shuffles out, carrying an impossibly tall stack of boxes that teeter with every step. Before I can ask if he needs help though, Perry hurries over to the front door to hold it open. When the top box threatens to fall, Perry grabs it for the delivery guy, and the two of them walk over to the idling van parked outside. David, who's been leaning across his desk watching the whole thing, beckons me over.

"Who was *that?*" he asks.

I smile reflexively. "A friend of mine. I'm kind of dating his brother."

"Well, if the brother is half as cute as that one, then *ding-ding*. Winner, winner, chicken dinner."

Laughter bursts out of me. "Thanks, David."

I take my irises back to my cubicle and arrange them on my desk. The earthy, sweet scent of irises mix with lavender, and I inhale deeply, closing my eyes. What a surprising turn of events. I never would have expected Perry to show up to my office and apologize in person, let alone bring me flowers. If this is the kind of family Devin has, that speaks well of him.

And now that Perry's on my side, I have one less hurdle to discovering whether this thing I have with Devin is real. If he's even half as thoughtful and self-aware as Perry, then he'll be well on his way to living up to my memory of him. Only time will tell.

My cell phone vibrates on my desk, and I pick it up when Devin's name flashes on the screen. I still can't believe it's been three weeks since we started dating. If you would have told postcoma Cass that her memories of Devin were actually a harbinger of events yet to come, she would have asked her neurologist to double her meds.

Not that what I've experienced over the past three weeks with Devin is *exactly* how I remember. Like, for our second date, he took me to see a show at Playhouse Square—something I could have sworn we'd never done before. And I was shocked to learn he doesn't own a bicycle, even though I distinctly remember us riding through the park.

But the thrill of getting to know him, complete with gut-fluttery anticipation every time I see him? Totally on point.

I tap the green accept button. "Hey, you."

"Hi there, gorgeous," his deep voice rumbles, igniting a shower of sparks in my chest.

"How are you? Sorry again for bailing last night."

"Not your fault. The boss asked you to help prep for a big-time case, which is awesome. I would have been mad if you ditched just to hang out with me."

"Well, I would have much rather been with you, trust me." I didn't leave the office until well after nine and continued working at home until nearly one in the morning. A yawn works its way up my throat and I muffle it with the back of my hand.

"Good. Because I have a surprise for you."

"Really? What is it?"

"Come downstairs."

"What, right now? But I'm at work.".

"Exactly."

I grin so wide my molars ache. "Devin Szymanski, what are you up to?"

"Come outside to the parking lot, and you'll find out."

Pushing back from my desk, I start walking. "Okay. I'll be right there."

"See you soon."

I end the call just as I round the corner of my cubicle . . . and collide with Mercedes.

"Oof," she grunts as our chests bump, and we both take a hasty step back. She smooths the front of her immaculate white blouse, crimson nails gleaming. Her cheeks are unusually pale and her fingers flutter when she tucks a lock of hair behind her ear. "Who were you talking to?"

I wrinkle my nose. Mercedes never asks me personal questions, let alone borderline invasive ones. "A friend."

"Are you heading out?"

"Why, do you need something?"

"No, I just wondered if you wanted to grab lunch."

"Oh, uhhh . . ."

Bustling around me, she snags her purse from her bottom desk drawer. "There's a new deli around the corner I've been dying to try. Shall we?" Her teeth flash and is that a . . . smile? Did I wake up in a parallel universe or did Mercedes Trowbridge suddenly decide to be nice to me?

"I'm sorry, Mercedes. I'm actually meeting someone right now. Rain check?"

"What, there isn't room for one more?" Her light laughter sounds like bells tinkling, but there's something off-key about it. In fact, there's something off-key about this whole encounter. Mercedes doesn't play nice with anyone—except for senior attorneys and partners—and she's certainly never played nice with me. I clutch my phone tighter.

"There's really nothing to join. My boyf—" *Boyfriend* isn't right. It's only been a few weeks and we haven't had the exclusivity talk yet. Not that I'm ready to be exclusive. I need to get to know *this* Devin, the real Devin, before going all in. And while things have been going well so far, it's still a work in progress. I clear my throat. "This guy I've been seeing, he stopped by to say hi."

"Well, isn't that sweet," she says through a thin-lipped smile.

"Hey, we could grab lunch after he leaves. How does that sound?"

Shrugging one shoulder, she plops her bag onto her desk and sweeps into her chair, crossing her long legs. "Don't worry about it. I wouldn't want to rush you and *the guy you're seeing*. We can go some other time."

Eyes glinting, she swivels to face her computer, signaling the end of the conversation.

The hairs on the back of my neck rise. "Okay . . . catch you later," I say to her back before hurrying down the hall. Summer associates are allowed to step out of the office for a breather from time to time—it's not like we're chained to our desks or anything—but I don't trust this new "nice" Mercedes. Based on, let's see, every single interaction I've had with her this summer, I wouldn't put it past her to find a way to make my brief absence take on the appearance of slacking. I should keep this meeting with Devin short.

Devin. The idea of a "surprise" for me, whatever it is, buoys my mood and fills my chest with lightness as I take the stairs, kitten heels clacking against each concrete step. I wave at David the receptionist, who salutes me back as he takes a call. Just as I reach the building's front door, my phone rings. Fishing it from my pocket, I check the screen. It's my mom.

"Really?" I groan. What timing. I hesitate with my shoulder against the door and my finger over the accept icon—she's already called twice this week and I haven't had a chance to call her back . . .

But I send her to voice mail. Devin's been waiting longer than he should thanks to Mercedes. I'll call Mom back as soon as he leaves.

Returning my phone to my pocket, I shove open the building's glass doors and a blast of heat and humidity smacks me in the face. You'd think we'd enjoy breezy, mild summers since Cleveland is next to a lake that borders Canada. Too bad that's not the case. Cleveland summers are as hot and sticky as the winters are long, cold, and dreary. Sweat gather on the back of my neck as I stride through the small parking lot and meander down the rows, scanning for Devin's car—a black BMW, I think—but it's not here. Did he leave already?

A car door clicks opens behind me, and I spot Devin stepping out of an unfamiliar white Lexus. He's wearing a sky-blue button-down that's open at his throat, gray slacks that hug his hips in the most oh-so-perfect way, and leather loafers the smoky color of burned wood. Closing the driver's door, he casually tosses an arm over the roof of the car.

"Hey, you." Crossing the distance between us, I plant a quick kiss on his cheek. Wrapping his arms around me, he pulls me into a lingering hug. I take the opportunity to inhale the spicy-rich scent of his cologne before stepping back. "Sorry you had to wait so long. I got cornered by a coworker on my way out."

"No worries."

"What happened to your car?" I nod at the Lexus, which is definitely not what he drove when he picked me up for our last date.

His full lips curve into a radiant grin. "It's back at the dealership."

"Did you trade it in or something?"

"No, that's the surprise."

I furrow my eyebrows. "I'm not following."

"Well, I know you still don't have a car, so I asked a buddy of mine who works for a dealership in Brook Park to let me know if any sweet deals cross his desk. He called me up this morning to tell me about a 2014 Lexus ES 350 he just happened to acquire." He pats the car's gleaming hood. "Apparently it belonged to an elderly woman who only drove it to church, poker nights, and the grocery store, and she maintained it like a pro. It's in perfect condition with only fifteen thousand miles on it."

He looks between me and the car with barely contained excitement, and a blast of shock barrels through me like a shotgun shell.

"And you . . . *bought it*?" I splutter.

"Ahhh, no. That'd be pretty over the top, don't you think?"

Oh thank God. I exhale a jittery laugh. "Yeah, just a little. So what's going on?"

Chuckling, Devin steps closer until our bodies are mere inches apart. "I didn't buy you a car, but I *did* convince my friend to let me take this one out for the afternoon so you can give it a test-drive. See if you like it."

A boulder settles over my chest. "Wow, that is so thoughtful of you, Devin. Thank you. But I'm not looking to buy a car right now."

"Really, why not? Is it because of money?"

I could lie and say yes. Not that I have big bucks in the bank, especially after the past year of medical bills and zero income, but a summer associate salary is nothing to sneeze at, and between the money I've saved from my law school scholarship and what I hope will be an impending full-time job offer at a top firm, I can afford a car—a used one, anyway. Blaming my budget would certainly be easier, and less painful, than telling the truth, but the truth would come out eventually and Devin deserves honesty.

"No," I say simply. "It's because I don't drive. Not since the accident."

"How do you get around then?"

I shrug. "Walk, Uber, bicycle."

"But what if you wanted to drive out to Chagrin Falls to visit your mom?"

"She picks me up or Brie takes me."

"And you think that's sustainable?" His voice is soft, but his words cut like ice picks.

Rubbing my arms, I take a step back. "I know it's hard to understand. Cleveland isn't exactly public-transportation friendly and, yeah, life would be easier if I had a car. I'm just not ready to drive yet."

"Wasn't the accident nearly a year ago? Not judging," he adds hastily.

Folding my arms across my chest, I force my voice to remain even. "It sounds like you're judging."

"What I meant was . . . have you tried driving since then?"

"Yes, several times. But whenever I get behind the wheel, everything seizes up and I can't breathe. I panic."

"I'm sorry." The tension seeps out of me at the sympathy in his gaze, and when he runs his palms down my arms and takes both my hands in his, I don't pull away. "That sounds hard," he murmurs.

"It is."

"But you know . . ." He leans in. "You've never tried driving with *me*."

"I don't think that will make a difference."

"Come on, just *try* it. I'll be right there with you and you don't have to go far. Just to the end of the parking lot."

I shake my head hard, but he tugs my hands, inching me closer to the Lexus.

"Come on, Cass. You'll never move forward if you don't at least try. You need to get back on the horse."

Molten anger bubbles up my throat. "No!" Yanking my hands out of his grip, I put a good six paces between us before whirling on him. "You don't get to tell me what I need. You barely even know me, and you show up unannounced with a *car* and tell me I have to do the thing that nearly got me killed a year ago? Who do you think you are?"

"Jesus, Cass. I'm just trying to help!"

"Yeah, well. I don't need your help."

We're facing each other in the parking lot, breathing hard. My cheeks are twin flames and sweat is officially coating every inch of my body, threatening to pit out my shirt. Devin's nostrils flare as his chest rises and falls. "Okay. I'll take it back then."

"Good."

"Fine."

"Cass? Is everything all right?" A female voice calls from over my shoulder.

I whip around so fast I nearly lose my balance. "Mom?" I splutter. "What are you doing here?" I'd been so absorbed in conversation I hadn't noticed her minivan parked at the edge of the lot—or her standing right behind me.

Mom adjusts her beige blazer. "You didn't get my voice mail? I had to run an errand on this side of town so I thought we could have lunch. I brought your favorite—a po' boy from Wiseman's." She holds up a brown paper bag.

A whole new level of panic threads through my veins. Snatching the bag, I mutter a quick "see you later" to Devin, loop my arm around her shoulders, and herd her toward my building. "Thanks, Mom. How about we eat in my office? I can give you a tour . . ."

Mom's never been someone to be pushed around, though, and she shrugs out of my hold with a *tut*. Her gaze flicks to Devin. "Is this one of your colleagues?"

"Oh! Uh . . . this . . . this is . . ."

Devin steps forward, hand extended. "Devin Szymanski."

"Devin," she murmurs. Realization lights up her features, followed by pure, unadulterated disbelief. "Devin? It can't . . . you aren't . . ." She touches her forehead and shoulders in the sign of the cross, something I haven't seen her do since I was a child.

"A figment of Cass's imagination? No, I'm not."

"So . . . you're real. Cass was right. You've been real this whole time." Her knees buckle and I reach for her automatically, but she steadies herself on the nearest car. Face pale, she waves me away. "She thought your name was Devin Bloom, though. Why?"

"I think she conflated my name with my brother's flower shop, Blooms & Baubles."

"I see." She's quiet for so long I'm afraid she's gone into shock. But then she straightens and lifts her chin. Uh-oh. I know that look. Warning bells sound in my head, but Devin continues to smile benignly as if a Tomahawk missile weren't headed his way.

"So—" Pushing off the car, she advances on him. "You date my daughter for three months, she gets in a near-fatal accident, and you disappear without a trace, making her believe you never existed at all?" For the first time, his confident expression falters. "Do you realize the *anguish* you put her through? Who the hell do you think you are? How *dare* you—"

I propel myself between them, arms raised. "Mom, pump the brakes. Let me explain."

"Now I see where you get your temper from," he mutters under his breath.

"Devin and I randomly ran into each other a few weeks ago, we got to talking, and neither of us remembered meeting before the accident. We decided to get together for drinks to try to pinpoint how we know each other, since I have so many memories of him. One thing led to another and—"

"—we started seeing each other," Devin finishes.

Mom's jaw goes slack. "You're . . . seeing each other. As in, dating?"

"Correct," says Devin.

"I don't believe it. It doesn't make sense. How could she remember you if you didn't meet until recently?"

"We're still trying to figure that out," I say.

She pinches her forehead between her thumb and forefinger. "I need to sit down."

"It's a lot to take in, isn't it?" Devin proffers his elbow.

Ignoring his offer of an escort, she marches through the parking lot and settles on a bench facing the river. Smoothing my skirt under me, I sit next to her. The quiet *slosh-slosh* of water lapping against the concrete embankment competes with the sound of drilling and hammering in the distance. Devin's footsteps approach, but he doesn't sit. He paces toward the river and back, opting to stand.

Mom stares out at the rippling brown water. "For the longest time, Cass was convinced you were real, and I didn't believe her. No one did. I'm sorry, Cass." Tears glisten in her eyes when she looks at me.

I pat her knee. "It's okay, Mom. It's a pretty unbelievable situation."

With a sniff, she swipes a finger under her eye, then shifts her attention to Devin. "How do I know you're not playing her?"

"*Mom.*"

"No, he could be taking advantage of you. You've suffered a traumatic brain injury, and suddenly a guy comes along who's supposed to be the man you thought was your boyfriend and now you're *dating*? It all sounds very convenient to me."

"Are you kidding me? It's not convenient at all. I'd finally moved on with my life, and *boom*, I meet Devin. And no, he's not taking advantage of me. He graciously agreed to hear me out when most people would have run for the hills. It's just a coincidence that we happened to hit it off."

Devin steps forward. "I care about Cass, honestly. I'd never do anything to hurt her." His blazing eyes settle on me, and my heart thumps painfully. He might not have intended to hurt me, but what he did today was heavy-handed and hurtful in its own way. I know he was just trying to help, but I still can't help feeling like I've been judged and found wanting. My gut twists like a wrung-out towel.

My mom stares at Devin for so long he's the first to look away. After what feels like an eternity, she shrugs. "God works in mysterious ways."

"Since when do you believe in God?"

"Just because we didn't go to church when you were growing up doesn't mean I don't believe in God. And I think he brought you two together for a reason."

"Mom," I hiss under my breath.

"I know, don't mind me. I'm still in shock. And I'm sorry, was I interrupting something?"

"No, you—"

"I brought a car over for Cass to test-drive," Devin says.

She whips her head in my direction so fast her hair swishes around her chin. "You're finally driving?"

"Not yet."

"Well, you should. It's been a year. You need to get back on the horse if you ever want to drive again."

Devin slides onto the bench next to Mom. "You know, that's exactly what I said."

"I like him," she says to me.

Yeah, yeah, Devin's great. "I *will* drive. Someday. But not today."

"I understand." He nods heavily. "Well, I should get going. I need to return the car and get back to the office by two for a meeting. It was nice to meet you—"

"Melanie," Mom says.

"Melanie," he repeats, taking her hand in his. Color flushes across Mom's cheeks. I don't remember the last time I've seen her flustered like this. Then again, Devin tends to have that effect on people.

"Likewise," she says.

"We'll talk later," Devin adds to me, standing.

Nerves pinch my gut and I force a tight smile. "Yeah. Later."

Mom and I watch him weave through the parking lot. Once he disappears into the Lexus and the engine revs, she whirls on me.

"You met him *weeks* ago and didn't tell me?" She slaps my arm.

I rub the spot. "Ow."

"I can't believe it. He looks exactly like your drawings. Is he the same as you remember?"

"Yes . . . and no."

"Well. Let me just say, I am impressed. He's polite, thoughtful, not to mention quite the looker. And he's encouraging you to step out of your comfort zone, which is exactly what you need."

"I'm sorry, is this reality, or am I living in an alternate universe? You actually *approve* of me dating? Who are you and what did you do with my mother?"

"Don't be so dramatic. I think it's perfectly fine for you to date."

"Since when?"

"Since now. You're a grown woman. You've earned your law degree, and you have a bright future ahead of you. I was hard on you when you were younger because I didn't want you to make the same mistakes I did."

"Like getting knocked up at seventeen?" She flinches like I've struck a physical blow. Guilt pools in my gut. "Mom, I'm sorry, I—"

"No, you're right. I didn't want you to become a teenage mom and struggle like I did." Gripping my shoulder, she stares into my eyes. "But don't think for a second I regret having you. You've been the most incredible, rewarding surprise of my life, and I wouldn't trade you for anything in the world. But still, having a baby so young was tough, especially after your grandparents kicked me out. I learned the hard way that the only person who can provide for you is *you*. That's why I push you. To make sure you can stand on your own two feet and live the life you deserve."

On an impulse, I throw my arms around her and squeeze. "I love you, Mom."

"I love you too, honey."

"You approve of Devin then?"

"Is he supportive of your career?"

"Very."

"Then *yes*. You need someone like him, someone who pushes you to be your best. He did something nice for you today, and it sounds like you didn't take it well."

"Don't you think it was kind of presumptuous though? He brought over a car without talking to me about it first because he assumed that's what I wanted."

"Cass, if the worst thing Devin has done is bring you a car to test-drive, it sounds like you have a winner on your hands."

Crossing my legs, I fold my arms over my chest and stare out at the river as a cluster of three yellow and orange kayaks slice through the calm water, passing us by. A breeze lifts a tendril of hair from my neck. Maybe Mom's right. Maybe I was too hard on him.

"Talk to him. Apologize if you overreacted. Don't let this one go," she says.

Snuggling closer, I rest my head on her shoulder. "Okay. Thanks, Mom. I'll talk to him."

11

I log off my computer and pack my bag at five thirty, even though I would normally stay another hour, at least. Mercedes is still working, and she gives me a sidelong glance when I leave.

I pull out my phone in the elevator and my fingers hover over my most recent text conversation with Devin. Mom's right, I should apologize—it's not his fault he didn't know about my driving-induced panic attacks.

Can we talk . . . . in person?

Sure. Meet me at B&B when you get off work? I promised Perry I'd swing by to help him with something.

Sounds good. See you soon

When I arrive at Blooms & Baubles ten minutes later, the door's locked even though the sign says it's open until six. I peer through the window—the interior lights are still on, but the store seems to be empty. I rap my knuckles against the door. A few seconds later,

Perry appears from the back. His eyes widen when he spots me, but he jogs over and opens it.

"Hey. What are you doing here?" he asks, leaning against the frame. The scent of roses and something woodsy—like pine mixed with rosemary—fills my nose, and I inhale deeply.

Shifting my weight, I peer over his shoulder into the empty shop. "I'm looking for Devin. Is he here?"

"Not yet. He said he'd swing by around six thirty to help with a few last-minute orders."

"Oh. He told me to meet him here." He probably assumed I wouldn't leave work until closer to my usual time of six thirty or seven. I shift uncomfortably in my flats. After my blowup earlier, I owe him that apology. Big-time. "I can come back later—"

"Cass, don't be ridiculous. Come in. Or would you rather melt into a puddle walking around in this heat?" Opening the door wider, he sweeps his arm in invitation. A blast of AC washes across my overheated skin, and I nearly moan.

"Okay, twist my arm." I step into the blessedly cool shop. A woof and a grunt sounds from behind the counter, and a familiar brown-and-white dog waddles over, tail wagging. Crouching, I stroke his short, thick fur. "Hey there, Captain."

"The Colonel," Perry corrects.

"Right. Sorry, The Colonel. I bet you run this place, huh." Snuffling my palm, he licks my wrist once, circles, and lies at my feet.

Perry chuckles. "Only for the past eleven years."

"Is he yours?" Straightening, I carefully step over The Colonel and mosey toward the counter.

"Sort of—he mostly belongs to Blooms & Baubles. Mom found him out back sniffing around the dumpster when he was a puppy and brought him into the shop. He made himself right at home, and he's been here ever since."

"Does he spend the night here?"

"Oh no, he comes upstairs with me."

"You live above the shop?"

"In the second-floor apartment, yes. We used to rent it out—well, technically, my grandparents used to live in it back in the fifties and sixties, before they had my mom and bought a house down the street. After they moved out, they started leasing the upstairs apartment, but when Mom sold the house last year to finance her relocation to Florida, I moved in. Saves me a bundle on rent, that's for sure."

Brushing my fingers across the pockmarked counter, I examine a display of hand-drawn greeting cards for sale next to the cash register. I wonder what Perry's apartment is like. Filled with green, growing things, I bet. And quirky art prints to match his offbeat personality. Unbidden, heat rises into my cheeks. Why am I imagining the details of Perry's living space?

"So it looks like we have some time on our hands. How would you like a tour of the shop?" he asks.

I look around the snug space filled with flowers and shelves full of trinkets for sale. "There's more?"

"There's the back. Want to see where the magic happens?" He pumps his eyebrows suggestively and I laugh.

"I thought you made your flower arrangements here." I motion toward the narrow space behind the counter lined with cabinets and bins of flowers. "That's where you made mine."

The tips of his ears turn pink. "Some of them, I do. But the larger orders require more space. Come on." Curiosity nibbles at me, and I follow him through the door marked Employees Only into a spacious, brightly lit room.

Inside, a massive, square worktable scattered with leaves and stray petals stands in the middle of the open space. Bins of flowers crowd beneath the bar-height table along with a pair of metal stools. A long wooden counter runs the entire length of two walls, and above the counter, shelves filled with colorful ribbons, vases, and baskets stretch to the ceiling.

A chill tickles my neck, and I notice the pair of glass-doored refrigerators hugging the wall to my right. They're the step-in kind you might see in a grocery store or gas station, and they're filled with even more flowers. And, tucked in the far back corner of the room, next to a tall filing cabinet and gray metal door, a cramped desk holds a clunky laptop, a wire lamp, and various stacks of papers.

The scent of flowers is stronger than in the front of the shop. I inhale deeply and imagine I'm standing in a spring meadow instead of a windowless back room.

Perry leans against the counter next to two vases holding bouquets wrapped in airy white tissue paper. "I just finished up the last couple arrangements that need to be delivered tonight before I tackle a big wedding order for tomorrow. One of them is for our longest-running customer, Mr. Johansson. Every year for the past forty-seven years, Mr. Johansson has ordered a bouquet of long-stemmed roses for his wife on their anniversary." He peels apart the tissue paper of the nearest bouquet, and I marvel at the velvety red blooms nestled among stunning evergreen leaves.

"She's a lucky lady."

He retucks the tissue paper into place. "She died seven years ago."

"And he keeps buying them?"

"To keep her memory alive."

"That's . . ." I clear my throat. "To experience a love that lasts beyond a lifetime. Hard to imagine."

"You don't know anyone who's had that kind of love? No one in your family?"

"Well, I was raised by a single mother. Don't know who my father is, and I only met my grandparents once."

"What were they like?"

"Religious fanatics."

"Yikes."

"Yeah. When my mom got pregnant in high school, they kicked her out. She reached out to them when I was five, hoping to mend fences, and we went to see them. I don't remember much, except for them calling me 'the daughter of a whore' and telling us they didn't want her sin in their life."

"Wow. They sound like horrible, miserable people. I mean, how could they not love their own grandchild? Especially you. You seem A-OK to me."

"Apart from a head injury and a stubborn streak a mile long? I can't think of anything not to like about me."

Perry chuckles.

Wandering around the table, I flick the end of one of the long ribbons hanging from spools on the lowest shelf. "So how many people work at Blooms & Baubles?"

"Besides me? Two. There's Alma, our weekend florist. She's a friend of my mom's and has been with the shop for over twenty years."

"And the other?"

"Our part-time delivery driver, Chuck. He's an ex-con, but a good guy. Highly dependable. We used to have more employees, but I've had to scale back since Mom transferred the business to me and I took over." A cloud passes over his expression, but it's gone in a blink.

"So you do most of the flower arrangements yourself?"

"I do indeed."

"And this is what you wanted to do with your life."

It's not a question, but he answers it anyway. "Shocking, isn't it?"

I shrug. "Not if you love flowers."

Perry pushes off the counter and saunters across the room. Settling onto a tall metal stool, he rests his elbow on the table. "It's not the flowers I love, exactly. I mean yes, I've always loved gardening and appreciate anything that grows in the dirt. But it's the joy that brought me to the job."

"The joy of arranging flowers?"

"The joy the act of giving flowers brings to others. Buying someone a handcrafted bouquet might seem old-fashioned, especially

these days—what with every grocery and dime-store drug mart selling cheap arrangements. And cut flowers only last a short time.
After a week—or two, if the flowers are ours—the blooms fade, and
what was once a beautiful bouquet shrivels up and dies. But the act
of giving someone even a small slice of beauty, and the thoughtful-
ness behind the gesture . . . that's permanent. That's what I love
about my job. Being a florist means celebrating the interconnected-
ness between people and the brief bouts of beauty in a world with
too much ugliness."

My skin tingles. "I never thought of it that way."

"Most people don't. I know I'm the odd one out." Perry flashes a
sheepish grin.

Finishing my lap around the room, I brush my fingers along the
table's worn, smooth edge. "So where do you get all your flowers
from? Do you grow them yourself, or . . . what?" I've never considered where flowers originate before they end up in a flower shop.

He chuckles. "Some I do, but I definitely don't have the space to
grow all of my own stock. I source the majority from a nursery in
Olmsted Falls—the same one my grandparents started buying
from back in the seventies. They're a small, family run operation
too. When the owners retired about twenty years ago, their son
and his wife took over. They're in their sixties now, but still going
strong, and they grow the best flowers in Northeast Ohio."

I nod thoughtfully. "You said you grow *some* of your flowers—
where do you grow them, exactly?" I look around as though a magical garden might poof into existence.

He raises an eyebrow. "Want to see?"

"Sure."

Perry leads me across the room to the back door. Sticky summer
heat washes over me as we walk down a short set of stairs that deposits us onto a moss-covered brick patio. I let out a breathy "*Oh!*"
I'm standing in Perry's fenced-in backyard, and half of it consists of
a metal-framed, glass-walled greenhouse. Between the patio's as-

sortment of cushy chairs, cozy fire pit, and the string of Edison lights zigzagging between the shop and the greenhouse, it's absolutely charming.

Beyond the tall wooden fence, a maple tree towers from a neighbor's yard. Its leaves rustle with the breeze, dappling the backyard in a kaleidoscope of ever-shifting shadows. We stroll down the pathway of paver stones set in the narrow patch of grass to the greenhouse. When I walk inside, an explosion of tropical colors and smells greet me. There are squat, miniature palm trees; tall, orange hibiscus; orchids in a variety of colors; and more types of potted plants than I can name.

It's *much* warmer in here than in the shop, which I guess is the point. Shrugging out of my blazer, I loop it over the bag tucked under my arm and stroll down the center aisle, studying each plant as I go. "I can't believe you did all this. How long have you had a greenhouse?" I ask.

Folding his arms over his chest, Perry leans against the nearest workbench. "Five years. My mom's garden used to be here, but when she brought me on to assist her with Blooms & Baubles when I was twenty-four, it had been ages since she'd touched it. I asked if I could build a greenhouse in this spot instead."

I bend over a particularly interesting-looking plant with long, spiky red-and-green leaves. "So how does one even become a florist? Besides inheriting the family business, I mean. Do they have floristry schools, or . . . ?"

He chuckles. "They do. I got my associate degree in floral design before transferring to Bowling Green for a bachelor's in ecology. Mom insisted on a four-year degree so I'd have options, even though I knew I wanted to follow in her footsteps," he explains.

"Smart." I run my finger along a white-and-purple orchid's large leathery leaf. "Do you sell everything you grow in here?"

"Some I sell, some I keep. It's part hobby, part business. One hundred percent labor of love."

"You know, I've never met someone as passionate about anything as you are about flowers."

"Too bad it hasn't helped my love life," he says with a sardonic smile.

"What do you mean? Why not?"

He hesitates, plucking at his collar. "Oh, well, when women hear what I do for a living, they usually assume I'm gay. Which is fine—it doesn't bother me—but it does tend to make dating more difficult. Selling flowers isn't the most stereotypically masculine profession, after all."

Unbidden, my fingers ball into a fist. "Screw stereotypes," I spit. "Any woman would be lucky to have you. You're a talented, successful business owner, and you make the most beautiful flower arrangements I've ever seen. If someone can't look beyond their own preconceptions to see what a catch you are, that's their loss."

A flush creeps up Perry's neck and his shoulders go rigid. Turning, he studies the hibiscus behind him before pinching off a spent bloom. "Thanks. That's nice of you to say." *Did my words strike a chord?*

But when he turns around several heartbeats later, his posture is relaxed again, his typical, adorable smile in place. Lifting his eyebrows, he snaps his fingers. "Hey, I have an idea. Want me to show you the ropes? Give you a minilesson in flower arranging before Devin gets here? We still have at least twenty minutes to kill," he says, checking the time on his phone.

My heart leaps. That actually sounds really fun. "Definitely."

When we return to the back room, I set my bag and blazer on the counter while Perry paces around the worktable, excitement oozing from every pore. "Okay." Clapping his hands once, he rubs his palms together. "First lesson: the key to an impactful arrangement is balance, but with an element of the unexpected."

"Like eucalyptus for scent?"

"Precisely."

I nod. "It's the same in art. As an artist, you want balance in a composition, but also something that grabs the viewer's attention. A unique detail or captivating approach that makes them linger."

"Exactly. Why don't you give it a shot?" Perry plucks a clear rectangular vase from one of the shelves and places it on the table in front of me.

"Really? Just . . . go?"

"You can pick from anything we have in stock." He sweeps his arm toward the bins of flowers on the floor.

"How do I even start?"

"Start with how you're feeling. Or how you want the bouquet's recipient to feel. Pick a feeling, any feeling."

Casting around, I settle on the first word that comes to mind. "Hope."

He nods. "Okay. Now when you close your eyes and picture hope, what do you see?"

Licking my lips, I close my eyes. "Rain."

"Rain . . . really?"

My head buzzes, and a scene forms in my mind. "Not gray, drizzly rain . . . The last raindrops at the very end of a storm. The way the ground smells fresh and alive. How the air is heavy with the promise of sunshine ahead because all the bad things have been washed away."

I blink open my eyes. Perry's staring at me, jaw slack. Embarrassment crawls up my throat. "I—"

"*Yes*. Boom. Perfect!" His lips split into a heart-melting grin. "Now, let your inspiration guide you."

I don't hesitate. I can see the colors in my mind, and I follow my gut. I select a variety of flowers in shades ranging from deep lavender to blush pink to coral, inserting them in the vase and adjusting as I go. Perry is quiet for the most part, offering advice when I ask for it. I change my mind several times, inserting a flower, removing it, putting it back in its bin only to pick another. After several attempts, I'm satisfied.

Perry's eyebrows knit as he rotates the vase, examining it from every angle. "Excellent. I love the pop of red you included here." He points to the single red Asiatic lily I included in my otherwise yellow, orange, and purple arrangement. "Normally, I would advise you to repeat elements—always use multiples of the same type of flower—but this works. It's an unexpected choice, and thoroughly stunning. I couldn't have done better myself."

My cheeks warm at the outlandish praise. "I doubt that, but thank you."

He peers at me from over the bouquet. "Why are you a lawyer again?"

I laugh. "What, like it's a bad career?"

"No, but you're obviously an artist at heart. Why did you choose law?"

"I've known since I was in elementary school that I was going to be a lawyer."

"Seriously?"

"Yep. My mom's a paralegal, so I've been around the law most of my life. It's a good career. Steady, rewarding. I might love art, but for all but a lucky few, it's not a viable career path. It's too uncertain, too mercurial. And if there's one thing I've learned being raised by a single mother, it's that you can't rely on anyone else to give you security. You have to build it for yourself."

"Do you enjoy being a lawyer?"

"For the most part. The law is fascinating. It's constantly evolving, and to argue a case you have to see the world in shades of gray instead of black and white. It takes a certain amount of creativity to interpret the law and use it to bolster the strengths of your client's case while downplaying its weaknesses."

"Isn't it all pretty dry though? All that reading, writing, and arguing?"

I shrug. "It can be."

"Please tell me you're still drawing on the side though. I saw your sketches of Devin—you're really good. Hell, I could even sell your work in the shop if you wanted. People would totally buy it."

I laugh. "I seriously doubt that." Unless they were drawings of Devin, in which case I bet every straight woman in the greater Cleveland area would line up for the chance to have his likeness gracing their wall.

"Are you still sketching these days?" he asks.

"Not for a few months. I haven't really had the time."

"I bet you wish you had the time though."

"Maybe not to sketch . . ." I meander around the table and settle onto one of the two empty stools. Taking a deep breath, I cross my legs and rub the goose bumps from my forearms. "Honestly? What I really miss is painting. Sketching was easier than painting when I was recovering from the accident, but in my brief stint as an art major, my preferred medium was acrylics. But painting requires even more time than picking up a pencil to doodle, plus I threw out all my painting supplies years ago . . . so pursuing art as a hobby simply isn't in the cards at the moment." I shrug.

"Hmmm." He nods thoughtfully as he rounds the table to stand next to me. "Well, for what it's worth, I hope you manage to find the time someday. Us creative types need to feed our souls, you know. Creating art clearly makes you happy, and you deserve to be happy, Cass."

Perry's green-hazel eyes bore into mine, and energy sizzles in my stomach. His slanted eyebrows are as mischievous as ever, but his grin fades as our gazes lock. The air between us charges, heavy with unspoken understanding.

"Thank you," I finally croak.

"You're welcome."

A metallic click and a slam jerks me out of my reverie. I blink. The Captain—no, The *Colonel*—woofs.

"Perry, you still here? Sorry I'm late," Devin's voice rings out.

Sliding off the stool, I stride to the other side of the room, smoothing my skirt down my thighs. I can't keep my hands from trembling. I turn around when Devin opens the door. "Hey," I choke out.

He blinks. "Cass. Hi. You're here. I thought you usually left work around six thirty."

"I took off early so we could talk."

"We can, for sure, but can you give me ten minutes? I promised Perry I'd help him with the last couple orders of the day." Devin pulls a double-take at the bouquet—my bouquet—on the table. "Are those for the Johansson order? Did he finally switch it up from roses?"

"No, Cass made that. For you," he adds, flashing me a hint of a smile from behind Devin's back.

My stomach flops. I hadn't had Devin in mind when I made the arrangement, but Perry's clearly trying to throw me a bone. I should roll with it.

"*You* did this?" Devin's eyes widen in astonishment.

"To say sorry for earlier," I say.

Devin's expression softens as he looks between me and the flowers. He shakes his head. "No woman has ever given me flowers before."

"Besides Mom," Perry says, correcting him.

"Right, but she doesn't count. Cass, these are beautiful." Gathering my face in his hands, he plants a kiss against my nose. "You're a natural."

"That's what I said. If the whole lawyer thing doesn't work out, you should consider a career as a florist. Or some kind of creative endeavor. Maybe painting?" Perry says softly. Our gazes connect for half a heartbeat before he looks away, rubbing the back of his neck. "Well, I should probably go deliver these." On the far side of the room, he scoops up the tissue paper–wrapped bouquets and balances one on either side of his slim waist.

"Do you need my help?" Devin asks.

"I got this. You guys have fun. Can you swing by in the morning to help me with the Leifkowitz wedding though? I still need to work up their invoice. Plus, I could use some help with the latest paperwork that came in from the state."

"You got it, bro."

With a nod, Perry strides across the room.

"Bye," I call when he's nearly at the door. "Thanks again for the lesson."

Pausing, he grins at me over his shoulder, but there's a hint of resignation behind his vivid eyes. "Anytime."

When the door clicks closed, Devin settles onto the metal stool and crosses his arms over his broad chest, legs spread wide. "Okay, you wanted to talk, so let's talk."

"Devin, I'm sorry about earlier. I shouldn't have—"

"Stop." He raises his palm. "Cass, *I'm* sorry. I shouldn't have surprised you with a car like that. I was overreaching. And then getting mad at you when you reasonably said 'thanks but no thanks'?" He shakes his head. "I'm an idiot, and I'm sorry. Can you forgive me?"

Stepping between his legs, I circle my arms around his neck. "Only if you forgive me."

He sweeps a kiss against my lips. "Of course I do. Next time, we'll decide if and when you'll drive—together. I won't push you into it. Just know I'm here and ready to help whenever you get up the courage to try."

My insides bristle at the inference that my refusal to get behind the wheel has to do with a lack of courage rather than debilitating anxiety I can't control. But we've already been in one fight today. Mincing words wouldn't be productive at this point, and I understand what he's really offering is help and support.

"Can I take you to dinner tonight?" he asks.

My stomach rumbles as if on cue. "Only if I can pay this time." Devin's paid for my meal the last two times we've been out, so it's most definitely my turn. This also feels like a good time to remind him that I'm fully capable of taking care of myself—which includes paying for meals.

Plus, it'll help me feel better about putting this afternoon behind us and simply enjoying our evening together. I hope.

12

"Mmm, this is delicious," I say to Devin. My lips tingle as I savor the explosion of spicy peppers and carnitas on my tongue. Swallowing, I wipe my mouth with a napkin. Conversations crest around us, filling the colorful tapas restaurant, while the wail of a trumpet accompanies the rhythmic notes of conga drums. I cross my legs under the bar, careful not to bump the woman sitting inches away from me. "I'm glad you talked me into the taco sampler."

Devin grins. "You can't go wrong with a sampler."

A bartender with a neatly trimmed mustache bustles over holding two glasses of champagne. "Here you are." He sets them in front of us.

"Thank you." Devin slides a twenty across the bar, picks up the glasses, and hands one to me.

"What's this for?"

"Surviving our first fight."

"I don't know if I'd call it a fight. More like a mutual misunderstanding."

"Still worth celebrating. I've been in relationships where misunderstandings turn into full-blown arguments pretty quickly, so I say we handled ourselves well."

"Yes, we did." I lift my glass.

"Cheers." We clink, and I take a sip. Bubbles tickle my nose as the crisp, effervescent liquid slides down my throat. Something Perry said the other week niggles at the back of my mind, and I put down my champagne.

"Is that how it was with your last girlfriend?"

Devin casts me a sidelong look.

"Perry mentioned you recently got out of a bad relationship with someone named . . . Susan? Samantha?"

"Sadie," he says darkly.

"What happened with Sadie?" Devin sucks in his cheek as though he's biting it and looks everywhere except at me. Happy, tipsy chatter fills the bar, and I scoot my stool closer to him. "You don't have to talk about her if you don't want to."

"No, it's fine. It's a fair question. We met at a bar in Columbus last year. I'd just graduated from my MBA program at Ohio State, and she was going into her third year of law school."

"I see you have a thing for lawyers," I say, teasing.

"They're smart and ambitious. What's not to love?" He offers me the ghost of a smile.

"How long were you together?"

"Eight months. I know it doesn't sound like a long time, but Sadie was like a keg of gunpowder. Being with her was . . . explosive. But we burned out just as quickly." He jabs a tortilla chip into a bowl of salsa and crams it into his mouth.

Jealousy claws up my spine like a slithering swamp monster, and I shove it back down. I have no right to be jealous. What he did, and whom he dated, before we met is none of my business. "What happened?"

Tipping his chin to the ceiling, he blows out a long breath. "She turned out to be a world-class liar. I didn't see it at first, but she manipulated me the whole time we were together. We broke up about three months ago. I haven't talked to her since."

"Is she still in Columbus?"

"No idea. I blocked her number and unfollowed her on Instagram. I have no desire to see or speak to her ever again."

Well, that sounds healthy.

"How about you? Any bad news ex-boyfriends I should be aware of?"

"Are we sharing our rosters?"

He chuckles. "If you like."

"Well, mine's pretty short. Besides a few short-term relationships in college, there was only Ben. We dated for a couple years in law school, but our breakup was blessedly free of drama."

"What happened with Ben?"

"We sort of . . . drifted apart emotionally. We dated for almost two years and even lived together our second year of law school, but after a while we realized that except for making fantastic study buddies, we didn't actually make sense together. I like museums, he likes sports. I wanted to travel, he wanted to stay home. My dream is to make partner at Smith & Boone, travel in my time off, and enjoy what city life has to offer—like art museums, live music, and festivals. His big dream is to become a tax attorney, get married, raise a couple kids in the suburbs, and score season tickets to the Browns."

"And you don't want that? A family, I mean. Not Browns tickets," he says.

"Someday, sure. But I want more than that too, you know? I want to be with someone I can have adventures with. Someone who shares my interests and wants to get out and explore as much as I do. I have such a small family that I'd like to have kids of my own—one day, in the far, *far* future—but I'm in no rush. I have a lot of living to do before then."

"Fair enough. So how did the end come about with Mr. Browns lover then?"

"We were eating dinner one night at home—with the game on,

of course—and he looked at me over a bowl of spaghetti and said, 'I don't think this is working.' And I said, 'You're right, it's not.' I moved out three weeks later."

"Wow. That's very mature."

I shrug. "We were in the same law school class and had the same circle of friends, so why make things harder than it had to be? I think we only stayed together for so long because it was comfortable, and it beat being alone, especially during such a stressful time in our lives."

"Hmmm," he grunts.

"What, you've never stayed in a relationship because it was easier than breaking up?"

"Ahhh, no. Before Sadie, my longest relationship lasted three months. Four, tops."

"Oh. Okay then."

"Not that I was a player or anything," he says.

My lips quirk. "No, of course not."

"Really!"

"With that face? I totally believe you." I give him a playful shove and his eyes twinkle.

"Believe what you want, but my one-night stands have been few and far between. I'm more of a serial dater."

"I'd say I am too, but that would require actually dating." At his questioning look, I clarify. "In law school there wasn't anyone after Ben, and then I had the accident. Kind of hard to date when you're in recovery. Plus, I've learned along the way that most men don't actually want to date smart women. They say they do, but when it comes down to it, more often than not they're secretly intimidated."

"Because they're insecure."

"And you're not," I say.

"Nope. When I think of the future, I picture a wife and kids." He adds, "One day," with a wry smile. "I'd love to move up in my dad's company and spearhead development projects that enhance communities and help revitalize the entire Northeast Ohio region. I want a partner who can stand side by side with me, not a step behind, so we can forge the best future possible together."

I take an overly large bite of my taco to cover my bemusement . . . because it sounds like Devin might want someone like *me*.

"Speaking of partners, how's work going?" he asks. "Have they given you a corner office with a gold nameplate on the door yet?"

I snort. "As if. I'm still just a lowly summer associate."

"But have they said anything about the fall? Whether your permanent job offer still stands?"

"No, but it's early days yet. Plus, there's this other summer associate gunning for my position."

"That scoundrel. Who is he?"

"*She* is another law school graduate, and she's hands-down the most cutthroat person I've ever met. She totally has it out for me."

"Don't let her get the best of you. If I were you, I'd do anything it takes to land the job. Be the first to arrive every day and the last to leave. Volunteer for extra work. Show them how badly you want it."

My shoulders stiffen. I've already been working such long hours I can't fathom putting in any more time than I already have. Perry's words from earlier float back to me.

You deserve to be happy, Cass.

Would working more make me happy? *No*, a little voice answers. Having fun with Brie, spending time with my Mom and brothers, and picking up a paintbrush every now and again would make me happy—not slaving away at a desk around the clock. I nibble my lip. But if it's only temporary—a push to help me secure the job of my dreams—the sacrifices would be worth it . . . right? I stuff another bite of taco into my mouth. "You might be onto something," I say thickly.

"Of course I am. There are hundreds of attorneys who would kill for a job offer from a firm like Smith & Boone. I'm proud they want to hire *you*." With a grin, he chucks me under the chin.

"Thanks, Devin."

Devin's car rumbles as he pulls in front of my house and cuts the engine.

"Thank you for the ride home," I say.

"Of course." Unbuckling his seat belt, he swivels to face me. "So hey, what are you doing for the Fourth?"

"The Fourth?" Right, I forgot the Fourth of July is this weekend. "Brie and I are going to the parade downtown, and then we're watching the fireworks from the rooftop of Marcus's bar."

"I see." His fingers play along my forearm, sending shivers down my spine. "My dad's throwing his big, annual Fourth of July party. He's good friends with the owner of a concrete plant downtown, so we get special access to a lakefront facility to gather and watch the fireworks. I'd love for you to come and meet my dad . . . if you're willing to change your plans, that is."

Devin's dark eyes contain a measure of vulnerability I haven't seen before. *He's nervous.* "You can bring Brie and Marcus too, if you—"

Before I can think twice, I unbuckle my seat belt, lean over the center console, and kiss him. He sucks in a surprised breath through his nose, but responds in earnest, his lips moving against mine. One hand tangles in my hair while the other runs down length of my back. Blood pounds in my ears at the swell of sensation. His lips are soft yet urgent as his tongue dips into my mouth, tasting me. Bright lights burn orange behind my eyelids and I pull back just as a car passes by where we're parked, its headlights cascading over us like a passing rainstorm.

"Is that a yes?" Devin asks, breathless.

My lips tingle. "A tentative yes. I have to talk to Brie first, but if she and Marcus are down, then we're in."

"Good." He smooths his thumb over my cheekbone. His eyes flick behind me, to my house. "So, can I come in?" His voice is pure, molten promise. But instead of melting, I tense.

Am I ready for that? I hold my breath, heartbeat skittering as I search his face.

My hesitation must be answer enough, because Devin clears his throat and drops his hand.

I touch his arm. "I want to. Honestly. It's just, given all that's happened to me, and how strange this situation is, I think I'd prefer to take it slow. I like you. I really do. I'm just not sure I'm ready for . . . *that*."

Devin's shoulders relax as he sweeps his thumb over my jaw. "Take all the time you need. I'm not going anywhere."

"Thanks for understanding." With a shaky smile, I gather up my bag from between my feet and crack open the door. "I'll text you later."

I'm halfway out of the car when he snatches my fingers. Bringing my knuckles to his lips, he presses a kiss against the tender skin. His dark eyes flash as his tongue darts out, setting my nerve endings ablaze. "Looking forward to it," he rumbles.

I somehow manage to exit the car without falling over—despite my quavering legs—and shut the door.

He waits until I wave from the front porch before driving away. Leaning against the screen door, I blow out a noisy breath, hand pressed against my chest. Devin is a perfect male specimen and the embodiment of every woman's fantasy: charming, kind, ambitious, and hotter than a clam bake on the Fourth of July. So why am I still hesitating?

There's the obvious: three weeks isn't a long time to date someone. I should get to know him better before diving whole hog into a relationship with someone I might still have very unrealistic expectations about. But it's not as if he's a stranger anymore. We've been on four, no *five*, dates now, and if it were any of the other guys I've dated, I would have invited him in for some grown-up sexy fun times by this point.

Unbidden, Perry's face floats into my mind—his shy smile, wavy brown hair, and the unbridled passion in his eyes when he talks about delivering joy to others. After the debacle at Marcus's bar and his drunken shenanigans at the pinball parlor, the last person I expected to find a friend in was Perry. But after tonight, I can call him a friend, and that's a good thing. I *should* get along with the brother of the man I'm seeing. It certainly makes things less complicated now that he's not overtly suspicious of me.

So why am I thinking about Perry . . . now? Minutes after kissing Devin?

With a huff, I open the screen door and twist the knob. The porch light is off and the door is locked. Either Brie's not home yet or she's turned in early. After a minute of fruitless searching in my bag for my keys, I pull out my phone and tap the flashlight app. A beam of concentrated light skitters across the porch, streaking across a package tucked next to the door. Frowning, I pick it up. It's not a delivery; it doesn't have an address or name on it, and it's surprisingly heavy. I flip it over, and find a small envelope taped to the back with one word on it: *Cass*.

Who in the world left this here? Did Mom drop something off for me? Judging by its rectangular shape and hard angles, I'm guessing it's a wooden box of some sort. I quickly find my keys, let myself in, and make a beeline for my bedroom. Down the hall, warm, yellow light seeps out from beneath Brie's closed door; she's in for the night.

Flipping on the ceiling light with my elbow, I deposit my bag on the floor of my bedroom before settling on the bed with my mystery package. Curiosity pounds through me with every beat of my heart as I tug off the envelope and slide out the card inside. On it, a handwritten message is scrawled in blue ink: *In case "someday" comes sooner than later. —Perry*

My jaw goes slack and I reread the note two more times before setting the card gingerly on the mattress beside me. My breathing accelerates as I rip open the package, peeling back the brown paper in strips. I was right; it's a wooden box—three times the size of a shoebox with a set of tarnished brass latches on one side. Flicking the latches, I open the lid.

And gasp. It's an easel. A portable one.

I tip it onto its side and something rattles inside the easel's boxy interior. I arrange the stand and extend the legs, adjusting several bolts to lock everything in place, and set the easel upright on the floor. A small groove in the center catches my eye, and I lift a thin panel to reveal a shallow drawer filled with twenty or so small tubes of acrylic paint. I remove them one by one and line them up on my desk next to the pitcher holding Devin's lilies, which are now dry and shriveled. At the bottom of the drawer, I discover several paintbrushes of various sizes, an oval mixing palette, and three blank, eight-by-ten flat-board canvases. Although the easel is old judging by the patchy stain of the box, the paints and brushes look barely used.

Tears burn behind my eyes. "Damn you, Perry." Laughing quietly, I pick up one of the brushes and drag its soft bristles across my palm.

This might be the most thoughtful gift anyone's ever given me in my entire life. And it's from *Perry*.

Excitement crackles through every cell of my body. Tossing the paintbrush onto my bed, I run down to the kitchen and fill a red Solo cup with water. I dig through the recycling bin under the sink, pull out a discarded neighborhood newspaper along with several rags, and carry everything upstairs. After changing into a T-shirt and a pair of old boxer shorts, I relocate the easel to a corner by my desk and arrange the newspapers beneath its spindly legs. My heart thunders as I place an empty canvas on the easel and step back.

Suddenly, my mind goes as blank as the stiff white canvas before me. It's been years since I picked up a brush. I used to lose myself in art for hours—the glide of paint on fresh canvas, the symphony of colors, the act of creation. But now, what if that part of me is as dusty and broken from lack of use as a busted clock? I imagine a knot of cobwebs around my soul, and instead of a heart, a clanking, groaning set of rusty gears.

My phone dings from my bag on the floor. Sighing, I dig it out. I have a calendar notification: 9:00 a.m. Friday, client mtg w/Andréa.

All the excitement seeps out of me. It's almost ten o'clock at night. I should pack the easel away and take the time before bed to review the notes Andréa sent earlier about the client we're meeting tomorrow and their case. That's what Devin would tell me to do—seize every chance to wow Smith & Boone so I land the job of my dreams.

My gaze drifts back to the blank canvas on my easel. Outside, thunder rumbles in the distance.

Screw it. I deserve to claim one night—one *hour*—for myself. I have Andréa's notes. I can review them in the morning.

Heavy raindrops splatter against my window. I sigh and let my eyelids flutter closed. *Another summer storm.* Sucking in a sharp breath, I open my eyes.

I know exactly what I'm going to paint.

13

"Cass. Hey, Cass! Are you awake?" Brie calls from somewhere above me.

"Go away," I groan, pulling my comforter over my head to block out the unwanted light.

She shakes my shoulder. "It's nine thirty. Shouldn't you be at work?"

My eyes fly open. "Did you say nine thirty?"

Bright sunlight cascades across Brie's worried face. "Yeah, are you—"

"Shit! I'm late!" Flinging off the covers, I launch out of bed. My toe catches on something lumpy, and I career into the wall. "Why didn't my alarm go off? Where's my phone?" I pat around my nightstand and under my pillow, but it's not there.

Brie squats to search through the tote bag on the floor, which is apparently what I tripped over. A second later, she holds up my phone. I snatch it from her and tap the screen. It's dead. "Noooo, I forgot to charge it last night." That must be why my alarm didn't go off.

She takes my phone and plugs it into my wall charger. "Get dressed, I got you covered." She jogs out of my room, brown leather booties squeaking against the wide-plank floor as I tear open my closet to grab whatever I see first. She reappears less than a minute later, when I'm in the middle of buttoning up a light blue oxford. "Take this, it's my portable charger. You can use it at work today."

"Thanks, Brie," I say, fastening the final button and returning to my closet.

She narrows her eyes at me. "Hey, what's with . . ." Her voice trails off when she catches sight of the easel in the corner and the freshly painted canvas filled with splashes of color. She whirls on me, eyes wide. "Holy shit, did *you* do that?"

"Yeah." I hop as I kick off my boxer shorts and yank on a navy pencil skirt.

"Cass, that's the first time you've painted in *years*."

"And now I'm paying for it." I have no idea what time I went to bed last night, but it was way later than I planned, and I overslept as a result. It's *not* okay for summer associates to be late. It's unprofessional, irresponsible, and certainly not the kind of impression I need to make if I want a job offer at the end of the summer. Something niggles at the back of my mind, compounding my urgency like gasoline dripping on a flame, but I can't recall what it is.

Grabbing my phone, bag, and a pair of navy heels from the closet, I scurry down the hall to the bathroom, Brie right behind me.

"What made you want to start painting again? Does Devin have something to do with it?" she calls before I close the bathroom door.

"Not exactly," I yell back. Inside, I brush my teeth at top speed, use the toilet, and throw my messy hair into a bun. There's no time for makeup—I'll have to do it at work. Brie's still standing in the hallway when I emerge. She falls into step beside me as we descend the stairs.

"Where'd you get the easel then?"

"Perry gave it to me."

"Perry, Devin's brother, *Perry*?"

"Yeah."

"Damn, Cass. What does Devin think about that?"

"He doesn't know. Or at least, I'm assuming Perry didn't tell him in the last twelve hours."

"So what, you have a secret thing with Perry now?"

I turn right, detouring to the kitchen. "No! It's not like that. Perry and I got to talking about hobbies yesterday while I was waiting for Devin at Blooms & Baubles. I mentioned that I used to paint, and when I got home from dinner, I found an easel and paint set on the porch with my name on it."

"That's really sweet."

"He's just being friendly . . . since I'm dating his brother and all."

"Pret-ty friendly, I'd say."

I purse my lips at her over my shoulder as I open the fridge.

"Wait, how does he know where you live?" she asks.

Good question. I shuffle through the possibilities. "Devin used Perry's phone to order an Uber for us the other week. The receipt probably listed my address since we stopped here first."

"That would explain it."

I swipe a Red Bull from the fridge and Brie tosses me a granola bar. I stuff them both into my bag.

"Come on. I'll give you a ride to work."

"Won't you be late?"

"Nah. I'm on flex time."

"You're a lifesaver. Thanks, Brie."

We hustle down the street to where her car's parallel parked and climb in. Her Ford Mustang's engine roars as she pulls out, and I take the opportunity to plug my phone into her portable charger and turn it on. My office is less than a five-minute drive from our place, and by the time my phone boots up we're nearly there. Two new messages flash across the screen.

Mom

How did your talk with Devin go?

Devin

Good morning 😊 Are we on for my dad's 4th of July party this weekend?

Right. I'd completely forgotten. "Hey, Brie, how would you feel about switching up our plans for the Fourth? Devin's dad is having a big party on the lake, and Devin invited us."

Brie's tires screech when she stops in front of my office. "Sounds lit. Let's do it."

"Great. I'll text him."

"What about Marcus?"

"He can come too. Can you pass along the invite?"

"Sure."

"Thanks."

Brie grins to herself as I shut the door. With a wave, I take off at a jog toward my building.

David looks up from reception when I bust through the doors. His thick black frames gleam in the light cascading from the lobby's wall of windows. "You're late."

"I know."

"Everything okay?"

"Ask me later," I call as I step into the empty elevator. I attempt to steady my breathing, but my heart thunders in my ears. When the doors open, I speed-walk through the gray-carpeted hallways toward my cubicle. Maybe I can make it to my desk without anyone else noticing . . .

"Cassidy?" Andréa's voice calls out.

Wincing, I turn slowly.

Andréa's standing in the doorway to her office, her full lips turned down in a frown. Behind her, Mercedes beams over her shoulder. Between her long, strawberry-blond hair, ivory shift dress, and cream jacket, she looks as beatific as an angel. Too bad deep down she's more like the devil.

"Where have you been, Cass? You missed our client meeting this morning," says Andréa.

Crap. So that's what I forgot. My stomach plummets to the basement. "I'm so sorry, Andréa. My alarm didn't go off and I accidentally overslept."

Andréa sighs. "Thank you for your help, Mercedes. I'm all set for now."

"You're welcome." Mercedes's ruby lips tilt into a smirk as she walks past me. Fury boils in my veins, and I tighten my hold on my purse strap.

Andréa settles her steely gaze on me. "Can I speak to you in my office, please?"

Despite my quavering calves, I force some iron into my spine as I follow Andréa into her office. She closes the door behind me, and the soft click rings through the silence like the clang of a jail cell. Sweat gathers at the base of my neck as she settles into her cushioned office chair, and I brush it away.

Taking a deep breath, she leans forward, grasping her hands on top of her desk. "Are you okay?"

I blink. "I'm fine. Just frazzled."

"It's not like you to miss a meeting."

"I know. Again, I'm so sorry. I would have called, but when I woke up my phone was dead, which is why my alarm didn't go off. I got here as soon as I could—"

"Take a deep breath. It's okay, you're not in trouble. Everyone oversleeps from time to time. It happens."

I slump in relief. "It won't happen again, I promise." I make a mental note to order a battery-operated alarm clock as soon as I get to my desk.

Andréa nods once. "Big law life is hard. It's a high-stress job, and the work is arduous. I just want to be sure you're balancing everything well."

"I am. Honestly."

Her chair squeaks when she leans back. "Good. Because I spoke to Glenn Boone about you the other day."

I sit up straighter. "Really?"

"He asked me what I think about renewing your offer to start as a first-year associate in the fall. I told him you were my top choice."

"Wow, Andréa. Thank you so much! I can't tell you how much I appreciate it."

She waves me away. "You deserve it. Your work product is excellent, and you have a knack for litigation. Your brief for the Lebow case was outstanding. Truly brilliant, creative legal reasoning. Smith & Boone would be lucky to have you."

Pride swells in my chest. "I appreciate it. I won't let you down."

"I'm glad to hear it. Now, as you know, we like to give our summer associates a chance to gain experience in different types of law . . ."

My eyebrows fly up my forehead. "You're moving me out of litigation?"

"Only temporarily. Mercedes Trowbridge has expressed an interest in shadowing me, so I'd like to cycle her in for few weeks and give you exposure to the public law group."

I nod, mouth dry. "Of course, whatever you want."

"This isn't a punishment, Cass. It'll be good for you to experience a different practice area."

"I understand, and I'm grateful. My undergraduate degree is in public administration, so a foray into public law should be pretty interesting for me."

"That's the spirit. And don't worry, I have full confidence in you. I know you'll continue your top-notch work and wow Frank as much as you've wowed me."

"Thank you, Andréa. I won't disappoint you. Or Frank."

Her eyes shine with pride. "I know."

I leave Andréa's office and trudge to my cubicle, emotions swirling and colliding like a paper boat pitched on storm-tossed waves. My shoulders tense when I spot Mercedes sitting at her desk.

She peers at me over her shoulder when I plop my bag onto the floor.

"Are you okay? You don't look so good," she simpers.

"Fine," I grit.

"Are you sure? I have concealer if you want some for those dark circles under your eyes." Her voice is nothing but pure concern, but I don't miss the infinitesimal curl to her lips.

Anger pounds hot and heavy through my veins. "Cut the crap, Mercedes. How long did you wait this morning before running off to Andréa's office when you figured out I was late? Was it thirty seconds or did you wait a whole minute?" Glaring, I sit heavily in my chair.

Her icy blue eyes flash. "Excuse me, it's not my fault you didn't show. And in fact, *she* reached out to *me*. If you don't like me covering for you, how about you do your job." Snagging a notebook from her desk, she storms away without a backward glance.

Groaning, I let my head fall on my desk with a *plunk*.

She's right. Even though I could have done without the hefty dose of smug satisfaction, it's not her fault I wasn't there and Andréa asked her to sub for my meeting.

Jiggling the mouse to wake up my computer, I punch in my password like I'm hammering nails. If only I hadn't stayed up late last night to paint.

I pound my armrest with my fist. *This is all Perry's fault.* I have one heartfelt conversation about art, and all sense flies out the window. I should have rewrapped that easel as soon as I opened it and delivered it straight back to Perry with a note: *Thanks, but no thanks. I'm too busy.* This is exactly why my mom has always cautioned me against distractions: they really do affect your career.

The overhead light catches my fingertips resting on my keyboard and I wrinkle my nose at the paint caked under my nails. I pick ineffectually at the splotches of cerulean, violet, and dusky gray, but they don't budge. Nostalgia washes over me like a cool breeze, and I curl my fingers into a fist.

How often did I walk around my freshman year of college with paint under my nails and a sense of deep contentment in my heart? When I finally rinsed my paintbrushes and turned in last night, I'd felt calmer and more at peace than I had in, well, *years*. It's probably why I slept so well. I didn't toss, turn, or otherwise flop around like a restless fish, and I didn't wake up even once in the middle of the night with my mind racing, ruminating on all the things I had to do the next day.

If it wasn't for me forgetting to charge my phone, I would have woken up rested—and arrived at work on time. It's not Perry's fault I missed the meeting. It was a by-product of my own cotton candy brain forgetting to plug in my phone.

And I just took it out on Mercedes.

Not that she doesn't deserve it a teeny, tiny bit—Lord knows she's been a thorn in my paw since day one—but if she's telling the truth and Andréa asked her to fill in for me, not the other way around, then she's right, it's not her fault.

Petty isn't a good look on anyone. Next time I see her, I'll extend an olive branch.

I just hope I don't forget.

14

"Are you sure this is the right place?" Marcus asks from the back seat when Brie turns onto an unmarked industrial road across from the empty parking lot next to the Browns stadium.

I reread Devin's directions on my phone. "I think so."

"It's not where I'd choose to throw a party, that's for sure," Brie mutters.

We bounce over a set of train tracks and drive past a series of long, low warehouses and stacks of rusted shipping containers until we reach a wide-open area filled with parked cars. The round white towers of a concrete plant rise in the distance roughly a hundred yards away. Beyond the towers, the blue-gray water of Lake Erie glints in the early evening light, countless boats bobbing on its surface.

Brie circles around, and I spot what must be the party. Down a hill from where the cars are parked, dozens of people dressed in their red, white, and blue finest dot a wide expanse of grass abutting the shore. Lawn chairs, blankets, and coolers are set up in clumps, and several people are playing cornhole farther down. Higher up on the hill, a long table is set out with containers of food covered in aluminum foil.

"I take it back. This is pretty sweet," she says.

We park at the edge of the lot and unpack our blankets and supplies. Brie grunts as she attempts to lift a cooler full of hard seltzers and beer out of her trunk.

Marcus takes it from her. "Here, let me carry that for you." He offers her a shy smile.

To my shock, the apples of her cheeks flush pink. "Uh, sure. Thanks, Marcus."

"Anytime. I'll find us a spot." Hoisting the cooler, he strides off in the direction of the party with a definite strut in his step. I swing my small blue daypack onto my back, grab the paper grocery bag full of snacks from the back seat, and shut the door.

"What's going on with you and Marcus?" I ask Brie as soon as he's out of earshot.

Looping a messenger bag over her head, she gathers a thick folded blanket to her chest and closes the trunk. "I don't know what you're talking about."

"Pi."

"Seriously? You're pulling pi on me?"

Lifting my eyebrows, I tap my toe.

"Uh, fine. We've been texting more lately since he came to my panel. I know what you're thinking, but we're just friends. Honestly!"

"I hate to break it to you, but I don't think Marcus wants to be your *friend*. I think he wants to get into your shorts."

Brie snorts. "Please."

"You really haven't noticed the way he looks at you?"

"It's called polite eye contact."

"Um, no. It's called he can't keep his eyes off you. Like you're a Popsicle on a hot summer day, and he's desperate to lick you up before you melt."

"Sheesh, graphic much?"

"It's the truth."

"Well, I don't see him that way."

"Why not?"

"I'm not dating at the moment."

"Still not over Sara?"

"No, I'm totally over her. We broke up months ago. I'm just . . . taking some me time right now."

Brie's a serial monogamist. Before Sara, it was Taylor. Before Taylor, it was Christopher. Each time she gets into a serious relationship, she's *all* in—she falls hard and fast, diving headlong into what she hopes will be the end-all, be-all of lifetime loves. Eventually, when the relationship sours or fizzles out, she's left feeling banged up and alone. This is probably a good thing for her, this "me time." The fact she's been single for six whole months is a miracle.

I nod, and we begin walking. "Fair enough, but whenever you're done with 'me time,' there's a perfectly adorable landlord-slash-bar manager who would love nothing better than to whisper sweet nothings in your ear . . . and ride the Brie-train to O-town."

"You're bad." She elbows me in the arm, but I don't miss the way she grins.

Even though the sun hangs low in the sky, the temperatures are still in the upper seventies, and I'm grateful I decided to wear a sports bra under my casual blue-and-white-striped romper. Pausing at the edge of the party, I scan the crowd of people until I spot Devin. He's talking to an older man wearing khaki shorts, a red polo, and loafers. Judging by his gray-streaked hair and the bone structure that's nearly identical to Devin's—same sharp nose, high cheekbones, and striking jawline—he must be Devin's dad.

I swallow. Meeting his dad is a big step. One I have mixed feelings about, although I'd never tell Devin that. He was so excited when I said yes to his invitation I didn't have the heart to tell him I was starting to have second thoughts. Formal parent introductions usually only happen after a couple has been dating seriously—and exclusively—for a while. Months, not weeks. So far, Devin and I are neither serious nor exclusive, although that certainly seems to be where things are headed.

Devin's face lights up when he catches sight of me, and he jogs over. "Cass, you made it!" He sweeps his lips against mine in a burst of a kiss. Heat climbs up my neck.

"Hey, Devin. You remember Brie, right?"

He nods. "You were at Zelma's the other week."

"That's me." She juts her hip in a mock curtsy. "Nice to officially meet you."

"Likewise. Is Marcus coming?"

"I'm right here." Marcus steps up behind us. "Thanks for the invite."

"Of course. Glad you could make it."

Behind Devin, the man I'm guessing is his father spots us. Excusing himself from his conversation with a pair of middle-aged men, he ambles over and claps Devin on the shoulder. "Introduce me to your friends, Devin." His piercing brown eyes peer at each of us in turn.

"Of course. Dad, this is Marcus Belmont. He manages Zelma's Taphouse in Ohio City. We play rec softball together. Marcus, this is my father."

Devin's dad looks Marcus over with a smile that doesn't quite reach his eyes. "Roger Szymanski." He extends his hand and they shake.

"And this is Cass Walker, the woman I told you about, and her roommate, Brie . . ." He trails off.

"Owens," she says.

Roger gives her the barest glance, then pulls a double take. "Owens . . . Owens?" he repeats. Squinting at her, he tilts his head. "Are you related to Charlotte Owens by chance? You're the spitting image of her."

Her lips quake with the effort to keep her smile in place. "She's my mom."

Roger's eyes light up. "Oh-ho! Devin, you didn't tell me your friends were so well connected. We're happy to have the daughter of Cleveland's most beloved newscaster at our little get-together."

From behind my bag of snacks, I grab Brie's hand and give it a surreptitious squeeze. She *hates* it when people fawn over her mother. The world might think Charlotte Owens is as sunny and sweet as her on-air persona suggests, but we both know the truth: she's Joan Crawford—controlling when it comes to her only daughter. Their relationship is strained, to put it mildly.

She squeezes back, and some of the tension leaves her. "Thank you. I'm glad to be here."

Roger nods, and turns his attention to me. "And this is the famous Cassidy."

"Cass," I correct automatically.

"Cass. Devin's told me a lot about you."

"Hopefully all good things." And nothing about my accident or the defies-the-odds coma memories. "It's a pleasure to meet you, Mr. Szymanski." I extend my hand and we shake. His grip is firm to the point of overpowering.

"Please, call me Roger. Devin tells me you're an attorney?"

"That's right."

"What kind of law do you practice?"

"Litigation, at the moment. I'm a summer associate at Smith & Boone, but I'm hoping to stay on full-time in the fall."

Widening his stance, he hooks his thumbs in his belt loops. "Smith & Boone is an excellent firm. They represent my business interests."

"Your business is in good hands then. You're a real estate developer, isn't that right?"

"Founder and CEO of Szymanski Enterprises. We operate mostly on the south side of the city and specialize in residential development, but we're in the process of expanding."

"How exciting. I bet you love having your son back in town to help run things."

Roger chuckles, and there's a sour note to the sound that makes my scalp prickle. "Help out? Yes. Run things?" He grunts. "Devin's coming along, but he has a long way to go if he wants to call the shots someday."

Devin's jaw tightens and his nostrils flare. "I don't know, Dad. I secured those two hundred acres in Medina County last month for 10 percent less than the seller was originally willing to take. And I got zoning approval for our new apartment project in Ohio City."

"Of course, you did, son," he says, his tone the verbal equivalent of a head-pat. "But success takes time, and you haven't developed that killer instinct yet."

"Not like you, huh, Dad?" someone calls from behind Roger. When he turns to locate the source of the voice, Perry emerges from behind a knot of people gathered near the food. My heart leaps.

Seeing Perry and Devin standing next to their dad, it's clear that Perry must take after his mother. He has the same jawline and lean, broad-shouldered build as his father and brother, but his features are softer, less sharp. His eyes, in particular, stand in stark contrast to Devin's and Roger's—and not just because theirs are a deep, rich brown, whereas his are clear emerald-hazel. There's a lightness behind Perry's eyes, a carefree amusement about the world that shines through every expression, like dandelion seeds dancing in the wind, whereas Devin's and Roger's piercing gazes are more like blown glass—smooth, solid, and untouchable.

Roger blinks. "Perry. You're here."

"I thought you said you weren't coming," says Devin.

Perry's forearm muscles jump as he slides his hands into the front pockets of his shorts. "I figured it was high time I make another appearance at one of Dad's famous Fourth of July parties. It's been a few years, after all. Marcus," he nods. "Cass." Our gazes connect and a smile whispers across his lips.

"Brie." She raises a hand in greeting.

Closing his mouth, Roger seems to recover himself. "Well, I'm glad you're here. It's been too long." He wraps Perry in an awkward one-armed hug and thumps him on the back with his fist. "How have you been?"

"Good. No complaints."

"And the shop? How's it going?"

Perry shifts his weight. "The shop's great. I've expanded my inventory, and second-quarter sales are up. We're doing better than ever."

Roger clears his throat. "That's not what Devin tells me." Even though he lowers his voice, we all catch his words.

Perry glares at Devin, who shakes his head imperceptibly.

"The offer's still on the table, Perry. Think about it. I can set you up, give you a chance to—"

Perry snorts. "Two minutes. I haven't been here for two whole minutes, and you're already doing what you always do. For the last time, the answer's no. Good to see you, Dad. If you'll excuse me, I'm going to grab some food." With an icy glance at Devin, he strides away.

"Perry, wait," Devin calls. "Be right back," he says to us before jogging after Perry.

"Roger!" A fortysomething blonde with shoulder-length hair beckons from a scrum of people gathered around a large red cooler about twenty feet away.

Roger waves back. Pasting on a tight smile, he returns his attention to Brie, Marcus, and me. "It was nice to meet you all. Please, help yourselves to whatever you'd like. And, Cass, I hope we have the chance to talk more soon. It'd be nice to get to know the woman my son is dating." His voice is deep and even, like Devin's, but his words hit me like the growl of a wolf. Because this man *is* a wolf, as cold, cunning, and calculating as one anyway—I'd bet my summer salary on it.

"Thank you," I blurt, but he's already gone.

"Well, that was awkward," mutters Brie.

"Tell me about it. What's the deal with Devin's dad?" I ask Marcus. He shrugs. "No clue. I just know he's some kind of big shot."

Brie snorts. "He's a big, douchey dick. Sorry," she adds to me. "I know he's your boyfriend's dad, but I call them like I see them."

"Not my boyfriend," I say. "But otherwise, yeah." I can't believe how Devin's dad belittled him, and in front of his friends to boot. And judging by Devin's stoic response, I'd wager it wasn't the first time it's happened either.

I glare at Roger through the crowd, at his broad back and the haughty lift of his chin. Mom might push me, but she'd never speak to me like that—alone or in front of other people—or intentionally try to make me feel small. Sympathy for Devin curls around my heart.

And *Perry*. No wonder he doesn't get along with his dad. I have no idea what kind of offer his dad was talking about, but clearly it's a sore spot between them. And it sounded like Devin told their dad something about Blooms & Baubles Perry didn't want him to know. I grip the bag of snacks so tightly against my ribs its contents crinkle.

This is going to be one interesting night.

15

Forty-five minutes later, Devin finally reappears. He flops down between me, Brie, and Marcus onto the thick navy blanket we've spread on the ground, hair windswept and cheeks rosy. "There you are. Where have you been?"

"Right here. Where have *you* been?" Draining the last of my hard cherry seltzer, I drop the can into the empty paper bag serving as our makeshift recycling bin and take a long drink of water from my Hydro Flask.

He lifts a bottle of Coors to his lips. "Sorry. I ran into my Great-Aunt Lydia and got roped into a very long conversation about, let's see, her fireman son, the state of her ulcer, and the failing health of her favorite Chihuahua."

"Did you find Perry?" I ask.

He shakes his head. "I think he left."

"That's too bad." My gut tightens. I was hoping I'd get a chance to thank him for the paint set, but it looks like that'll have to wait.

Devin shoves to his feet. "Come on. I want you to meet some friends of mine. I saw them earlier but haven't had a chance to say hi yet."

"Are you guys okay here for a bit?" I ask Brie and Marcus.

Brie salutes me with a potato chip. "For sure. You go on ahead. Marcus and I are going to play cornhole."

His dark eyebrows bounce. "We are?"

"Yep, and I hope you're good . . . because I hate to lose." Grabbing him by the bicep, she yanks him off the ground and toward the three cornhole sets farther down the shore.

Devin proffers his hand. I take it, and he hauls me to my feet. "Come on, let's go." Slipping my canvas bag onto my back, I follow him.

"Are you okay?" I ask Devin after we start walking.

"Fine. Why?"

"I don't know. Your dad . . . he's hard on you, isn't he?"

He gazes out at the shimmering lake dotted with boats. "Sometimes. He just wants me to be my best."

"By belittling you in front of your friends?" I say quietly.

"He wasn't belittling me. He's right. I still have a lot to learn if I want to be as successful as he is some day." His neck stiffens, tendons straining.

"I have no doubt you will be. Even more so, I bet."

After a long moment, he takes my hand. "Thanks, Cass."

Devin leads me through a maze of folding chairs and blankets until we reach a group of twentysomethings sitting in a row of lawn chairs facing the lake, sipping drinks as they talk. There are four of them, three men and a woman, and with their polo shirts, twill shorts, and the woman's immaculate pink sundress, they all look like they could have stepped out of a J.Crew catalogue. They stand when they catch sight of Devin and me.

"Devin, you dirty dog!" one of the twentysomethings calls. He's ruddy faced and stocky, with close-cropped blond hair. "How the hell are you?"

"Mikey," Devin drawls.

Clasping hands, they bump shoulders.

"Need a refill?" Mikey asks.

Before Devin can answer, Mikey exchanges Devin's empty beer bottle for a fresh one from their cooler. Devin attempts to pass it to me, but I shake my head. I've had two hard seltzers already, and between those and the heat, I already feel a bit woozy. Shrugging, he cracks it open. "Thanks."

"Where's Sadie? Is she here?" Mikey peers around as though Devin's ex-girlfriend is going to pop out from behind a beach chair.

"Ahhh, no. We broke up."

"Oh man, I'm sorry. Sadie was the tops, the whole package. When you guys started talking about moving in together, I thought a ring wasn't far behind. What happened?"

I stare at Devin. *They were going to move in together?* He never told me that.

Devin's nostrils flare. "It didn't work out."

"But—"

"Mikey, I'd like you to meet Cass," he says loudly. "Cass, this is Mike Howitzer. Mike and I went to high school together. He's the one I told you about who works at a car dealership in Brook Park."

Mike covers his mouth. "Oh shit, is this your new girlfriend?"

"We've been seeing each other for about a month," I say.

"Sorry, sorry, sorry. I can be a real jackass sometimes."

"Isn't that the truth," says the man next to him, grinning from beneath a neatly trimmed auburn beard. "Dev, it's been too long." He pulls Devin into a back-slapping hug.

"Gavin, good to see you. How's med school?"

"Hard as hell." He laughs, pushing his Ray-Ban sunglasses farther up his pointed nose. "I'm starting rotations in the fall, then hopefully a residency in cardiothoracic surgery. I heard you're back in the C-L-E working for your dad. What does he have you doing?"

"A little bit of everything. Scouting properties, negotiating deals as part of our new expansion. That sort of thing."

"Come on, you're being modest. I bet you're his right-hand man."

The tips of Devin's ears turn pink. "You know it."

The guys laugh, and Devin grins when Mikey jostles him playfully. "Attaboy."

The woman with long black hair and a pink sundress steps forward with a little wave. "Hi there, I'm Anisha Patel. This is my husband, Jai," she says to me.

"Hi. Nice to meet you." I wave back. "So, did you all go to high school together?"

"That's right," says Jai.

"St. Isaac, baby!" Mikey whoops.

St. Isaac is one of the most prestigious Catholic schools in Cleveland. It certainly explains the preppy vibe.

"Is that how you two met?" I flick a finger between Jai and Anisha.

Anisha smiles, revealing dazzling white teeth. "Jai was my senior prom date. We lost touch in college, but reconnected when we both started as analysts for Key Bank five years ago. We got married last summer," she explains, patting her husband's chest. A diamond the size of a small marble sparkles on her ring finger.

"Congratulations."

"So, what do you do, Cass?" Anisha's long, sleek ponytail falls over one shoulder as she takes a dainty sip of hard seltzer.

"Cass is a trial lawyer for Smith & Boone," says Devin. Pride shines out of his every pore.

"Nice! Where'd you go to law school?" Jai asks.

"I went to—"

"Case Western," Devin cuts in. "She was the editor of their law review journal *and* the captain of the mock trial team."

A muscle jumps in my neck. "Devin, you're making me blush," I say through a tight smile.

Wrapping his arm around my waist, he tugs me closer until my side is pressed against his. "Come on, let me brag. You deserve it." His tone is sincere, but the way his gaze drifts to his friends makes me feel like his words aren't actually meant for me. My stomach twists.

"Cass." Mikey snaps his fingers. "You're the girl who was interested in the 2014 Lexus ES 350, right? Devin told me about you! Wait, weren't you in a *coma*?"

Ice fills my veins, despite the heat. "Uh, yeah."

Anisha pushes her sunglasses to the top of her head. "Oh my God, that's terrible. What happened?"

"I was in a car accident last summer. I'm fine now."

Mikey leans closer like he's hypnotized. "What was it like being in a coma? Were you trapped in your body? Was it torture?"

Gavin punches him in the arm. "Jesus, Mikey!"

"What? I'm curious. I've never met anyone who's been in a coma before."

Everyone's attention settles on me like I'm a specimen in a petri dish.

My throat squeezes and I suck in a breath. "Me neither." I force a laugh, and it pierces my throat like a knife. Everyone laughs along with me.

"I'm sorry, I need to use the restroom." I back away. "It was nice meeting you all." With a little wave, I bolt out of there as fast as I can without it looking like I'm fleeing. I'm vaguely aware that Devin's following me, but I keep going.

"Cass, hold up," he calls.

I don't stop.

"Cass!"

I turn on him, heart thundering. "What the hell was that?"

He balks. "What do you mean?"

"Why did you tell your friends I was in a coma?"

"I didn't know it was a secret."

"It's not, but it might have been nice if you warned me. Now every time they see me, they'll think of me as 'that girl who was in a coma.' Do you know what that's like? Having the most traumatic experience of your life reduced to a topic of casual conversation?"

"No, I don't," he says quietly.

"And what was with the bragging? I didn't even recognize you, the way you interrupted me, trying to impress your friends."

"Cass, it was just talk."

"Are you sure?" I scoff. "Look, I don't know why you invited me, but I didn't come here to be your arm candy. My résumé isn't some tool you can use to impress your friends, and my medical history certainly isn't a curiosity people can trot out for entertainment."

His eyes blaze. "I invited you because I like you, and I wanted to introduce you to my dad and some of the other important people in my life. I bragged about you because you're *worth* bragging about. Everyone should know what an incredible person you are." Scrubbing the back of his neck, he lets out a noisy breath. "I'm sorry if I made you uncomfortable back there."

Folding my arms across my chest, I nod once.

"And I'm sorry for telling Mikey about your coma. I mentioned it in passing when I picked up the car from the dealership, but I should have known better. Mikey's heart's in the right place, but he has a big mouth."

"It's not just that," I say quietly. "If you haven't noticed, I don't exactly enjoy talking about my coma, or the accident. I've worked hard to move past it, and once people find out what happened, it's all they see."

Inhaling deeply, he closes the distance between us. He reaches out, slowly, deliberately, as though giving me the chance to back away. When I don't, he runs a palm up and down my bare arm. My skin prickles under his touch. "I didn't know. I'm sorry." Sincerity swells behind his eyes.

After several long seconds, my muscles unfurl. "It's okay. Apology accepted."

Lips tilting into a grin, he gives me a lingering kiss. "What should we do now? Want to challenge Brie and Marcus to a game of cornhole?"

"Sure. But first, I really do need to use the restroom." I wince.

"I'll walk you—"

"No, it's okay. Stay, hang out with your friends. I'll find you when I get back."

He nods. "There's a bathroom in the concrete plant, on the side closest to the lake. The door should be unlocked."

"Thanks. See you in a bit." Hooking my fingers around the straps of my backpack, I walk in the direction of the two white towers looming in the near distance. I try not to replay the conversation with Devin's friends in my head.

Or the way a stone settled in the pit of my stomach when he kissed me.

His apology was heartfelt and I do forgive him, but a tiny, nagging part of me wonders if it was enough.

16

I wind through the myriad partygoers, keeping a sharp eye out for Devin's dad. I really don't feel like talking to Mr. Bigshot Developer again, especially after the debacle with Devin and his buddies. I've had my fill of making nice with strangers for the night. Just as I pass the food table, a woman's voice cuts through the music pumping from a set of nearby speakers. "*Cass?*"

I crane my neck, searching for the source of the voice, until I spot a woman wearing white shorts, a loose red T-shirt, and a familiar wide grin.

Recognition zings through me and my eyes bug out. "Val?" I splutter.

"Cass! It's been forever!" The guy next to her, a lanky thirty-something with a long, thin nose and a full head of chestnut hair, takes her plate, and she wraps me up in a bone-crushing hug. She's a head shorter than me, and the tips of her tightly coiled black hair tickle my chin. "I heard about the accident. I'm so sorry. How are you doing?"

"Good. Great. Fully recovered." Physically, at least.

She squeezes my shoulder. "I'm so glad to hear it."

"How about you? What have you been up to?"

"Working for the city of Cleveland mostly. I run the Permits and Zoning Department now."

"You're not practicing law?"

"Nah. I figured out pretty soon after graduation that practicing law isn't all it's cracked up to be. My background is in community development, so the job's a good fit. The hours are steady, the stress is fairly low—compared to firm life, at least." She chuckles. "I like it. What about you?"

"I recently started at Smith & Boone."

She whistles low. "Damn, girl. If anyone has the brains and stamina for big law life, it's you. Cass was a year below me in law school, and we were on *Law Review* at the same time," she explains to the man standing next to her, who nods. "Oh, this is my fiancé, Eric, by the way."

"You're engaged? Congratulations!" I hug each of them in turn. "How do you know the Szymanskis?" I ask.

"I'm one of them." Eric grins, and I see the family resemblance in his high cheekbones and broad-shouldered build. "Roger Szymanski is my uncle."

I raise my eyebrows. "So you're Devin's cousin?"

"On my mom's side. How do you know Devin?"

"We started seeing each other about a month ago."

"Nice. Well, I'm very glad to meet you, Cass."

"Same here." An idea coalesces, and I sidle closer to Val. "So hey, random question. Can you remember if there was ever a party or law school event over the last few years that Devin and I would have both attended? Maybe something you or Eric hosted?"

She cocks her head. "I don't think so. Why?"

"When Devin and I first met we both had this strange flash of déjà vu, like we'd met somewhere before." My gut twists at the white lie, but I keep going. "We've been racking our brains ever since, trying to figure out where our paths might have crossed. You're only the second mutual connection we've found. Any ideas?"

Pinching her eyebrows together, Val taps a finger against her lips. "No, sorry. I know Devin through Eric, and Eric and I didn't meet until after I graduated law school."

I haven't seen her since she graduated, which means she can't be the connection we're looking for. My stomach sinks, the flash of hope that we finally had a lead gone. I smooth my features. "No biggie, I was just curious."

"Val?" a man calls from several yards away. "I thought that was you! What are you doing here?"

"Victor, hey. One second." Turning, she leans in. "What am *I* doing here? What is *he* doing here?" At my confused expression, she clarifies. "That's my boss. He's in charge of community development projects for the city of Cleveland."

"He's probably friends with my uncle. Roger knows *everyone*," says Eric.

"We should go say hi." She sighs. "Cass, it was *so* good to see you. Let's hang out soon, yeah?"

"For sure. Are you still on Instagram?"

She shakes her head. "My therapist recommended I take a break from social media for my mental health, and I haven't looked back." That explains why she didn't pop up as a mutual contact when Devin and I compared social media accounts last month. "I'm pretty sure I still have your number though . . ." Checking her phone, she nods. "Here's mine, just in case."

From inside my bag, my phone buzzes. "Text me. We'll do lunch."

"I'd love that."

"See you later." Taking her plate back from Eric, she disappears into the crowd.

A pleasant breeze wafts from the lake when I finally reach the concrete facility, cooling my overheated skin. The building is located on the edge of a short cliff, and I peer down the eight-foot decline to the rocky shore below. No one else is around, and I'm grateful for the quiet. My mind's still buzzing from my encounter with Val. For a second, I thought I'd finally found the connection that could explain how and why I imagined Devin, but I was wrong.

Back to square one, I guess.

My bladder reminds me why I'm here, and I pick up the pace. After all the seltzers and water I drank, I really do have to pee. Following the curve of the squat, round towers, I scan for a door. After fifty or so feet I find one. I tug the handle. The door doesn't budge. I knock, pressing my ear against the thick metal. No one answers. I walk around the entire facility, trying every door I find, but none of them are unlocked. "Damn it," I mumble.

I head toward the end of the building that's farthest away from the party until I find a weedy nook that offers sufficient concealment from prying eyes. This will have to do. Cursing under my breath, I drop my bag, peel the top of my romper down along with my underwear, and squat. Why I thought wearing a romper to an outdoor party was a solid choice, I have no idea. It might be cute as hell and on-theme, since it's blue and white, especially paired with my red espadrilles, but now I'm virtually naked, peeing out in the open, wearing nothing but a sports bra.

Something crunches nearby. Is someone coming? Breathing hard, I fumble with my romper.

A vague form rounds the corner, not ten feet away.

"Don't come over here!" I scream.

"Oh shit, sorry!" A male voice yells. I catch a vague impression of someone tripping before disappearing with a yelp. It all happened so fast I couldn't quite catch it, but I think someone just rolled down the hill . . . and possibly into the lake. I finish as fast as I can, pull up my romper, grab my bag, and scurry to the edge of the hill. "Hey, are you okay?" I call down to the man several feet below me.

Lurching to his feet with his back to me, the man smacks wet sand off his shorts. "Fine. I'm fine." He looks up.

"*Perry?*" I gasp.

His cheeks flame pink. "Oh, Cass. It's you. I'm so sorry . . . I didn't know anyone was back here or that they'd be . . ." He swallows.

Heat scorches my face. "It's fine. No big deal."

Behind him, the setting sun reflects off the water, washing his features in golden light. Rubbing the back of his neck, he offers me a lopsided grin. "I didn't see anything. I promise." With his arm lifted, his short-sleeved denim shirt rides up, revealing a hint of flat, smooth stomach. Saliva fills my mouth and I swallow.

Okay, Perry is low-key officially hot . . . so what? It's a dispassionate, empirical observation. It doesn't mean anything. Acknowledging the fact that he's physically attractive—and based on those muscles, jacked to boot—doesn't mean I *like* him. I'm simply appreciating the male form. Anyone with an artistic eye would do the same.

A shrill *eeep-eeep-eeep* cuts through the silence, and a small brown bird with a white chest and dark stripes zips through the air, dive-bombing Perry's head. He ducks.

"Watch out for the killdeer. I think you're near her nest," I say.

"I think you're right." Eyeing the slope, he begins traversing the incline's loose scree, the *eeep-eeep-eeep* of the bird spurring him on. I take a small bottle of hand sanitizer out of my bag and quickly squirt some of the clear, potent gel onto my palms and rub them together. By the time I stash it away, Perry's almost at the top of the hill. He grins at me as he takes his last step, but his foot slips. I lunge for him automatically and yank him up by the shirt. I pull a little too hard, and he tumbles into me. "*Oof.*" I stumble back, and he steadies me by the shoulders. The pressure of his palms cause sparks to flit around my belly like grasshoppers.

Backing up, I clear my throat. "Devin will be surprised you're still here. We all thought you left."

"I decided to take a walk."

"Thank you for the paint set, by the way," I blurt. "And the easel."

His eyes twinkle. "You found it then."

"It was kind of hard to miss. Where did you even get one—an easel like that?"

"The back of my closet."

"It was yours?"

"My mom got it for me. I went through a painting phase when I was in high school before realizing I have zero talent for studio art," he explains. "The kit's been collecting dust ever since. I wanted you to have it."

How do you express gratitude for a gift that's unlocked a part of yourself you've suppressed for years? I lick my lips. "Thank you. It was a really thoughtful gesture."

Perry's entire posture seems to relax. "You're welcome."

"I'm glad you didn't leave. I have something for you." Hoisting off my pack, I unzip it and pull out the small, thin canvas I brought on the off-chance I'd run into him. Before I can chicken out, I flip the canvas around and thrust it toward him. "It's a thank-you gift."

Lips parting in surprise, he takes it from me. He studies the painting for so long a bead of sweat trickles down my neck. Every beat of my heart echoes in my ears, and I resist the urge to snatch the canvas and chuck it into the lake.

I can file an appeal, draw up a contract, and argue the merits of a case without blinking an eye, but I'd forgotten how soul-crushingly terrifying it can be to share my art. How personal it is, like revealing a little piece of my soul.

"Hope," he finally murmurs, eyes widening. "You painted the rainstorm you picture when you think of hope."

"That's right." Edging closer until we're side by side, I peer over his shoulder at my creation—at the moody cerulean and indigo clouds, the abstract gray-pink raindrops giving way to a hazy golden sunrise.

"Cass, this is beautiful. I . . . I can't keep this."

He tries to give the painting back to me, but I push it toward him. My fingers brush his, and the sensation burrows into my blood.

"You were the one who encouraged me to take the leap and start painting again. I'd forgotten how much I love it. How it makes me feel . . . alive. I painted this the night I found your easel on my porch. I want you to have it."

"Thank—" His voice cracks. "Thank you."

His clear emerald eyes meet mine, and my calves tense. We're close—only a foot of space between us. At this distance, Perry's woodsy scent dances across my senses and my head feels curiously light. Like I'm standing on the pinnacle of a mountain or poised to deliver the closing argument to a jury, heart pounding with anticipation.

Chin quavering, I step back and swing my bag onto my back. "You're welcome. I would have thanked you sooner, but I don't have your number."

"Let's remedy that." Tucking the painting under his arm, he takes out his cell and taps the screen several times. From inside my bag, my phone beeps. "I just AirDropped you my contact info. Feel free to call me anytime. I mean, if you ever need anything, or whatever." Scratching his nose, he looks away. "I bet Devin's missing you. Don't you think you should head back?"

I wave him away. "He's fine. He's with his high school friends," I say.

"Ahhh, you met 'the crew'?"

"If you mean the 'one-up club,' then yes." I immediately wince. "That wasn't fair. They were actually pretty nice." For the most part.

"Don't judge Devin too harshly," he says. "I know he doesn't act like it, but Dad's criticism gets to him. And sometimes he overcompensates by trying to prove how great and successful he is, you know? But it doesn't come from a bad place, believe me."

"Why don't you come back to the party with me? I know he wants to talk to you."

Perry's expression darkens. "I'm sure he does."

"You can't solve your problems if you don't talk them out." I tap Perry's chest to punctuate my point.

"There's no problem, not really. I mean, I'm not thrilled he's been telling my dad about the state of Blooms & Baubles, but I'm not surprised. It's all part of a longer-term disagreement we have."

"About what?"

"Devin thinks I should liquidate and close down the business."

I furrow my brows. "Why is he helping you with the books then?"

"On the off-chance I might decide to sell it someday instead. Nobody wants to buy a business that's struggling. Strong finances mean a better sale."

"But you don't want to quit the business, do you?"

"No, but I might not have much of a choice. Mom struggled for years before I even took over. It turns out she owed a bundle in back property taxes. I've been working on paying it off, but the fact is, we're in debt."

"What about your dad? Couldn't you take him up on his offer to help?"

Perry lets out a derisive laugh. "He doesn't want to help. He offered to *buy* Blooms & Baubles—the business, the property, everything—to take it off my hands so I can do something 'worthwhile' with my life," he says, complete with the air quotes.

"Screw him. What you do *is* worthwhile. I'm sorry he doesn't see that."

Perry lifts and lowers one shoulder. "Truth be told, it's not really about me. A lot of his feelings about the shop are wrapped up in his feelings about my mom. B&B was her life. When we were little, he begged her to sell the shop so they could move out to the suburbs and start his development company, and Mom refused. She said she wouldn't give up what made her happy. Even though they've been divorced for nearly twenty years, I think he still resents that she chose the shop over him. And now he resents me for keeping it going . . . and that I love it as much as she did."

"Resentment is a poison."

"Too true." Crouching briefly, Perry picks up a flat, smooth rock. Weighing it in his hand, he whips it toward the lake. It skips across the water twice before sinking beneath the surface.

"Have you talked to him? Explained why running the business is so important to you?"

"I've tried, but that would require him listening for once."

"I'm sorry," I say again.

"It's not your fault. It's just one of those things."

"Is there anything I can do to help?"

His eyebrows quirk. "Not unless you know the number for the best family therapist in Ohio. Or a quick way to make twenty thousand bucks."

"Is that how much you owe in taxes?"

"More or less."

"Hmmm." I squint at the horizon. "You could sell a kidney. I hear the going rate on the black market these days is pret-ty good."

"Yes! Why didn't I think of that? Who needs two kidneys anyway? I could totally sell one."

"There you go. Your golden ticket."

Perry's rich laughter is infectious, and I join in.

"You're a gem, you know that? Devin's lucky you dreamed of him." The sun catches his profile, illuminating his tanned skin and the auburn streaks in his birch-brown hair. Warmth spreads through me like an ink drop in water.

My phone dings from inside my bag. Blinking, I pull it out and read the text that pops up. It's from Brie.

> Cass, where are you? Devin said you went to the bathroom. Did you fall in? DO YOU NEED ME TO RESCUE YOU???

> Sorry, I ran into Perry and we started talking. Back in a jiff!

> Ohhhh that explains it then 😉 Well hurry up and get back here. The fireworks are starting soon!

> Is Devin with you now?

> He was, but he took off a few minutes ago to look for you.

I return my phone to my bag and squint at the darkening sky. Brilliant orange crowns the horizon where the sun is sinking into the waves, and deep blue is spreading out from the sunset's golden edges like a cloak. "Devin's looking for me. Are you sticking around for the fireworks?"

"Wouldn't miss it. That's the one good thing about this party. The city of Cleveland sets off the fireworks right there—" He points over my shoulder to a low building about a hundred yards down the shore with the words Port of Cleveland painted in giant green letters across the roof, a fire truck peeking out behind it. "There isn't a better vantage point in the entire city."

"Let's go then." I begin trudging over the uneven ground, but Perry's not behind me. I stop.

"You go ahead. I think it's best if I stay here," he says.

"Nonsense. You can't watch fireworks alone. It's the law."

"Oh really?" He chuckles.

"Oh yes. Ohio Revised Code, section 375, subparagraph D,

clause twenty-nine." Sticking my finger in the air, I clear my throat. "No person shall witness, observe, or engage in any public display of fireworks, unless in the presence of at least one other person, of any age, at a distance of no greater than ten feet."

"I can't argue with that."

"Smart move. I'm a lawyer. Arguing's kind of my thing." I wink.

"I thought painting was your thing?"

"Only on nights and weekends." I grin. "And hey, we can avoid your dad if that's what you're worried about. You don't have to talk to him if you don't want to."

"It's like you can read my mind." Perry cocks his head as he studies me. "Okay, you win. Give me a minute to run to my car—I wouldn't want anything to happen to my new favorite painting." He taps the canvas against his chest. "Then we can find Devin."

My gut scrunches as I return his smile. "Sounds like a plan."

17

Finding our way back through the party is considerably more difficult than I anticipated. By the time Perry stashes my painting in his car and we hike back from the concrete plant, full dark has settled in. More people have arrived in the last hour—there's at least two hundred people milling around in the moonlight—and the mood has turned downright bacchanalian.

Searching for Devin, we pass half a dozen middle-aged women dancing drunkenly along to music from a Bluetooth speaker, and a pair of twentysomethings engaged in a chugging contest with a crowd cheering them on. Empty beer cans, plastic forks, and napkins litter the trampled grass. Someone must have brought an industrial-sized box of glow-in-the-dark accessories, too, because neon necklaces and glow sticks dot the night like Technicolor fireflies.

I spot Mr. Szymanski lounging in a lawn chair next to the same blond woman who beckoned him earlier, and I quickly tug Perry in the opposite direction. There are so many people I gather a fistful of his shirt at his waist just so I don't lose him. A bottle rocket whistles nearby, momentarily illuminating the sky in a burst of red sparks.

"Coma Girl!" someone croons. I stiffen. A swirl of neon green, pink, and blue bobs toward us, and I recognize the newcomer as one of Devin's friends from earlier—the short-haired blond.

"What did you just say?" Perry's voice is sharper than I've ever heard it.

The guy—I can't remember his name—squints one eye in Perry's direction. "Holy shit, is that Perry? What's up, Pear Tree?" He lifts his hand, offering a high five.

Perry folds his arms across his chest. "Not much, Mikey." Even in the meager light cast by Mikey's multiple glow-in-the-dark necklaces, which he's wearing on his head like a lopsided crown, I can tell Perry's face is as stony as a statue.

Mikey drops his hand. "Long time no see. Still slinging flowers?"

"Still crushing beer cans with your face?"

"You know it." Tipping his head to the sky, he howls like a coyote.

"Where's Devin?" I say, cutting in.

"Dunno. Last time I saw him, he was over there." Mikey motions widely, indicating half the party. Helpful.

My phone vibrates against my hip. Maybe it's Devin.

It's not. It's a text from my mom wishing me a happy Fourth of July. A photo pops up—a selfie of her, Rob, and the twins waving tiny American flags while they stick their tongues out at the camera. My chest aches. I miss my brothers. At least I'll get to see them tomorrow when I go to Mom's house for brunch. I text her back, Thanks, you too 🖤 🤍 🖤 Hug Liam and Jackson for me! and fire off a text to Devin.

> I'm back. Where are you?

I stare at the screen for a few seconds, but he doesn't respond. Sighing, I add another text—Meet me by our cooler, k?—before stashing my phone in my pocket.

"We should get going," I say.

Mikey sways as he lifts his beer. "Right on. Catch you later, Coma Girl—"

"*Cass*. Her name is Cass." Perry looms over the shorter man, his hand balled into a fist at his side. Gratitude fills me, as warm and sweet as honey.

Mikey backs up a step. "Sorry. Cass. Got it." Saluting us with two fingers, he clicks his tongue. "Gavin, you son of a bitch, where'd you go with my brownie?" he shouts as he stumbles away.

Perry watches him leave with narrowed eyes. "Sorry about Mikey," he yells over the drunken chatter.

"It's okay."

"No, it's not. People shouldn't make light of what happened to you. Calling you Coma Girl isn't cool."

Unbidden, tears prick my eyes. I blink them away. I didn't realize how good it felt for someone to understand my situation without having to explain. "Thanks for sticking up for me."

"Anytime." His eyes gleam in the moonlight.

"If you had waited another second, I would have grabbed his beer and dumped it on his head."

Perry chuckles. "Too bad. That would have been a sight."

I take two steps before my curiosity gets the better of me and I turn. "Pear Tree?" I ask.

"Oh, that," he grunts. "I started a gardening club in high school, and 'Pear Tree' sort of stuck. Mikey's the only one who still calls me that though."

I shake my head. "Some people never leave high school, even after they graduate."

"Isn't that the truth. Any word from Devin?"

My stomach flips. I check my phone again. "Not yet. I told him to meet me by our stuff."

"Good call."

We continue on through the crush of bodies. A minute later, I spot the place where we set up camp. "There it is." I squint through the darkness, but I can't tell if anyone's still there.

I catch sight of an indistinguishable mass stretched out on our blanket, no more than a dim shadow writhing in the dark. I frown. *What the . . . ?* Perry keeps walking and I throw out my arm to stop him. "Wait," I whisper, heartbeat accelerating.

I click on my cell. Pointing the screen toward the ground, I edge forward slowly. Lifting the phone by degrees, I focus the screen's dim light on the blanket . . . and immediately clutch my phone to my chest. I double-time back to Perry.

"Let's go."

"What's wrong?"

"Nothing. Just, come on." Ten steps away I can't hold it in anymore. I burst out laughing. "It's Brie and Marcus. They're having a *moment*."

Perry raises his eyebrows in question.

"By 'moment,' I mean they're making out like sex-starved teenagers."

"I didn't know they were together."

"They're not. Or maybe they are now?" Based on our conversation earlier, it didn't sound like Brie was ready to end her moratorium on dating. Then again, maybe Marcus is more persuasive than I give him credit for. "It's complicated."

A woman stumbles down the hill nearby and bumps into me when she passes, not noticing that she nearly knocks me off my balance. Perry steadies me with a hand at my waist, and the sensation delves straight to my core.

What the hell is happening to me?

I pluck at the hem of my romper. "Is it always this crowded?"

"I assume so. Dad doesn't do 'small.' What's the point of having a party if you don't invite everyone you know?"

"Why didn't *you* bring anyone to the party? Devin invited his friends."

He shrugs. "There was no one to invite. Most of my friends have moved away, and the ones who are left already had plans with their partners and families."

"Bummer. Why not invite someone new? Maybe some cute customer from the flower shop?" My tone is teasing, but I can't stop my thighs from clenching.

Perry's hand closes around my wrist. His touch is feather-light, but I freeze like I've been zapped with fifty thousand volts. "Because she's already here." His voice is low, but his words echo through my head like a shout down a hall. We're so close I can sense every rise and fall of his chest, feel every cool, spearmint breath as it fans across my cheek. My stomach tightens like a vise.

"Perry, I—"

"Cass, there you are!" Devin shouts, ambling toward us through the dark as he holds his cell phone aloft like a makeshift torch. A green glowstick dangles around his neck from an invisible cord, illuminating the white box he's clutching against his chest.

Perry's fingers slip from my wrist, and my skin tingles where he touched me.

"I've been looking all over for you," says Devin.

"Same here. Sorry I took so long. I tried to find a bathroom, but the facility was locked. Then I ran into Perry."

Devin stops short. "I thought you left," he says to Perry.

"I decided to stick around. Cass talked me into staying for the fireworks."

"She can be persuasive, can't she?" He grins at me. "Hey, Per, I'm sorry about Dad. I mentioned one time that I was helping you with taxes, and he must have put two and two together."

"Don't worry about it. I know you have my back when it counts." With a tense smile, Perry clasps Devin's shoulder. His eyes drift down. "What's in the box?"

"Something for Cass." He turns to me. "To say sorry again for earlier." Handing his phone to Perry, he lifts the box's lid. Inside is a sizable slice of strawberry cheesecake—Devin must have snagged the last piece from the food table, box and all. "Your deepest desire if I recall," he murmurs.

"You remembered."

"How could I forget?"

My heart flutters even as a tingling sensation skitters up my spine. A vague, half-forgotten memory rises to the surface of my consciousness, like the ghost of a dream. A white gleaming plate. A slice of decadent cheesecake, sweet sauce oozing down its side, sliced strawberries fanning out across the top. Devin, leaning across a narrow table, smiling at me as though I'm the most beautiful woman in the world.

I jolt. This is the first memory flashback I've experienced in weeks. Perhaps the real memories I'm making with Devin are crowding out the fake ones.

"You're the best. Thank you," I say, taking the box from him and closing the lid.

Beside Devin, Perry's face is an inscrutable mask. I inhale, but my breath sticks in my throat.

A dull boom sounds close by. A whistle. Then an explosion of red lights up the sky like a waterfall of fire. *Ooooo*s rise up from the party. Someone switches the music, and the brass notes of "Off We Go, into the Wild Blue Yonder" swell through the night. The myriad glow-in-the-dark accessories still by degrees as people settle in to watch the show.

"Come on, let's sit down," Devin shouts over the crackling booms of the fireworks. He starts toward our blanket, but I touch his arm.

"Not there. Brie and Marcus are . . . occupied. This way." I head toward the hill, find a wide, empty spot, and sit. Devin puts down the box and settles onto the grass on my right. Perry sits on my left. Swallowing, I wrap my arms around my knees, tucking them to my chest.

A succession of blue, silver, green, and gold bursts swallow the sky. The fireworks are so close they unfurl straight toward us, dripping through the stars and dissipating in a fizzle of sparks and smoke. Bits of detritus rain down, plinking softly in the grass all around us. I've never seen fireworks like this before—larger than life, filling my entire field of vision like the sky is our own private IMAX theater.

Beside me, Perry leans back to recline on his elbows, chin tilted toward the sky. It isn't long before my neck begins to ache from craning it to look nearly straight up, and I stretch out on my back on the hillside's soft grass, crossing my feet at the ankles. A heartbeat later, Devin follows suit. Once he's settled, he twines his fingers through mine. His palm is rough and warm, and I focus on the comforting familiarity of his touch.

Just as the music changes again, this time to a twangy, America-loving country song, Perry lays back as well. His arm brushes against mine as he settles into place . . . and stays there. It's only an inch or two of contact above our elbows, but my skin flames where we meet. I don't shift away. Neither does Perry. He must not register that we're touching . . . right?

The boom of fireworks reverberates through my rib cage, mirroring the thudding of my heart. A massive firework explodes directly overhead, its trailing gold sparks sweeping down like the branches of a willow tree. I seize the opportunity to steal a glance at Perry. My heartbeat stutter-steps.

He's not watching the fireworks. He's watching *me*. His nostrils flare when our gazes connect. My lips part automatically. Our chests rise and fall in tandem, the point of connection between us blazing brighter than the rockets above.

Guilt cleaves me like an axe, and I look away. I'm here with Devin, *holding hands* with Devin, but every fiber of my being is focused on the minuscule point where Perry and I are touching.

What does it mean? I can't deny that Perry and I have a connection, although I'm not sure yet whether it's friendship or something . . . else. But Devin and I are connected too—and on a deeper, inexplicable level. Perry shifts subtlety beside me, increasing the surface area of contact. Heat rises in my face, but I don't shift away.

By the time the finale begins what feels like an eternity later, my heart is hammering so hard I'm sure Devin and Perry can hear it above the 1812 Overture finale's opening strains. Fireworks explode in such quick succession I can barely track them. Red, blue, green, silver, violet, and gold bursts illuminate the sky. Devin runs his thumb along mine and my gut tightens.

After a final, dizzying display of fireworks, the sky turns black—and stays that way. People applaud as smoke wafts through the moonlight. Releasing Devin's hand, I push myself into a sitting position. Devin and Perry do the same. Even though I'm no longer touching either of them, I'm acutely aware of them flanking me in the dark.

"Best fireworks ever," I say. Shoving to my feet, I brush grass off the back of my romper before shouldering my bag and edging around Devin to pick up the box containing my cheesecake.

"Hold up, aren't you sticking around for the afterparty?" asks Devin, springing to his feet. "A bunch of us are walking over to Punch Bowl Social on the East Bank of the Flats."

I gnaw the inside of my cheek. My mind is a muddled mess of confusion, and right now I need to talk to Brie more than anything. "I don't know. I have to get up early tomorrow—my mom's picking me up at nine and taking me to her house for brunch . . ."

Devin gathers my hand in his, and I resist the urge to pull away. "Come on, it'll be fun."

I flick a glance at Perry. His features are cloaked in darkness, but I can still make out the barest hint of a frown in the light cast by the glowstick hanging around Devin's neck.

"Let me talk to Brie first and see what she wants to do. She's my ride home, after all."

"Cass, is that you?" Brie's voice floats through the dark a few yards away. She must have heard me say her name.

"Brie!" I blurt, grateful for the interruption. I head toward the sound of her voice, but before I take three steps, a shadow bounds toward me through the dark and Brie's small body wraps me in a breath-stealing hug.

"Where have you been? You missed the fireworks!"

"I saw them. We watched from over there." I motion toward the hill.

"Why not with me?" She frowns.

"You and Marcus seemed busy."

"Oh. Yeah, we were." She giggles.

About a hundred questions are poised on my tongue, but before I can get even one of them out, Marcus joins us, looping an arm around Brie's shoulder. "What's up, ladies?" he says.

"Afterparty is what's up," Devin chimes in. "Punch Bowl Social. You in?"

"Hell yes, we're in!" croons Brie. "Right, guys?" She bumps Marcus's hip. Even through the dark, I swear I can see his cheeks turn red. He's officially off-the-charts adorable with how hard he's crushing on Brie. "If you and Cass are game," she adds. "Cass, what do you say? Party time?" She's practically radiating hope.

I force a smile even as my calf muscles bunch. "Sure, sounds fun."

Devin loops his arm around me. It rests on my shoulder like a bag of potatoes. "That's more like it."

Perry steps forward. "If you'd rather go home, I'd be happy to drive you," he says quietly.

I glance at Brie, but her attention has already shifted back to Marcus. Pushing onto her tiptoes, she nudges a curl off his forehead with her finger. She's finally taken the plunge, and me telling her I'd rather go home right now would be like tossing a bucket of water onto a nascent flame. She'd insist on driving me herself, and even if I managed to convince her to stay and let Perry take me home, she'd probably be all up in her head about why I didn't want to go in the first place instead of focusing on the cute guy who's clearly head-over-heels interested in her. No way am I standing in the way of them having a good time tonight. "No, it's okay. I'll stay. Thank you though."

Devin's phone trills from his pocket and he answers it. "Yo, Jai. Are you and Anisha coming to Punch Bowl? Wait, Mikey did *what*?" Plugging his other ear, he strides away toward the thick of the party, which is a jumble of boisterous shouting, shuffling, and clanging as people pack up and trickle toward the parking lot.

I turn toward Brie and Marcus, but they're already deep in conversation. I might as well be a hundred miles away.

Perry clears his throat. "Well, I'm taking off. Have fun." He begins to leave, but I stop him with a touch to his forearm. His muscles jump under my fingertips.

"No afterparty for you?" I ask.

"Nah. I've already had one encounter with drunk Mikey tonight, which means I've met my quota for the year."

I laugh softly. "I understand."

"Cass—I . . ." He clears his throat again, and my gut seizes. We stare at each other, my heart thumping harder with each passing second. Finally, he shifts his weight and looks away.

"Be careful with Devin, okay?"

My stomach sinks. I thought we were past this. "I know you're protective of him, but really, you have nothing to worry about. I'd never do anything to hurt him."

"I meant be careful for yourself. I don't want to see *you* get hurt either."

I blink back my surprise. "You think Devin is going to *hurt* me?"

"Not on purpose."

"I thought you said earlier I should cut him some slack. But now you're telling me to watch out?"

He sighs. "I love Devin, but he tends to have a short attention span where women are concerned. When things start getting serious is usually when he bails."

"That's not how it was with Sadie though."

"She was the exception."

And apparently, if Mikey is to be believed, at one point he considered proposing—before whatever happened between them happened.

Perry shifts his weight. "Look, you're the first woman he's shown an interest in since Sadie, and, well, his track record with women generally hasn't included long-term relationships. I—I just thought you should know."

Emotion swells in my chest. Here's Perry, offering me a warning he certainly doesn't owe me. The connection we experienced during the fireworks blazes hot and bright between us, and I don't know whether to fling my arms around his neck or take off running into the night. Goose bumps prickle my flesh and I settle for stepping back and rubbing my arms instead.

"Are you sure you don't want to come to the afterparty?" I ask, despite myself.

"Nah, it's not my scene. Besides, you don't need me there. You have Devin." His words are light, but there's a wistful note in his tone I can't miss.

With a little wave, he disappears into the darkness, and I'm more confused than ever.

18

Despite its vast, airy interior, Punch Bowl Social is a loud, sweaty cluster. Music blares through the multistoried bar, thick with partygoers high on holiday celebrations. We weave through the dancing, heaving crowd, buy a round of drinks, and stake our claim at a tall, circular table when it's vacated by an older couple. There are only two chairs and at least seven of us who walked over from the party—mostly Devin's friends and a couple of others I don't recall meeting—so we opt to stand around the table instead of sit.

Brie and Marcus quickly fall into deep conversation, heads bent together as Brie sips from a glass of water. Marcus's eyes are over-bright, and he's grinning in a slightly stunned way like either he can't believe his luck, or he's been hit over the head with a sledge-hammer. I chuckle softly. Brie tends to have that effect on people.

Devin casually drapes his arm over my shoulder as he chats with Jai about their fantasy football league. It's hot in this crowded bar, and I resist the urge to put some space between us when sweat threatens to gather on the back of my neck. Jai's wife, Anisha, joins us then. She's pulled her long black hair into a high messy bun, and I notice she's switched from hard seltzers to a clear cocktail. The scent of lime wafts in the air between us.

"You guys . . ." she says, flicking her finger between Devin and me, "are *too* cute together."

Devin chuckles softly.

"Thanks," I murmur.

"Just don't let Sadie find out," she adds to me with a wink. "She was always the jealous type."

Devin's expression immediately shutters. "Don't worry, she won't. I blocked her months ago."

Anisha shrugs. "She's in Cleveland now, you know."

"*What?*" splutters Devin.

"Yeah. She moved here not too long ago. At least, I don't think it was that long ago." Anisha taps her full lips as she thinks. "May, maybe? She posted a picture of her new apartment on Instagram— I think it's in Slavic Village."

Jai sticks his finger in the air. "I thought you said it was Old Brooklyn."

"You're right, duh. Old Brooklyn," she repeats.

Holy shit. The Old Brooklyn neighborhood is only ten minutes away from mine.

The color leaches from Devin's cheeks as he unloops his arm from my shoulders and clears his throat. "Jai, you knew about this? Why didn't you tell me?"

Jai's eyes widen. "I'm sorry, man. I thought you knew."

"No. I didn't." His voice is so low it's barely above a rumble.

My gut squeezes like a wrung-out towel as I study Devin's face. Confusion, anger, and something I can't quite name flickers across his expression. I lean in and lower my voice. "Can I talk to you outside for a sec?"

Devin blinks down at me and nods.

"Well, it's officially sweltering in here. I could use some air," I say to the group as I fan myself. "Come with me?" I add to Devin with a smile I hope isn't too forced.

I lead Devin away from his friends and up a set of stairs to an open-air patio. It's not as crowded out here, and I suck in a deep lungful of clear summer air, grateful for the breeze cooling my overheated skin. We settle next to a concrete wall that overlooks a vast parking lot and, beyond, a smattering of skyscrapers.

Leaning my hips against the wall, I face Devin. "Are you okay?"

"Sure. Why?" His smile doesn't reach his eyes.

"You seemed kind of . . . upset . . . over the news about Sadie."

"Why would I be upset? My ex-girlfriend decided to move ten minutes away and none of my friends told me."

I wince. "I'm sorry."

We fall silent for several long seconds. Laughter and music from a myriad of restaurants and bars tangle in the night, creating a cacophonous buzz. "Why didn't you tell me you and Sadie were so serious?" I finally ask.

His eyebrows furrow momentarily before he nods in understanding. "You're referring to what Mikey said earlier."

"Right. It would have been nice knowing that before meeting your friends."

"Sorry. It's not something I like to talk about."

"I get it. I feel the same way about my accident." I scoot closer until we're only a few inches apart. "Look, if there's some big, ex-girlfriend-shaped skeleton in your closet that's going to come after us, I should know about it, right? Whatever happened, you can tell me. I'm here for you." I lay my hand on his and squeeze.

He sighs. "Fine. Sadie is a wild card, and I wouldn't put it past her to try to get at me through someone I'm dating—she's *that* kind of person . . ." He sucks in a deep breath. "So basically, she faked a pregnancy in an attempt to get me to marry her."

My jaw falls open. "*What?* No way. That's ridiculous. No one actually does that."

"*She* did."

"How do you know she was faking it? What happened?"

"We'd been together for about seven months when one day she tells me, *surprise*, she's pregnant."

"She wasn't on birth control?" I blurt out the first thought that comes to mind and immediately grimace.

"Yeah, she was, which is why I was so shocked. I didn't think getting pregnant was a real possibility, especially since we'd been taking other precautions. But even though it was a complete surprise, I had no reason to think she'd lie. And she seemed genuinely excited about it."

"Were you? Excited, that is?"

"Not at first," he admits. "I was pretty freaked out when she broke the news and showed me a picture of the pregnancy test, but I loved her. I thought she was the one I'd end up with in the long haul, so a pregnancy simply fast-tracked our plans by a few years. So when she said she wanted to keep the baby, I supported her choice. We even started looking for an apartment together and talking baby names . . ."

By the faraway look in his eye, I'd bet he was more excited about the prospect of a baby than he's letting on. My heart constricts and I rub the center of my chest. Poor Devin. To have his excitement over becoming a father build up only to have it ripped away? I can't imagine what that feels like.

"That's when she began pushing marriage. Asking if we could get married before the baby comes, how soon, when could we set a date, that sort of thing. She was relentless." His expression hardens. "Then about a month later, I was at her apartment helping her pack—we were about to sign a lease on a two-bedroom condo in the suburbs—when I went into her bathroom and noticed a spot of blood on the toilet seat and the wrapper for a pad in the trash can," he says softly.

The hairs on my arms stand on end, but he continues.

"I asked her if she was okay, and she said she'd been bleeding a little, but it was normal and nothing to worry about. Well, of course, I was worried—because it didn't look like just a little blood to me, it looked like a lot—so I insisted she call her doctor. That's when things got weird. She refused point-blank to call her doctor and accused me of overreacting. She said she knew her body best and everything was fine. Well, I wasn't willing to chance it, so I found her ob-gyn's number in her phone and called for her. It was after-hours, so the nurse on call told me she needed an ultrasound as soon as possible and that I should take her to the ER."

"What did Sadie do then?" I say, almost afraid to ask.

"When I told her what the nurse said she turned as white as a sheet and could barely even speak." He shakes his head. "It's funny—looking back, I thought her reaction was concern for the baby, but now I see she was freaking out because she knew she couldn't keep up the lie anymore. There was no way she could reasonably refuse to go to the hospital once her doctor's office suggested it, so I drove her. That's when I found out she wasn't actually pregnant. An ultrasound confirmed it."

Devin sighs. "Not that Sadie would have told me herself. She did everything in her power to keep me out of the hospital room and far away from the doctor—manufacturing things she wanted so I would get them for her, inventing errands. But I was there when he shared the results. No baby."

I squeeze his arm so hard my fingers ache. "I'm so sorry, Devin."

He nods heavily. "Her lies unraveled after that. Like why she only showed me a *picture* of a positive pregnancy test instead of the test itself—probably because she never actually took one and must have pulled a picture off the Internet. Or how she miraculously became pregnant despite being on birth control, and conveniently right around the time we'd started arguing more. I broke up with her that night and haven't seen her since."

"Unbelievable." I shake my head. "Not you—I don't blame you at all for breaking up with her. What she did was *nuts*. I just can't understand why she'd want to strongarm you into marriage. That seems like a recipe for a miserable life."

"My best guess? She did it for the money." He shrugs. "Her family has always struggled financially, and her student loans put her pretty deep underwater. Even with a high-paying law job, it would have taken her decades to pay them off. She knew about my dad's business and talked all the time about us moving to Cleveland so I could work for him and take over the company someday. So when we started fighting more, maybe she thought her golden ticket to a better life was about to disappear and decided to take any risk to keep me around . . . even if it backfired."

"But how did she think she'd be able to keep a fake pregnancy a secret?" I press. "You were bound to find out a few months later when, whoops, no baby."

His jaw muscles tighten. "I'm guessing she was planning to tragically 'lose' the baby as soon as she had a ring . . . there's no other explanation."

I blow out a long breath. "That's messed up."

"Tell me about it. Honestly, the whole thing messed me up for a while, but I'm doing a lot better now. Especially since I met you." He gathers my hand in his and presses a kiss to my knuckles. "Enough about Sadie. She's in the past. What do you say we head back inside?"

"You go ahead. I'd like to stay out here just a couple minutes longer. It really is *so* hot in there." I pluck at where my romper clings to my waist and laugh.

"How about I get you some water?"

"Water would be great, thank you."

Flashing a heart-melting smile over his shoulder, Devin strides across the patio and back into the bar. My shoulders slump as soon as he's out of sight. He truly is so incredibly thoughtful. And I can barely fathom how difficult things have been for him over the past few months. So why can't I shake the feeling that something's still not quite right between us?

My phone buzzes against my hip and I pull it from my pocket. My chest lightens at the name on the screen: *Perry Szymanski*.

He's texted me a photo. I tap it to make it larger, and my cheeks immediately warm. It's a picture of my painting—the one I gave him earlier. It's hanging next to a framed black-and-white family photo and a watercolor painting of what looks like Brandywine Falls. The bright colors pop against the soft white wall behind it, and the corners of at least three other frames peek out from the edges of the photo. He must have a gallery wall somewhere in his apartment, and he's already added my painting to it. Sparks fizz in my chest like bubbles from a freshly opened can of pop.

Three dots appear quickly followed by a new text.

> Check out the new crown jewel of my apartment: a Cass Walker original. Can you believe it? It was a gift from the artist herself. She's quite talented, so I bet it'll be worth a bundle someday.

> P.S. Thanks again for the thoughtful gift. I love it 😊

Emotion chokes my throat, and with a shaking finger, I "heart" his text. I don't know what else I could possibly say in response.

A wave of music rolls over the patio as someone opens the door, and I look up to spot Devin returning with my water. I stuff my phone back into my pocket just as he reaches me. "Here you go." He extends the tall glass of ice water toward me and I grab it. Condensation slicks my palm as I take a sip. "Thanks."

"You okay?" he asks, eyebrows furrowing as he studies me.

I paste a wide smile on my face, even though my chest aches. How can a simple, sweet text from Perry make me feel like someone's yanked on a loose thread in my heart, splitting it down the middle like a seam? I can't be feeling this way about Perry *and* be with Devin. What is wrong with me? "Never better."

"Good. Let's go." He tilts his head toward the door, a sweet, mischievous grin tugging at his lips. I follow him back into the bar with a heaviness I shouldn't feel, and a foreboding I can't ignore.

Devin is my dream man—I can't deny it. But I'm starting to wonder if maybe not all dreams are meant to come true.

19

My phone dings from the counter at the exact moment my toast pops out of the toaster. Ignoring the notification, I butter my two pieces of golden-brown brioche, carefully take my two cloud eggs out of the toaster oven, and scoop them onto each slice of toast. Grabbing my plate and coffee, I'm about to sit at the kitchen table when I remember the painting I'd laid out to dry last night. I return my plate and mug to the counter and carefully pick up the eleven-by-fourteen canvas.

Eyebrows knitting, I study my latest creation: a painting of a mother and daughter walking along the shore of Lake Erie, based on a sketch I did a few weekends ago when Brie and I drove out to Edgewater Park. We'd taken blankets and a picnic lunch, and while we were eating, I noticed a little girl squatting in the sand nearby, looking for beach glass while her mom gazed out at a sailboat in the distance, arm lifted to shade her eyes. It reminded me so much of me and my own mom that I took out the small sketch pad I've taken to carrying around with me and drew a quick sketch. Last night when I was flipping through my sketchbook, the image struck me again, and I decided to bring the scene to life on canvas.

The colors are right, but the little girl could use more definition. I'll work on that later. I prop the painting against the wall in the corner, so it's out of the way, and settle in at the table with my breakfast. I swipe open my phone as I take a bite of eggy goodness, and groan at the text that appears on the screen.

Devin

Are we still on for lunch today?

Brushing the crumbs off my fingers, I type a reply.

Yep!

Good. I haven't seen you in days and I miss you 🖤

My stomach hollows, guilt gnawing at the edges. It's been five days since the Fourth of July party, and I've turned him down both times he's wanted to hang out since then. Not that my excuses weren't legitimate. On Monday, he asked if I wanted to have dinner, but Brie and I already had plans. Sure, the plans involved chicken fried rice and pedis at home, but we were overdue for a girl's night.

And yesterday, I was in my mom's car heading to watch my brothers' soccer game when he texted with an offer of Netflix and chill. I could have changed my plans, but Jackson and Liam would have been disappointed, and Mom would have pestered me with questions about Devin and our relationship if I picked him over my family . . . questions I wasn't sure I was ready to answer.

So yesterday, when Devin asked if we could have lunch today—Thursday—there was no reason not to say yes. So I did.

I "heart" Devin's last text before tossing my phone onto the table, screen down.

"What's with the face?" Brie asks, shuffling into the kitchen. She's still wearing her pajamas—a loose black T-shirt and leopard-print pants—and her hair is lifted in tangles around her face like a blond cotton ball. Plunking into the seat opposite me, she snags one of my eggs on toast and takes an oversized bite, but I don't mind. Brie's been snatching my food since middle school.

"Nothing," I say around my own mouthful of eggs. "I'm having lunch with Devin today."

Her eyebrows raise. "And that's why you look like you just choked on a grapefruit?"

Lifting and lowering one shoulder, I take another bite.

"You haven't seen him since the party, and you don't seem that excited to see him today. What's going on with you two?"

"I don't know. Everything's good, but . . ."

"Do you not like him anymore? Wait . . . was he a dick to you? Want me to key his car?" Her eyes gleam behind her glasses and her smile is as vicious as a feral kitten's.

I snort back a laugh. "No, he's been amazing. The perfect"—the word "boyfriend" sticks to my tongue and I swallow—"gentleman. I'm excited we're having lunch today. Truly."

"So why have you been avoiding him all week then?"

"I haven't," I say, lying.

Brie drops her chin and shoots me an *oh-really* look. "Don't make me pi you."

"Okay, maybe I've been avoiding him a little," I mumble.

"Does it have something to do with a certain sexy brother? You two seemed pretty chummy at the party."

Damn Brie for being so perceptive. *Wait . . .*

"You really think Perry is sexy?"

"Um, yeah. He's got this sexy-rascally thing going for him. Like a grown-up Peter Pan. Not in a weird way," she quickly corrects. "He's like a tall Tom Holland or—what's that guy's name from *Dune*?"

"Timothée Chalamet?" I say.

She snaps her fingers. "Yes. Must be the eyebrows," she muses. "And Perry's jacked. Have you *seen* the guns he's toting? He's a hottie with a naughty body, for sure."

I suck in a surprised breath only to choke on my toast. "I can't believe you just said 'hottie with a naughty body.'" I splutter in between coughs. Brie thumps my back and I take a hasty gulp of coffee to clear my throat.

"If you're not into Devin anymore, you should tell him. Rip the Band-Aid off."

The problem is that I *am* still into him . . . I'm just not sure how much. Devin is my literal dream man—giving up on him after only a month would be like tossing a gift-wrapped blessing from the universe into the garbage. I owe it to both of us to give this thing between us a real chance. Even if I might be feeling . . . *things* for his brother.

I'm not prepared to confront my tangled web of feelings right now though, so I just say, "Duly noted." I cover my hesitation with another sip of coffee. Time to change the subject. "So hey, why are you up so early anyway?" According to the clock on the microwave it's 8:10, and Brie doesn't usually roll out of bed until closer to 8:30 or 9.

Her expression shutters. "I woke up early and couldn't get back to sleep. I've been up since six."

I notice the dark smudges under her eyes for the first time and frown. "Are you okay?"

"Yeah, I'm just freaking out a little bit, but it's fine. Nothing a hot shower and a kick in the pants won't solve."

"Is it work related?"

She shakes her head. "It's Marcus."

Ever since the party, Brie's been floating around the house with her nose in her phone, a goofy lovestruck grin on her face. Could things have soured that fast? "I thought everything was going well with him."

"It's going *amazing*. That's the problem."

"Remind me . . . how is that a problem again?"

"Because, Cass, I like him *so* much. He might be the nicest person I've ever met—besides you, of course. And, you'd never guess it, but he's actually *funny*."

My eyebrows bounce up my forehead.

"I know, right? He's constantly cracking me up—although now that I think about it, I'm not sure it's always on purpose." She shakes her head. "Anyway, he's thoughtful, sweet, and he makes me feel . . . special. And not because I'm the daughter of Charlotte Owens, the pride of Cleveland's nightly news, but because I'm *me*."

"Brie, those are all good things. What are you so worried about?"

"Oh, you know. The usual. That I'll fall in love way too fast, like I always do, and then everything will go to shit and I'll end up with my heart smashed to pieces. I don't think I can go through that again. Not after Sara."

My chest squeezes painfully at the memory of Brie showing up at my mom's house the night Sara dumped her six months ago, a sobbing, hiccupping mess. She'd said Sara had ended things because she felt they'd "grown apart," but a few days later, Brie found out the real reason courtesy of Instagram: Sara had met someone else. Although I don't know for sure, I still suspect her of cheating on Brie toward the end. I think Brie does too, which is probably why she stayed single for so long afterward.

"Not to mention," Brie continues, "Marcus is our *landlord*, so if things go bad, like they always eventually do, it'll be super awkward to have my ex living upstairs and cashing my rental checks."

Brie drags a finger under her glasses, her eyes shining with unshed tears. Heart aching, I clamp my chair under my butt and edge around the table—a difficult feat given the pencil skirt constricting my legs, but I manage—and wrap her in a tight hug. She sniffs into my shoulder once before letting go.

Dipping my chin, I look into her pink-rimmed eyes. "Brie, the fact that you're capable of loving so easily is one of the most amazing things about you. It's hard to put your heart out there, but you do, over and over again. And that's a *good* thing, even though I know it doesn't always feel that way. You can't find love if you're not willing to try. But because you are, heartache is just one of the inevitable potholes along the way."

She blows out a long, slow breath. "You're right."

"I know." Grinning, I clasp her shoulders and give them a little shake. "So, listen to me: quit worrying so much about hypothetical futures and enjoy what you have with Marcus today. Maybe it'll work out in the long run, or maybe not. But if you like him, don't torpedo your chances in the first week by getting all up in your head about it. And hey, if things don't work out and shit gets awkward, we can always move. It wouldn't be the end of the world."

"True." Her shaky laughter bounces around the small kitchen as she stands. "Okay, so maybe I was being a tad melodramatic. Thanks for the straight talk. I needed it." Ambling to the coffee-maker, she lifts out a chipped blue mug from an upper cabinet and then whirls on me, brandishing the mug like a wagging finger. "But don't think you're getting away that easy with ignoring the Perry problem. I know you, and I know when you're avoiding something." Grimacing, I scratch my nose. *Busted.*

"So here's some straight talk for you," she says as she pours herself some coffee. "Don't stay with Devin just because you believe you owe it to him, the universe, fate, or whatever. Sure, I think you guys are good together, and from what I can tell, he's a catch, but if your gut says otherwise . . . you should listen."

The happiness extinguishes from my heart, a sour, crumpled-up feeling taking its place. How Brie always manages to see through me straight to the core of my problems is a mystery to me, and right now, not entirely wanted. "I know." Scooping up my plate, I scrape my half-eaten breakfast into the trash; my appetite has abandoned me. "I should finish getting ready for work. Have a good day, all right?"

"You too," she calls back, but I'm already in the living room. Stomach hollow, I trudge up the stairs back to my bedroom.

Too bad giving advice is a lot easier than taking it.

"Are there any further questions?" The dozen other summer associates gaze attentively at Glenn Boone, who's standing at the front of the conference room next to one of the firm's junior partners, a brunette wearing a no-nonsense expression and a gray power suit. Shifting in my seat, I recross my legs. Sweat has gathered at the back of my knee where it had rested for the last forty-five minutes against my chair's pleather fabric. When no one raises their hand, Glenn nods. "All right. Thank you, Karen, for that fascinating presentation on the future of environmental justice legislation. Very enlightening."

Applause fills the room. Tucking my pen into the notebook on my lap, I ignore the doodles I've made in the margins as I sweep it closed and join in. The woman shakes Glenn's hand and leaves the room, briefcase tucked under an arm.

"Now—" Glenn claps his hands once. "Before you all run off to lunch, I'd like to remind you of the July Social coming up in a little more than a week from now, next Saturday the eighteenth. Thank you, Jeremey, for suggesting laser bowling. It sounds quite refreshing."

The pinch-faced twentysomething across the table from me nods.

"The purpose of these monthly socials is to give you all a chance to relax, unwind, and mingle with Smith & Boone staff in a less formal setting. Since these events are an integral part of your summer associateship with the firm, I like them to be driven by the summer associates themselves. So far, we've only had one suggestion for the August Social, attending an Indians, I mean, Guardians, game—thank you for that idea, Bradley—and while that's a fine thought, I'd like to hear from more of you before making a decision.

"You only have another six weeks left of the program, so we should end the summer with a bang. Please don't forget to share your ideas with me no later than July 31. As an incentive, the person who submits the winning idea will receive a special gift from me." Everyone sits up a little straighter. "Thank you," Glenn concludes.

Closing my notebook, I push back from the oval conference table and stand. The rest of the summer associates are filing out of the room along with Glenn. When I turn around, I find myself face-to-face with Mercedes. Her red lips peel back from her gleaming white teeth. "Hey Cass, how've you been?" she asks.

"Hi. Good," I say automatically, forcing myself not to put more space between us. I haven't seen much of Mercedes this week since I switched into the public law group three days ago. She's been working out of one of the conference rooms downstairs—probably on something far more interesting than anything I've encountered in my new assignment—while I've spent most of my time in our cubicle. "How about you?" I ask, despite myself.

"Ugh, *so* busy." She flips her long sheet of strawberry-blond hair over one shoulder. "Andréa has me working on the Ervin case. I haven't been able to leave the office before eight ever since we switched groups." She sighs dramatically, as if the statement isn't a humble-brag. "What are you working on?"

My nostrils flare, but I quickly smooth my expression. The Ervin case was supposed to be *my* case. Andréa had told me I'd be assisting with discovery . . . before she decided to swap me for Mercedes. Even if it's just temporary and the reason is legit—to give us exposure to different areas of the law—it still stings.

I lift and lower one shoulder. "I just finished a memo on recent developments in eminent domain case law. Pretty complex stuff." Not really, but I'm not about to admit that to Mercedes.

"Oh wow, that's it? You're lucky Frank's not overloading you."

No, I'm *not* lucky, and Mercedes knows it. When it comes to summer associates, the busier, the better. Busy means your skills are being recognized and utilized. A bored summer associate is most likely to be one without an offer come fall, and so far, my workload has been considerably lighter than it was in litigation.

A blur whizzes past the open door, stops, and edges into the room. It's Frank Carlson, Mercedes's former boss and the lead attorney of the public law group—aka, my new boss. The bright overhead lights gleam off his smooth skull, highlighting what remains of his short, wispy gray hair. "There you are, Cass. Are you free for lunch today?"

My stomach bottoms out; this will be the third time I've flaked on Devin this week if I cancel now. But it can't be helped. Even he would agree that saying no to a lunch invite from a senior attorney isn't wise.

I ignore the relief fanning across my skin and stand up a little straighter. "I can be. Why?"

"One of our clients is pitching a proposal to a city council member and wants someone from Smith & Boone to attend. I'll be there, but your eminent domain memo might come up, so I'd like you there too so you can help field questions if needed. Stellar work on that memo, by the way."

Mercedes's smile falters at the same time I widen mine. "Thank you. I'd be happy to join."

He raps his knuckles against the door frame. "Good. We're meeting at Sullivan's Steakhouse at one o'clock. Do you want a ride?"

"No, it's okay. I can walk."

"Do you know where it is?"

"Just a couple blocks down the street, right? The place with the maroon awning?" The only reason I know it is because I've passed it every day on my way to work for the past six weeks. Realization makes my jaw tighten—it's also right next door to the deli where Devin and I had planned to meet for lunch today.

"That's right. I'll see you there at one." Frank disappears from the doorway. Everyone else has left; only Mercedes and I remain in the conference room. "I can't believe Frank sprung this on me so last minute. Now I have to cancel my lunch plans." Now it's my turn to sigh dramatically.

"Did you have a hot date or something?" She sniffs.

"Well, yes, actually."

"With the same guy you've been seeing?"

"Mmm-hmm."

"Do tell. Is it serious?" She blinks her wide, guileless eyes. Unease trickles through my veins.

"Not really; we'll see. We're just having fun for now."

"Well, good luck. See you later." I don't know if she's wishing me luck in my love life or with my lunch meeting, but before I can respond she flounces out of the room.

Shaking my head, I slip my phone out of my bag and add the time and location of my lunch meeting to my calendar, complete with an alarm set for fifteen minutes beforehand so I'm not late. Then I text Devin.

> Hey, I'm SO sorry for the last-minute notice, but I can't make it to lunch. Work stuff, UGH!

Three dots appear. Disappear. Then reappear a few seconds later.

> No problem. Something came up for me too so that actually works out well.

Guilt prompts my fingers to move.

How about you swing by my place after work?

We can have dinner out, order in, whatever you want.

Sounds like a plan. I'll text you when I get off

Clicking off my phone, I stuff it into my bag and exit the conference room. Maybe hanging out with Devin one-on-one tonight will help me sort through my feelings. *Or maybe not*, says a tiny voice inside my head. Guilt squirms in my chest, but there's no time to think about that now. I have a client meeting to prep for and a boss to wow, so I'd better get to it.

20

Forty-five minutes later, the alarm on my phone goes off just as the printer spits out the final page of my memo. I tuck the just-in-case hard copy into my bag, make a quick detour to the restroom to touch up my makeup, and leave the office at exactly 12:51. The restaurant's only a five-minute walk from here, so I should be on time, even at my slower-than-usual pace thanks to making the trek in heels instead of the flats I usually wear to and from work. At least the sky is overcast, a welcome change from the sunbaked weather we've experienced all month.

I mentally review the principal elements of eminent domain as I turn the corner onto the street where Sullivan's is located. *Eminent domain allows the state to seize an individual's private property, but only if the property is acquired for a public use, the owner is paid the fair market value for the property, and the property's owner receives due process.*

Due process requires that the property owner receive notice of the eminent domain action, and the opportunity to present objections . . .

"Cass?" The sound of my name makes me jump, and I nearly catch my heel on a jutting corner of sidewalk. On my left is the glass front of a restaurant topped with a maroon awning—Sullivan's

Steakhouse. I twist around, looking for the source of the voice, and my mouth pops open in surprise.

Devin is striding toward me, dark eyes as round as dinner plates. Across the street, his dad shuts the door to a black Lexus, his ear pressed to his cell phone.

"Devin?" I splutter. "What are you doing here? I thought you agreed we weren't having lunch today."

"I know; we're not. My dad invited me to a business lunch last minute."

"At Sullivan's?"

He narrows his eyes. "Yeah."

"What a coincidence! I'm actually here for a work meeting with my boss too."

"Wait. Is your boss Frank Carlson?"

I blink. "How do you know Frank?"

Devin's face pales. "He's been consulting with my dad on something. Wait, I thought you said you were assigned to the litigation group. Frank doesn't do litigation." His voice is entirely too sharp, and I balk.

"I was, but I'm doing a rotation for a few weeks in public law. Why does it matter? What's going on?"

Devin closes his eyes briefly and curses under his breath. When he opens them again, his usual, charming expression is back. "You know what? Why don't we just get out of here? I'll ditch my dad and you can call in sick from your work meeting. Maybe we can—"

"Cassidy, is that you?" Roger Szymanski's graying eyebrows flick upward as he approaches, tucking his cell phone inside his blazer. Except for the formal gray suit, he looks the same he did at the Fourth of July party—same perfectly styled hair, imperious air, and cold, calculating expression. "Did Devin invite you or . . . that's right, you work for Smith & Boone, don't you? Will you be joining our meeting today?"

"Meeting?" I repeat, blinking. Is the client we're meeting with . . . Roger Szymanski?

Frank pulls up in his car then, a navy Cadillac, and parallel parks along the sidewalk next to us. Cutting off the engine, he steps out, briefcase in hand. "Ahh, Cass. You made it. And I see you've already met our clients. This is Roger Szymanski, founder and CEO of Szymanski Enterprises, and his son Devin."

The gears start turning in my head. The memo I wrote was about eminent domain, which involves real estate. Devin's dad is a real estate developer. I frown to myself. But that still doesn't explain why they're here. Eminent domain can't be used by private companies to seize someone's property; it can only be used by the government to take private property when it's needed to serve the public good—like widening roads, building schools, or burying utility lines. So why are we meeting with Szymanski Enterprises to talk about eminent domain unless . . . wait. Didn't Frank say our client is proposing something to a Cleveland City Council member? Could the proposal involve eminent domain somehow? It's a bit strange, but not entirely out of the realm of possibility.

Devin edges closer to his father until they're elbow to elbow. "Hey, Dad, are you sure Cass should be in this meeting? She's only a summer associate. She doesn't need to be bothered with this, does she?" His voice is quiet, but I can still hear his words—and so can Frank, because he's standing right next to me.

My jaw goes slack even as ice slices through my lungs like a spear. I can't believe Devin just belittled me in front of his dad *and* my boss. I narrow my eyes at him even as unease crawls up my spine. Why the hell is he trying to keep me out of this meeting?

Frank adjusts his briefcase under one arm. "Ms. Walker is a bright young attorney with the firm and has researched the relevant case law thoroughly. If it's all right with you, I'd like her to sit in."

"Of course, Cassidy is welcome to join us," booms Roger, shooting a frown at his son. "Shall we?" He motions toward the restaurant. Frank opens the door for Roger before following him inside. I toss a withering glare over my shoulder at Devin, whose eyes widen.

"What's wrong?" he murmurs in my ear as we wait in the entry for the hostess to seat us.

"Are you serious? You just talked down to me in front of my boss," I hiss under my breath.

His cheeks go pale. "I—I didn't mean it like that. I was just trying to get you out of a boring meeting. I thought I was doing you a favor."

"Well, you weren't." Even if his intentions were noble—which I'm not certain they were given how shady he's been acting since he got here—his words were completely thoughtless. I rub my temple before the hostess shows us to a round table in the back where a fiftysomething Black man is already seated, reading a menu. He stands when we approach.

"Councilman Truman, good to see you," says Roger, shaking his hand.

"Likewise. How have you been, Roger?"

A brief round of introductions follows, and we take our seats. My gut hardens when I end up sitting with Frank on my left and Devin on my right. Devin tries to catch my eye, but I ignore him. I can't let my annoyance put me off my game. I'm meeting with a prestigious client and a prominent local politician. Professionalism is a must . . . even though I'd like nothing better than to haul Devin out back and strangle some answers out of him. A few minutes of innocuous small talk follows before a server comes over and we place our orders.

"Are you sure you only want a salad, Councilman? Please, order whatever you like," says Roger. "My treat."

Councilman Truman folds his hands over the thick maroon menu and peers at Roger over his wire-framed reading glasses. "Now, Roger, even if I wasn't watching my cholesterol, you know I can't do that. I don't accept gifts from constituents, and even if I could, I wouldn't. Propriety and all."

"You and your propriety." Roger chuckles, but there's an edge to the sound. Like glass mixed with gravel.

Once the server takes our menus and leaves, the councilman leans back in his cushioned chair. "Now, what's this big idea you wanted to discuss?"

Roger gives him a wide smile that feels about as warm as a barracuda, reaches into his briefcase, and produces a thin stack of stapled papers. Beside me, Devin shifts his weight. He's gripping his armrest so tightly his tendons strain. I furrow my eyebrows and return my focus to Roger, who slides the papers across the table.

"As you know, the city of Cleveland has already approved zoning for our new apartment complex going up on West Twenty-Eighth Street," he says.

"I know. I voted to approve it," says Councilman Truman.

Roger nods solemnly. "Yes, because you know the city is in dire need of revitalization. Every year for the past four decades, people have been moving out of Cleveland and into the suburbs. If we want a bright future for the city, we need to reverse that trend. We need to entice people to move back in order to build up the tax base."

The councilman drums his long fingers against the arm of his chair. "What are you getting at?"

"We need more amenities. More businesses, more recreation, and more educational opportunities. *If you build it, they will come.*"

"Spoken like a true developer. What are you suggesting we build?"

"To start with? A new satellite campus for Cleveland's community college right here in the heart of Ohio City. It would bring revenue to the neighborhood in the form of new residents, and by extension, the city of Cleveland, while offering a much-needed educational facility for college students."

"We already have a community college branch downtown, located less than five miles away, so I wouldn't say a new campus is strictly 'needed.'" The councilman rubs his chin. "Then again, it certainly wouldn't hurt given the increasing demand for affordable college courses. But Ohio City is highly developed. Hell, it took you five years to secure the real estate necessary for your new apartments. Where do you think we could build a campus?"

Roger reaches across the table and flips several pages of the packet before stopping at a black-and-white street map. "West Twenty-Eighth and Providence," he says, tapping the map twice. "There are three properties ripe for development. Two of them I already own. I purchased them when they went into foreclosure a few weeks ago, but I'd be happy to transfer ownership to the city of Cleveland for below market value. And the third building owes a significant amount of money to the state in back property taxes, which—as I understand from my attorney, Frank, here—you could use as a basis to acquire it through eminent domain. Combined, the three buildings' footprint would offer enough land to build a multistory community college facility that would benefit the entire city."

Wait . . . West Twenty-Eighth and Providence . . . money owed in back taxes . . .

My heart nearly stops beating. *Roger is talking about Blooms & Baubles.* He's proposing that the city of Cleveland take Blooms & Baubles away from Perry—against his will—using the legal doctrine of eminent domain.

I stare at Devin, openmouthed. He looks everywhere around the restaurant . . . except at me. Betrayal beats a hot, heavy drumbeat in my chest, and I swallow back the nausea slithering up my throat.

He knew. Devin *knew* what this meeting was about—that his dad was going to use his connections to take away Perry's beloved home and store. *That's* why he didn't want me here. Why he tried to prevent me from sitting in on this meeting. He knows I'm friendly with Perry, and by the guilt-ridden look on his face, he understands what his dad is doing is wrong.

But he didn't do a damn thing to stop it.

The Devin I thought I remembered postcoma would never have betrayed anyone like that, especially his brother.

This Devin? It seems I don't know him at all.

"Wait," I say before I can stop myself. "The building you're talking about at Twenty-Eighth and Providence, it houses a business—a flower shop—isn't that right?"

Roger's eyes blaze. "Correct. I know the owner personally, which is why I can promise that if the city acquires the property it would be a blessing for both parties. The business has been in decline for years. The money he'd receive in exchange for the property would improve his life."

"What if he disagrees? I'm certain he would oppose an eminent domain action. Most property owners do," I hastily add, so Frank doesn't catch on to the extent I'm personally enmeshed with the parties involved in this proposal.

Roger chuckles. "Isn't that what lawyers are for? The city's attorneys could handle any objections the owner might have. Right, Frank?"

Frank clears his throat. "Potentially. The Constitution stringently protects property ownership as a right, which is why the government can only seize private property through eminent domain for a compelling public purpose. Building a community college would satisfy the 'public good' requirement as long as the city's justification for exercising eminent domain in this case is a solid one. Especially since the owner is behind on their taxes, which the city could argue makes it a 'blighted' property, and justifiable to seize." He turns to me then. "Would you agree, Cass?"

The last thing I want to do is weigh in, but Frank put me on the spot. I don't have a choice. I swallow. "It depends on the amount of money owed in back taxes. If it's less than the fair market value of the property, then the property wouldn't necessarily qualify as blighted, which could give the owner a stronger basis for an objection." If I remember correctly, Perry owes somewhere in the ballpark of twenty thousand dollars—likely less than what the property must be worth, even given the structure's age and location. At least he has that going for him.

"But according to the research you conducted this week, the city of Cleveland could proceed with an eminent domain action here with a strong chance of success, right?" presses Frank.

My mouth turns dry as hot, angry tears burn behind my eyes, but I don't let them fall. Sipping my water to cover my whirlpool of emotions, I silently curse Devin for making me an unwitting accomplice in his father's selfish plans. Because as much as I want to lie, I can't. My printed memo burns like coals from the depths of my bag. The law is the law, and I can't change it. "That's correct," I finally say.

Beside me, Devin closes his eyes briefly, but he still doesn't say anything.

Roger's triumphant smile needles me like pinpricks, and it takes every ounce of resolve not to walk out of the restaurant on the spot.

Councilman Truman nods thoughtfully, steepling his fingers under his chin. "I have to say I'm intrigued, Roger. This plan could be good for the city's residents—depending on the cost, of course. We'll have to take a close look at the numbers." Lifting his chin, he narrows his eyes at Roger. "One question though . . . what's in it for you?"

Roger leans back in his chair. "Me? Nothing. I'd simply like the chance to put in a bid to build the school should the project move forward—the same as any other developer. Besides that, students need a place to live, and my new apartments are going up only a few blocks away, so you could say it's a win-win for everyone."

Yeah, except for Perry. My blood runs cold. If the city seizes Blooms & Baubles, Roger will finally get what he really wants: to exercise control over the son who refuses to live his life according to his father's vision—and stamp his ex-wife's cherished business out of existence to boot. That controlling, arrogant *bastard*.

The rest of the meeting passes by in a blur of strategizing and political talk. At least Frank doesn't ask for my input again, which I'm grateful for. My stomach is a knot of anger, resentment, and shock, and I only manage a few bites of my Caesar salad when it arrives. Finally, roughly an hour later, the server brings our checks. There are only two, since Roger insisted on paying for my meal along with Frank's and Devin's. Part of me wants to refuse—I don't want to accept a damn thing from this monster. The other part wishes I'd ordered the most expensive thing on the menu, just to stick it to him.

My phone buzzes from inside my bag. Frank is talking to Councilman Truman while Roger signs his credit card receipt, so I slip my cell out and check the notification in my lap. My throat squeezes at the text that appears.

Devin

It's not what you think. Please, let me explain.

I glance at him; he's clutching his phone in a white-knuckled grip, his eyes silently pleading. With a glare, I click off my phone and stuff it roughly into my bag.

Pushing back from the table, Councilman Truman stands. "Well, I need to get back to my office. Have your people send an electronic copy of your proposal to my assistant, and I'll put it on the agenda for the next closed city council session in August."

"Of course. Devin will see that it's done," says Roger, shaking the councilman's hand.

Devin's eyes flash as he stares at his father, jaw tense. But even now, he remains silent. A fresh wave of disgust rolls through me, and I ball my hands into fists in my lap.

With a curt nod, Councilman Truman leaves the restaurant. Once he's gone, Roger swivels to face my boss. "Frank, do you have a few extra minutes? I'd like to talk strategy—"

I clear my throat. "Excuse me, Frank? If you don't need me for anything else, would you mind if I head back to the office? I'm not feeling well," I add quietly. It's not a lie. If I sit here another second longer, there's a real possibility the revulsion flooding my gut will wind up all over the table.

Frank's eyebrows pinch together in concern. "I'm sorry to hear that. Please, why don't you take the rest of the afternoon off?" I begin to protest automatically, but he holds up his hand. "Rest up. We'll reconnect tomorrow."

I should keep arguing—insist I'm fine to finish out the day—but I don't. Instead, I murmur a thank-you, collect my bag from the floor, and walk out without a second glance. I'm not two steps from the restaurant when the door whooshes open behind me.

"Cass, wait," Devin chokes out, voice strained.

All of the anger, shock, and disgust that has been boiling in my chest the past hour solidifies into a sharp, jagged mass and I whirl on Devin.

"How could you." My voice is pure ice.

"You don't understand—" he begins, but I cut him off.

"What don't I understand? That you've been pretending to help Perry with his shop all while plotting with your dad behind his back to take away his business—his *home*?"

"It's not like that—"

"How could you do this to him—to your own *brother*?" Nostrils flaring, I stare at Devin. Even though his features are as familiar to me as my own, for the first time, I feel like I'm looking at a stranger.

He reaches for me, eyes glistening with unshed tears. "Please, it's not what you think. Just let me explain."

I back away. The thought of him touching me makes my skin crawl. "There's nothing to explain. We're done." Turning on my heel, I march away, skull pounding with every step.

"Cass—" he calls.

"Leave me alone," I yell.

And he does.

21

"Devin did *what*?" Brie freezes with her wineglass halfway to her mouth. Xerxes clicks softly in her lap while a breeze filters through our wood-planked front porch.

"I know. I still can't believe it." I top off my own glass with another hefty pour from the half-empty bottle by my feet. When I arrived home after the meeting nearly four hours ago, my head was a roiling mash of emotions, so I forced myself to take a long, calming walk and an even longer bubble bath before settling on the front porch with a bottle of cheap Riesling to drown my sorrows at the socially acceptable hour of five o'clock. Brie took one look at me when she arrived home nearly an hour later, grabbed Xerxes from his cage and a wineglass from the kitchen, and settled in next to me.

Sprawling in my Adirondack chair, I take a long sip. A car zips down our street, its engine cutting through the quiet evening air. Brie sets her glass on the armrest of her own folding Adirondack, which she's pulled up next to mine. She stares at me intently. "Tell me everything."

I recount the entire lunch—the proposal, Devin's attempts to keep me out of the meeting, and his silence once I found out his dad's plans.

"So, this whole time he's been secretly trying to screw his own brother out of his business? That *asshole*," she breathes.

"Yeah, that about sums it up."

"Did you confront him? What did he say?"

"He followed me out of the restaurant when I left and tried to offer some kind of excuse, but I didn't stay to listen; I'm sure it would have been bullshit. I told him we're done."

"I'm so sorry, Cass."

"Thanks." Tears blur my vision and I take another gulp of wine. "I really thought for a second Devin might have been 'the one,' you know? Like maybe my memories of him was the universe's way of bringing us together. I was wrong."

And now I'm alone . . . again. Tears gather at the corner of my eyes and I swipe them away.

Brie leans over to hug me, and my heart lightens a fraction. A rustle and a flap precedes a soft weight settling onto my lap. When Brie pulls away, I discover that Xerxes has hopped onto my thigh, his talons dully pinching my skin through the thin material of my leggings. He peers up at me through one beady pale-yellow eye, but his usual malice is gone. Irony climbs up my throat and I hiccup. This might be the first time in fourteen years that Xerxes has ever voluntarily interacted with me. Maybe parrots can sense emotion and my misery is too much, even for him.

Reaching over to the small bowl of sunflower seeds on Brie's armrest, I pick one out and offer it to Xerxes. He nips my finger before taking the seed, but the bite is markedly gentler than his typical bloodthirsty pecks. "Still couldn't help yourself, huh?" I murmur as he cracks the seed in his beak. Smiling despite myself, I run my fingertips along the short gray feathers on his back. I'll take all the comfort I can get right now—even from Xerxes.

Brie smiles at her parrot like a proud mother before returning her attention to me, expression shifting back to concern. "Did you tell Perry what's going on?" she asks.

I'd considered calling Perry the second I left the restaurant, but anger makes you do rash, stupid things, and I knew I needed to calm down first to think through the best way to break the news to him. In a perfect world, Devin would have immediately told Perry about his dad's selfish plans the second he learned of them, but of course he didn't. So now it's up to me. "Not yet, but I will. He deserves to know."

A black BMW pulls up in front of our house then, parking neatly next to the curb. Every muscle in my body tenses when I spot the face through the driver's side window.

Devin.

"What's wrong?" asks Brie, frowning at my strained posture.

"He's here," I breathe.

Devin's walking up the sidewalk toward our house now, steps jerky as though uncertain. I set my glass on the flat, expansive armrest and shift to stand, momentarily forgetting about Xerxes. He flaps indignantly before Brie snatches him and settles him on her shoulder. Standing, she folds her arms over her chest and widens her stance like a tiny, disgruntled bodyguard.

Devin's heavy footfalls thud up the steps as he approaches. When he reaches the porch he pauses, glancing from me to Brie and back again. "Hey," he says, stuffing his hands into his pockets.

Brie marches right up to Devin until they're practically nose to nose. "You have some nerve showing up here." Xerxes gnashes his beak menacingly, and Devin wisely takes a hasty step back.

"I need to talk to Cass," he says.

"I don't think she wants to talk to you."

"Cass, come on. You didn't let me explain earlier," he says around Brie's shoulder. "Give me five minutes, please. If you don't like what I have to say, I'll leave and never bother you again. I promise."

For a brief moment, I have the ludicrous urge to shout, "Sic him, Xerxes!" But I don't. I owe it to myself to hear him out, if for no other reason than to gain closure in this relationship.

After tonight, I'll never have to see Devin again—a fact that makes my stomach squirm in equal parts disappointment and heavyhearted relief.

I sigh. "Fine. Have a seat." I motion to Brie's empty chair.

"Want me to stick around?" she asks, stroking Xerxes's feathered chest.

"No, it's okay. I got this."

"I'll be inside if you need anything." Scowling at Devin, she makes a "V" with two fingers, points to her eyes, and then to his in an *I'm-watching-you* warning before leaving us alone on the porch.

Once she's gone, Devin lowers himself into her abandoned chair, but I don't sit next to him. Snatching my wine, I cross to the opposite side of the porch directly across from him and lean against the wooden railing. It creaks under my weight.

"I know what happened today looks bad—" he begins.

I snort. "That's an understatement."

"—but I never intended to let Dad go through with it."

Fresh anger beats through my veins and I slam my stemless metal glass on the railing behind me. "Oh really? Is that why you were at the meeting? To stop him? Because I didn't hear you say a single word against his plan *to convince the city to steal your brother's property.*"

"I couldn't. You know what my dad is like. If I called him out in front of a Cleveland City Council member, he would have fired me the second the meeting was over. He doesn't put up with people undermining him in public, not even me."

"Would that be such a bad thing—getting fired? Why do you even want to work for someone so underhanded, so backstabbing—"

"Because I have to if I want to get ahead, okay? I know my dad's a difficult man, but if I want to take over the business someday, I have to put up with his bullshit."

"So what you're saying is that it's okay to betray your brother because your own personal success is more important than his," I spit. "You know what I think? I think you'd do anything for your dad's approval because you're jealous of Perry and the fact he doesn't have to answer to anyone else for his success." Jaw tight, I fold my arms across my chest.

Devin shoves roughly to his feet, nostrils flaring. "You don't know what it's like. The lengths I have to go to prove myself to *both* my parents. My mom simply doesn't understand why I'm not more like my brother. And when it comes to my dad, he's never happy with me. Nothing I do is ever good enough. Do you know what that's like?"

"No, but it's no excuse to hurt the people you love—your own family."

"I told my dad from the beginning that his idea was insane and I didn't approve."

"But you still went along with it."

"I didn't know he'd already contacted someone from the city council! I thought the meeting today was only with our lawyer, and that Frank would shoot down the idea on the spot. I had no clue the law actually allows the government to take someone's property, or that someone on the city council would be into the idea."

"You would have if you'd confided in me from the start. I could have told you your dad's plan had legal merit. But you didn't. And you didn't tell Perry either. Why is that, exactly?"

"I didn't want him to worry unless there was actually something to worry about. Dad's tried to convince Perry for years to quit the business, and has even offered repeatedly to buy it from him, but I didn't think he'd go to such extremes to control Perry's life—even with a legit business opportunity to use as an excuse. And like I said, I never thought his idea would actually go anywhere. He does this sometimes—hatches some big plan or other, gets really excited about it, but abandons it just as quickly when the roadblocks are too big. I thought that's what would happen this time too. I never thought it would go this far."

He takes a deep breath. "And Perry's relationship with Dad has been rocky for a long time. The Fourth of July party was the first time he's shown up at a gathering with our dad in over two years, and I didn't want to see all that progress disappear overnight. I don't want to have to choose between my dad and my brother; I want them to get along. I didn't want to give Perry more fuel to hate our father when nothing might actually come of his plan."

"You don't see how that's selfish? Even if your dad never followed through on his idea, Perry deserves to know how desperately his own father wants to control his life—even if it means that Perry cuts him off for good. No one should have to put up with that kind of toxic behavior, not even from family. And did you never consider that if Perry knew, he might have confronted your dad and eventually, maybe, it could have led to some healing?" I shake my head. "No, you didn't. And now you've sucked me in as an unwitting sidekick, and there's nothing I can do about it."

Devin staggers back and sags into the chair behind him, face pale. "You're right. I'm sorry."

"Have you even told Perry what happened today?" I press.

"Yeah. I called him this afternoon when I got back to the office."

My stomach clenches into a fist. "What did he say?"

"A lot of things. Let's see . . . that he can't believe I sided with Dad, how could I do this to him, and, oh yeah, my personal favorite: that I can lose his number because we're no longer brothers," he says miserably.

"Did you tell him I was at the meeting too?"

"I left you out of it."

"Why?"

"I'm the one he should be angry with, not you. It wasn't your fault you ended up at Sullivan's. Unlike me, you didn't know what was coming." Shaking his head, he clenches his jaw. "I can't believe I was so naive to think my dad wouldn't be willing to dick over Perry if he thought it was 'what's best' for him. Because everything he does, no matter how much it hurts, is for our own good. At least that's the way he sees it." Nostrils flaring, he slams his fist against the armrest. "*Damn it*, I should have known better. I could have warned Perry weeks ago. Except I can't, and now——" His voice cracks, and he pinches glistening tears from the corners of his eyes. "Now I've ruined Perry's life."

Yeah, you kinda did. I keep the rebuke to myself. Guilt oozes from every pore of Devin's pained expression. He clearly regrets his actions, and it wouldn't be helpful—or kind—to pile on at this point.

Sighing, I pace the length of the porch. I imagine Perry's face when Devin delivered the news—the sadness, anger, and betrayal etched into every line, zapping every ounce of happiness from his mischievous features. All Perry wanted was to bring joy to others, and now he might lose his beloved flower shop *and* his home. I gnaw my thumbnail.

There has to be a way to fix this.

I think back to my memo, to the eminent domain cases the courts have heard in recent years. The loopholes, the successful challenges . . .

I pause a few feet away from Devin. "Maybe there's a way you can help Perry."

Devin snorts. "Once Dad sets himself on a course of action, there's no changing it."

"No, that's not it. The city's ability to seize Perry's property depends on whether they can show there's a strong public need for that particular land, which can be bolstered if they prove the property is blighted. The fact that Perry owes money in back taxes is a mark against him. But if he could make a significant dent in what he owes, bring the sum down even further, it would make the city of Cleveland's case that much harder."

"How could he possibly do that? He barely has enough money to sign his employees' paychecks, let alone pay down tens of thousands of dollars in debt."

"What he *does* have though are connections. You both do," I murmur to myself, thinking back to all the people I met at the Fourth of July party. An idea suddenly hits me with the force of a 747 and my eyes widen. "What if Perry hosted an event . . . a festival for the community?"

"What, like a flower festival or something?"

"Yes, exactly!" I snap my fingers. "But it could be more than that. The theme could be flowers—he could sell them, offer free flower-arranging workshops, consultations for special events, that sort of thing—and he could charge a fee for local artists to set up booths at the festival and sell their wares."

"I don't know. Dad said the next closed city council session is a month from now. Planning an event like that on such short notice is next to impossible. For starters, Perry would need an event permit from the city—"

"I can help with that."

"Okay, but even assuming the permit would come through in time, we'd need to find dozens of people to sign on within the next week or two if we want to get this thing off the ground. How do you propose we do that?"

"Are you serious? You are quite possibly the most charming person alive in the greater Cleveland area. And you know *everyone*. You can't tell me that you don't think you could sweet-talk some local businesses into joining a festival that would—hopefully—make them money and bring in new customers?"

"I guess I can be pretty persuasive."

"Damn straight you are."

His lips flicker into the barest hint of a grin. "Marcus does owe me a favor," he muses. "Maybe he can convince the owner of Zelma's to let them serve as the official food and alcohol vendor for the event. Wait . . ." Pinching his bottom lip, his eyes flick back and forth. "That gives me an idea. Not everyone likes flowers, you know. I mean, if I saw an ad for a 'flower festival' I wouldn't exactly be hopping up and down. What if we framed it as a flower *and beer* festival? We could invite a few local breweries to set up booths and offer beer tastings. I think it'd draw in more people, for sure."

"That. Is. Genius," I breathe.

"And I could look for corporate sponsorships to defray the hosting costs too—like Key Bank, since Jai and Anisha work there."

"And I'll help with publicity and planning! I'd be happy to sketch out a logo, call local vendors, order tables, whatever Perry needs. If we tap everyone we know and we all work together, I really think we can pull this thing off."

Devin lifts his eyebrows. "So you'll help then?"

I open my mouth to speak, but no words come out. From a professional standpoint, I shouldn't. Attorneys are ethically bound to zealously represent their clients' interests, and in this case, Szymanski Enterprises is my firm's client. But then again, we've already completed the work the client requested—offering legal advice on eminent domain case law. If the city council moves forward with an eminent domain action against Perry, the city's attorneys will handle it, not us. But Smith & Boone likely won't approve of me actively trying to undermine a client's objectives, even if the situation falls into an ethical gray area. If they found out, it would be all the reason they'd need not to offer me a first-year associate position . . .

I clamp my jaw. Screw it. Some things are worth the risk, and helping Perry is the right thing to do. Plus, I have another idea that could help Perry's case, and I'm the only one who can oversee it. I'll just have to make sure I keep my involvement quiet so Frank doesn't find out.

I swallow the lump rising in my throat. "Yes, I'll help. But I can't let Frank or anyone else at Smith & Boone find out about it."

"Deal." Devin smiles as he stands. "Thank you, Cass. I can't tell you how much I appreciate it." Striding toward me, he extends his arms as though about to wrap me in a hug. I push my finger against the center of his chest, stopping him.

"Let's make one thing clear. This does *not* mean that we're together. I accept your explanation for what happened, but I still don't know if I can fully trust you after today. I need to take a step back from . . . us."

"I understand." He nods heavily, but when he glances at me, a spark lights his eyes. "I guess I'll simply have to earn your trust back then."

My stomach squirms. Honestly, I'm not sure whether I'll ever be able to trust Devin the same way again. It's too soon to tell. But putting our relationship on ice is definitely the right choice given all that's happened. Plus, without the romantic obligations—and drama—I'll be freed up to focus on helping Perry save his business. I can sort out my feelings later.

"We'll see," I finally say.

The dazzling smile he gifts me would have made me weak in the knees only a week ago. Now? I don't feel anything except a faint strum of guilt. But I'm not making any promises at this point, so I'm not breaking any either.

Pushing back my shoulders, I nod once. "To start with, let's talk to Perry."

Devin's expression shutters. "He definitely doesn't want to see me right now."

Picking up my phone from where I stashed it next to the wine bottle on the porch, I open my messages app and pull up the last text conversation I had with Perry. "Leave that to me."

22

Devin drops me off in front of Blooms & Baubles an hour later. "The door to Perry's apartment is around the side there." He points to a narrow iron gate beside the store that I hadn't noticed until now. Nodding, I step out of the car and shut the door. The clouds have cleared, and the sun cuts through the sky, making me squint.

"Hey, Cass?" Devin calls, and I bend down to peer at him through the open passenger-side window.

"Thanks again," he says.

I force a smile. I'm not doing this for Devin, but I don't want to tell him that. "I'll let you know what he says."

"I'll be here." He rolls up the window.

I walk up the familiar path to Blooms & Baubles. It's after seven now and the sign in the window reads Closed. Instead of going through the front door like I usually would, I unlatch the side gate and follow the building around through a narrow alley until I reach an unlocked gray door toward the back, revealing an interior stairwell leading to a white door—Perry's second-floor apartment. At the top of the stairs, I catch the savory scent of chicken and spices along with faint strains of music coming from inside. He's definitely home.

Lifting my fist, I hesitate, thinking back to the text I sent Perry an hour ago: I heard what's going on. I'm so sorry. Can we talk?

He never responded.

I can't blame him. As far as he's concerned, I'm his brother's girlfriend, and his brother just royally screwed him over. He probably thinks I only want to talk to him to plead Devin's case, which I imagine he doesn't want to hear. If I were him, I wouldn't want to talk to me either.

Disappointment lances my chest and I rub my thumb over my knuckles. Coming here tonight was a gamble, but I have to try. If Perry wants to save his business and his home, he needs to act now. And I won't let him give up without a fight. I just hope he's willing to hear me out.

Forcing some steel into my spine, I rap my knuckles against the door. A dog barks from somewhere inside—it must be The Colonel. I jolt. *The Colonel.* I can't believe I remembered his name for once. The music switches off, footsteps approach, and the door swings open to reveal Perry standing in a dim hallway.

He's barefoot and wearing his usual worn jeans and T-shirt, but his expression is completely foreign—the antithesis of the Perry I've come to know and like. The joy has winked out of his eyes like an extinguished candle, his cheeks are hollow, and his lips are twisted into a pained frown. "Oh, it's you," he says flatly. The Colonel saunters up from behind him and wags his tail when he sniffs my sneakers.

"Can I come in?" I ask.

"Is Devin with you?" Perry peers around my shoulder to the empty staircase behind me.

I swallow hard. "He's outside."

"Whatever excuse he sent you to make, I don't want to hear it." Stepping back, he begins to close the door, but I shoulder forward, blocking it with my foot.

"I'm not here to make excuses for him. What he did was wrong. He should have told you about your dad's plan from the start."

Perry knits his eyebrows. "Why are you here then?"

"Because I have an idea for how you can save Blooms & Baubles."

Perry's lips part and he stares at me for so long I have to resist the urge to fidget. Finally, he shrugs and opens the door wide. "Come in then. I have to warn you though, I'm not the best company at the moment."

I step into the apartment and follow him down a short hallway into a clean, light-filled space consisting of a kitchen and living room. A long wooden countertop with a farmhouse sink and a four-burner stove stretches along the entire back wall of windows. It's dotted with flowering potted plants and overlooks his backyard greenhouse and the stately maple growing just outside his cracked wooden fence. A mishmash of multicolored dishes, mugs, and cups occupy the open shelves that flank the white, magnet-filled refrigerator, while a tall butcher's block island doubles as a table, two low-backed stools pushed neatly underneath it.

In the living room, a television is tucked into a corner between a potted palm tree and a carved fireplace, which is capped by a round antique mirror. Two armchairs, one high-backed and blue and the other short, round, and forest green, sit kitty-corner next to a worn cognac leather sofa pushed against a wall filled with artwork and framed photographs—Perry's gallery wall. Warmth fills my belly when I spot my painting among the eclectic mix. It's located near the center, a clear focal point illuminated by a pair of skylights overhead.

Perry's apartment isn't quite how I imagined it, but somehow it suits him perfectly. His family's deep connection to this place is evident in every piece of hand-me-down furniture; every mismatched vintage dish; and in every scuffed, weathered floorboard, worn smooth in sections by the innumerable people who have trodden the same paths for decades.

The Colonel trots over to a beige dog bed in front of the fireplace and flops into its cushiony center with a huff while Perry strides over to the thick mahogany coffee table, scoops up a plate of half-eaten chicken and risotto, and deposits it in the sink. His jerky movements ignite a fresh wave of nerves, and I hover in the space between the living room and kitchen, unsure whether to sit, stand, or give him the hug he so clearly needs. I split the difference by taking a hesitant step forward.

"How did you even find out about the whole property-stealing plan anyway?" he asks with his back to me. "I can't believe Devin told you."

My thighs tighten painfully. "He didn't. I was at the meeting with your dad and Councilman Truman today."

The dish he's washing clatters in the sink. "*What?*"

"I didn't know I was meeting with Devin and your dad, or that a member of the city council would be there," I say hastily. "My boss asked me to sit in because I recently researched eminent do-main, the legal doctrine that would enable your dad's plan to work, but he didn't tell me who the client was that we were meeting or what exactly all my research was for."

"So you were just as blindsided as I was," he murmurs. "I'm so sorry, Cass. You don't deserve to be dragged into the middle of my family's drama."

I stride forward until the only thing separating us is the kitchen island. "Why are you apologizing? *I'm* the one who's sorry. Your own father is trying to leverage his political connections to take away your business. I can't imagine how you must feel right now."

Turning fully to face me, Perry leans his hips against the cabinet behind him, fingers squeezing the countertop. "Furious, of course. But not surprised. My dad has been trying to control me my whole life. But Devin . . ." His jaw flexes so tightly it trembles. "I thought he had my back."

"He does," I say.

Perry's eyes flash.

I raise my palms. "I know it's hard to believe, and you have every right to be angry with him. He should have told you right away what your dad was planning—he admits that. But he didn't tell you because he thought your dad's idea was so far-fetched it wasn't even possible, and he didn't want you to worry prematurely. Misguided, I know," I add at his dubious expression. "For what it's worth, he feels horrible. He said he should have realized your dad would go to any lengths to control your life, and he regrets not trying to stop him sooner."

Sighing, Perry scrubs a palm over his jaw. When he looks at me, some of the tension has seeped from his posture, but there's still a hard edge to his smile. "I thought you said you weren't here to make excuses for him."

"You're right, I'm not. But I do think you should give him a chance to explain himself and apologize—in person."

Perry's quiet for a long, tense moment. Finally, he rolls his shoulders and pushes away from the countertop. "I'll think about it."

I exhale a long breath.

"But first, tell me how you think I can save Blooms & Baubles. Fair warning though: if it turns out you were serious about me selling a kidney, I'll have to pass. I'm pretty attached to mine." A flicker of amusement crosses his lips, and the knot in my gut loosens a fraction.

"No black-market organ sales required. Scout's honor."

Grabbing a beer from the fridge, he motions toward one of the low-backed stools at the kitchen island, and I sit.

"Want a beer?" he asks over his shoulder.

I shake my head. "I'm good, thanks."

He fills a glass with ice water and sets it on the table in front of me. Twisting open his beer with a *phfffz*, Perry drags the other stool out from the opposite side of the island and sits so we're facing each other. The tall wooden island is long but narrow—only two feet wide or so, which means even though we're sitting on opposite sides we're still close. Under the makeshift table, Perry's knee skims mine and my nerves buzz at the contact.

Rather than sitting in Perry's cozy kitchen, I suddenly feel like we're back at the lakeshore, lying side by side in the grass, pretending not to notice our skin grazing as fireworks explode in the sky above—or the undeniable connection blooming between us.

Perry sips his beer. The movement shifts his knee away, breaking our contact, and *no*, that is not disappointment I feel. Nope.

Dipping his chin, he peers into my face. "Okay, talk to me."

Taking a deep breath, I launch into my festival idea. His eyes widen with every passing minute. Soon, he's leaning forward, his strong forearms braced flat against the tabletop, fingers clasped. It's only when I've finished that I register I've unconsciously mirrored his pose and my hands are resting a mere inch from his. The realization ignites a wave of tingling heat in my belly. Cheeks warming, I lean back, tucking a lock of hair behind my ear.

"Cass . . . this . . . is . . ." He lets out a breathy laugh. "You came up with this idea for a festival all on your own—*tonight*?"

I nod. "It was Devin's idea to add beer plus look for corporate sponsors, and I think it's a good one. A well-publicized, corporate-sponsored community event would help bring in new customers and make you a decent amount of money in a short amount of time. If you can pay off what you owe in back taxes, or even make a significant dent in the amount, it would make the city's case that much harder—"

"But the rest of the idea . . . that was all you?" he presses.

"Um, well, yeah."

"Damn," he breathes. His lips tilt into a wry smile as he assesses me.

I resist the urge to fidget under the intensity of his gaze. "So? What do you think?"

"I think you're the most impressive woman I've ever met." His voice is so low I'm not sure at first whether I heard him correctly.

But then he winks and takes a long swig of beer. "But I don't think the festival will work."

"Why not?" I splutter.

"First of all, I don't have enough flowers."

"What about your greenhouse?"

"Even if I emptied it, I still wouldn't have enough stock on hand to accommodate so many customers."

"Can you place an extra order from that one nursery you told me about?"

"Maybe. I'll have to talk to the owners to see what they can do. And maybe a few other plant nurseries in the area too. But even if I could get my hands on enough flowers, there's the matter of cost. I'd need to purchase everything in advance, on credit, and if the festival flops and no one buys my flowers, I'd *lose* money. It's a risk. Not to mention I'd need help arranging all of the flowers once I bring them in. I have Alma, my part-time florist, but she's not enough. The flowers would need to be prepped and arranged within a few days of the event so they're fresh, and I don't have the manpower to tackle such a big job on such a tight time frame."

"You have me. I'd be happy to help. You were the one who said I was a natural at flower arranging, remember?"

"I did say that, didn't I?"

"And Devin would help too, I'm sure of it—he'd do anything to make it up to you. So would Brie and Marcus."

Perry's jaw muscles tense, a flicker of anger resurfacing at the mention of Devin. I quickly shift gears. "What if you sourced potted plants to sell in addition to bouquets? People love a nice perennial, and potted plants don't require arranging—just watering."

"That's not a bad idea. It would help cut down on the prep time, for sure."

"Okay, so assuming you're able to get the flowers and the plants *and* the help you need—do you think we could find enough vendors in time? I know it's a lot of pressure, but Devin said he'd talk to local businesses for you, and I'm happy to make calls, chase down leads, whatever you need. Do you know enough local artists who might be interested in signing on to make it worthwhile?"

"I know artists, weavers, knitters, candle makers, glassblowers, wood carvers—you name it." He laughs. "Most of the local makers whose work I sell in the store would probably be interested—a lot of them routinely sell their products at festivals—so that's well over a dozen vendors right there."

"There you go. No more reasons not to take the plunge." I spread my arms out wide.

"Sometimes I forget you're a lawyer. It's hard to argue with you."

"Exactly. So why even bother?"

Perry laughs then, and the sound washes over me like melted caramel. After a long moment, he quiets, his expression turning serious. "Why are you helping me?"

"Why wouldn't I?"

"Apart from your big-time law career and general lack of free time?"

My gut tenses. How *am* I going to juggle this festival with my job at Smith & Boone? I only have six more weeks left in my summer associateship, and if I want them to invite me to stay on permanently, I can't slack now . . . but heck, I survived law school. Even if it means less sleep for a few weeks—and no painting—I can do it. I wave him away. "*Pshh.* You let me worry about that."

"I know you're with Devin, but you don't owe this to him. Or me. Or anyone. I hope you don't feel obligated to help."

"Actually, Devin and I aren't together anymore," I say primly, not quite meeting his eyes.

He goes very still. "You're not?"

"I ended things about an hour ago. We're on a break . . . an indefinite break."

"I see," he murmurs, expression unreadable.

My thighs threaten to sweat and I shift uncomfortably on my stool. "Anyways . . ." I clap. The sound pierces through the quiet apartment, and The Colonel wakes up with a snort. "So what do you say—is next month's first-annual Ohio City Flower & Beer Festival a go?"

Perry drums his fingers against the table, considering me for a long moment. "Yes, maybe—*if* the stars align and we can bring all the pieces together in time. I'd still be taking a financial risk, but if there's even the smallest chance this festival of yours can save my business *and* show my dad he can't control my life? It's worth it."

"So, is that a yes?"

Grinning, he smacks his palm on the table. "Yes."

I let out a happy shriek. I can't help it. "This festival is going to be a hit. I can feel it." Springing off my stool, I circle the island and wrap him in a tight hug.

His arms twine around my waist and he tugs me closer. "Thank you," he murmurs, his breath stirring my hair against my neck.

"For what?" I whisper.

"For being you."

Grinning to myself, I let out a long, slow breath that comes out more like a sigh. I *should* step away now, disconnect from the hug, but something inside me resists. His arms are sturdy and warm against my back, and his rich, woodsy scent invades my senses. After the emotional roller coaster of the day, Perry is as solid and reassuring as an anchor. And I don't want to let go.

Apparently . . . neither does he.

His arms tighten around me slightly, and my breath catches in my throat. He's still sitting on his tall barstool, and I'm standing between his legs. Our bodies are fitted together so tightly I can feel every rise and fall of his chest like the rolling waves of an ocean. His thumb strokes the dip of my waist—a small, seemingly unconscious gesture—and my heartbeat accelerates like a rocket.

What am I doing?

Perry is Devin's *brother*. And I ended things with Devin barely an hour ago, and now here I am . . . with my arms around Perry . . . and . . . I . . . I want . . .

I don't know what I want.

A few weeks ago, I thought Devin and I were cosmically connected thanks to the universe depositing him into my life like a Christmas gift in a stocking. But now, I can't ignore that I feel something very different standing here with Perry. Something I can't quite name—or explain. But I also feel guilty.

Devin thinks he can earn back my trust—and rekindle our relationship someday—and maybe we will, but maybe we won't . . . And I'm also most definitely feeling *something* for Perry, which I refuse to admit because, hello, it's *Perry*, and . . .

Clearing his throat, Perry loosens his hold. The movement snaps me back to myself. *Right*, we've officially been hugging for way too long and now it's awkward. As I begin to unloop my arms from around his shoulders, I glance at his face and *ohhhh shit, that was a mistake.*

Longing burns in the emerald depths of his eyes like twin coals. My lungs seize. The intensity of his gaze simultaneously knocks me back and draws me in like a butterfly to a bloom. My eyes drift downward, and I stare at the sensual line of his upper lip, as sleek as a bow, and the glistening fullness of his bottom lip. I bet they're exquisitely soft, like silk. Before I can stop it, my tongue sneaks out and I wet my own lips. Perry's nostrils flare and his fingers squeeze my hip, igniting a wave of heat in my belly.

"Cass?" he whispers.

"Yes?" I ask, still drunk on Perry's nearness and the imagined softness of his lips.

"You're standing on my foot."

"Huh?" I blink up at him.

Raising his eyebrows, he nods meaningfully at his feet. Sure enough, I'm standing on him; my right sneaker is completely covering the toes on his left foot. Horror crashes over me like a bucket of ice water.

"Oh God. Sorry." I hop back quickly—too quickly—and catch the rubber sole of my shoe against the slick wood floor. Perry steadies me by the arm before I can lose my balance. His palm burns against my overheated skin.

"It's okay," he says through a sardonic smile. The apples of his cheeks are flushed and his eyes are curiously hazy. He clears his throat a second time before letting go of my arm. "Well, I should probably talk to Devin."

Right. *Devin.* He's still sitting outside, waiting to hear whether Perry is willing to forgive him or not.

"Yes. Good idea. I'll tell him you want to see him on my way out."

He frowns. "You're not staying?"

"I should probably go." Smoothing my T-shirt, I begin backing toward the door. "I'm sure you guys have a lot of ground to cover, and I don't want to get in the way. We can start hashing out specifics for the festival tomorrow."

"Hold up. Cass?" Perry says when I'm nearly at the mouth of the hallway. He crosses the space between us in five long strides and pauses in front of me. My mouth turns dry as I stare into his sparkling green eyes.

Exhaling, he rubs the back of his neck. "I'll talk to you tomorrow."

"Bye." I practically bolt out of Perry's apartment and don't slow down until I reach the narrow alley outside. Leaning against the brick wall of the building next door, I flatten my palm against the center of my chest as I stare at the darkening sky. Over the next four weeks, I'll be in constant contact with both Devin *and* Perry to help them plan the festival that could save Blooms & Baubles. And I can't let Smith & Boone know what I'm doing in the process.

So these fluttery feelings in my stomach, which I certainly don't want or need, will have to take a back seat. There's too much at stake and too much to do in too short a time to start catching even the slightest hint of feelings for anyone, let alone the most inconvenient person in the world.

It's way past time I stop dreaming of relationships and romance and focus on the one thing I *can* control: my choices. Shoving off the wall, I open the gate and march toward Devin's car, which is still idling where he parked it half an hour ago.

Time to tell him he can make it right with Perry after all.

Then tomorrow, the planning begins in earnest.

23

The box of discovery materials from the Ervin case glares at me like an evil eye from the corner of my desk. Damn the defendant for providing hard copies of their records instead of digital. It's going to take me at least twice as long to process these.

It's been a week since Andréa switched Mercedes and me back to our original groups, and three weeks since I started helping Perry plan his two-day Flower & Beer Festival to save Blooms & Baubles, and I have a literal mountain of work to tackle. But my personal email beckons me, along with the seemingly endless tasks that still need to be accomplished before the festival launches next Saturday: one short week from tomorrow. What's a summer associate slash event planner supposed to do?

The fact that we've even come this far is a miracle. Over twenty artisans and other local makers have purchased booths for the event, plus we have musical entertainment lined up for each day. Marcus's bar—Zelma's Taphouse—is serving as the official food vendor, three microbreweries have signed on to sell beer and offer tastings, and over a thousand people have indicated their interest in attending our event on Facebook.

But some critical pieces are still missing. Like media coverage . . . and the event permit itself.

I check my phone for the dozenth time this morning. No new emails.

"Come on, Val, don't fail me now," I mutter under my breath.

I'd called Val nearly three weeks ago, the Monday after Perry, Devin, Brie, Marcus, and I spent the weekend power-brainstorming for the Flower & Beer Festival. Within three days of proposing the idea, we had a detailed plan complete with task lists and timelines. My first action? Help Perry complete the application paperwork and reach out to my old friend from law school—who just so happens to run Cleveland's Permits and Zoning Department—to see what she could do to expedite his application. She was only too happy to help, so it was *very* lucky I ran into her on the Fourth of July.

But city government runs slowly even with connections at the top, so I've been sweating ever since. Without the permit to close down a block of West Twenty-Eighth Street for our weekend event, we won't have anywhere to host the festival, and all our efforts will have been for nothing.

Sighing, I reach for the box and pull it toward me. Time to catch up on my *real* work. I haven't been slacking, exactly, but I haven't been pulling ten- or twelve-hour days like I used to either. Andréa hasn't said anything, but I'm pretty sure she's noticed my hours have shrunk to a more manageable nine to five . . . even while my workload hasn't.

But at least I've been *happy*. The past few weeks helping Perry and Devin plan this festival have been the best of my entire summer. I have something to look forward to every day that doesn't involve work, and I feel like I'm making a real difference to someone—other than our corporate clients, who, let's face, already have deep pockets and enough vacation homes to make Leonardo DiCaprio jealous.

My phone dings just as I lift out the first stack of papers, and I nearly knock the box off my desk in my rush to check the notification. My heart lodges in my throat. I have one new email: it's from Val. I hold my breath and quickly read her message.

Hi, Cass,

Hope you're having a good week! Just wanted to let you know that I was able to fast-track your friend's permit application, and his two-day event (12 p.m. – 5 p.m. on Sat 8/14 and Sun 8/15) has been approved. He should receive his permit by the end of the day.

Cheers!
Val

P.S. The festival sounds super fun—can't wait to see you there!

"Yes!" I squeal under my breath.

I brace myself for the typical disapproving cough, but my cubicle remains silent. Peering over my shoulder, I frown at Mercedes's empty desk. *Huh.* I hadn't noticed she'd stepped out. The last few weeks have been relatively quiet on the Mercedes front. We seem to have settled into a mutually accepted stalemate of surface-level politeness and general avoidance, which is perfectly fine with me. I have enough on my mind without worrying about cutthroat co-workers.

Shoving back from my desk, I stand. I need to call Perry.

Well, I don't *need* to. I could just text him. But this kind of news deserves a phone call, right? So what if the thought of hearing the smooth tenor of his voice has my heart hopscotching?

Swallowing hard, I walk to the women's bathroom, phone in hand. Cubicles aren't exactly private, and I don't like to make personal calls at work—especially not about the festival, since I'm still trying to keep my organizer role under wraps. Even though I'm no longer working for Frank Carlson in the public law group, I can't be too careful.

When I reach the restroom, I glance around briefly to make sure I'm alone and promptly call Perry. He answers on the first ring.

"Hey, Cass. What's up?" His silky voice pulls my lips into a smile as though on a string.

"Oh, I don't know. Just the best news *ever*."

"The Browns won the Super Bowl? Oh wait, their season hasn't even started yet. Never mind. What is it?"

I laugh. "Remember my friend I told you about—the one who runs the Permits and Zoning Department for the city? I just found out she was able to fast-track your event application and you'll receive your permit by the end of the day. The Ohio City Flower & Beer Festival is officially a go."

"Seriously? Cass, that's amazing. You're a miracle worker."

"Just doing what I can."

"I'd say you're doing way more than that."

I gnaw my lower lip through my smile. "How's the search for corporate sponsorships going?"

"Great. In fact, I have some good news of my own. Mikey came through with his car dealership this morning: they're in. That brings the total number of sponsorships up to five, including Key Bank. And they've all agreed to cover the cost for tents, signage, and the fee for the event permit as long as we feature their logos prominently on all publicity materials."

"That . . . is . . . awesome!" I pump my fist in a victory dance. I make a mental note to revise my opinion of Mikey—maybe he's not such a goon after all. "We are *killing* it with this festival planning," I croon.

"*You're* killing it. You drew the logo for the event, got us a great deal on table and tent rentals, followed up with local artists and breweries to confirm they submitted their booth fees, and now you snagged us the permit we need. We never would have made it this far without you."

My cheeks warm even as I bask in his words. My phone beeps, and I blink at the familiar number on the screen. "Oh hey, I gotta go. My stepdad's calling me."

"No problem. Hey, are you still coming to the prep meeting next Thursday? With all the extra flowers I'm having delivered, it's an all-hands-on-deck kind of situation to get everything arranged in time for the festival. I'd sure appreciate your help if you have time."

"Of course. I wouldn't miss it."

"You're the best." His words thread through my heart, igniting a wave of happiness that drips through my veins like honey.

I grin at my reflection. "See you later." Tapping the screen, I switch over to the new call. "Hi, Rob," I say, leaning against the sink.

"Helloooo there," my stepdad drawls. "How's the big-time lawyer doing?"

"Good, thanks. How's my favorite Realtor?"

"No complaints—I feel great, all is well. It's a beautiful day to be alive." I chuckle at Robert's response, which is his standard, regardless of the weather. "So you know that property search you wanted me to run? I have something interesting for you."

I stand up straighter. "Oh yeah?"

"I found two vacant commercial buildings in Buckeye-Shaker that are currently for sale and listed at below market value—just what you're looking for."

"That sounds perfect. What's their condition?"

"A little run-down, but salvageable. One housed medical offices and the other used to be leased by a church. I swung by earlier today to see them in person and the bones are good. Most of the work needed is surface-level only. The owner is retiring and wants to unload them as soon as possible, so I'm pretty sure he'd accept an offer below listing. Want to tell me again what this is all about? Are you planning on secretly switching careers and becoming a real estate investor? You know what, don't tell me. I'm incapable of keeping secrets from your mother. She knows all my tells."

I chuckle. "No. Just trying to give the Cleveland City Council new ideas for possible community college locations so they don't make a huge mistake."

"How very mysterious. I can't wait to hear all about it."

A toilet flushes and my heart hammers against my ribs. *Oh my God. I'm not alone.* "Thanks again, Rob. I'll call you later."

"Okay, b—"

I end the call at the same time one of the stall doors swings open to reveal Mercedes. My calves tighten. I hadn't noticed that the farthest stall was occupied, *damn it.* Her smile is way too wide as she strolls to the sink next to me and begins washing her hands. "Hey," she says.

"Hey," I reply. My shoulders tense but I force them to relax as I readjust the bobby pin holding back Rogue Curl. Maybe she didn't hear anything . . .

Shaking the water droplets off her hands, she yanks a paper towel from the wall dispenser between us. "So, what's all this about you finding properties for the city of Cleveland? What in the world does Andréa have you working on? Sorry, I couldn't help but overhear." She titters.

Overhear? More like eavesdrop. "Nothing. Just a little side project. It's personal."

"Oh, because for a second there I thought it had something to do with Szymanski Enterprises and their proposal to the city council for a new community college at West Twenty-Eighth and Providence."

All the color drains from my face. Did Roger ask Frank to do additional work on that? He must have, and Frank must have assigned it to Mercedes. *Shit.* I force my eyes to widen in what I hope passes for innocence. "Nope. Totally unrelated."

"Oh. Okay." Studying her reflection in the mirror, she finger-combs her hair, fluffing it at the roots. "Good luck with your . . . what was it? 'Flower Festival'? I'm surprised you have time to volunteer for a planning committee with your workload. Andréa must be impressed."

"What I do in my personal time is my business, Mercedes."

"You're not on personal time right now, are you? But here you are . . . making personal calls." Her eyes glint with something that looks suspiciously like victory.

Something inside me snaps, and all the frustration and anger she's elicited this entire summer boils to the surface. I can't believe I ever thought extending an olive branch to Mercedes was a good idea. Narrowing my eyes, I square up to face her. "What is your problem? You've been horrible to me since the first day we started here. What did I ever do to you?"

Her lips part and for a moment she actually looks startled. She closes her mouth, her usual frosty expression sliding back into place. "Don't be so dramatic. I just don't want to be besties with the competition. I can't afford to sit around and braid your hair or whatever and lose sight of why we're both here: to land a permanent job. The likelihood that both of us will be chosen to stay on as first-year associates is slim. I *need* it to be me. I don't even think you want it that badly anymore."

Her words hit me like a slap and I stumble back a step.

Do I still want to work for Smith & Boone? Of course I do.

Sure, I've found myself thinking more and more about Perry's festival—jotting down ideas and reminders when I should be researching case law, sketching sign designs in the margins of my notepads, daydreaming during meetings about the impact the festival is poised to have. But securing a job at a top law firm is what I've worked for my whole life. The past three weeks have only been a blip—a summer project before the real career grind begins in the fall.

But if my actions at work have made Mercedes think I don't want a permanent offer anymore, what does Andréa think? Or Glenn Boone? Am I blowing my chance for a successful career right when it matters most?

Mercedes flips her hair, bringing me back to the present. "Anyways, don't worry. I won't tell Andréa about your little *extracurriculars*." She waves vaguely at my phone, which I'm still clutching in my bloodless fist. "I don't need to." She smirks.

What the hell does that mean? Does she know something I don't, or is she bluffing?

With a final imperious glare, she marches out of the bathroom, leaving me alone with a feeling of unshakable foreboding. Now more than ever, I'll have to watch my back. And step up my hours if I don't want Mercedes to swoop in and snatch a job offer right out from under me. I just hope at this point my efforts will be enough . . . and Mercedes will stay far, far out of my way.

24

The following Thursday, I burst into Blooms & Baubles, legs aching from jogging almost the entire way from my office. I can't believe I'm over two hours late, but Andréa needed help prepping for a cross-examination so of course I stayed. I just hope my tardiness hasn't put Perry too far behind on all the flower arranging that needs to be done by this weekend's festival.

The door to the shop is unlocked, but the store is as dark and empty as the street outside. Maybe Perry's holding the meeting in the back. Hiking my bag higher on my shoulder, I cross the shop to the Employees Only room. Bright lights momentarily blind me when I open the door, and I squint. "Hey guys, sorry I'm late. What'd I miss—*oh*!" My voice catches when I walk straight into a mountain of pure muscle.

I look up into the looming, craggy face of an unfamiliar middle-aged man, and immediately jump back. His head is closely shaved and he has a snake the size of a fist tattooed on his neck, directly above the collar of his gray Script Ohio T-shirt. My breath abandons me and I freeze.

"Hey, Cass, you made it!" Perry calls from behind the boulder of a man standing in front of me, and my heart starts beating again. "Meet Chuck."

Chuck? Oh right, Chuck. "You're Perry's delivery driver." I nearly laugh in relief. I knew Chuck was an ex-con, but I wasn't expecting him to look like, well, someone off *Dateline*. But then again, if Perry hired him, I can trust him. Looks are only skin deep, after all. "Hi. I'm Cass."

"Nice to meet you." His voice is gruff, but his smile is kind, if a bit hesitant.

An older woman with short, black-streaked gray hair and copious wrinkles around her soft brown eyes sidles up next to Chuck. "This must be the famous Cass. At last we meet." She thrusts a tanned hand at me, and we shake. "Alma Fernandes. I've known Perry here since he was in diapers."

"Alma." He groans.

"What? It's true."

"You're the part-time florist, right?" I ask.

"I would be full-time if my grandkids didn't keep me so busy. My daughter just had her third in May, and with three babies under the age of four, she needs all the help she can get." Her crisp laughter tugs a smile from me. "We thought you'd be here earlier. What kept you?"

"I had to stay late at work."

"Gotta draw lines, honey. Gotta draw those lines. If you don't, your bosses will walk all over you. Isn't that right, Perry?"

I peer over Alma's shoulder through the open door to where Perry is sitting at his desk in the far corner. His lips twitch as though he's suppressing a smile, and he nods solemnly. "Alma doesn't let me put a single toe out of line."

She chuckles. "I'm only teasing. Perry's one of the good ones. Excuse me," she suddenly barks, and I jolt. "Don't think I don't see you trying to sneak off, Chuck. You're having dinner at my place tonight and that's the end of it."

I'd been so focused on Alma I hadn't noticed that Chuck had edged past me into the store. He freezes a couple of feet behind me, lips pursed. "Alma, honestly. You don't have to feed me. I have leftover pizza—"

"Cold pizza for dinner? Not on my watch. I've got a pot roast in the Crock-Pot and no one to share it with. I'll even send you home with some extra for tomorrow. Come on now, no more arguing. Let's go."

I step back so Alma can pass me.

Chuck rolls his eyes, but I don't miss his grudging smile. "Some advice?" he says to me. "Don't argue with Alma. She's always right."

"I don't know," calls Perry. "She's never gone toe-to-toe with Cass. Alma, you might have finally met your match."

Alma's eyebrows bounce as she looks me up and down. "Oh really? You must be quite the spitfire then. I approve. I look forward to getting to know you better, Cass. You'll be at the festival this weekend, of course?"

"Absolutely," I say.

"See you then. Come on, Chuck," she adds. "A pot roast waits for no one." Slipping her arm through his, she tugs him in the direction of the front door.

"Bye," I call.

Chuck tosses a wave over his shoulder, and they disappear into the darkened shop. Smiling to myself, I step into the back room and plop my bag onto the floor. The door shuts behind me with a heavy *clack* and my stomach hollows when I take in the full scope of the room.

It's empty save for Perry . . . and a mind-boggling number of buckets stuffed with bouquets in every shade from blush white to sunset orange to baby-blanket pink to deepest scarlet. There must be at least thirty buckets crowding the floor, table, and counter space in the back room, filled with countless bouquets. There are even more in the refrigerated units along the wall—likely hundreds of arrangements in total.

I groan despite my awe. "I'm too late, aren't I?"

"Cass. You're never too late." The smile he gifts me sends a tingle all the way down to my toes, despite the rising tide of guilt I feel. Is this always how it's always going to be throughout my entire career? Personal sacrifices, skipped commitments, and perpetually late arrivals?

Tiptoeing around the buckets, I pick my way through the bins until I reach Perry and plop into the empty metal chair pulled up beside him. I motion around the room. "I mean, I was too late to help you with the arrangements and now you're done."

"Don't sweat it, honestly. You've done so much for me already. And besides, I had plenty of help. Marcus and Brie swung by for an hour around six, and between them, Alma, Chuck, and Devin, we were able to knock everything out quicker than I thought."

"Devin was here?"

"Since five. He just stepped out to grab us dinner."

"Still, I wish I could have been here too. I would have much rather been making bouquets than doing what I was doing, believe me."

He wrinkles his nose in sympathy. "Tough day at the office?"

I snort. "Always. But tonight was just . . ." I make a disgusted sound in my throat and shift to face him fully. "I had to help my boss prep for her trial tomorrow, so we were reviewing depositions and running through her cross-examination questions and I realized . . . *I don't care.* I don't care that our client was sued by a former employee for wrongful termination because, let's face it, our client is a scumbag. And the only reason we're in court to begin with is because he refused to settle, even though he easily could have paid the amount the plaintiff was rightfully asking for. I mean, I know everyone deserves zealous legal representation, and it's our job as lawyers to present evidence and make the strongest case we can for our client then let the court decide the outcome, but it's *exhausting.* Especially when I don't see how I'm doing much good for anyone except our rich, entitled client, you know?"

"Hmmm." Perry nods thoughtfully. "It definitely sounds like you had a rough day. Okay, turn around." He twirls his finger in the air.

"Um, what?"

"Come on, scoot your chair around. Trust me, you need this." I half stand, and he drags my chair until the back of it is facing him. When I sit, his fingers close around my shoulders. "Perry, you don't have to . . . *ahhhhrgh*, okay maybe just a few minutes."

I can't remember the last time I had a massage, let alone from a cute guy. Ben wasn't exactly generous with the back rubs—he'd grudgingly give me one if I asked, but he usually burned out after a few minutes. And in our short few weeks of dating, Devin's never casually offered any kind of massage: back, shoulder, or otherwise.

I sink lower in my chair as Perry's strong fingers knead the stiff muscles of my neck, and my eyelids flutter closed. Oh God, I needed this. "Enough about me. How was your day?" My voice is as languid as my limbs.

"Busy, but good."

"What'd you do? Besides all this." I point my foot toward the flowers.

"Let's see . . . well, I woke up early, around seven. Showered. Ate breakfast: a whole wheat bagel with avocado and peanut butter. Took The Colonel for a walk—"

Tutting, I reach back and smack him on the arm. "That's not what I meant."

"Oh, you don't want to hear about every mundane minute of my day?" He laughs softly, and the sound does funny things to my insides. Between his rich voice and clever fingers, I'm roughly three seconds away from melting into jelly. "Well, in between filling orders and handling customers, I finalized the volunteer schedule for the festival."

My eyes fly open and I sit up straighter. "Oh yeah? Can I see it?" I don't want him to stop, but we've been chipping away at the volunteer schedule for the last two weeks. I'm dying to know how it turned out.

"Sure." His fingers slip from my neck as I shuffle my chair back around to face his desk. I steal a glance at Perry's face as he reaches for his clunky ancient laptop. His tawny brown hair is mussed, like he's raked his fingers through it one too many times today, and his cheekbones are tinged with pink. Our chairs are so close together that his leg brushes mine as he swivels his laptop to face me, and I swallow hard.

On the screen is a neatly typed spreadsheet. "We had fourteen people volunteer total—eight on Saturday and six on Sunday—not counting Alma or Chuck. I figured we should have volunteers work the ticket booth in pairs, in case anyone needs to step away for any reason, and I assigned each pair to work one- to two-hour shifts," he explains.

I scan the spreadsheet and smile at the roster of familiar names—Jai and Anisha, Brie and Marcus, Mikey and Gavin. But there are a host of unfamiliar names as well. "Who are all these people?"

"Friends. Mostly from high school, but a few are from our rec softball league too." My chest fills with warmth at how many people in Perry's life have rallied to help him in his time of need—even bigmouthed Mikey.

"What about Alma and Chuck then? What will they be doing?" I ask.

"Alma will staff the store so I can man the Blooms & Baubles booth outside. And Chuck is going to manage setting up and tearing down the tents both days and take over the Blooms & Baubles booth whenever I need a breather."

I nod. "What about me though? My name's not on there."

"I thought you could serve as an unofficial coordinator with Devin. We could use someone else to help direct volunteers and vendors, announce when the musical performances are starting, troubleshoot any problems that come up, that sort of thing."

My eyebrows raise. "You sure I can handle such a big job?" With my short-term memory still on the fritz, I'm not exactly the safest choice.

"You practically planned the entire thing. I can't think of anyone better."

My cheeks flush. "I'd love to then. You can put me down for both days." Something nips at my memory. "Oh, wait a sec."

Springing from my seat, I retrieve my bag from beside the door. Returning to my chair, I plop my bag onto my lap. I dig around its depths, removing my wallet, Hydro Flask, and pocket sketchbook, and set them on Perry's desk as I rummage.

Perry picks up my sketchbook and his eyes widen as he holds it up. "May I?"

Nerves pluck at my spine, and I lick my lips. "Sure."

I watch him carefully as he flips through the pages. He pauses on one of the drawings, studying it carefully. Finally, he flips the book around. "I love this," he says, tapping the page. "Who is it?"

"Just an old woman I see by the office every now and again. Sometimes when I take my lunch outside to eat on the bench by the river she's there." Her deeply lined face is angled to the side as her deep-set eyes gaze into the distance, her wrinkled hands clasped on top of a cane.

"It's beautiful. I'm so glad you're drawing again."

"Painting too, thanks to you." A flush creeps up my neck when he smiles at me, and I hastily return to the mission at hand: finding my phone. When I finally locate it at the bottom of my bag, Perry hands me my sketchbook and I toss it and my wallet and keys back inside. Plopping my bag onto the floor, I gnaw the inside of my cheek as I pull up my calendar app.

"Shoot, I was right. I might have to cut out early on Saturday." I look up at Perry. "I've been meaning to tell you: one of the managing partners asked us the other week to block off this coming Saturday from noon to 8 p.m. for this stupid mandatory social event thing for work, and with everything else going on, it completely slipped my mind. The event should only last two or three hours, but I don't know exactly what we're doing yet or what time it starts. They're announcing the details tomorrow. I'm sorry if I can't be there the whole time." I wince.

"Cass, stop apologizing. You've done more than anyone. Devoting nearly your entire weekend to the festival is above and beyond. So, thank you, for whatever time you can make it. And no more apologies." Perry covers my hand with his where it's resting on my knee. I try not to notice how the edge of his pinkie skims the bare skin peeking out from under my skirt's hemline. I stare at his long fingers . . . and frown. Thin red scratches mar his lightly tanned skin.

"Oh my God, what happened to your hand?" Snatching it, I hold his hand up to the light.

"Hazard of the profession, I'm afraid." He flashes me a wry smile. "Rose thorns. I have a tool to strip them off the stems, but they're sneaky little fuckers." Flipping over his hand, I study his palm. More red and pink scratches crisscross his fingertips. I wince. Even though the cuts aren't deep, I bet they sting. I suck in a sharp breath. *And he gave me a shoulder massage*—despite the pain.

"Does it hurt?" Drawing the tip of my index finger lightly across his skin, I trace the pattern of angry red lines.

"Not when you do that."

The husky, raw tone of his voice settles into my bones, releasing a flood of heat.

Slowly, I still my finger, and drag my gaze up to his face.

His hooded eyes bore into mine, and the intensity behind them nearly makes me swoon. He's never looked at me like this before. Like a giant, invisible hand is all that's keeping him from tackling me to the ground like a tiger pouncing on his prey. His chest rises and falls sharply as his gaze lowers to my parted lips.

I'm breathing just as hard as he is, and our whooshing breath is the only sound in the silent room. My nerves tingle. Every cell in my body screams out in want.

He curls his fingers around mine, and the pressure ignites the sparks in my belly. "Cass . . ." he rasps, and it's like the word was ripped from the very depths of his soul.

We reach for each other at the same time. His hand closes around the back of my neck at the same moment I cup his stubble-roughened jaw. I close my eyes. His rosemary and pine scent envelopes me, draws me in.

Our breath mingles. Our lips touch in the barest whisper of greeting.

The door behind us opens with a rusty squeal, and we jerk apart.

"Dinner's here," Devin announces as he walks into the room, wearing his typical fitted polo and holding an overstuffed plastic take-out bag. I drag the back of my wrist across my mouth automatically. Perry clears his throat as he settles back in his chair. He doesn't look at me.

Devin's eyebrows pinch together briefly when he catches sight of me sitting knee-to-knee with Perry, but then he smiles. "Hey, Cass. I didn't think you were coming."

I laugh nervously. Devin, my ex-but-not-really, almost just walked in on me *kissing his brother.*

Well . . . sort of. Does half a second of lip-to-lip contact count as a kiss? It doesn't matter. What matters is that I can't deny my feelings for Perry, whether I want to or not. And he's obviously feeling *something* for me—he's made that abundantly clear.

But Devin's still hoping we'll get back together, and I can't keep kicking that can down the road, expecting my romantic entanglements to magically resolve themselves. I need to make a choice.

But not tonight. The festival kicks off in two short days and we all have enough to worry about without me throwing a drama-bomb in the mix.

I inhale deeply in an attempt to calm my runaway heart. "Better late than never, right?"

"Are you hungry?" Devin lifts the take-out bag, and I catch the spicy scent of Thai food.

"Starving."

"Good. Because I bought plenty." Sliding one of the buckets of flowers over to clear space on the large square table in the center of the room, Devin deposits the bag in the corner. "Did you tell Cass about the T-shirts?" he asks over his shoulder.

Perry and I look at each other and quickly away. My thighs tense even as guilt pounds through my veins.

"Not yet," murmurs Perry.

"What T-shirts?" I ask, voice entirely too bright.

"We had T-shirts made for all the festival volunteers. One of Perry's artist friends does silk-screening, and she gave us a sweet deal. We got one for you too."

Grinning, Devin slides a cardboard box out from under the table. After a few seconds of digging around its depths, he pulls out a kelly green T-shirt and tosses it to me. "Here you go."

Unballing the soft fabric, I hold up the shirt. The event logo I drew weeks ago is on the back. Flowering vines twine around the words "Ohio City Flower & Beer Festival," which are written in blocky, old-timey font, while the logos of our five corporate sponsors form a line underneath. I flip the shirt over on my lap to study the front and I let out a bark of laughter. "It even has my name on it." Printed on the left side of the chest below the V-neck collar, "Cass" is printed in the same blocky font as the logo.

"That was Perry's idea—including each volunteer's name on their shirt," says Devin.

I lift my eyebrows at Perry, who scratches the back of his neck. "I know the accident has made it harder for you to remember people's names. I figured that you'd want to help out in-person during the festival, and this way you won't have to worry about names because everyone's will be right there, on their chest." With a sheepish smile, he shrugs.

I stare at him.

Perry tenses, eyes creasing. "I'm sorry, I didn't mean to offend you," he says quickly. "I just thought—"

I launch out of my chair and wrap my arms around him in a brief, heartfelt hug. His muscles stiffen beneath me, and I quickly resume my seat, neck warming. Gripping the T-shirt in my fist, press it against my chest, directly over my heart. "Thank you," I say, putting every ounce of appreciation I can muster into the words.

"You're welcome," he says, ears turning pink.

"Oh!" I snap. "That reminds me. I have something for you too. Can I borrow your computer?"

"Of course." Perry slides his laptop over to me at the same moment I reach for it, and for a brief moment, our arms brush.

I suck in a sharp breath. Perry shifts quickly, rubbing the spot where we touched. His gaze lands briefly on me before darting away. *Okay, don't panic. This is fine.*

"Thank you." Squaring my shoulders, I open a new browser window and log on to my personal email. I pull up the email I drafted last night, open the pdf attachment, and angle the computer toward Perry. "I wanted to wait until Devin was here before sharing it since it pertains to both of you."

With an inscrutable expression, Perry begins reading. After several seconds, his jaw goes slack. "When did you do this?" he breathes, eyes flying across the screen.

"What is it?" Devin asks. Striding over to the desk, he leans down to read over Perry's shoulder.

"A *new* community college idea for Councilman Truman. One that doesn't involve tearing down Blooms & Baubles or using eminent domain to get the city the property it needs," I explain. "My stepdad's a Realtor, so I asked him a couple weeks ago to run a search for commercial properties in Cleveland that are currently available at or below market value in neighborhoods that could truly *use* a community college, along with the opportunities it will bring residents. Because let's face it: Ohio City is comparatively more affluent—and white—than a lot of other areas. He found two side-by-side commercial buildings for sale in the Buckeye-Shaker neighborhood that would only need retrofitting to turn them into an educational facility. Not only would it cost significantly less than building from scratch, but it would actually be helping a neighborhood that needs it way more than ours does."

Perry stares at me, openmouthed.

Straightening, Devin lets out a breathy laugh. "Holy shit."

"Don't get me wrong. I have complete faith that this festival will be a success and save Blooms & Baubles. But as every good attorney knows, you don't file a brief with only one legal argument; you present backups and backups to those backups. And if the city council decides to move forward with your dad's idea? Well, now you have the ammunition to argue that the city doesn't *need* your property, per se. Because there are other options available."

"I didn't think it was possible, but you continue to surprise me." Perry's voice is so hoarse he coughs. "How are you planning to share this with Councilman Truman? Email it to him?"

"I was planning on asking my friend Val, the one who works for the city, to forward it to his office—from an anonymous constituent. I can't have my name associated with the festival since my firm represents your dad. It could be seen as a conflict of interest."

Dipping his head, Devin squeezes the back of Perry's chair. "Let me give the proposal to Councilman Truman in person."

"What? Why?" Perry demands.

"Because he already knows me, and I can get a meeting with him. He can ignore an email. He can't ignore someone talking to him face-to-face."

"But Dad will know you're involved then, and you'll lose your job and your chance to take over the company someday," Perry protests.

"Good! Cass, you were right. I shouldn't work for him—not if this is how he treats his family. It's not worth it," Devin says softly.

"Devin, no."

"I'm doing the right thing for once, and don't you dare try to talk me out of it."

Pushing back his chair, Perry stands and faces his brother. They stare at each other for a long, tense moment. Finally, Perry wraps his brother in a back-thumping hug. "Thank you."

"Love you, brother," he murmurs before disconnecting. Scrubbing a hand through his hair, he holds his arms out wide. "Well, should we eat?"

Perry blinks several times. "I'll find us some plates." I track his movements as he crosses the room to one of the far cabinets, squats down, and rummages in its depths.

I feel Devin's eyes on me, and I quickly pick up my phone and pretend to check my email, heart thudding.

Despite the cluster of a situation I landed myself in tonight, I can't help thinking about the last surprise I have up my sleeve—a backup to the backup, of sorts. I *could* tell Perry and Devin what I'm planning, but right now it feels safer to keep it close to my chest. I don't think I can handle giving or receiving any more surprises.

Besides, if I'm being honest, I'd rather see the look on Perry's face when he discovers what I have in store for Blooms & Baubles.

And boy, is he going to be surprised . . . in the best possible way.

25

The lobby is several degrees warmer than usual with all the summer associates plus another dozen or so attorneys milling around, and I unbutton my jacket. Glenn called us all here at noon to announce the time and location of tomorrow's August Social, and it's already ten minutes past the hour. He sure does love to wind us up.

One of the other summer associates, Bradley, elbows me in the arm. "Where do you think it's going to be?"

Drumming my fingers against my thigh, I shrug. "My money's on an escape room." The idea of locking us all up together and requiring us to use our wits to get out seems exactly like the fun sort of "game" Glenn would enjoy. "Either that, or a casino night downtown."

I overheard one of the other summer associates talking about how he suggested happy hour at Jack's casino for our final social, which honestly doesn't sound so bad. At least a casino night would be likely to start later in the day, closer to five or six, versus an escape room, which feels more like an afternoon activity—and would therefore cut into my festival time.

The elevators on the far side of the lobby open, and a hush falls over the crowded lobby as Glenn Boone steps out. Wobbling over to stand in front of the reception desk, Glenn clears his throat. "Hello, everyone," he begins. "I'm sure you're all anxious to know where we're going tomorrow for our last summer associate social. Thank you for blocking such a wide time frame on your calendars, by the way. Until yesterday I was considering two possibilities, and after discussing it with the other partners this morning, I've made a decision."

General murmurs filter through the lobby.

"Casino night. Please say casino night," Bradley chants under his breath.

Glenn pumps his arms for silence. "But before I reveal the surprise, I promised a gift to the person who made the winning suggestion." He pauses for dramatic effect. "Andréa Miller, come on up."

A smattering of applause accompanies Andréa's clacking heels as she strides over to Glenn. He pulls a small, flat box from the inside of his suit and holds it out to her. Grinning, she takes it from him, opens the lid, and holds the box up for all to see. Inside, what looks like a very fancy pen winks in the overhead lights.

"Would you like to tell them where we're going tomorrow, Andréa?" Glenn asks her.

"Absolutely. But first, I have a confession. The idea I submitted for the social wasn't originally mine. One of our summer associates told me about it earlier this week. I thought it sounded perfect, so without her mentioning it to me, I never would have shared it with you. So, Glenn, if it's all right with you, I'd like her to have the prize."

Glenn's jowls wobble as he nods slowly. "How magnanimous. Which summer associate can we thank then?"

"Mercedes Trowbridge," she announces. "Come on up, Mercedes."

Mercedes's smile is blinding when she reaches Andréa and Glenn, and I force myself to clap along with the rest of our colleagues as she takes the pen from Andréa. When her gaze drifts to me, rather than her usual smirk or extra show of teeth, her shoulders tense and her smile falters. My spine prickles with unease.

"Don't keep us in suspense, Andréa. Where are we going?" Frank calls genially, and several of the other attorneys laugh.

"Mercedes, would you like to do the honors?" Andréa asks.

"No, you go ahead," she demurs.

I blink. Since when has Mercedes ever turned down an opportunity to be in the spotlight?

"Okay then." Andréa claps. "Tomorrow, we're celebrating community. The community we've built at the firm over the past three months with our group of talented up-and-coming summer associates, and the community in which we work—Ohio City."

My unease morphs into full-blown panic as a creeping, unavoidable suspicion settles into place.

"To celebrate and support those communities, we're attending a festival in our very own neighborhood hosted by a local, family owned flower shop that's been in operation for three generations. There will be food, music, beer, and, of course, flowers, for anyone looking to beautify their living space or make a loved one smile. We'll meet tomorrow at Twenty-Eighth and Providence at noon, where everyone will be provided with lunch and two free drink tickets, courtesy of the firm. So get ready: we're going to the Ohio City Flower & Beer Festival!"

My mouth is still hanging open when the first group of people file into the elevators to return to their offices.

I'm going to the Flower & Beer Festival. Tomorrow. At noon. With everyone from work, including my boss and managing partner.

My heartbeat accelerates and sweat gathers on my neck.

Pacing to the window, I unbutton my jacket and brace my hands on my hips. Maybe it's not such a bad thing. Sure, I still need to keep my role as a coordinator under wraps, but at least I'll be able to help set up beforehand and stick around once my co-workers leave. And starting at noon? I'll just have to provide moral support and plenty of thumbs-ups from a distance.

I hang back until only a handful of attorneys are left in the lobby before getting in line for the elevator. I catch sight of Mercedes several feet in front of me and glare at the back of her blush-colored blouse.

She did this on purpose. I know it. When she overheard me talking in the bathroom about the festival she must have connected the dots to Szymanski Enterprises. She probably thought she was pretty smart filtering the festival idea through Andréa so I wouldn't find out she proposed it for our social. She didn't count on Andréa handing the credit back to her at the moment of truth though.

The elevator dings, and the next group shuffles in. When the doors close, there are only four of us left in the lobby: me, Mercedes, and two junior partners I don't know well. Narrowing my eyes at her, I pull my phone from my pocket and text Perry and Devin.

> Just found out where my firm's social is tomorrow, and you're not going to believe it . . .

> WE'RE GOING TO THE FESTIVAL 💀💀💀

Perry

> Are you serious??

> Yep. The big boss just announced it.

> Me and 20+ other attorneys from Smith & Boone will be there starting at noon.

Devin

> Sweet, 'cause we could sure use your help

My gut twists.

> I have to keep my participation on the DL, remember?

Perry

> We can't let anyone find out Cass helped plan this thing. Her job might depend on it. Got it, Dev?

Devin

> Right, sorry. I forgot.

I'm in the middle of tapping out a response when the elevator doors open once again. Reluctantly, I return my phone to my pocket and step inside. The two junior partners are talking with their heads bent together, so Mercedes and I wind up standing next to each other in the back. She takes half a step away from me when the doors close. The elevator ascends.

"Congratulations on the winning idea, Mercedes," I grate.

"Thank you," she says primly, squeezing the small, narrow box in her clasped hands.

The elevator dings when we reach the second floor, and the junior partners step out. As soon as they're out of sight and the doors close, I drop the fake smile and turn on her. "What are you playing at?"

"I don't know what you mean."

"I mean suggesting the flower festival to Andréa for our summer social?"

"What's wrong with that?"

I narrow my eyes at her. Is she trying to make me confess? Is her phone in her pocket set to secretly record me? At this point, I can't count anything out. Shrugging, I turn away from her to face straight ahead. "Nothing, I guess."

Staring resolutely at the elevator buttons, she licks her red lips. "For what it's worth, I didn't think Andréa would take the idea to Glenn. She asked me the other day if I had any fun plans for the weekend, and I mentioned I *might* swing by a flower festival in Ohio City, and she ran with it. I wasn't trying to . . . make anyone's life harder. I swear."

I study her out of the corner of my eye. Her expression is as smooth and serene as always. But then she swallows, and I notice the tightness around her lips and the quiver in her jaw.

Is she . . . telling the truth?

The number three appears above the doors, and the second they open she fast-walks out without a backward glance. I stare after her for so long the doors start to close, and I have to shoulder my way through to force them to open again.

I am suddenly *so* over it. Over everything. The long hours, the cutthroat competition, the untrustworthy colleague who has me questioning her intentions when I have so many other, more important things to worry about.

Tonight—and the final surprise I have in store for Perry and his business—can't come soon enough.

And then I just have to get through tomorrow.

"How did I let you talk me into this?" Brie mutters later that night, pulling her baseball cap lower down her forehead. Crickets chirp from the overgrown side yard, while the Twenty-Eighth Street warehouse's white exterior shines in the dim streetlights.

My heart sinks. "If you're having second thoughts, I don't blame you. What we're doing isn't exactly legal, and—" I say, but she cuts me off.

"Oh no. Bring on the misdemeanor. I meant *that*." She wrinkles her nose at the jars of paint lined up on the grass as though they hold arsenic instead of acrylics. Brie's artistic skills extend to mathematical modeling and the occasional whimsical cross-stitch, and that's about it. Art—more precisely, paint—has never been her thing.

"I'll handle the painting. If you could just hand me what I need as I go and keep a lookout for bystanders, that would be great."

Grinning, Brie rolls up the sleeves of her loose long-sleeved shirt. "No problem, boss. Bystanders, get ready to check yourself. Move along!" she shouts into the night. Her words bounce down the empty street, echoing off the darkened windows of Blooms & Baubles next door.

"*Shhh.* Are you nuts? I don't want to get caught!"

"Oh, we'll be fine. You're not robbing an ATM, you're painting a wall. Banksy does it all the time."

"Banksy is an international icon. He can paint whatever and wherever he wants."

She swats the air at what's probably a mosquito. "Why are you doing this, anyway? I mean, it's awesome, but this is the biggest risk I've ever seen you take—trespassing, defacing private property. Why do it? Do you like Perry that much?"

"It's not just for him. It's for me too. I *want* to do this. I can't explain it, but I have to." I don't say that I can't explain because I don't fully understand it myself. The festival starts tomorrow, and this is my last chance to do something that can make a real, tangible difference.

Yes, part of me is doing this simply because I know it will help Perry, and the thought of making him happy makes me happy too. But it also feels like my own personal revolution. My way of veering off my predetermined track and doing something that speaks to my soul, even if it's risky. After a year of struggle and a lifetime of doing what's expected of me, I need this more than I can articulate, even to Brie.

Grinning at the blank wall in front of us, I nudge Brie with my elbow. "Joy of painting aside, picturing the look on Roger Szymanski's face when he sees his warehouse this weekend gives me life."

"Well, I can't think of a better reason than that," Brie says, lifting her hand to high-five me. She gathers up the bag of paintbrushes. "Let's get to it. Darkness is our friend, and the night won't last forever."

"Neither will Roger's plan." Unfolding the sketch I'd tucked into my back pocket earlier, I attach it to the wall with painter's tape—the blueprint for my mural. I examine the jars of paint on the grass, pick one, and gently shake it before twisting off the lid. Brie hands me a flat, three-inch brush, and I dip it into the jar's dusky purple depths. Lifting the paint-laden brush to the bare white wall before me, I make the first strokes of what I can only hope will be a game changer—for me, for Perry, for the city of Cleveland, for all of us.

26

I know the moment Brie and I arrive at West Twenty-Eighth and Jay Avenue at 10:40 on Saturday morning that something's off. Twenty-Eighth Street is blocked off with traffic barricades between Providence and Jay, exactly like it's supposed to be. But besides the dozens of tables and handful of volunteers dotting the street, the block is otherwise empty.

My lungs seize. *Where are the tents?*

I grab the nearest person wearing a green shirt. "Where are the tents?" I accidentally shout in the volunteer's face, and he flinches.

His name is Alec, according to the name printed on his chest. I don't recognize him, so he's probably one of Perry and Devin's friends from softball. "I'm sorry, um, but the event doesn't start until noon," he stammers.

Oh, right. I unbutton my white linen jacket and flash my own green volunteer T-shirt at him. I figured it'd be a good idea to wear it for the hours I *can* help today, and simply cover up when Smith & Boone attorneys start arriving.

Alec's eyes widen in understanding. "Oh, you know the Szymanskis. Sorry, I thought you were just some random person."

Brie circles a finger at her own green shirt. "Hello, we're *volunteers*."

"The tents?" I press.

"I don't know where they are, sorry. Devin's on the phone with the rental company now."

"Where is he?"

Alec points at a spot halfway down the block, and I take off at a jog. I silently curse myself for not arriving earlier. But Brie and I didn't get home from our painting escapades until almost three in the morning, and ten o'clock seemed like a reasonable time to set our alarms.

"What's wrong?" Brie asks, trotting at my heels.

"The tents aren't up. They were supposed to be delivered this morning and setup should have started by now."

"Ohhhh, that's not good."

No, it's not. I spot Devin farther up the block with his phone pressed to his ear, but it's what's in the distance behind him that makes me stop abruptly. Brie collides with my back with an *oof*. At the end of the street, behind the barricades at the corner of Providence and Twenty-Eighth, is Roger's warehouse . . . and my mural.

It looks even more beautiful in the daytime than I'd ever hoped. Along the top of the white wall, "Blooms & Baubles" is painted in the same large purple font that's on their sign, and the words "Delivering Joy to Ohio City Since 1946" are painted underneath with a large black arrow pointing directly to Perry's shop. Below the words are a collage of people—old and young, Black and white, of every size, shape, and color—grouped arm in arm in front of a background of multicolored flowers raining down on them like swirling snowflakes.

A couple with a small child about Jackson and Liam's age pauses to study the mural. The little boy points up at it, and his dad picks up him to give him a better view.

Brie loops her arm around my shoulders. "It's beautiful, Cass. Truly."

I let out a shaky laugh, my heart so full it threatens to burst like a piñata filled with rainbows. I almost forgot what it felt like to put a tiny piece of my soul on display . . . the joy of seeing others, even complete strangers, connect to it in some small way.

"Still no word from Perry yet?" she asks.

My smile fades. "No." When I woke up this morning, I expected to find a voice mail or at least a text from Perry expressing his delight at the mural that appeared overnight on the side of his dad's warehouse. But I haven't heard a peep from him since yesterday. Maybe he doesn't like it? Or maybe he thinks I stepped out of line and now he's angry with me?

Brie bumps me with her hip. "I bet he didn't realize you painted it. And besides, I'm sure he's been swamped with festival prep today. What with the tent debacle and everything."

"That's right, the tents." I let my own mural distract me. "Come on. Let's see what's going on."

We hustle the last few yards to where Devin is pacing the street, talking on his phone. His words become clear as we approach. "What do you mean you can't deliver the tents until twelve? Our event *starts* at twelve. They should have been here an hour ago! No, I won't hol—" Punching the air, he curses.

"Is that the rental company?" I ask.

He shifts the phone away from his mouth. "Yeah, and they've completely dicked us over. They're giving me some line about not guaranteeing their delivery window, even though the contract specifically said ten *and* I confirmed with the manager yesterday that everything would be delivered on time."

"Did you get the confirmation in writing?"

"Does 'email' count as writing?"

I beckon for the phone. "Let me talk to them."

He raises his eyebrows, but hands it over. "Okay. Good luck."

Wedging a hand under one arm, I lift Devin's phone to my ear. Several seconds later, a bored voice speaks. "Yeah, so I just talked to my manager, and there's nothing we can do. Sorry."

"Hello, this is Cassidy Walker. I'm Blooms & Baubles's attorney. With whom am I speaking?"

"Uh, Jeffrey."

"Hi, Jeffrey. Thank you for your help so far today. Can you put your manager on the phone, please?"

He sighs heavily, his breath blustering in my ear. "Sure. Hold."

I tap my toe as I wait.

"Hello," snaps a gruff male voice.

"Hello, sir. I'm an attorney calling on behalf of Blooms & Baubles in regard to the order they placed for twenty-eight tents for a public-facing event this afternoon. It's my understanding that you promised delivery by 10 a.m. this morning, and it is currently 10:45—nearly an hour past the contracted delivery time."

"Look, lady, like I told the other guy, the delivery driver's running late so the earliest we can get them there is noon."

"You're telling me you have no one else on staff who can make the delivery?"

"That's what I said."

"So neither you, nor your associate, Jeffrey, is capable of driving a delivery truck to the corner of West Twenty-Eighth and Jay Avenue?" Silence fills the line. "Are you aware that you're currently in breach of contract, and my client would be well within his rights to sue you?"

"Hang on a sec—"

"My client paid a significant sum of money to rent twenty-eight tents to be delivered by ten o'clock this morning. Not ten thirty. Not eleven. Not twelve. And we have a written record of you confirming the delivery time yesterday, which my client has relied on to his detriment. And as the result of your breach of contract, he now stands to lose thousands of dollars in income, for which I will ensure you are *personally* held responsible." I take a deep breath. "Now. Let me ask you again. Is there anyone else at your facility who can deliver the tents my client ordered—immediately?"

A heavy beat follows. "They'll be there in twenty."

"Thank you. We'll be waiting."

Ending the call, I hand the phone back to Devin. His mouth is hanging open and he's staring at me like I've sprouted gills and a fish tail. "The tents will be here in twenty minutes," I say, shrugging.

"Damn, girl. Remind me never to get on your bad side," breathes Brie.

"Seriously." Grinning, Devin shakes his head. "By the way, Brie, any updates from your mom about whether her station can send someone out to cover the festival this weekend? Cass mentioned yesterday you were still working on her."

Her face falls. "It's a no-go, sorry. Unfortunately, the great Charlotte Owens didn't think a small community festival was newsworthy enough to merit live coverage. Although I did convince her to have the station include it on their website's 'What to Do around Town' series. So there's that."

Devin shrugs. "It's something. Thanks for trying."

"And don't sweat your mom," I say. "The publicity would have been great, but we both knew it was a long shot." The concept of helping others when there's nothing in it for her is as foreign to Charlotte as snow is to the equator.

"Tell me about it," grumbles Brie.

I squeeze her arm before turning my attention to Devin. "Okay, so we have a little less than an hour until the festival kicks off. What else needs to be done?"

Devin's mouth twists. "Plenty. Follow me."

"Is that the last of them?" Straightening, I swipe at the sweat on my forehead.

Chuck adjusts the final tie along the ticket booth tent's white folded flap. "Should be."

I check the time on my phone: 11:54 a.m. I gaze down the length of the block, at the festival that *finally* looks like a festival. The peaks of twenty-eight tents rise above the street like billowing sails, signaling the arrival of a day filled with flowers, food, and fun. All of the local artists have arrived and are in the final stages of setting up their booths, and at the farthest end of the block inside the largest tent—next to Blooms & Baubles's, which is the second largest—Marcus, Brie, and the crew from Zelma's Taphouse have arranged grills, kegs, and multiple industrial coolers. The scent of grilled meat wafts through the air, making my mouth water.

I still haven't talked to Perry, although I've seen him in passing several times. While we were all scrambling to set up the tents once they arrived at 11:05 sharp, he was dealing with another mess: finding a last-minute replacement for the cover band that was supposed to perform. Apparently, the lead singer *and* drummer woke up with the "stomach flu" (aka a hangover, I'd bet my paint set on it), so Perry spent the last hour calling every musician he knew trying to find a backup.

Through the general murmur, a crackle fills the air. "*One two, one two. Check, check,*" intones a female voice through a set of speakers. A guitar strums. The notes shift as the instrument is tuned, and several heartbeats later, guitar chords fill the street and a woman begins singing. Her lilting alto is mesmerizing, and I smile. Looks like Perry found a replacement act after all.

"Hey, Cass. You're here early." I jump at the sound of David the receptionist's voice, my hand flying to my chest. *Here we go. It's Smith & Boone time.* With fumbling fingers, I quickly button my jacket to hide my volunteer T-shirt.

"Hi, David," I say, turning around. "You look nice."

Cocking a hip, he adjusts his pink-framed sunglasses. "Thank you. I wasn't sure about the fanny pack. Is it too much? It's too much." Tugging at the hem of his black-and-white-striped T-shirt, he adjusts a neon green fanny pack over his cut-off jean shorts.

"No, it's perfect. Not everyone can rock a fanny pack, but you're totally pulling it off."

Pursing his lips in a smile, he taps my shoulder. "You're so sweet. I'm loving this outfit, too, by the way. Very *Emily in Paris* meets *Love & Basketball*." He wags his finger between my white Adidas, high-waisted khaki linen shorts and matching belt, tucked-in T-shirt peeking out from my white linen jacket, and hair piled into a loose bun on top of my head. "Aren't you hot though? It's like a thousand degrees out." He flicks the corner of my lapel.

My mind races to find a convincing lie. "I have a sunburn. On my arms," I say quickly, because my legs are clearly normal colored. "Yeah, I went to the lake after work yesterday and forgot to put sunblock on my arms. So stupid." Rolling my eyes, I force a laugh. "So I have to keep them covered today. Boo."

"Well, at least linen breathes," he says. "So, I'm supposed to buy the lunch and drink tickets for everyone. Do you know where to go for that?" Unzipping his fanny pack, he pulls out a shiny black credit card—probably a company card.

"Oh, um . . ."

"Hey, there you are!" A familiar female voice rings out. Devin's friend Anisha is waving at me from thirty feet away and approaching fast. "Devin's been—"

"I think you buy tickets inside this tent." I say to David as I unceremoniously push him into the ticket booth tent we just set up.

"Goodness!" he blurts.

I poke my head in after him. "Wait here. I'll see if I can find a volunteer to help." I don't wait for his response before making a beeline toward Anisha in her green volunteer shirt. I intercept her not ten feet away.

"Cass! I've—"

"*Shhh.*" I make a slicing motion at my throat. "One of my coworkers is right there," I say in a hoarse whisper, pointing at the ticket tent behind me.

Her hands fly up to her mouth. "Oh my God, I'm so sorry. I forgot we have to pretend like we don't know you today. Perry filled us in."

"I mean, you don't have to pretend like you don't *know* me. It's just, a few dozen people I work with including my bosses will be here today, and I don't want them to find out I helped plan this event. It's complicated."

"No, no, I get it. Devin was looking for you, but I'll remind him you're officially off the clock until your coworkers leave."

"Thanks, Anisha. If you could remind the other volunteers too, I'd appreciate it. Oh, and do you know who's scheduled to work the ticket booth at twelve?"

"Me and Jai."

"Perfect. My colleague is in there right now—he's here early to buy lunch and drink tickets on behalf of my company. When you sell him the tickets, can you set them aside in the booth? Then when a Smith & Boone person arrives, ask them to show you their work ID in exchange for their allotted tickets. Oh, and don't forget to card them if they want an alcohol wristband."

To simplify sales on Zelma's end so they wouldn't have to handle money and card people while also serving food and drinks, Marcus suggested selling tickets at a separate booth for two dollars apiece that festival-goers could use at their tent—five tickets for a burger and fries, three tickets for a beer, etc. That way, Zelma's and the other breweries could provide faster service and we could card people up front and give out wristbands to those twenty-one and over. Plus, it gave us the perfect opportunity to put out a "suggested entry donation: $2" jar for anyone who wants to throw a couple of bucks toward festival costs.

"Great. Jai and I are on it. And don't worry—" Pinching her thumb and forefinger together, she drags them across her lips like a zipper.

"Thank you," I mouth, tapping my chest twice above my heart.

Glenn Boone's unmistakable voice rises up from the festival's entrance behind us. I turn and spot him greeting Andréa and two other people I assume are Smith & Boone attorneys on the far side of the ticket booth. With their typical professional attire swapped for casual summer wear, it's harder to recognize them. Even Glenn is dressed down in crisp gray trousers, an ironed white polo, and loafers.

Checking that my jacket's single button is still fastened, I push my shoulders back and take a deep breath. Time to make an appearance at the last required work function of the summer. I just hope none of the other volunteers slip up and ask me questions in front of anyone, especially Andréa, Frank, or Glenn.

I roll my shoulders back and take a deep breath. This might be the ultimate "worlds colliding" scenario, but it's only for a couple of hours. I'll get through it. I have to.

27

When I join the group of Smith & Boone attorneys, Andréa greets me with a hug. "Hey, Cass. How's it going?"

"Good."

"Excited for the festival?"

"Yeah, can't wait."

"Oh, hold on . . ." Craning her neck, she lifts her arm. "Mercedes! Over here!" I look in the direction she waves, and sure enough, there's Mercedes. Even on her day off, she looks impeccable. She's traded her signature red for a flowing gray, knee-length sundress, sparkly sandals, and the largest sunglasses I've ever seen outside a tabloid magazine. Her normally loose hair is tied up into a tight bun, while a violet-and-red patterned scarf is wrapped around her head like a makeshift headband. She's walking up West Twenty-Eighth toward Providence, which is the wrong way, since the entrance is at Jay Avenue, but pauses when she spots me and Andréa.

Pushing her sunglasses up her nose, she hikes her small white purse higher on her shoulder and walks over to us. Frank joins us a couple of minutes later, and soon, over two dozen summer associates and senior attorneys are milling in the street just outside the festival's barricade. Glenn's voice pierces through the chatter, music, and nearby traffic noises, and the Smith & Boone contingency quiets.

"Thank you all for being here! It's delightful to see you outside of the office, and on such a beautiful August day. As I understand it, the Ohio City Flower & Beer Festival has more than twenty local vendors selling art and handcrafted items ranging from photography prints to paintings to artisanal baked goods, in addition to a variety of cut flowers and potted perennials. And three local microbreweries are offering beer tastings as well."

My heart lifts. Hearing Glenn describe the festival makes it sound impressive. Despite the constant, low-level thrum of nerves I feel, pride trickles through my chest.

"David has purchased tickets for everyone, which you can use to buy lunch up to a twenty-dollar value, plus vouchers for two alcoholic beverages, should you choose to partake. Show your work identification at the entry booth to collect your tickets . . . and enjoy!"

Clapping follows Glenn's pronouncement, and the Smith & Boone crowd begins to disperse.

Andréa turns toward me and Mercedes. "Well, what do you think? Do you want to grab lunch first, then check out the vendors?"

"Oh, you want us to have lunch . . . together?" asks Mercedes.

Frank leans forward. "Of course. You've both been stalwart associates this summer. Andréa and I thought it would be nice to have lunch—the four of us. What do you say?"

"Sure," I blurt.

"Yes, thank you," Mercedes murmurs.

Frank claps. "All right then. Shall we?" His blue-gray eyes sparkle as he exchanges an unreadable look with Andréa, whose lips crinkle in a tight smile. What are these two up to?

Before I can question further, we're shepherded into the ticket booth. Jai and Anisha are sitting behind the table, checking ID's, running credit cards for the other festival-goers, and handing out tickets. Jai winks at me when he catches my eye, but otherwise doesn't say anything, for which I'm grateful. Before I can reach the table, someone tugs on my sleeve. Mercedes is behind me. Even though the tent is shaded, she's still wearing her sunglasses. "I need to use the restroom. Can you collect my tickets for me?"

"Um, well, if you want to drink, you'll need to show your ID."

She waves me away. "I'm not drinking. I have to drive later. If you could pick up my lunch tickets, though, I'd appreciate it. Thank you."

Without waiting for me to respond, she bustles out of the tent in the direction of the three portable toilets lined up at the corner. I shake my head in bewilderment. When you've gotta go, you've gotta go.

I step up to the table in front of Anisha, who smiles placidly as she looks at my driver's license, giving away no hint that she knows me, bless her, and hands me a yellow wristband and a dozen red tickets. I almost walk away before I remember Mercedes. "Oh, and can I get six tickets for my coworker please?"

"Six tickets, coming right up," she says, then catches sight of Frank peering at her curiously. "Oh, I mean. No, sorry. We can only give out prepurchased Smith & Boone tickets with a corresponding work ID. I'm afraid your friend will need pick up her tickets herself."

Frank smiles genially. "You run a tight ship. I admire that. But I'm a senior attorney at Smith & Boone, and I can vouch that my colleague's request is valid. The tickets are for Mercedes, right?" he adds to me.

"Yeah. She ran to the bathroom."

He nods. "If you get any blowback for it, I'll take the blame, okay?" Fishing his wallet out of his pocket, he produces a business card and hands it to Anisha. She blinks as she takes it, and looks between me and Frank. He has no idea that the person she'd get any blowback from is standing right here. The irony is almost enough to make me giggle.

She tears six more tickets off from the designated Smith & Boone roll and hands them to me. "There you go."

"Thank you. Much appreciated." Tipping an imaginary hat, Frank walks out of the tent. Anisha flashes me quick thumbs-up as soon as his back is turned. I give her doubles in return, and quickly catch up with Frank and Andréa. We wait just inside the festival until Mercedes returns a couple of minutes later. She takes her lunch tickets with a murmured "Thanks," and we head toward the food tent.

More people are beginning to trickle into the festival now, and I marvel at the kaleidoscope of colors, scents, and sounds bursting from every corner of the tent-packed block. A young couple with a toddler and an infant stroll past us before diverting into a tent filled with hand-stitched stuffed animals. An older, hunched man wearing a faded trucker's cap shuffles into another tent filled with baked goods at the same time a trio of college-aged women walk out, each holding a decadent cupcake. One of the women has a bouquet tucked in her tote bag—an assortment of pink and white blooms peeks out from between the straps.

Everywhere I look, people are smiling, strolling, laughing, and generally enjoying being outside in the sunshine on a beautiful Cleveland summer day. As I pass one of the microbrewery tents where a man with a ponytail is lining up a beer-tasting flight for a pair of twentysomethings, someone grabs me by the elbow. It's what's-his-face from earlier . . . Alec, the volunteer who didn't know anything about the tents.

"Hey, I thought that was you," he said. "Can you help me with something for a sec? I—"

"I'm sorry, I think you have me confused with someone else," I say through gritted teeth. Widening my eyes, I give the tiniest shake of my head.

Alec furrows his eyebrows, clearly not picking up what I'm putting down. "But, before—"

"Please excuse me." Shooting him a meaningful glare, I aboutface, only to find three pairs of eyes staring at me.

Andréa's dark eyebrows raise. "Everything okay, Cass?"

"Oh yeah. That guy thought he knew me. He had me confused with someone else." At her blank stare, I continue. "He thought I was one of the festival volunteers." I roll my eyes, all *can-you-believe-that?* Andréa looks at me then at Alec, who, after a bewildered beat, shakes his head and walks away.

"Must be your shirt," Mercedes says, and I feel bile rise in my throat. *She wouldn't.* "It's green, like the shirts all the volunteers are wearing."

Frank laughs. "Bad luck for you, Cass. It probably won't be the only time someone mistakes you for a festival worker today."

"Yeah, bad luck." I chuckle through the wave of relief washing over me. *That was a close one.*

Andréa and Frank resume walking, and Mercedes and I fall into step behind them. "Thank you," I murmur under my breath.

Sticking her nose in the air, she shrugs. "I told you I wasn't out to get you." Maybe she really *was* telling the truth in the elevator about not intentionally trying to sabotage me. Could I have been wrong about her this whole time?

"I just want your job. And I'll earn it fair and square," she adds with a sniff. *Ah. There she is.* "Anyways . . ." She hesitates, chewing her bottom lip. "How did you get involved with"—she motions around us—"all of this anyway. Was it your boyfriend's idea?"

"No, we're not together anymore."

"You're not?"

"We broke up about a month ago." I have no idea why I'm telling her about my love life, except a certain camaraderie has blossomed between us in the last ten minutes, and I kind of like it. It's nice not to be constantly at odds with Mercedes, and to trade favors even.

"I'm sorry to hear that," she says softly.

"It's okay. He wants to give it another try, but I'm still deciding whether I want to."

"No, don't," she snaps.

I jolt. "Why?"

"Because . . . when is it ever a good idea to give an ex another chance to break your heart? If you broke up, it was probably for a good reason. You should follow your instincts."

I'm about to correct her assumption that *he* broke *my* heart, which he didn't, when Andréa stops short. We've arrived at the Zelma's Taphouse tent. Behind the long set of tables, I spot Marcus pouring beers from a tapped keg. Brie's beside him, handing over food orders to waiting customers. They don't see me, which is just as well. The way they move in tandem, shifting and sidestepping one another, is as seamless as a dance. Since Brie's freak-out last month, things between her and Marcus have been better than ever. And for the first time in a long time, I really, really think they might stay that way.

"Should one of us grab a table?" Andréa asks us.

"I can, sure," I reply.

"Great! What do you want for lunch? We'll get it for you."

I scan the menu board and blurt out the first thing I read. "A chicken sandwich, thanks."

"And to drink?"

"Whatever's on tap. A pale ale if they have it."

She grins. "You got it."

I give Andréa my tickets with another heartfelt thanks, and meander through the rapidly filling metal picnic tables clustered at the mouth of the tent. I steer away from where Glenn and five other summer associates and attorneys are sitting, toward a table in the far corner . . . near the Blooms & Baubles booth.

Perry's tent is set up directly next to Zelma's, and it sports a six-foot-tall, vertical Blooms & Baubles sign in brilliant purple and

green. I can't see Perry from where I'm standing, but several potted perennials and bins of bouquets peek out from the tent's
white flaps.

Stepping over one of the picnic table's benches, I yank my
phone out of my back pocket and sit with a huff. I glance at Frank,
Andréa, and Mercedes who are already moving up in line, then
back to the Blooms & Baubles tent.

Maybe I could duck in for a second to see how Perry's doing . . .

No. Too risky. I've already had more than one close call being
outed as a festival volunteer; I don't need another. And I certainly
wouldn't earn any points if I left the table only to have it snatched
up by someone else.

Jiggling my foot, I swipe open my phone. I attempt to distract
myself with Instagram, but I barely see the images as I scroll.
Clicking off my phone, I tap it against my palm, my eyes sliding to
the Blooms & Baubles tent again.

Maybe I should text Perry . . .

He still hasn't said anything about the mural. Granted, we've
only exchanged pleasantries between frantic bouts of festival setup,
but still . . . I wonder what he thinks about it. We also haven't ad-
dressed our almost-kiss the other night or what that might mean
for me and him . . . or for me and Devin and our future, or possible lack thereof.

Unexpectedly, the hair on my arms stands up. A green shirt and
head of copper-brown hair flickers in the corner of my vision.

I look up to find Perry standing at the entrance to the Blooms
& Baubles tent, talking to a customer, and my mouth goes dry.
His smile is as carefree as ever, his posture relaxed as he chats.
When the customer finally leaves, he turns and our eyes lock. Even
with twenty-some feet and the odd person weaving between us, I
feel the scorching intensity of his gaze down to my toes. It's as
though we're the only two people in the world.

Perry thumbs over his shoulder—to the mural glowing in the

bright afternoon sun—then points to me. His mischievous eyebrows raise in question. *Was that you?* he silently asks.

Smiling, I shrug. *Maybe.*

Shaking his head with a wry grin, he places his hand over his heart.

And I'm a goner.

"Cass. Cass?"

"Huh?" I jerk toward the sound of the voice.

Andréa is holding out a cardboard to-go box—my sandwich. "Your lunch," she says, eyebrows pinching in concern. She, Mercedes, and Frank are all staring at me, probably wondering why I'm just sitting here staring into the distance like my mind wandered off for a vacation.

"Oh, thank you." I quickly take the box from her along with the plastic cup of beer Frank offers me. "Sorry. I thought I saw someone I knew." I scoot down the bench, and by the time I look up again, Perry's disappeared inside his tent.

Once everyone is settled in, Frank plants both palms on the table and leans forward. "So, Andréa and I wanted to have lunch with the two of you today for a reason."

"Apart from the chance to enjoy your sparkling company," Andréa adds, causing Frank to boom a laugh.

"Exactly." He looks at her, and she prompts him with a nod. "We have some exciting news to share. You weren't supposed to find out until next week, but Glenn gave us permission to spill the beans early."

Mercedes's back is so stiff she looks like she might shatter at the tiniest tap. My own heartbeat accelerates. *Could this be . . . ?*

Frank's eyes light up until they practically twinkle. "We'd like to officially welcome both of you to the Smith & Boone family . . . as first-year associates."

28

Oh my God, I did it. They offered me my dream job—the one I thought I'd lost a year ago. My mouth falls open and I can't seem to form words beyond a vague croaking sound. Mercedes looks as stunned as I feel. Her blue eyes are wide, and her hand is fluttering against her chest as though she's trying to keep her heart from spilling out.

"Frank, I'm honored. Thank you so, so much," she breathes.

"Yeah," I finally manage to say. "Wow. Thank you."

Laughing genially, Andréa shakes each of our hands in turn. "Allow me to be the first to say, welcome to the firm."

"Assuming you accept, of course," interjects Frank. "Your formal written offers are coming next week, which I'm sure you'll read with a fine-toothed comb. You'll want to know all about your pay, billable-hour requirements, bonuses, benefits, vacation time, that sort of thing."

Fluffing out her paper napkin, Andréa lays it across her lap and flips open her takeout box to reveal a hearty salad. "As a heads-up, vacation time isn't really a thing. You get personal time off, which includes sick leave, but most first-year associates don't use it. Not unless they don't want to make their billable hours," she says with a laugh.

Frank pauses with his burger halfway to his mouth. "True. But the good news is, once you have enough years under your belt to take some time off, you'll have enough money in the bank to go wherever you could possibly want."

"Like Fiji, right Frank?" says Andréa.

"Exactly. That's where the wife and I went for our twentieth anniversary last summer. Two weeks of nothing but sun, sand, and snorkeling."

"And the Seymour case," she says with a smile.

He nods thoughtfully. "Oh yes, the Seymour case. That was a tough one. I remember one day I had to set my alarm for three in the morning so I could dial in to a client meeting from our on-the-water bungalow. My wife was *not* happy with me that day." He chuckles. "Oh, Andréa, but we're probably scaring them." He flashes me and Mercedes an apologetic smile.

Andréa takes a bite of salad. "Nah, they know what they're getting into. Or else they wouldn't have applied for our summer program in the first place, right guys?"

Mercedes sits up straighter. "Exactly. Big-firm life isn't a problem. In fact, my job is my first priority. And Smith & Boone is where I want to build a career. I won't let you down." She takes a shaky sip of what looks like iced tea and licks her lips. "Out of curiosity, to which group will I be assigned?"

"Mine," says Frank. "You proved you're a capable hand at public law. I'm thrilled to have you on board."

"And you'll be in litigation, with me," Andréa says to me.

Beside me, Mercedes's leg tenses. I know she had her heart set on litigation. Does this mean the competition is back on? If so, then there will never be a finish line. As long as we're working at the same firm with me in litigation and her in public law, she's going to be gunning for a spot in my coveted practice group.

A headache forms at the base of my skull. "Thank you, Andréa. I can't wait." I lift my beer and take several long, long gulps. Frowning, Mercedes glances at me out of the corner of her eye.

Why do I suddenly feel bone-deep weary? This is everything I've hoped for, and more. Smith & Boone is one of the most prestigious firms in the state, maybe even the country. It's where countless members of Congress and appellate court judges started their careers. I'll be respected, well paid, and challenged every day. I'll never have to worry about finances or not being able to pay my bills, especially since I'm starting with a clean financial slate thanks to my college and law school scholarships.

I can have the life other people only dream about.

But what kind of life will I have time to live once I leave the office?

I know the hours Andréa works—I've witnessed it all summer. Leaving at six thirty is considered early for her. Eight or nine is more her norm, especially when she's working a big case, and—let's face it—she's always working a big case.

Does *she* ever paint? Help plan community festivals? Go on vacations without bringing work with her? Beer curdles in my empty stomach and I fight back a wave of nausea. Fumbling for my phone, I stand.

"Cass, are you all right?" Andréa asks, eyeing me closely.

No. Not even a little bit. "Yeah, fine. Sorry. Um, the chicken isn't sitting so well."

Her eyebrows knit together. "You haven't eaten any."

"I mean my breakfast. I made eggs this morning and I thought they smelled a little weird, but I ate them anyway because breakfast is the most important meal of the day, you know? And now I'm feeling off. I'm going to find a bathroom," I mutter.

Mercedes half stands. "Do you want me to come with you?"

"No," I quickly say, stepping backward over the bench. "I'll be fine." I stumble a step before turning back around. "Thank you again, Andréa. This opportunity really does mean the world to me." I put my hand over my heart. "I'll be right back."

I catch a glimpse of Mercedes's creased forehead before I walk away from the table into the ever-shifting crowd.

Air. I can't get enough air. Running my knuckles along the center of my chest, I force myself to take deep, calming breaths.

What is *wrong* with me? Why does it feel like an elephant decided to sit on my chest?

I pass the Blooms & Baubles tent. Inside, Perry is talking to Devin. He pulls a double take when he spots me. I keep walking. I can't deal with Perry or Devin or my twisted web of romantic feelings at the moment.

I don't head for the portable toilets—the thought of their rank stench only increases the churning, sick feeling in my gut. Instead, I walk to Blooms & Baubles, the shop. I just need a few minutes to collect myself. Somewhere cool and calm.

My tennis shoes thud dully against the sidewalk as I pass my mural, but I don't stop to admire my handiwork. Accepting the position at Smith & Boone will mean no more murals, that's for sure. Maybe some small-scale painting here and there—I won't be working 24/7 after all—but just like in law school, I know the busier I get, the less I'll paint . . . and the unhappier I'll be.

Dodging a middle-aged couple on the sidewalk, I practically run up the path to Blooms & Baubles. The bell tinkles when I open the door, and I stop dead. The shop is busier than I've ever seen it. At least half a dozen people are meandering through the cramped store, and two more are in line at the counter—one holding a handblown vase, the other a small art print and ceramic mug. Alma looks up from behind the counter when I approach.

"Cass!" she says, but her smile fades as she studies me. "Hey, are you okay?"

"Can I use your bathroom?"

"Of course. You know where it is, right?"

Nodding, I sidestep the line of customers, walk past The Colonel, where he's dozing in his dog bed, and veer through the door on my right into a tiny white bathroom. Locking the door behind me, I brace my hands on the vinyl vanity and stare into the mirror.

My cheeks are flushed pink and my eyes are overbright. For once, Rogue Curl remains firmly in place, trapped by the extra bobby pin I used to secure it.

"What am I doing?" I ask my reflection. She stubbornly provides no answers.

Closing my eyes, I tilt my chin to the ceiling. Why does it feel like at the moment of victory, the world is crashing down on me?

You know why, says a little voice inside my head.

I shake my head hard, dispelling the tears that have formed. They trickle down my cheeks, cutting a stinging path.

I don't want this. The job. Or big law life.

The realization has been creeping up on me for weeks, poking and prodding at the edge of my consciousness, but I've been fighting it. How many years have I felt depleted to the bone from simply existing? From the moment I wake up to the second my eyes close in uneasy sleep, I'm thinking about the job—obsessing about what I could do better or differently. And what has it given me? Clinical anxiety and permanent frown lines. Every Sunday night before I drift off to sleep, tears threaten to flood my cheeks because I dread waking up on Monday morning. What kind of life is that?

My climb to the top of the legal profession has defined me for so long that somehow I've lost myself along the way, unable to focus on anything but that one singular goal. Until recently, all I saw when I looked in the mirror was that picture-perfect definition of success—the one my professors, family, and classmates convinced me I wanted. But when was the last time I felt truly happy?

An image of Blooms & Baubles floats into my mind. Not that I want to be a florist—I don't—but I've never been so happy as I have working to save Perry's business. I've thrived putting my training and intuition to work for a goal that's poised to make a real, tangible difference to the community. Helping Perry plan this festival to save Blooms & Baubles these past few weeks has finally cracked the illusion of my life. There's more to me than a pile of law books and a windowless office. *I* get to choose what makes me happy—who *I* want to be.

So, if I'm not Cass Walker, up-and-coming lawyer at a big-time firm . . . who am I? Setting my jaw, I stare hard at my reflection.

How about . . . Cass Walker, the person who uses her law degree to *help* people—to help communities? Cass Walker, who fights against self-serving corporate interests and advocates for those who actually need it? How about Cass Walker, painter? Cass Walker, Sunday brunch eater and family visitor and friend?

I don't *need* a job at Smith & Boone to find career success, achieve financial security, or live my best life. In fact, I know that accepting this job offer will bring me nothing but anxiety and regret.

I have to turn it down.

Suddenly, the roiling nausea in my gut is gone. My chest feels light and airy like it hasn't since . . . since I started painting again. A laugh bursts out of me. So *this* is what it feels like when you take charge of your own life.

Tearing off a paper towel from the roll sitting on the sink, I swipe the tears from my cheeks. Studying my reflection, I tug the bobby pins out of my hair and take down my bun. Rogue Curl is just long enough now so it doesn't stick straight out anymore, although it still protrudes slightly compared with the rest of my curls.

I don't care. Rogue Curl isn't perfect, and neither am I. And that's okay.

Wetting my lips, I open the door and turn out the light. Time to claim my future . . . the one I actually want.

The moment I step onto the sidewalk outside of Blooms & Baubles, someone shouts my name. My heart leaps. I'd know that voice anywhere—it's Perry's.

He's standing several yards away at the corner of Providence and Twenty-Eighth Street. Our eyes meet, and we walk toward each other as though connected by an invisible string. We meet in the middle, directly beneath my mural. His hair is windswept and his shoulders tense as he looks me over.

"Are you okay? I saw you walk past the booth earlier and you looked upset."

I grasp his forearms. "I'm fine. Everything's great, in fact. Smith & Boone offered me a permanent job."

His lips part in surprise. "Wow, Cass, that's great news. Congratula—"

"I've decided to turn it down."

"Hold up. What are you talking about?"

"Next week when they deliver the formal written offer, I'm going to decline it. Which means when my summer associateship ends, I'll be unemployed . . . but that's okay! There is a whole world of possibility out there. I still have my license to practice law, and I'm going to do something meaningful with it."

"But . . . I thought working for Smith & Boone is what you've always wanted?"

"I had an epiphany just now. In your bathroom, actually." I laugh softly. "I don't think I ever wanted to work for a big firm, not really. Everyone thinks working for a big firm is the pinnacle of a law career because big firms are the most prestigious, and therefore the best. I've strived for so long to be the best at whatever I do that it was only natural for me to want a career in big law as well."

Stepping closer, I run my palms down his arms and gather both of his hands in mine. "But over the past few weeks, you helped me realize something: working at Smith & Boone doesn't make me happy. It makes me pretty miserable, actually. The hours, the stress, the clients. The lack of time to pursue hobbies and friendships and . . . other things." I nibble my lower lip, and Perry's nostrils flare.

"I've loved helping you plan this festival, and I loved drafting a proposal for the city council to open a community college in Buckeye-Shaker. There are a lot of ways to use a law degree that can help make a real, meaningful difference to people—everyday people who are simply trying to pay their bills, feed their families, or run a small business." I squeeze his hands. "So that's what I want to do. And I don't know if I ever would have realized any of that if it weren't for you. You encouraged me to look inside myself and question what really makes me happy. Like painting."

A sly smile crosses his lips. "I can't believe you painted that mural. I mean, I suspected, but I wasn't sure until I saw you at the picnic tables. *Thank you*. I'm stunned."

"I had some help. Brie was my lookout." I let out a breathy laugh. "If you thought it was me, why didn't you say anything sooner? Why didn't you text me this morning?"

"I had to see you first—to ask you something face to face." Glancing at our clasped hands, he inhales deeply. When he looks up again, his eyes blaze brighter than the noonday sun. "Why did you paint it?"

My heart gallops and I swallow hard. "Well, to stick it to your dad, for one. Painting a ten-foot-tall advertisement on his warehouse for his son's business he's trying to destroy felt like karmic justice, don't you think?"

He dips his chin to look into my eyes. "Is that the only reason?"

"No," I whisper. "I did it for myself, because it felt right . . . and I did it for you."

He sucks in a jagged breath like I've punched him in the stomach. His fingers tighten around mine as he pulls me closer.

"Cass?" There's an unspoken question in his voice.

I can't hold back anymore. Pushing onto my toes, I close my eyes and bring my lips to his. The moment they touch, the simmering attraction that's been building between us all summer explodes into being, as bright and all-consuming as fireworks on the Fourth of July.

With a groan, he hauls me flush against him. And then his mouth is moving against mine and . . . ohhhh my God, *bliss*. Cupping his smooth jaw, I put every ounce of repressed feeling I can muster into the kiss. His fingers tangle in my hair and he returns my intensity with interest.

I'm swimming in Perry—his rich, woodsy scent, the soft press of his lips, his hips fitted tightly against mine. His tongue dips into my mouth and I moan at the sensuous glide. He tastes spicy and sweet, like a cinnamon bun. My lips part and he deepens the kiss, coaxing pleasure with every swirl of his tongue and scrape of his teeth. When I suck his bottom lip between my teeth, nipping slightly, he smiles against my mouth. But he doesn't stop. With a growl, he tilts my chin and kisses me again and I'm drowning in a pool of pleasure and need.

Because I *need* this. I need Perry, his lips on mine, and this feeling of heady, unbridled joy that's threatening to send me spinning off into another universe. My blood is on fire and my soul is screaming out with rightness at his every touch.

This is what a kiss a supposed to feel like. Not a textbook recreation of technical mastery like it was with Devin, each move calculated to produce an expected physical response. It's a meeting of souls, an exchange of promises. A revelation.

And now I know, undeniably and unequivocally, I want Perry. *He's* the one.

I think I've known it since the first moment I saw him in his shop, but I was too blinded by dreams and fantasies to realize it. I don't want Devin, and I never will.

Devin. I have to tell him. He deserves that much.

With a gasp, I break away. Perry's lips are kiss-swollen and pink, his emerald eyes wide with wonder. "Devin," I choke.

He jerks like I've slapped him. His expression hardens, and he lurches away from me. My heart trills in panic.

"Wow," he rasps. "It's never going to be me, is it?"

"What? No." I reach for him, but he backs away.

"Even when you're kissing me, you're thinking about him. I'll never be able to compete with a dream, will I?"

"Perry, no. That's not what I meant . . ."

But he's already walking away. He glances briefly to his left, and whatever he sees makes him pause. But the next heartbeat he's moving again. I run after him. "Please, wait!"

"Cass?" Devin's voice makes me stop so fast I nearly trip. He's standing at the corner on the opposite sidewalk, staring at me. His mouth is open, his face a mask of shock. My stomach bottoms out.

He saw us. He saw everything.

I crane my neck, looking for Perry, but he's disappeared into the crowd. As much as I want to chase after him and *make* him understand, the explanation I owe Devin is long overdue. And after what he just witnessed, I owe him the truth. Now more than ever. Blowing out a shaky breath, I force my feet to carry me across the street.

But before I reach him, Mercedes rounds the corner. Pushing her sunglasses to the top of her head, she jogs over to where I'm standing in the street and grips my shoulder. "Hey, I've been looking all over for you. Andréa and Frank are worried. Are you o—?"

Devin steps hesitantly off the sidewalk. "*Sadie?*" he blurts.

Mercedes whirls, and her face goes stark white. "Devin."

Wait . . . what? Mercedes is *Sadie?* *The* Sadie? The nickname makes sense, but I can't quite process the possibility that I've been working all summer alongside Devin's pregnancy-faking, manipulative ex.

He steps back, every muscle tense. "What the hell are you doing here?" His voice is low and dangerous.

They face each other on the sidewalk, wearing twin expressions of disgust. I look from Mercedes to Devin and back again.

The back of my neck tingles. The tingle intensifies until it burns like I'm on fire. *This isn't the first time I've seen them together.* Present blurs with past. Images float through my memories—my *real* memories—along with strains of music. The scene before me shifts and flickers. Dim lighting. Crowded tables. Devin and Mercedes.

My vision goes fuzzy. I stumble forward and my knees connect with the sidewalk—hard.

I remember.

I remember *everything*.

29

When I walk out of the bar exam testing center, I don't feel happy, relieved, or anything, really. I'm sure I passed—I know in my bones I knocked it out of the park—but there's only a dull heaviness left.

I don't feel like making the two-hour drive home to Cleveland yet, so I spend the afternoon exploring the Short North district of downtown Columbus, drifting from one little art gallery to the next until blisters threaten to form on my feet and my stomach protests at its emptiness. I spot a little restaurant—Italian, I think. It's close, I'm hungry, I go in.

The host gives me a pitying look when he seats me, as though a young woman eating alone is a travesty. I ignore him. My head is too full of other doubts to care. He seats me at one of the small, two-person tables crowded together along the back of the restaurant. A few minutes later a server arrives, and I place my order. As soon as he leaves, the ruminations start churning again.

It's like I've run a marathon and finally crossed the finish line only to realize there's nothing else on the horizon. What do you do with your life when your only goals have been to graduate from law school, pass the bar, and land a job at a high-profile firm . . . and you achieve all of those goals by the age of twenty-five?

My job as a first-year associate at Smith & Boone starts a few short weeks from now. What will the next twenty or thirty years of my life look like, I wonder.

I imagine slaving away in an office, working evenings and weekends until I finally make partner at age . . . who knows? Will my career leave me time for family? Friends? Art? Or will my life be the job: the single, overarching trait that defines my existence?

Mom would say it doesn't matter. I can fill in the gaps with the things I love, and as a successful attorney at a top firm, I'll have the financial security to do it.

But will it be enough?

Emptiness creeps through me until I'm so hollow you could ring me like a bell. Gazing out across the crowded restaurant, I've never felt so alone.

A couple walks in then—a stunning blonde wearing a fitted burgundy dress and a man who steals the attention of every person he passes, he's that beautiful.

I shift uncomfortably when the hostess seats them at the two-person table directly next to mine. Our tables are so close together there's only a foot and a half of space between them, if that. Edging sideways, the woman squeezes into the booth next to me, primly smoothing her dress beneath her. The man sits opposite her, unwinding his red scarf with white squares from around his neck and looping it on the back of his chair.

I study the man out of the corner of my eye. He and his date are dressed up nicer than the restaurant calls for. Did they just come from a show? Is this their first date, their fifth, or their fiftieth? They're not married, judging by their lack of rings, and there's something about the hesitancy in the woman's posture that has me guessing it's their first date.

I soon discover I'm right. Sonny and Cher's "I Got You, Babe" drifts through the restaurant, mingling with the myriad conversations humming around us, but at this distance, it's impossible not to overhear this couple's every word. Sipping my ice water, I pretend to study my phone while I listen.

As far as first dates go, it seems to be off to a good start. He's brought her a bouquet of fresh white lilies, which she's propped on the booth next to me. Plastic wrap crinkles every time her elbow brushes them. They ask each other all the typical first-date questions: where are you from, what do you do, what do you like to do . . .

At one point she laughs at a story he tells her about falling off a trampoline in the third grade and breaking his pinkie finger. "Oh, Devin. You didn't." She covers his hand with hers on top of the table, obscuring the crooked finger, and my stomach hardens into a ball. When's the last time I experienced such a sweet, simple gesture of affection? The smile he gifts her is so radiant it's blinding.

He tells her about his family. How his mother runs a flower shop in Cleveland—Blooms & Baubles—but how he wants to work for his dad, a developer on the south side, and help deliver the business into the future. She says she's always wanted to move to Cleveland.

He does most of the talking, charming her with story after story, and a life unfolds before me—rich, complex, and beautiful in its meaning and uncertainties. He talks about high school and his love of soccer and baseball and long bike rides through the Metroparks. She listens intently, but prompts him with follow-up questions and measured laughter.

When the server approaches my table for the third time asking if I'm ready for the check, I finally nod. The couple is nearly finished as well. The man—Devin—has gone to the restroom and the woman is scrolling through her phone. I check the time; it's after nine o'clock, and I still have a long drive ahead of me before I can finally crawl into bed and surrender to exhaustion.

Gathering my bag, I reluctantly leave. On my way out, I veer toward the restrooms—a pit stop is always a good idea before a long drive—and pause at the mirror in the back hallway to study my reflection.

My cheeks are hollow and the purple smudges under my eyes that have become a permanent fixture these last few months are bruise-dark. Today might have been the end of one long, arduous journey, but it marks the beginning of another. Sighing, I turn at the same moment the door to the men's room swings open beside me, and I find myself face-to-face with the man from the next table over—Devin.

He glances at me, his smile stretching across his model-worthy face. "Excuse me," he murmurs. The lights above us flicker twice as I watch him pass me in the mirror until he disappears from view.

Ten minutes later, I steer my car onto I-71, the highway that will take me home, and suppress a yawn that feels like it's birthed from the depths of my very marrow. Only two hours until bed. I can make it . . .

I never make it.

I vaguely recall exhaustion tugging at me throughout the drive, but I stubbornly refuse to stop. I crack the windows, blast music, and think about the couple on the date next to me. Their stories, their history, their lives. The man's beaming smile and intoxicating confidence . . . my own loneliness . . .

The next thing I know, I'm in the hospital and Brie is holding my hand, imploring me to come back to her.

"Cass, what's wrong?" Devin's face blurs into focus. He's kneeling in front of me on the sidewalk and gripping my shoulders, mouth a slash of concern. Mercedes is standing beside him, wide-eyed and rigid.

"I'm okay." Using his body as leverage, I heave to my feet. My knees ache where I slammed them on the pavement, but I ignore the pain. Devin stands.

"I remember you. Both of you," I add, nodding at Mercedes.

"What are you talking about? We've been working together all summer. I should hope you'd remember me," she says, a skeptical look of concern on her face.

"No. I don't mean that." Shaking my head, I return my attention to Devin. "I finally know why I woke up from my coma thinking I knew you. I was there, on your first date with Mercedes. I was sitting at the table next to you, and I overheard everything. Your entire conversation."

Devin's mouth falls open and his arms go slack at his sides. After several seconds of stunned silence, he shakes his head. "No, that's . . . that can't be."

"It can. Last July, I was in Columbus for the bar exam. I'd finished earlier that day, and decided to explore the city. After touring a couple galleries, I treated myself to dinner. You were seated next to me at one of those tiny two-person tables they squash together—Mercedes, you sat in the booth beside me, and Devin, you were across from her. The tables were so close together I could see you clearly, which must be why I was able to draw Devin so accurately. Except for the scar, which I must not have noticed since he was seated on my right and his scar is on the left side of his face."

"That still doesn't explain why you woke up thinking I was your boyfriend," he splutters.

Pursing my lips, I rub my forehead. "My brain must have scrambled my memories when I had the accident, conflating actual events with imagined ones. You told Mercedes . . . Sadie"—I correct; the name tastes strange on my tongue—"all about your life, your interests, your parents, Blooms & Baubles, everything. You wore your scarf—the red one with white squares. And you brought Mercedes flowers. I didn't have anything better to do, so I listened. Later that night, I was driving back to Cleveland when I fell asleep at the wheel and crashed my car. I guess I'd been thinking about your date, and your stories sort of soaked into my consciousness. When I saw you two standing together just now, it all came back to me."

"Holy shit," he breathes. "I can't believe you finally figured it out."

Mercedes raises her hand like she's in class. "Excuse me, what in the world is going on here? Cass, when were you in a *coma*?

And what's all this about thinking Devin was your boyfriend? I thought he *was* your boyfriend. You two were together this summer, right?"

"Yeah, but it's complicated . . ." I trail off, looking at her hard. "Wait. How did you know that? I never told you Devin was my boyfriend. In fact, I made it a point not to mention his name because, honestly, I didn't trust you."

Her cheeks flush. "I overheard you talking to him on the phone last month. The day he stopped by the office to see you."

"Why didn't you tell me he was your ex then—that *you* were Sadie?"

Devin snorts. "Because she wanted to manipulate you. That's what she does."

"Screw you, Devin," she spits, eyes blazing with hatred. "I *wasn't* trying to manipulate anyone. Cass, I wanted to tell you, but I didn't know how."

"I'm sorry, but I find that hard to believe."

"Put yourself in my shoes for a minute. You find out that your colleague, who appears to strongly dislike you, is dating your ex-boyfriend—the same ex-boyfriend who left you bleeding at the hospital on the most traumatic day of your life, and who has since made it his singular mission to convince everyone he knows that you're a monstrous, lying harpy." Her voice cracks, and I'm alarmed to find tears streaming down the side of her nose. "Would you have believed me if I tried to warn you that Devin is an arrogant, self-righteous know-it-all? That you should run far, far away because he can't be trusted? Or would you think I was just playing to character and trying to manipulate you?"

With a derisive snort, Devin folds his arms across his chest. "*I* can't be trusted? I can't be trusted. Wow, Sadie. That's rich. I'm not the one who faked a pregnancy and lied about it."

"For the last time, it wasn't fake!" She screams so loud people thirty feet away shoot us questioning looks from inside the festival.

"You were there when the first doctor delivered the news: I wasn't pregnant. But you left before they sent in an ob-gyn to explain what she actually saw on the ultrasound: an empty gestational sac. *Gestational sac*. Which means I *was* pregnant, but I lost the baby early on, around six or seven weeks."

"Why didn't you tell me you miscarried then? Why keep it a secret for another month?"

"Because I didn't know. I had morning sickness up until a week before we went to the hospital. When it started going away, I thought it was normal because I was getting closer to the second trimester. I had no idea that it was possible to lose a pregnancy but for your body not to get the message. Even though the embryo stopped developing around week six, my uterus continued growing a placenta and pumping out pregnancy hormones for another month, tricking me into believing I was still pregnant."

Devin's eyes flick back and forth across her face. "Why didn't you want to go to the hospital when you started bleeding then?"

She throws her hands in the air. "I was scared. I didn't want to believe my body had failed at the one thing on this earth it's biologically wired to do. I know it sounds stupid, but I thought when I got pregnant despite being on the pill that it was fate—that this baby, *our* baby, was meant to be, even though we never planned it. Do you understand how much it destroyed me when I lost it? No. Of course you don't. Because you left me in the hospital without so much as a goodbye or even a ride home. I didn't even know we were over for good until I found the box you left on my doorstep two days later with all my stuff from your apartment. And then I couldn't contact you to explain what really happened because you blocked me on everything, even LinkedIn. You completely ghosted me."

Devin's jaw loosens and his arms fall limply at his sides. "Oh God. Sadie . . ." He blinks several times, and a tear trickles down his cheek. "I'm so sorry. I thought you were lying. I thought—"

"It doesn't matter anymore. You had your shot, but you blew it." Lifting her trembling chin, she faces me. "I'm sorry you had to hear all that, but I'm not sorry things didn't work out between you and Devin. I know I wasn't that friendly with you this summer, but that's just how I am, I guess. I'm not used to trusting people or making friends in professional settings; between my student loans and helping my family with their bills, there's always been too much at stake. And I'm not what you'd call a 'bubbly' person anyway. But I'm not the villain here either."

Gripping her purse strap like a lifeline, she marches back toward the festival and fades into the crowd.

Devin stares sightlessly after her, chest rising and falling. He's quiet for so long I consider tiptoeing away when he suddenly thrusts his fingers through his hair. "Sadie, wait." He takes off running after her, leaving me alone on the sidewalk.

30

Perry, where are you? We need to talk.

I clutch my phone as I weave my way back through the festival. I need to find him, and he wasn't in the Blooms & Baubles tent or with Marcus or Brie. So much has happened in the last twenty minutes my head might explode, but one thing's clear: I can't let Perry think I'd ever choose Devin over him.

Things are over between us for good. I might not have had the chance to tell him yet, but given the way he sprinted after Mercedes, I don't think my feelings for Perry will be an issue.

My phone vibrates and I check the screen.

Turn around

My heart skips a beat. Perry's not ten feet behind me, standing beside the entrance to a booth filled with watercolor paintings. Sunlight glints off his tight, inscrutable expression.

I run to him. "You didn't leave." I try to take his hand, but he slips out of my grasp. My stomach twists into knots.

"You're right. We need to talk." He beckons for me to follow him, and he leads me out of the festival until we're standing directly behind his Blooms & Baubles tent. Farther down Twenty-Eighth Street, cars turn onto side streets, detouring around the blocked section of road.

"Look, Perry," I say in a rush. "When I said Devin's name, I didn't mean it like *that*. I realized that he still harbored hope that I'll take him back someday and I needed to tell him the truth: he's not the one for me. I even know now why I remembered him after my coma."

Perry's eyebrows fly up his forehead.

"It turns out I was at the restaurant where he took Sadie on their first date, and I overheard everything—I sat right next to them—which is why I knew so much about him. It all came back to me when I saw Devin and Sadie standing together on the sidewalk after you left."

"Wait, you saw *Sadie*? She's here?"

"It doesn't matter. None of that matters. The point is: I choose *you*, Perry. I want to be with you. Will you give me another chance?"

His throat constricts as he swallows, and I hold my breath, every muscle tense.

"I'm afraid . . . not. I'm sorry, but I'm not sure my heart could take it." His smile is as wobbly as his voice, and it's like an arrow through my gut. He steeples his hands over his nose and mouth briefly before sucking in a shuddering breath.

"Cass, from the very first moment you walked into my shop, I was hooked. Done for. Thoroughly enamored. And that doesn't happen to me often. I tend to guard my heart at the best of times, but there you were: long legs, hair pulled back revealing the most gorgeous smile, and that voice you used with The Colonel . . ."

I swipe my fist over my eyes. "Utterly ridiculous."

"And endearing. You weren't afraid to be yourself or show who you really are. And when I looked into your eyes, you enchanted me. *Who is this woman and how did she end up here . . . in* my *shop?* We talked, and I thought for a brief, shining moment that maybe you were just as interested in getting to know me as I was in getting to know you. Then you fainted, and whose name did you call? Devin's. And my hopes shattered."

I open my mouth to speak, but he continues. "You have to understand, there's never been a single time in my life when someone has chosen me over my brother—not even our own father. Most of the time, I couldn't care less. Devin's his own person and so am I. We're not in high school anymore, competing for the same small pool of prom dates. But for once, I thought I'd met someone who existed outside of his sphere—someone funny, kind, and completely disarming. But then you said his name, and I knew it was too late. And that was before your whole coma story came out and it seemed fate had destined you for my brother."

Scrubbing a hand over the back of his neck, he sets his jaw. "But then we spent some time together. At first it wasn't ideal, like when I crashed your not-really-a-date, date. And then there was that night you came by the shop and we talked about the hopes and dreams we have for our lives. Then the Fourth of July party happened and the painting you gave me and . . ." He hesitates, and our eyes lock. *The unspoken connection between us.*

"A tiny speck of hope came back, even while I pushed it down. You were with Devin. That was your choice, and I respected it. But then you painted that mural and you *kissed* me and I thought . . . this is it. You chose me. But then you said *his* name."

"Perry, it was a *mistake*."

He holds up his hand, silencing me. "Please, let me finish," he says softly. "I know you didn't mean to, but it's true, you admitted it—you were thinking about him while you were kissing me. And I can't help but think: Was your subconscious trying to tell you something? Was it fate at work again, steering you toward your soul mate and here I am, simply in the way?"

"*No*, fate has nothing to do with it. The fact I coma-remembered Devin was a coincidence. I—"

"I'm sorry, but I can't live with the doubt. I've worked too hard to accept and appreciate who I am, independent of my father and brother, and I need to be with someone who leaves no room for doubt in my mind of our possible future together. I care about you Cass. I always will. But I can't be with you. I know my heart couldn't survive if you decided to choose him again. I can't take that chance. I'm sorry."

Then, without so much as a backward glance, the man I care about more than anyone in the world walks away from me forever.

I somehow manage to keep it together for the remainder of the festival, although I have no idea how. After taking several minutes to collect myself behind Perry's tent, I eventually emerge and find Frank and Andréa, who inform me that Mercedes had to leave early due to a family emergency. I trail behind them as they float from booth to booth, dutifully smiling when they look my way, and pretend to be excited for Andréa when she finds the perfect birthday gift for her mother—a whimsical crocheted purse. I studiously avoid going anywhere near Perry's Blooms & Baubles tent, and I don't see Devin again either.

Once the two hours of forced fun are up and Frank and Andréa and the other Smith & Boone attorneys say their goodbyes, I drag myself to the food tent, where Brie is still helping Marcus. She takes one look at my face and scurries over to me.

"What's wrong?"

"I have to talk to you," I choke out.

Marcus appears at her shoulder. "Are you okay?"

Pressing my lips tightly together, I shake my head. "No." A silent sob rips through me and my shoulders tremble.

Marcus shouts instructions to one of the people working the

Zelma's booth, and together Marcus and Brie guide me out of the festival and down a side street while I unsuccessfully attempt to hold back my tears.

We pause in front of a beat-up red truck that must belong to Marcus, and he helps me climb into the back seat. Brie follows me in. "Thanks, Marcus. I got this," she says before shutting the door behind us. The engine revs and cool air flows through the vents; Marcus must have remote-started his truck.

Brie takes off her sunglasses and looks me in the eye. "Now, what happened? Tell me everything."

And I do. I tell her about Perry, our kiss, my revelation about Devin, and how I said his name after I kissed Perry and it ruined my chances with him—everything. I even tell her about the job offer from Smith & Boone, my decision to turn it down, my memories returning, and the Sadie surprise. By the time I'm finished, her mouth is hanging open and her expression is dazed.

"Jesus, Cass. I leave you alone for two hours and you experience an entire soap opera season's worth of drama."

"Tell me about it." Plucking a napkin from the center console, I blow my nose. "I just can't believe I screwed things up so badly with Perry."

She shrugs. "Well, if you ask me, he's acting like a little bitch."

"Hey!" I slap her on the leg.

"Sorry, but it's true. It's like you told me: heartbreak is only a speed bump on the way to finding love. I get he has emotional baggage—who doesn't?—but he's giving up the chance to be happy because he's afraid he'll get hurt. He needs to grow a set and realize what a goddamn gift you are and how lucky he is to have you."

"I don't think that's the issue. I know how he feels about me." Our kiss earlier left no doubt about that. "I think I need to prove, beyond a shadow of a doubt, that I'm choosing him, and not Devin. Screw dreams, fate, the universe, all of it. He thinks I'm cosmically fated for his brother, even though my Devin memories have a perfectly logical, scientifically sound explanation. So I need to show him that it's our *choices* that make our fate, not the other way around."

Flopping against the seat back, Brie clicks her molars. "That's not going to be easy. A simple conversation won't do it—clearly. What you need is something *big*. Like a banner across the sky written in fifty-foot letters: Cass loves Perry."

I open my mouth to protest, but her words sink into my skin, burrowing until they're branded on my heart, as permanent as a tattoo. *Cass loves Perry.*

And holy shit, I think I do love him.

When I wake up in the morning, he's the first person I think about. When we're not together, I count down the hours until I get to see him again. He always manages to make me smile, even when I'm feeling down or stressed. He understands where I'm coming from because he actually *listens*, and he doesn't pass judgment or try to fix my problems, but rather gives me the space and freedom to be fully myself.

He's carefree, conscientious, and kind, and *oh my God*, I'm in love with Perry.

The feelings I've been trying for so long to ignore have somehow grown into something larger than life and utterly precious.

And now he's slammed the door on any kind of future together before I even had the chance to tell him how I really feel.

Brie jerks forward suddenly, her eyes going wide. "I have an idea. A very, very big idea." She winces. "But I don't know if you're going to like it. When I say big, I mean BIG. And you're going to need Devin's help to pull it off."

"I don't care. What is it?"

I have to steady myself against the window once she's done explaining. Holy mother of pearl, this might just be the nuttiest thing Brie's ever proposed.

"What do you think?" she asks. "Too crazy?"

"It's perfect." Terrifying, but perfect.

She whoops. "I have some calls to make then, and so do you. Reconvene back at the house later?"

"It's a plan."

I throw my arms around her and squeeze until she squeaks, and climb out of the truck.

No more drifting along in my own life, floating wherever the current takes me. I'm behind the wheel and I make my own choices. And right now? I'm choosing to show Perry with actions, instead of words, how much I love him.

I just hope it'll be enough.

31

The following morning arrives with a blistering headache and limbs trembling with nerves. After Brie arrived home late last night and confirmed that our plan is officially a go, I couldn't sleep. I finally closed my eyes around four, and when I opened them again it was already nine thirty in the morning. I should feel exhausted, but instead I'm wired like I've guzzled an entire pot of coffee. My knees bounce as I wash my hair in the shower, and I nearly poke myself in the eye with my mascara, my hands are trembling so badly.

Today will change everything. Not just for Perry, but for me too.

When it's time to leave at eleven, Brie insists on driving us to the festival, even though it's only a ten-minute walk.

"You look too gorgeous to ruin your makeup walking around in this heat," she explains, and I don't protest.

We pull along the curb behind a white news truck that's parked outside Blooms & Baubles. Turning off the engine, she stashes her key in the glove compartment before locking the door—the benefits of keyless entry. When I step out of the car, I stare up at the shop's dusky purple siding and my heart flutters.

On the corner, a news crew is setting up equipment. A burly

man positions three tall black stools on the sidewalk in front of my mural, while another sets up a large camera. Off to the side, Brie's mom—Cleveland's very own Charlotte Owens—is reapplying lipstick using a pocket mirror.

Farther up the street, I catch sight of my mom and half brothers with my stepfather, Robert, behind them. I wave. "Mom! You made it!"

"Cass!" Jackson and Liam squeal in tandem as they sprint over to me. Squatting down, I brace myself as they fling their tiny bodies at me in a tackle hug.

"I missed you guys," I murmur into their hair.

Jackson hugs me extra tight. "I missed you too, Cassy."

"Hey, little dudes," says Brie. She ruffles Liam's hair, and he swats at her. She grins.

Mom and Robert join us then. "Boys, let Cass breathe," Mom says, and they reluctantly let go. "Good to see you, Brie," she adds.

"Always, Mel."

Straightening, I smooth the front of my pink skirt. "Thank you so much for coming."

"Of course. You said you wanted us here by eleven, so here we are." Robert's wide face splits into a grin as he scrubs his close-clipped hair.

Mom *harumphs*. "What is this all about anyway? You were very cryptic on the phone last night."

Robert looks between me and Mom and clears his throat. "Jackson, Liam, how about you and me go check out that painting over there . . ." He's already shepherding them away, despite their protests.

Brie checks her watch. "And I'm going to see if my mom's ready for you. See you in a bit," she says to me.

My mom squints after her. "Is that Charlotte over there with the news crew? Cassidy Walker, what in God's name is going on here?"

I clamp my hands on her shoulders. "Smith & Boone offered me the job as a first-year associate." My mom's eyes light up like a pair of sparklers. "I'm going to turn them down." The light fades just as quickly.

"Why would you do that?" she demands.

"Because working for a big firm doesn't make me happy, Mom. I learned that this summer. I learned a lot of things, actually," I mutter to myself. "Big law life isn't for me, and really, it was never my dream in the first place. In fact, I think it was more your dream all along."

"Cass, what are you talking about? This is what we've been working for—"

"No, Mom. It's what *I* worked for. Not that you haven't supported me every step of the way—you have, and I'm grateful. I know how much you sacrificed to move us to a good school district and find educational opportunities for me. I never would have made it this far without you. But you also taught me to stand on my own two feet and take responsibility for myself, so that's what I'm doing. Which is why I can't take this job. If I do, I'll be miserable."

"Cassidy." Tutting, she runs her hands up and down the length of my arms before pulling me into a hug. "I had no idea you felt that way. Did you think I'd be mad if you didn't end up at Smith & Boone?"

I nod against her shoulder.

"I want you to be successful, but more important, I want you to be *happy*." Leaning back, she looks me hard in the eyes. "I'm so sorry if I ever made you feel like I pressured you into big law. I'd never want you to do something that makes you unhappy just because you think it's what I want. You come first, always. I'm so sorry."

"It's okay. Really."

Eyes shimmering, she tucks my hair behind my shoulder. "So now you know what you don't want to do—what *do* you want to do?"

"I'm not sure yet. Work for a nonprofit, maybe? I'd love to use my law degree in a way that helps people. Maybe get into community development."

"Well, if a career at a nonprofit, or even a different field altogether, makes you happy, then *I'm* happy."

"Thanks, Mom. And you know . . . it's never too late to go back to school. Melanie Walker, esquire, has a nice ring to it, don't you think?"

She laughs. "Ask me again when the twins are older." Her gaze catches on the news crew, and she frowns. "But really, what *is* Charlotte Owens doing here? God, she's the worst."

"Cass, they're ready for you," Brie shouts from farther up the street. Behind her, Charlotte eyes me with sharp-edged hunger. Next to her, Devin is off to the side, talking to—*Perry?* My heart thunders. Whereas Perry is wearing his green festival T-shirt, Devin is dressed in a sleek polo and jeans. I suck in a deep breath.

Gathering my courage, I pat Mom's shoulder. "You'll find out soon."

A small crowd has formed outside the barricade the crew set up around the camera and stools, and I have to squeeze my way through the gathering people.

A familiar face crosses my vision—Val. She'd texted this morning that she was planning on swinging by the festival around noon today, and I told her she might want to arrive early. Looks like she made it. "Hey! Val!" I call, and her sunglasses-covered face swivels in my direction.

She bobs over to me, the silver threads of her T-shirt shining. "Cass! What's going on here?"

"A surprise." I give her a quick hug. "So good to see you. Thanks again for your help with the events permits. I have to go right now, but let's connect after this, okay?"

"For sure." She waves as I slip through the crowd.

One of the news crew members briefly stops me, but Charlotte waves me past the barricade. "Cassidy, Cassidy, Cassidy. It's been too long." She air-kisses my cheek, and I try not to gag at the over-powering smell of her perfume.

"At least eight years," I say.

"I was shocked when Brie called me last night. I can't believe she didn't tell me your story before now. If I'd have known, I would have invited you on the show weeks ago. This is seriously compelling stuff. People are going to *love* it."

"Well, thank you for accommodating our request to film here."

"No problem. It's perfect, actually. The background is gorgeous and it really sets the scene. Gary here will fit you and your boy-friend for a mic, okay?" She waves at the shorter of the two crew members, who sidles up holding a tangle of wires and a small black box. He clips a small lapel mic to my collar, helps me run the wire inside my blouse down my back, and instructs me to clip the small box at the end to the waistband of my skirt.

Devin steps even with me just as he finishes with his own mic, Perry right behind him.

"Cass," Perry murmurs, and my heart nearly breaks all over again. His hands are jammed into his pockets and dark shadows ring his eyes, like he didn't sleep much last night. "Devin told me Brie finally convinced her mom to cover the event, but that she wants to do an interview with you and Devin?"

I shrug. "Yeah. It's bananas, isn't it?"

"Yeah."

"Well, I should probably go. Good lu—"

I grab his arm. "Stay. Please. I don't think I can do this if you're not here."

He nods. "Sure. I'll be cheering you on from the sidelines. Quietly, of course."

Gary checks Devin's mic, and gives the thumbs-up to Charlotte.

"All right. Let's take our places, people," she says.

"You got this," murmurs Brie before stepping off to the side with Perry.

The cameraman shows Devin and me to our respective seats: Charlotte on the left, Devin in the middle, and me on the right.

As they do a sound check, I lean over and whisper in his ear. "Thank you so much for doing this for me."

His lips quirk. "Like I said last night when you called, it's not just for you. It's for Perry too."

"You're sure you're okay with this? Until yesterday, there was a chance you and I . . ."

He shakes his head. "I've known since the day we met with Councilman Truman it was never going to work out."

"You did?"

"I mean, I'd hoped maybe you'd come around? But I've come to realize that we're better off as friends. You're an amazing person and I'm grateful for the time we spent together, but something about us just doesn't—"

"Click," I finish. "Just because we're two good people doesn't mean we're good together."

"Exactly. And come on." He nudges me with his elbow. "I can see the way you look at Perry. You never looked at me like that. And you sure as hell never *kissed* me like that."

Heat climbs up my neck and I look away. Time to change the subject. "Did you hear back from Sadie?"

"I tried calling her again last night and left her a voice mail, but she hasn't called me back. I can't believe what a monumental asshole I was to her, which I detailed at great length in my message."

"Give her time."

"Are you ready?" Charlotte interrupts us, eyebrows raised expectantly.

Devin and I exchange wry grins. "As we'll ever be," he says.

"All right then. If we could have quiet, please," the cameraman shouts at the crowd of people. "We're going live in five, four . . ." He holds up three fingers, then two, then points to Charlotte, who pastes a beaming smile onto her face.

"Good afternoon, Cleveland! This is Charlotte Owens, Channel Six, coming to you live from the Ohio City Flower & Beer Festival. I'm with local attorney Cass Walker and development manager Devin Szymanski, and they're here to share a story of wonder, fate, and true love. So, Cass, you were in a car accident a year ago that landed you in a coma for six days, isn't that correct?"

My heart hammers so fast I'm sure it's pulsing visibly beneath my blouse, but I force myself to smile. "That's right, Charlotte."

"And while you were in a coma, you dreamed of this man here, Devin Szymanski. Except—here's the kicker, folks," she says directly to the camera, "you had never actually met him before?"

"Correct. Although he wasn't only in my dreams. When I woke up, I *remembered* him, as though we knew each other well and had been dating for several months."

"So you remembered going on a first date together, heartfelt conversations, months of getting to know each other?"

"Exactly. But that was over a year ago, and until this June I thought I'd imagined him—that he wasn't real. I had no evidence to suggest he was. My doctors agreed. My case was even featured in a peer-reviewed journal article my neurologist wrote several months later titled 'Coma-Induced False Memory Generation: A Case Study.'"

"Except I am. Real, that is." Devin winks at the camera, turning up the charm to eleven.

Charlotte blushes—actually blushes—at his smile.

"So tell us, what happened?" she asks Devin.

"We met for real in June. Cass had recently moved to Ohio City and stopped by my brother's flower shop, Blooms & Baubles, the host of today's Flower & Beer Festival." He turns to the camera with a dazzling smile. "If you haven't already, come on down to West Twenty-Eighth and Providence. The festivities will run until five this evening." Charlotte's lips thin in apparent annoyance. She probably doesn't appreciate Devin hijacking her interview with his own personal ad, but she seems to let it slide.

"And then you started dating," she prods.

Devin nods. "I was skeptical at first. I mean, what a story, right? But all her claims checked out, and the more time I spent with her, the more I wanted to get to know her. Now here we are, two months later, and we couldn't be happier."

"There you go, folks. A beautiful story of fate bringing people together."

I find Perry in the crowd. His face has gone ashen and I stare at him, willing him to trust me. To stay and listen, just a little longer.

"Not exactly, Charlotte," I say with a smile.

Her long, false lashes flutter against her cheeks. "Oh? How would you describe it then?"

"I don't know, to be honest. I struggled for a very long time over the question of fate and its role in the events of my life. Was my car accident and the resulting months of gut-wrenching struggle part of fate's plan? If so, what does that say about the nature of fate, that it would condone such pain? And then there were my memories of Devin. Can you imagine what it's like to wake up from a terrible car accident only to discover that the one person you want to see is, in fact, not real? And how difficult it is when your own *mind* is untrustworthy, when you begin to question the very basis of who you are?

"And then finally, after a year, when it turns out that this person is real after all—to meet the guy you imagined but still not know why or how you knew him because he doesn't remember ever meeting *you*? At first, I convinced myself that the answer to the puzzle was fate. Why else would I dream up a man who turned out to be real, if he wasn't my soul mate sanctioned by the universe?"

I steal another glance at Perry. He's holding very still, watching me so closely I feel it in every nerve ending. I refocus on the camera.

"But then something miraculous happened. I met someone else. Devin's brother, Perry. Our connection wasn't as cosmic or immediate, but the more time we spent together, the more I realized that this person, this *stranger*, might just fulfill me even more than the one I dreamed about. Not because I don't like Devin—in fact, he's an incredible person I'm honored to call a friend. But the workings of the heart are as mysterious as the universe itself. Is it chemical, the feeling of attraction we experience for another person? Is it emotional? A combination of pheromones and the brain recognizing an inherent compatibility with another person on a subconscious level? I don't have the answer. But what I do know is that I've found that kind of soul-deep connection people dream about. And it's not with Devin."

With a sardonic smile, he shrugs and the crowd chuckles.

"It took me a while to recognize it, but *Perry* Szymanski is the man who speaks to my heart. His entire mission in life is to bring joy to others through the simple act of giving. He recognizes and celebrates the connection between people because he understands the fleeting nature of life and the powerful bonds we forge while we're here. And even though his own father, Roger Szymanski of Szymanski Enterprises, is trying to use his power and influence with the city of Cleveland to close his son's beloved business, Blooms & Baubles, Perry's light still shines. He laughs easily, he makes the most beautiful flower arrangements you'll ever see, and his trust is hard to earn, but worth its weight in gold once you have it.

"You said earlier that this story was one of fate bringing people together. I think you might be right, Charlotte. I don't know if fate or God or forces beyond our understanding exist in the universe. But if they do, I believe they brought me to Devin so I would meet Perry—the man I've fallen in love with."

Silence falls across the crowd. Even Charlotte is speechless for a full three seconds. Finally, she flashes her newscaster smile. "Well. That was quite a story."

32

As soon as the camera stops rolling, the makeshift set erupts into chaos. "What the hell was that?" Charlotte screeches, but I'm already unclipping my mic. Pushing onto my toes, I search the undulating sea of spectators, but I can't find Perry. My chest aches. Did he leave?

Brie scurries to my side. "Oh my God, *Cass*—"

"Where's Perry?" Unfastening the mic box from the back of my skirt, I yank the wire out of my blouse and drop it onto my stool.

Blinking, she looks around, frowning. "He was just here."

"I need to find him." Before I can take a step, however, Charlotte Owens is in my face. Her blond, shoulder-length bob crackles with anger.

"How dare you blindside me like that. I interviewed you as a favor to Brie, and you—"

Brie inserts herself between us. "Shut up, Mother." She's several inches shorter than her mom, but her expression is so venomous Charlotte takes a hasty step back. "Quit pretending like you did me some big favor. You only agreed to interview Cass when there was a big, juicy story at stake. You wouldn't even send your most junior reporter to cover the festival when I asked you about it weeks ago, and then again just the other day. So stop acting like you're such a saint and be thankful that Cass probably just handed you a viral video."

My throat constricts. "You think it'll go viral?" I ask, horrified.

Wincing, Brie shrugs. "It's pretty compelling stuff."

"Excuse me. What is going on here?" A deep voice booms. The crowd in front of us parts, revealing Roger Szymanski. His hair isn't as neat as usual, and his Lacoste polo is wrinkled on one side, like he tucked it in in a hurry. Nostrils flaring, he glares at the mural behind us, then at Devin. "My assistant called this morning to inform me that *someone* painted *my* warehouse, and that there's some kind of festival going on associated with Blooms & Baubles. And now I find *you* here with a news crew? Explain yourself," he hisses.

"Why, Dad? So you can fire me? Threaten to ruin my life like you're trying to ruin Perry's?" Devin spits, chest puffing.

He flinches. "How *dare* you—"

I step forward. "How dare *you*." My heart's beating so hard my vision blurs around the edges. "You act like you care about your sons, but you don't. Fathers who care don't try to control their children's lives. Fathers who care don't lie, scheme, and plot. And they don't wield their political connections to execute personal vendettas at the cost of the city."

Behind Roger, Charlotte motions quickly to the cameraman, who swivels the camera in our direction.

I shake my head. "The sad thing is, you have no idea how wonderful, hardworking, and thoughtful your sons are—both of them. And because you can't see past your own selfish whims, you're going to lose them. You'll wind up an old man, bitter and alone because you drove your family away."

"Well," he sneers. "I see you were in on this too. You can kiss your career at Smith & Boone goodbye. Because once I inform Frank—"

With a snort, I fold my arms over my chest. "Do your worst. I see right through you, Roger Szymanski. And now everyone else does too."

Charlotte snatches a microphone from the cameraman before smoothing her hair. Arranging her expression into one of cool journalistic focus, she strides up to Roger, microphone to her chin. "Excuse me, Roger Szymanski?"

"What?" He turns, and the color leaches from his face.

"Charlotte Owens. Channel Six News. Can you comment on the allegation that you used your political connections with the city of Cleveland to execute a personal vendetta—and against your very own son?"

Roger's face turns so red it's practically eggplant. "No comment." Shoving through the crowd, he storms off in the direction of the festival, Charlotte dogging his heels. The cameraman hoists the massive camera onto his shoulder and follows them at a trot.

"Is there grift at city hall?" she shouts. "What does Szymanski Enterprises stand to gain?" Her voice trails off as they disappear into the distance.

Vindication washes over me, as warm as a heated blanket. Serves Roger right. Maybe he'll even learn something from all this. For Perry's sake, I hope he does.

I turn to Brie, who's staring at me, mouth hanging open.

"I need to find Perry. Now," I say.

She closes it with a snap. "He was over there a minute ago." She motions to where he was standing before. "I'd offer to come with, but you're on a roll. Go get him, girl."

Grinning, I slide into the murmuring crowd.

"Cass?" Devin shouts after me, and I look back. His chin quivers as he smiles. "Perry's a lucky guy."

"Lucky to have you for a brother," I call back with a grin before pushing forward. I search every face I pass, but none of them are Perry's. Mom waves at me through the scrum of people, but I don't go to her. I'll fill her in about everything later. Once I break free from the throng, I take off at a run toward Blooms & Baubles—the most logical place for Perry to have gone. The soles of my stone-studded sandals slap against the sidewalk in time to my thundering heart.

Why didn't he stay to talk to me after the segment? I know he missed me telling off his dad, but did he hear me say I love him?

Maybe it doesn't matter. Maybe this was all a mistake . . . maybe I'm too late.

I see it then, in the far distance: a splash of Kelly green a block away. My heart leaps and I skid to a stop in front of Blooms & Baubles. Squinting, I can just make out a man wearing a green T-shirt with white writing on the back. He's walking up Providence Street—away from the festival . . . and me. His golden-brown hair shines in the afternoon sun.

Perry.

Turning the corner, he disappears onto West Twenty-Seventh Street.

"No, no, no."

Without thinking, I run to Brie's car. I know her keyless entry code by heart—4937, the last four digits of her home phone number when she was little—and punch them into the keypad. Opening the door, I launch myself into the driver's seat and take two deep breaths. My heart hammers and my hands shake as I fish her key out of her glove box and stick it in the ignition. I'd rather face down a hundred Roger Szymanskis than drive, but I have to do this. For Perry. Before it's too late.

I turn the key, and the engine roars to life. Sweat trickles down my spine, but I grip the steering wheel. I shift into reverse, backing slowly. My tire bumps the curb and I hit the brakes. My thighs tremble and I dry heave. No, that wasn't an accident. I only grazed a curb. I'm fine. I'm safe. I can do this.

Breathing hard, I shift into drive and turn the wheel. As soon as I clear the news van, I hit the gas. A flash of green darts across my vision, and a man leaps into the road in front of me, spreading his arms wide. Screaming, I slam on the breaks.

Chest heaving, I stare through the windshield. At Perry.

He's standing directly in front of me, a tissue paper–wrapped bouquet gripped in his fist.

Our eyes connect and my soul temporarily leaves my body.

He's here. He didn't leave after all. Fumbling with the gearshift, I put the car in park, turn off the engine, and step out. He's at my side in a heartbeat.

He looks me over, presumably for signs of injury. "Are you okay? I thought you don't drive—what's going on?"

"I thought you left. I saw you walking up the street. I had to talk to you, so I jumped in Brie's car. I couldn't let you leave without you knowing . . . I love you. I love you, Perry. I don't know how to make it any clearer that I don't want to be with Devin because I love *you* and—"

Without warning, he crushes his mouth against mine in a searing kiss. My skin tingles and my chest expands with giddy joy as he wraps his arms around me. Breaking away, he smooths his thumb over my cheekbone. "I'm sorry for acting like such an idiot. I made a mistake yesterday, giving in to my insecurities. I never should have walked away from you because . . . I love you too, Cass."

A sob threatens to rip through my chest, but before I can speak another word, he kisses me again and I melt into him. His lips are a promise fulfilled, and a glimpse of adventure-filled days to come.

A snicker steals my attention, and I look over my shoulder to find a pair of teenagers filming us on their phones from behind the news van. When they see us looking, they quickly stash their phones and run off in a flurry of giggles. Laughing softly, Perry shakes his head. "I think you and Devin made quite the splash with that interview."

"Brie thinks it might go viral."

Tightening his arms around me, he tugs me closer. "Does that upset you? You never liked to talk about your accident, or your coma, so I know what a sacrifice it was for you to go on live television and share your personal experience with the world."

"It was surprisingly cathartic, actually. Especially when I called your dad out to his face for being a self-serving jerk."

He laughs, but quickly stops, tilting his head. "Wait, what?"

"I'll tell you later." Grinning, I lean forward to kiss him again, but paper crinkles under my chin. Perry's bouquet is wedged between us. "Are those for me?" I ask.

"Of course. I arranged it for you last night. I planned to give it to you today while I begged you to give me a second chance, but that was before you went on live TV and I realized I hadn't lost my shot after all. As soon as your interview was over, I ran up to my apartment to get the flowers I thought you deserved."

Gathering the bouquet in my arms, I admire the silken violet petals interspersed with light and dark green . . . it's exactly like the bouquet he made for me the first day we met, down to the eucalyptus scent. "They're beautiful. So that wasn't you walking down the street?"

"No." Wrapping his arms around me, he kisses me softly on the lips. "I'll never walk away from you again."

And somehow, I know he never will. Because while Devin was the man of my dreams, Perry is the man of my heart.

And for the first time in my life, I'm choosing to follow my heart. And I couldn't be happier.

EPILOGUE

TWO AND A HALF YEARS LATER

Brie pounds on the bathroom door. "Cass, if you don't hurry up, you're going to be late to your own show!"

I quickly loop my purse over my head and drape my wool coat over my arm. I automatically check my hair in the mirror one last time out of habit, even though Rogue Curl has long since grown out, blending in seamlessly with the rest of my long chestnut curls. Stepping into the hallway, I turn in a circle. The wood floorboards creak under my suede boots. "What do you think?"

Adjusting her glasses, Brie smooths one of my sleeves before brushing a speck of lint off the hem of my knee-length, curve-hugging black dress. Stepping back, she gives me a chef's kiss. "Perfection. Perry's not going to know what hit him."

"Thanks, Brie. And that goes double for Marcus." Flicking the hem of her hot-pink tulle skirt, she juts her hip in a mock curtsy and giggles.

It's been almost a year since I moved into Perry's apartment above the shop, but Brie insisted I get dressed at her place tonight, for old time's sake. As much as I wanted to enjoy every minute of tonight with Perry, I couldn't say no. Brie is my first love, after all.

We stroll down the hall arm in arm, and my chest twinges when I pass my old bedroom. Instead of a bed, nightstand, and dresser, it's filled with books, a large, L-shaped desk, and a secondhand armchair. Brie converted it to an office after I moved out—and Marcus moved in a year and a half ago—once she started her part-time aeronautics PhD program at Case, but it's still strange not to see my own furniture in there.

Marcus is waiting at the bottom of the stairs for us, wearing a suit coat and the same goofy-in-love grin he always does whenever he's with Brie.

He bows, doffing an imaginary top hat. "Ladies, you look lovely this evening. Shall we?"

"Does our chariot await, sir?" asks Brie.

"If by chariot you mean Uber, then yes."

Xerxes whistles from his cage in the living room as we leave. Outside, it's snowing. Tugging on my coat, I gaze into the tar-black sky swimming with dancing swirls of white. How lucky am I to exist in a world with such beauty? We pile into the waiting silver sedan, and my phone dings with a text from Val.

> Congrats on the show!!! Sorry I can't be there tonight. Jake has a cold. Sending you my best though! Can't wait to swing by the gallery next week!

> Thanks! Hope the little one feels better soon 🖤

> Tell Eric I say hi!

> Will do

> P.S. Did you see this yet?? All because of you, girl!

Her next text is a link to a local news article: "New Community College Campus Set to Open in Buckeye-Shaker in June." Even though I already read the article earlier today, my chest still strums with triumph. After calling out Roger Szymanski on live television, the city had no choice but to trash his proposal. With propriety, and the city council's reputation, on the line, Councilman Truman was particularly opposed to the idea once he found out the true motives behind Roger's proposal . . . and read a certain thoroughly researched alternative that Devin shared with him the week after our interview. My lungs expand at the thought of how much good a new community college will do for the residents of Buckeye-Shaker . . . and the city of Cleveland as a whole.

Five minutes later, we pull up to West Twenty-Eighth and Providence, in front of the warehouse that once belonged to Roger Szymanski. I smile at my Blooms & Baubles mural. It's faded over the years thanks to the elements, but it's still here, as meaningful as the night I painted it. We circle to the front of the building to a door with a sign that reads Ohio City Artists Co-op. Marcus opens the thick wooden door, and my heart pounds as I step across the threshold and into a cocoon of warm air.

My lips part in surprise. Inside, twinkle lights flicker above a curved white desk. Beyond it, the open gallery is packed with people.

Brie squeezes my hand. "They're all here for you, sweetie."

We hang our coats on the rack next to the desk and walk into the white-walled gallery.

"Cass!" Jackson calls, and he and Liam run over, their dress shoes pounding against the parquet floor.

"Did you really do *all* of this?" Liam's wide eyes rove over the walls filled with artwork—*my* artwork. Canvasses of all sizes line the walls, filled with abstract portraits and multimedia collages, each one telling a story. My story. From my accident to the coma to my memory struggles—which, although they've improved over the years, haven't faded completely—to my revelations about life, love, and finding joy through the choices we make and the people we call family.

I flick a curl off Liam's forehead. "Yeah, can you believe it?"

"I sure can," says Robert, sidling up to us, his arm around my mom.

Eyes shining with tears, Mom wraps me in a bear hug. "I'm sorry I ever thought your art was a waste of time. I'm blown away by you. And so, so proud."

I hug her back before stepping away. "Thanks, Mom. Have you seen Perry, by the way?"

"Did I hear my name?" Strong arms snake around my waist, and I'm pulled backward into a firm chest. I smile up at Perry as he kisses the column of my neck. His familiar woodsy and floral scent envelopes me, and I sigh. "You're late," he whispers, nipping my earlobe.

"Hey, it takes time to look this good."

He turns me in his arms and plants a kiss on my lips. "You always look beautiful."

"Right back at you." And *damn*, but he does look good tonight. He's wearing a full suit and tie, loose around the collar in typical Perry fashion, and his cheekbones gleam in the soft overhead lights.

Jackson pretends to stick his finger down his throat and makes a retching sound. Mom laughs.

"There she is!" a voice booms, and half a dozen of my coworkers from the Cleveland Community Foundation crowd around me. After a round of hugs and "congratulations!" that leave me a little breathless, my boss, Tom, a kindhearted man in his fifties, shakes my hand. "I knew you were a talented lawyer, but an artist too? I'm stunned."

"How did you not know Cass was an artist?" blurts Rosie, our intern. "Didn't you ever see that one video that was all over the Internet a couple years ago? The one that was taken right outside? Cass is famous!"

Tom's eyes widen. "Wait, *you're* Coma Girl?"

There was a time when the moniker would have stung. But ever since my interview with Charlotte went viral, along with the cell phone video of me and Perry kissing, the name has taken on a whole new meaning, one that's near and dear to my heart. Because if it weren't for my coma, I never would have met the love of my life, found my true purpose, or helped him save his business, which is now the most renowned flower shop in the state of Ohio. "That's me."

The next half hour passes by in a blur of handshakes and introductions, well-wishes and thanks. And through it all, Perry never leaves my side. He guides me through the room, his hand at the small of my back, stealing kisses when no one is looking.

An art critic for the *Plain Dealer* introduces herself, and asks me a series of questions, jotting my responses in a little notebook. I excuse myself when I spot Devin and Mercedes walking into the gallery. Her strawberry blond hair is cut shorter now and it's wavier, less styled—not the perfectly smooth sheet it was when we first met. Her pale blue dress swishes around her thighs as Devin takes her coat.

"There's the woman of the hour," says Devin. Grinning at Perry, he gives me a one-armed hug.

"And here's the man of the hour," I say. "This never would have happened if it weren't for you."

Devin shrugs, his smile as charming as ever. "Hey, after all the money came in from the talk show circuit we did, how could I not buy this place—through a secretly created LLC, of course, so Dad wouldn't find out and scuttle the sale. And turning it into an artists' cooperative with a gallery and studio space only felt right, given everything you did for Perry and me." Slipping his arm around Mercedes, he squeezes her hip, and she smiles up at him.

A caterer approaches us, holding a tray. "Champagne, anyone?"

Perry hands one to Devin and me, but when he reaches for two more glasses, Mercedes waves him off. "None for me, thanks."

I look at her sharply. "You're not drinking? Wait . . . are you . . ." I stare at her belly, searching for a bump.

"No." She laughs. "But . . ." She gazes up at Devin, who nods encouragingly. "We started trying."

"Oh my God, guys! That's so exciting! I won't say congratulations, since there's nothing to congratulate . . . *yet* . . . but I'm so happy for you."

"Thanks," says Devin. "Our therapist agrees we're in a really good place, and we're both ready, so why not give it a go? On purpose, this time," he adds, kissing her sweetly.

I raise my champagne. "Cheers to futures full of possibility."

"Cheers," they echo. We clink, and the smoldering look Perry gives me over his glass makes my calves tense and my toes curl inside my boots.

Three hours later, the gallery is mostly empty. Brie finds me chatting with my mom in the corner and gives me one last hug. "Marcus and I are heading out. Congrats again."

"Thanks, Brie."

"Enjoy the rest of your evening." Dropping her chin, she slides a sly look to Perry. He's kneeling on the floor on the other side of the room with Jackson hanging off his back while Liam yanks his arm in an apparent two-on-one wrestling match. They're all laughing. My chest fills with warmth.

"Bye, Mel," she says as she backs away.

"Good night," Mom calls back. Sighing, Mom checks her watch. "It's getting late, and I should get the boys to bed."

"Thanks again for coming, Mom. It means a lot."

She pats my cheek. "I wouldn't have missed it for the world. You've got a good one there, by the way," she says, nodding at Perry. "You're lucky to have each other."

My responding smile comes straight from my soul. "I know."

After Perry and I say goodbye to my family, he slings an arm over my shoulder. "Ready to go home, Ms. Artiste?"

"Definitely."

Gathering our coats, we make the short trek through the snow to our apartment next door. The Colonel hefts himself out of his bed and waddles over when we arrive. At thirteen, he's slowed down quite a bit, but he still greets us in the living room with his typical tail-wagging bark. "*Who's a good doggie?*" I croon as I rub his soft ears. My fingers connect with an unfamiliar collar. Craning my head, I let out a honk of laughter. "Is he wearing a *bow tie?*" I ask Perry.

Loosening his own tie, he drops his keys on the kitchen table. "Just because he couldn't come to the show tonight, doesn't mean he didn't want to celebrate."

Standing, I twine my arms around his neck. "That was sweet. Thank you, Perry. For everything. Tonight was perfect." After two and a half years, I still can't believe how much I love this man. Being with him is just so . . . *easy.* As effortless as breathing.

I kiss him then. It starts out slow and languid, but heat ignites between us, and soon Perry's tugging off my coat. My fingers find the buttons of his shirt and I run my palms along his bare chest.

"Wait." He drags himself away, panting. "I—I have another surprise for you."

"Can't it wait?" I fumble for his belt buckle, but he holds me firm.

"One minute," he says. "Wait here." Eye twinkling, he runs his tongue along his bottom lip and disappears into the bedroom.

Plopping onto a stool in the kitchen, I unzip each boot and slide them off my aching feet. I tap my fingers against my thigh. Gnawing my lip, I meander toward the bedroom and press my ear to the closed door. *What is he up to?* Suddenly, the door opens, and I tumble into Perry's arms with a squawk.

Catching me, he laughs. "You couldn't wait, could you?"

"Patience isn't my strong suit."

Grazing his knuckles along my cheek, Perry steps back, and I gasp. Our candlelit bedroom is filled with flowers. Vases of roses fill every available hard surface from the dresser to the nightstands, while hanging garlands drip from the ceiling. And on the bed, our white comforter is sprinkled with ruby-red petals.

"Perry," I breathe. "When did you do all this?"

He chuckles low in his throat, circling in front of me. He's removed his tie, shoes, and socks, and his cheeks are tinged with pink. "Earlier tonight. That's why Brie asked you to get ready at her place."

Shaking my head, I laugh. "She was in on it?"

"Totally." He runs his thumb along my knuckles, swallowing. "And . . . there's one more thing."

Reaching into his pocket, he pulls out a small black box, and drops to one knee. Inhaling sharply, I cover my mouth.

"Cassidy Walker, the last two and a half years with you have been the best of my life. When you chose me that day at the festival, I felt like I'd won the lottery on a cosmic scale. But what I didn't know is that every day after that would be even better than the last. The way you see the world, and the possibilities within it, inspires me to be my best self because that's what you do—uplift everyone around you simply by being yourself. You're courageous, caring, kind, and the most brilliant person I've ever known. Each day with you is a gift, and I don't want to spend the rest of my life anywhere except by your side."

He flips open the lid to reveal a silver band holding a square-cut emerald. It's the same shade of green as his eyes, which he knows all too well is my favorite color. "Will you marry m—"

I throw myself into his arms. "Yes!"

Standing, he takes my trembling hand and slides the ring onto my finger.

"I love you, Perry." I look up at him, and he kisses me—long, slow, and sweet. Smiling against his lips, I flatten my palms against his chest and push him onto the bed. We both laugh, and he tugs me down on top of him. Rose petals scatter around us like falling snow.

The mood changes, urgency blooming between us. Gathering the hem of my dress, he yanks it up and over my head. In between kisses, I manage to remove his shirt, pants, and boxers. He groans when I curl my fingers around his hard length, and the sound burrows into my belly. Eyes shining in the candlelight, he unlatches my bra and tosses it aside before scooping me up and flipping me over so I'm stretched out beneath him.

I moan as he drags kisses over my jaw, down the line of my neck, along my collar bone, and lower still. When he traces his tongue along the curve of my hip, I arch my back, and he peels off my panties in one fluid motion. My skin flames everywhere he touches me. His delicious weight, the friction of skin against skin, and every sinful swirl of his tongue sends me spinning closer to bliss. But I can't get close enough. Can't get enough of *him*.

Blood pounds through my veins. "I need you," I rasp. "Now."

"Okay," he whispers, dragging his thumb over his glistening lips. Climbing up my body, he nudges my legs wider, positions himself, and enters me in one long, slow slide. I gasp at the sudden sensation of fullness. Stilling, he runs his fingers through my hair, gazing at me in pure reverence. "I love you so much."

While his kisses are tender, his pace is not. We move together, faster, more desperate, until we're both panting with need. The pleasure builds. I'm close. So close.

When he reaches between us and circles his fingers where I want them the most, I tip over the edge. Several thrusts later he joins me, and we collapse in a satisfied, sweaty heap.

"You know," I say between heavy breaths. "I think I'm the lucky one here."

"Oh yeah? Why's that?" He's equally out of breath. Arm tossed above his head, eyes half closed, hair disheveled from my raking fingers—this is my favorite Perry. Perfectly happy, utterly unguarded, and authentically himself. I don't think I've ever seen anything so beautiful.

Rolling onto my side to face him, I prop myself up with one arm. My emerald ring winks in the flickering light of the candles, sending tingles down my spine. It couldn't be more perfect if I'd picked it out myself. Smiling, I trace my fingertips along his chest. "Because I get to spend the rest of my life with *you*."

Turning over my hand, he kisses my open palm. "And what a life it will be."

What a life, indeed. Nestling against his bare chest, I close my eyes. He presses a kiss to my temple, and I sigh.

Perry is my fate, my forever.

He's my dream come true.

Acknowledgments

Dream On started as a literal dream, and I feel fortunate beyond words for all the love and support I've received from so many, without whom this book never would have come to fruition.

Huge thanks to my agent, Jess Watterson, for cheering me on every step of the way, even when the (pandemic) going got tough. You're the deliverer of dreams and my publishing journey guru. I'm so very grateful to have you in my corner (#bestagentever).

To my wonderfully talented editor, Molly Gregory: working with you is an honor and a dream come true. This story never would have come together the way it did without your insightful feedback, brainstorming help, and support—thank you. Heartfelt thanks to the entire Gallery Books team for their support as well: my publisher, Jen Bergstrom; deputy publisher, Jen Long; publicity/marketing director, Sally Marvin; publicist, Lucy Nalen; marketing specialist, Mackenzie Hickey; managing editor, Caroline Pallotta; production editor, Christine Masters; copyeditor, Faren Bachelis; art director, Lisa Litwack; and editorial director, Aimée Bell.

To my UK publisher, Headline Eternal, and editor, Kate Byrne: thank you, once again, for bringing my words to readers across the pond! I'm thrilled and deeply grateful.

To anyone who's experienced pregnancy loss and felt moved to talk about it: from the bottom of my heart, thank you. I patterned the pregnancy loss in *Dream On* after my own miscarriage a few years back, and I never would have mustered the courage to revisit the experience and reflect it in the pages of a book if it weren't for the many brave individuals who have chosen to share their stories. (P.S. If you're reading this, and you're among the one in four who have encountered pregnancy loss and experienced the complicated trauma that can accompany it: please know I see you, I feel you, and I care. Support is out there. You're not alone.)

Much love and thanks to Karen Cullinane, Erinn Ervin, and Katy Holloway for buoying me every day with our group text antics. You're my boxing gloves, my glass of wine at the end of a hard day, and my springy cushion when I fall. I love you guys.

Thank you, Megan Keck, for FaceTiming with me at the height of the pandemic to talk about all things restaurants and the service industry. While the story ultimately took a turn away from that particular plotline, I'm grateful for your willingness to let me pick apart your brain—and that I get to call you a friend.

To Amanda Uhl, thank you for reading early chapters of *Dream On* and letting me bounce ideas off you. And thanks to my good friend Lindsey Davis for accompanying me on a mini–writers' retreat to Ohio City, and for your friendship over many years (and ever-willingness to commiserate about all of life's speed bumps). Cleveland buds for life!

Thanks to my street team of enthusiastic readers, aka the "Shippers," for your time, energy, and continued support. I adore and appreciate you so very much!

Thank you to sweet-as-pie Gracie from the Flower Shoppe in Strongsville for serving as the loose inspiration behind The Colonel—lily pollen splotches and all! And thanks to Mike Dunn for inviting me to your Fourth of July party at the lake all those years ago! It was a blast drawing on my memories of the location for the setting of the lakeside party in *Dream On* (if not the company, because you and your friends are straight-up awesome and pure fun—no Roger Szymanskis in sight).

To Wellesley College alums near and far: I feel lucky beyond measure to be part of such an empowering community. Thanks to you, I believe I can *do*.

Gratitude to the city of Cleveland, and all the folks who are working so hard to uplift and strengthen communities throughout Northeast Ohio. The grit, heart, and tenacity of this city, and the people who call it home, have inspired me deeply. I couldn't imagine setting *Dream On*, and Cass's journey, anywhere else.

Finally, to my family—my bedrock of support—I couldn't have written this book without you!

Thanks to my mom, Sandy, for always believing in me and encouraging me to step outside my comfort zone and simply *go for it*. I feel fortunate to have been raised by such a strong, hardworking single mom (and badass boss bitch to boot!). Thank you for being my number one cheerleader on this roller-coaster journey!

To the best in-laws ever and my resident Cleveland experts: I can always count on you for an encouraging word and genuine insights on life. Thanks for making me feel like I'm the daughter you never had.

To my stepdad, Don: thanks for your unwavering love and support. Your presence is like a warm blanket in a chaotic world. I appreciate you.

Thank you, Grandma, for your rock-steady support and lifelong love. We're kindred spirits, you and I, and had we been born at the same time, I'm convinced we would have been like Brie and Cass, getting up to countless shenanigans together. I love you.

To my son, Cooper, aka the light of my life and the funniest little dude I know: being your mom is the greatest of adventures, and you make me smile every single day. Thank you for filling my heart and motivating me to be my best self.

To my husband, Jimmy: how lucky am I to have you as a partner? Thank you for doing the laundry . . . and the dishes . . . and the grocery shopping . . . and bedtime routines, cleaning, organizing, dog walking, and basically tackling more than your fair share of household chores when the rubber hit the road with this manuscript. *Dream On* never would have happened if it weren't for you stepping up to the plate and offering your unconditional support. I love you.

Thank you to the booksellers, reviewers, bloggers, Bookstagrammers, BookTokers, librarians, educators, and everyone who shares their love of reading and encourages people to pick up a book. I'm eternally grateful for what you do!

And finally, to all of the readers out there who gave *Dream On* a chance: thank you, thank you, thank you! You mean the world to me, truly. I feel privileged to have the chance to share this story with you, and I sincerely hope you enjoyed it. Thank you for reading!

It's About Time

LIZ EVERS

It's
About
Time

From CALENDARS and CLOCKS to
MOON CYCLES and LIGHT YEARS
– A HISTORY

METRO BOOKS
New York

METRO BOOKS
New York

An Imprint of Sterling Publishing
1166 Avenue of the Americas
New York, NY 10036

METRO BOOKS and the distinctive Metro Books logo are
trademarks of Sterling Publishing Co., Inc.

Cover design by Ana Bjezancevic
Designed and typeset by K DESIGN, Somerset
Illustrations by Greg Stevenson

Maps on pages 108 and 125 by David Woodroffe

ISBN 978-1-4351-6121-4

For information about custom editions, special sales,
and premium and corporate purchases, please contact
Sterling Special Sales at 800-805-5489 or specialsales@
sterlingpublishing.com.

Manufactured by CPI Group (UK) Ltd, Croydon, CR0 4YY

2 4 6 8 10 9 7 5 3 1

www.sterlingpublishing.com

Contents

Acknowledgements

My sincerest thanks to all at Michael O'Mara Books, especially to my editor Anna Marx for her support, enthusiasm and input, Ana Bježančević for her ever-lovely design work, and Greg Stevenson for his wonderful illustrations. Thanks also to Dan O'Grady and my brother Peter Evers for all their useful suggestions. And finally the biggest thank you goes to my great friend and editor-extraordinaire, Silvia Crompton, for all the precious time she has given to me these past few years.

Introduction

A few years ago some startling images were captured by Brazil's Indian Affairs Department. Taken from a plane flying high above the Amazon near the border of Brazil and Peru, the images showed members of an 'uncontacted' tribe. Some were painted red, others black, but all were looking up curiously at the metal bird cutting through the sky above.

Looking at these images felt a bit like time travel; looking at the past in the present, or two dimensions co-existing. These people do not know that it's the 'twenty-first century'. To them, we are the weird creatures from another time, possibly even another world. How long this 'past' in the Amazon can continue is uncertain, as modern man encroaches ever more into these ancient tribal lives, sometimes violently, in the name of progress.

A few months after these images entered the public domain I came across another story, this time about a recently contacted tribe, the Amondawa in Brazil. First 'discovered' by anthropologists in 1986, the Amondawa do not have an abstract concept of time. They have no word for time, or divisions of time – such as months or years. Rather than talk about age they assign different names to each other to indicate the different stages of their lives or their status within their community. They have no 'time technology' – no calendars or clocks – and only a limited numbering system.

What struck me is just how difficult this kind of life is to comprehend. And I realized how obsessed we modern people are with time – especially not having enough of it – and just how unique the Amondawa are in the absence of this obsession. I also realized how little I understood about time, how we capture and create it, and how our Earth and our bodies interact with it.

We each live in our own psychological time – memories of the past, anticipation for the future – and these 'time zones' co-exist with our present, our now. And we experience time subjectively – an hour is a long time in a doctor's waiting room, but can fly by with good friends.

This book goes back to the beginning of time as we know it – right back to the beginning of the universe and starts from there. It pieces together the history of time as perceived and processed by our forebears and by the great scientific minds of our current age – and it also tries to have a little fun along the way.

We'll journey through geological ages, meet dinosaurs and distant cousins, tell time by the Moon and the Sun, and learn about the clocks within us which dictate the rhythms of our daily lives. We'll look at the evolution of time technologies, from the earliest calendars etched on the bones of eagles' wings to quantum clocks. We'll see how time is speeding up and how it's slowing down, we'll travel into the future through wormholes and black holes, span light years and peek into parallel dimensions. And for aspiring time travellers, there will be tips and tricks for journeying into the past and future along the way.

1
The Land Before Time

Happy Birthday Planet Earth

In 1654, the Anglican Bishop of Armagh, James Usher, announced that the universe was created at six o'clock on the evening of 22 October 4004 BCE. He reportedly came to this rather definitive conclusion after years of studying the Bible and world history. This theory of the Earth's age was pretty popular right up to the nineteenth century, when the study of geology and Darwin's theory of evolution made it clear that the world was considerably older.

It is now widely believed to be 4.54 billion years old – or written out in full – 4,540,000,000 years old. That's a lot of years. The 4.54 billion figure has been reached using rather complex mathematics combined with the methods of 'radiometric' dating – which include radiocarbon dating, potassium-argon dating and uranium lead dating.

At its most basic, radiometric dating looks at radioactive decay. It compares the amount of a naturally occurring radioactive chemical component (isotope) and its decay products – we know, for example, that the radioactive component uranium decays to become lead, so looking at the amount of lead left in a rock one can calculate how much uranium there would have been to start with and so how long it has taken to produce the lead.

Applying these techniques to really, really old rocks and minerals – including meteorites and lunar samples – the magic figure of 4.54 billion has been reached and agreed upon. For now.

The oldest known terrestrial materials are zircon crystals found in Western Australia. These have been dated as over 4.4 billion years old. The oldest known meteorite matter is 4.567 billion years old. It is believed that our solar system can't be much older than these samples.

Which brings us to the time before there was an Earth, or a solar system to house it. To when our

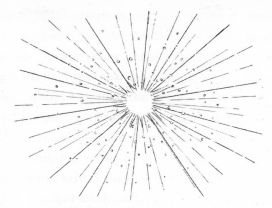

The Big Bang is dated as starting 13.5 and 13.75 billion years ago

universe was born. The prevailing theory is that of the Big Bang, when the universe started expanding from a dense and hot state – and continues to expand into space, which is itself continually expanding.

The geologic time scale

Coming back down to Earth again, something called the 'geologic' time scale is used by earth scientists, geologists and palaeontologists to describe timings and events in our Earth's past. It relates time to 'stratigraphy' – the study of layers of rocks (stratification).

There are many wonderful examples of stratification bearing testament to the Earth's long history. Examples are found in chalk layers in Cyprus, the stunning Colorado Plateau in Utah, exposed strata on mountain faces in the French Alps, and the amazing Stratified Island near La Paz, Mexico, to name but a few.

The units used to describe geologic time are very long. They include Eons (half a billion years), Eras (several hundred million years), Epochs (tens of millions of years), and Ages (millions of years).

Taking it as read that the Earth is 4.54 billion years old, the deposits of our old pal zircon, the oldest known mineral, were found during the Hadean Eon in the Cryptic Era. This is when the Moon and Earth were formed. Between 500 and 600 million years later in the Eoarchean Era, simple single-celled life came into being, evidence for which is found in microfossils – that is, fossils which are not larger than four millimetres, and often smaller than one millimetre, and which can only be studied using light or electron microscopy.

Skipping ahead to the Proterozoic Eon, geologic evidence shows that our atmosphere became oxygenic (specifically during the Palaeoproterozoic

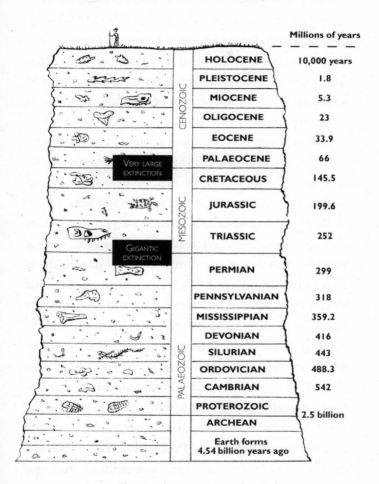

		Millions of years
	HOLOCENE	10,000 years
	PLEISTOCENE	1.8
CENOZOIC	MIOCENE	5.3
	OLIGOCENE	23
	EOCENE	33.9
	PALAEOCENE	66
	CRETACEOUS	145.5
MESOZOIC	JURASSIC	199.6
	TRIASSIC	252
	PERMIAN	299
	PENNSYLVANIAN	318
	MISSISSIPPIAN	359.2
	DEVONIAN	416
PALAEOZOIC	SILURIAN	443
	ORDOVICIAN	488.3
	CAMBRIAN	542
	PROTEROZOIC	2.5 billion
	ARCHEAN	
	Earth forms 4.54 billion years ago	

VERY LARGE EXTINCTION

GIGANTIC EXTINCTION

The geologic time scale

Era some 2.05 billion years ago), then the first complex single-celled life, protists, came into being around 1.8 billion years ago.

It took another 1.2 billion years for the first fossils of multi-celled animals (worms, sponges, soft jelly-like creatures) to show up during the Neo-proterozoic Era (around 635 million years ago) and these evolved into yet more complex fishy creatures during the long Palaeozoic Era (between 541 and 255 million years ago). By the end of this Era the landmass known as Pangaea had formed, comprised of North America, Europe, Asia, South America, Africa, Antarctica, and Australia. Various reptiles and amphibians were roaming about and basic flora, mosses and primitive seed plants had developed, while a host of marine life flourished in shallow reefs.

Thence to the Mesozoic Era. During its Triassic, Jurassic and Cretaceous Periods (between 252 and 72 million years ago) the dinosaurs, first mammals and crocodilia appeared. Then flowering plants and all manner of new types of insects. Towards the end of the Cretaceous Period there were many new species of dinosaur (though not for long) and creatures equivalent to modern crocodiles and sharks. Primitive birds replaced pterosaurs and the first marsupials appeared. Plus atmospheric CO_2 was close to our present-day levels.

Which brings us to our own Era – the Cenozoic – which started some 66 million years ago and is often referred to as the 'age of mammals'. In the early part of this Era, the dinosaurs were extinct (more on this to follow) and mammals were diversifying, but it would still be another 40-plus million years before the first apes, our evolutionary ancestors, appeared.

And it wasn't until just 200,000 years ago that the first anatomically modern humans appeared and only 50,000 years ago during the Holocene Epoch (which we're still in) that we started tinkering with stone tools.

The bottom line is the Earth is very old, and we are very young upon it. To put things in perspective, if you think of the age of the Earth as a 24-hour clock, the first humans appear just 40 seconds before midnight at 23:59:20.

So what happened to the dinosaurs?

It is now generally agreed that the catchily titled 'Cretaceous-Palaeogene extinction event', which happened approximately 65.5 million years ago, led to the mass extinction of the dinosaurs.

However, the actual nature of the event is still a matter of considerable discussion. Theories range from a massive asteroid or meteor impact to increased volcanic activity altering the biosphere and significantly reducing the amount of sunlight reaching Earth.

Whatever it was, the event left behind a geological signature known variously as the Cretaceous-Palaeogene boundary, K-T boundary or K-Pg boundary. Non-avian dinosaurs were wiped out, their fossils lying below the boundary, indicating they became extinct during the event. The small number of dinosaur fossils that have been found above the boundary have been explained as having eroded from their original positions and preserved in later sedimentary layers. You can see exposed areas of the boundary in wilderness areas and state parks, such as at Trinidad Lake, Colorado, and Drumheller in Alberta, Canada.

Ice ages

Technically, we are still in an ice age. Admittedly at the tail end of it, the worst was over around 12,500 years ago. It began 2.6 million years ago, but the presence of ice sheets in Greenland and the Antarctic signal its continued existence.

The Swiss geographer and engineer Pierre Martel (1706–1767) was the first to posit the theory of ice ages. On a visit to the Chamonix valley in the Alps, he observed that the dispersal of boulders pointed to the fact that the glaciers had once been much larger, but had contracted with time. And this phenomenon was observable in other parts of Switzerland, Scandinavia and later noted in the Chilean Andes. But it wasn't until the 1870s that the theory was widely accepted as fact.

In addition to the erratic dispersal of large boulders, other evidence of ice ages comes in the form of rock scouring and scratching, valley cutting, the creation of small hills called drumlins and unusual patterns in the distribution of fossils.

There have been at least five ice ages in our Earth's history – and outside of these ages the Earth appears

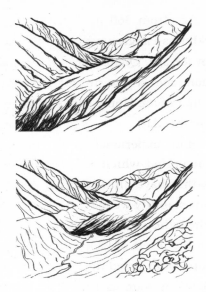

Contraction of a glacier in Chamonix

to have been free of ice, even at high latitudes. The first ice age was the Huronian, which is thought to have extended from 2.4 billion years ago to 2.1 billion years ago (that's before the existence of complex single-celled life forms). This was followed by the Cryogenian from 850 to 635 million years ago (when multi-celled creatures were evolving); the relatively short Andean-Saharan from 460 to 430 million years ago (as more complex marine life was evolving); the

Karoo Ice Age from 360 to 260 million years ago (as the landmass Pangaea was forming); and finally the current ice age, Quaternary, which started 2.58 million years ago (a few hundred thousand years before the first of the Homo genus had evolved) and continues to this day.

We are now experiencing a relatively stable 'interglacial' period, which has provided the climate conditions that have allowed our race to flourish. Without this stability we may not have survived.

As to when the next ice age begins in earnest depends on the levels of CO_2 in the atmosphere. A sudden drop would speed up the arrival of the next ice age – even as soon as 15,000 years hence. But estimates based on rising CO_2 (the more likely case given our penchant for fossil fuels) suggest that our current interglacial period may persist for another 50,000 years or even considerably longer.

Human evolution

It is astonishing how recent is most of our knowledge about ourselves and our planet. As mentioned above, the concept of ice ages was only first posited in the mid-1700s and generally accepted in the 1870s.

The ideas of the 'evolution' of species, including humans, and 'natural selection' have only been knocking around since the mid-1800s, and only brought to the fore in 1859 when Charles Darwin (1809–1882) published *On the Origin of Species*. Even so, it took many more decades for Darwin's ideas about evolution to become mainstream and be incorporated into life sciences. Thinking about the Earth's age as a 24-hour clock again, the most infinitesimal units of time measurement would be required to place these discoveries in our planet's natural history.

There was uproar just a century and half ago when Darwin more explicitly outlined his theories about human evolution in his seminal 1871 book *The Descent of Man, and Selection in Relation to Sex*. In it he suggests that human races evolved from a common ancestor – and that common ancestor from a succession of animals over millennia. It was an idea appalling to the majority of the day.

But with close study and uncovering ever more substantive evidence, the proof for many of Darwin's ideas became too compelling to deny. The evolutionary theory that emerged is now widely accepted as fact by the scientific community, if not by various religious communities. To this day 'Creationists', like our friend James Usher (1581-1656), Bishop of Armagh, believe the world was created by God in six days around 4004 BCE.

Our now considerable knowledge of the geologic time scale and fossil records gives us a fascinating portrait of the development of life on Earth. And discoveries in archaeology, palaeontology and DNA research continue to provide a vivid picture of our evolution as a species. We've seen already that it was just 200,000 years ago that the first anatomically modern humans appeared.

The Homo genus

It is thought that primates, from whom humans are descended, diverged from other mammals about 85 million years ago, though the earliest fossil records we have are from around 55 million years ago. The first bipeds diverged around 4 to 6 million years ago, splitting from cousin primates like chimpanzees with whom we share a common ancestor, and eventually evolving into the genus, or biological classification, Homo. There is no definitive timeline for the Homo genus, and there are many candidates for the evolutionary links in our chain:

25

HOMO HABILIS
(3 TO 2 MILLION YEARS AGO)

The first documented members of the genus Homo, *Homo habilis* evolved around 2.3 million years ago in South and East Africa. It is thought to be the earliest species to use stone tools. *Homo habilis*'s brains were around the size of a chimpanzee's. In May 2010, a new species, *Homo gautengensis,* was discovered in South Africa and may have evolved earlier than *Homo habilis*, but this has yet to be agreed conclusively.

HOMO RUDOLFENSIS AND HOMO GEORGICUS
(1.9 TO 1.6 MILLION YEARS AGO)

These are proposed species names for fossils from about 1.9 to 1.6 million years ago but whose relation to *Homo habilis* is not yet clear. There is just one *Homo rudolfensis* specimen – an incomplete skull from Kenya, which may or may not be another *Homo habilis*. *Homo georgicus* comes from Georgia, in the Caucasus region, and may be an intermediate form between *Homo habilis* and *Homo erectus*.

HOMO ERECTUS
(1.8 MILLION TO 70,000 YEARS AGO)

Homo erectus had a long evolutionary lifespan. Records indicate that the species lived from about 1.8 million to about 70,000 years ago, possibly being largely wiped out by the so-called Toba catastrophe (a volcanic super-eruption in Indonesia, where many of the significant *Homo erectus* fossil finds are). It is thought that some populations of *Homo habilis* evolved larger brains and started to use more elaborate stone tools – leading to the new advanced classification *Homo erectus*. Other key physiological changes include the evolution of locking knees and

27

a different location of the foramen magnum (the hole in the skull where the spine enters).

HOMO HEIDELBERGENSIS
(800,000 TO 300,000 YEARS AGO)

Homo heidelbergensis (also 'Heidelberg Man', after the University of Heidelberg) could be the direct ancestor of both *Homo neanderthalensis* (Neanderthals, see page 29) in Europe and *Homo sapiens*. The missing link, if you will. The best evidence found for these hominines dates them to between 600,000 and 400,000 years ago, but it is thought that they may have lived from about 800,000 to about 300,000 years ago.

Homo heidelbergensis used stone-tool technology that was very close to those used by *Homo erectus*, and recent findings of twenty-eight skeletons in Atapuerca in Spain suggest that this species may have been the first of the Homo genus to bury their dead. It is also thought that *Homo heidelbergensis* may have had a primitive form of language, although no forms of art (often equated with symbolic thinking and language) have been uncovered in relation to this species.

HOMO SAPIENS
(250,000 TO 200,000 YEARS AGO TO PRESENT)

The most important evolutionary period for our species occurred between 400,000 and 250,000 years ago – the period of transition from *Homo erectus* to *Homo sapiens*. During this time, our cranial sizes expanded, meaning bigger brains, and we began to use ever-increasingly elaborate stone tools. As a species *Homo sapiens* are highly homogenous, genetically speaking. This is relatively unusual in any species so widely disbursed and is seen as evidence that we evolved in a particular place (Africa) and migrated from there. But we have evolved certain region-specific adaptive traits such as skin colour, and eyelid and nose shapes, for example.

Neanderthal man

Named after the Neander Valley in Germany where the species was first discovered, Neanderthals are alternatively classified as a subspecies of *Homo sapiens* or as a separate species but of the same Homo genus.

The earliest Neanderthals are though to have appeared in Europe 600,000 to 350,000 years ago (no evidence of Neanderthals has been found in Africa) – and to have survived there until around 25,000 years ago. Often characterized as primitive creatures with low brows and weak chins, they in fact used advanced tools (projectile points, bone tools), had a language and lived in complex social groups. The Neanderthal cranial capacity is thought to have been the same size as modern humans, possibly bigger. And when it comes to brains in the Homo genus, size really does matter.

Neanderthals disappeared from the fossil record about 25,000 years ago. Theories abound as to what happened to them. But apart from hypotheses about a volcanic 'super-eruption' or their slowness to adapt to rapid changes in climate leading to their demise, it seems that the worst thing for Neanderthals was us. It is thought that Neanderthals were most likely driven to extinction because of living in competition with ever-expanding human populations. However, there is also evidence to suggest that we absorbed them through interbreeding. This latter idea is particular intriguing and DNA sequencing evidence from 2010 suggests that modern non-African humans in Europe and Asia share 1% to 4% of their genes with Neanderthals.

Hobbit or human?

Nicknamed the 'hobbit' because of its small size, *Homo floresiensis* is a recently discovered species said to have lived between 100,000 and 12,000 years ago on the Indonesian island of Flores. In 2003, a female *Homo floresiensis* skeleton was found and dated as approximately 18,000 years old. When alive, she would have been under one meter in height. She could just be a modern human with pathological dwarfism – after all, there were pygmies living on neighbouring islands until 1,400 years ago. Though the fact that this female had a particularly small skull size and therefore brain may keep the debate open a while yet.

The Three Ages

Human prehistory is frequently divided up into three ages: Stone, Bronze and Iron.

All members of the Homo genus, from *habilis* to *sapiens*, existed within a period broadly defined as the 'Stone Age'– which lasted 3 million years or so and only ended between 4500 and 2000 BCE with the advent of metalworking at different times among different human populations.

Because of the enormous length of the Stone Age relative to the metal ages that followed (Bronze and Iron), it has been subdivided into three eras: the Palaeolithic (itself divided into lower, middle and late – characterized by control of fire and use of stone tools); the Mesolithic (first use of advanced technologies including the bow and canoe); and the Neolithic (pottery, general domestication and significant burial/religious site building).

Following the length of the Stone Age, the Bronze Age was a mere blink of an eye. Characterized by the ability to smelt and fashion metals such as copper and bronze to make weapons, utensils and jewellery,

the Bronze Age started at approximately the same time in the most populous regions of the Earth, between 3750 and 3000 BCE in Europe, the Near East, India and China, but later in other areas (800 BCE in Korea, for example) and it ended between 1200 and 600 BCE. Writing is considered to have been invented during this period in Mesopotamia and Ancient Egypt, and the oldest known literary texts date from 2700 to 2600 BCE. Civilizations developed during this period – most notably in Mesopotamia which included Sumer and the Akkadian, Babylonian, and Assyrian empires, all now part of modern-day Iraq.

Next up was the Iron Age, which wasn't just about iron, but also the use of steel. This period started earliest in the Ancient Near East (Anatolia, Cyprus, Egypt, Persia) around 1300 BCE, then Europe and India around 1200 BCE and later in other parts of Asia: China (600 BCE), Korea (400 BCE) and Japan (100 BCE). The Iron Age lasted into the Common Era, ending around 400 CE in Europe and as late as 500 CE in Japan. Significant texts dating from this period include the Indian Vedas, the Hebrew Bible (Old Testament) and the earliest literature from Ancient Greece.

BC or *BCE?*

Because of its Christian connotations, BC (meaning 'Before Christ') is now often changed to BCE (meaning 'Before Common Era'). AD (Anno Domini, meaning 'In the year of our Lord') is increasingly replaced with the secular CE (meaning 'Common Era'). But whichever way one pitches it, the origin of 'Year One' is unchanged, coinciding with the assigned birth year of Jesus.

Time-Travel Tip
Visit the Grand Canyon!

An astonishing wilderness of rock, the Grand Canyon in Arizona is considered one of the Seven Natural Wonders of the World. A trip to the 277-mile-long canyon is also a trip to 2 billion years of the Earth's geological history – exposed in glorious layer after layer of rock record. Journeying into the perfectly preserved caves and cliff dwellings takes you back to the time when the ancient Pueblo people populated the region around 1200 BCE.

2
Marking Time

Nature's timekeepers

The Earth, the Sun, the stars and the Moon were following their own cycles and rhythms long before humans invented the notion of timekeeping. The planet's rotation, the seasons, the gravitational effects of the Sun and the Moon, the growth patterns of trees and plants, are all part of an intricate and interconnected natural timekeeping that the world does all by itself.

The Sun and the Moon

Every day as the Earth spins on its axis, the Sun rises in the East and sets in the West. The planet completes

35

an annual orbit of the Sun following a pattern that demarks the seasons across the world and dictates the behaviour of all the plant and animal life that draw their nourishment from the Sun. The Sun rises and sets at radically different times depending on where you are. In the tropical areas north and south of the equator, it rises around 6 a.m. and sets at 6 p.m. with reassuring predictability – creating a near-perfect 12-hour day. But at the Earth's poles the lengths of days vary considerably. Sometimes the Sun never sets and sometimes it never rises.

The Sun lights different parts of our Moon each day of the month, though we always see the same 'face' of the Moon. About 29 days and 12 hours elapse between full moons, when the whole face is visible, and from this duration humans created months – though we've since tampered with the length to suit our solar-based calendars, with months now averaging 30.4 days.

The Moon's close proximity to the Earth (some 380,000 km away) creates a significant gravitational pull – strong enough to cause the tides in our oceans. 'High tide' occurs as the Moon passes over the world, pulling the water in its seas up into a hump, which follows around the planet behind the Moon. The

Earth itself is pulled by the Moon, leaving another hump of water on the side away from the Moon that forms the second high tide. So as the Earth rotates there are two high tides every day in coastal areas.

Because it is further away from the Earth, the Sun's gravitational pull is less influential. But when the Sun and Moon align with the Earth, the two gravitational pulls combine to create stronger 'spring' tides. This happens every fourteen days. Because the Moon takes a little more than 24 hours to orbit the Earth, the gap between tides is around 12 hours and 25 minutes.

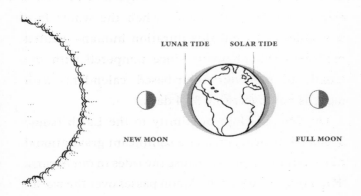

Spring tides result in higher than average high waters and stronger tidal currents

But the Moon's influence on the sea doesn't end with the tides. It extends to creatures living within it. Oysters open and shut their shells in response to the gravitational pull of the Moon. And apparently the best time to go fishing is at the time of the new moon, when the Moon passes between the Earth, and the Sun is either completely invisible from Earth or visible only as a very narrow crescent.

Once in a blue moon

A 'blue moon' is indeed a rare thing. But it does happen every now and then – twice in every five years or so – when two full moons appear in a 1-month period. If there's a full moon on the first of a month with thirty-one days, then there'll be a second full moon, or blue moon, on the last day of that month.

The phrase can also relate to something a lot more literal, when pollution and dust from volcanoes or fires fill the atmosphere and alter our perception of the moon's colour, making it appear blue.

Tree rings

Every year trees grow during the summer and stop during the cold winter months – creating a new annual growth ring. Thinner rings show that growth was unimpressive in a given year, while the opposite is true of thicker rings. Rings can help us to find out the age of the tree and to gauge the weather conditions in certain years.

The oldest known living tree bears the appropriate name Methuselah. It is a Great Basin bristlecone pine located in Inyo County, California, and in 2013 was estimated to be between 4,845 and 4,846

Methuselah, the oldest known living tree

years old. However, it is believed that an olive tree known as 'The Sisters' in the Batroun district of Lebanon is older still – anything between 6,000 and 6,800 years old.

The so-called Bodhi tree, a sacred fig located in Anuradhapura, Sri Lanka, was planted in 288 BCE and is the oldest living tree to have been grown by humans. According to legend, it was under a sapling from this tree that Buddha became enlightened.

Sun worship

The Sun as a deity appears throughout most of the known ancient religions. Our Neolithic ancestors built great monuments to it to celebrate significant astronomical events. The ancient Egyptians personified it as Ra or Horus, the ruler of the sky, the Earth, and the underworld. The Aztecs had Tonatiuh as their sun god and the leader of heaven, a god that required bloody human sacrifice in return for moving around the world. The Greeks had Helios, a handsome sun god crowned with a shining aureole or halo who drove his chariot of the sun around the world each day.

There are four key dates for our sun-worshipping forebears during the year: the Spring Equinox

*Helios, the personification of the Sun in
Greek mythology*

(20 or 21 March), Summer Solstice (20 or 21
June), Autumn Equinox (22 or 23 September) and
Winter Solstice (21 or 22 December). In Europe,
two of our most treasured Neolithic monuments,
Stonehenge in England and Newgrange in Ireland,
were constructed to channel the Sun's rays in a
symbolic way on the Summer and Winter Solstices
respectively. The Summer Solstice marks the
longest day of the year, when the Sun is highest in
the sky, the Winter the shortest day, when the Sun is
at its lowest. The Equinoxes occur when the centre
of the Sun is in the same plane as the equator.

A large proportion of the planet continues to mark the Winter Solstice though many are unaware that that is what they are doing. It is no mistake that Christmas Day is in such close proximity to the Winter Solstice – being a deliberate attempt to co-opt the existing pagan festival. The same can be said of Easter (Spring Equinox) – which is why both celebrations are such a strange blend of Christian and pagan traditions.

Seasons

In the Western world we divide our years up into four distinct seasons (winter, spring, summer and autumn or fall), which tie in with shifts in the weather, and the behaviour of plants and animals in relation to it, and are handily marked by Solstices and Equinoxes.

But such seasons are geographically unique. For example, India recognizes six seasons: hot, rainy or monsoon, autumn, winter, cool season and spring. And in many parts of Africa there are two seasons: dry and rainy. The ancient Egyptians talked of three: flood, winter and summer – each made up of four months. And for a long time the ancient Greeks didn't have an autumn season to go with their spring, summer and winter. Germanic peoples living in the more extreme conditions of Iceland and Scandinavian countries had just two seasons: winter and summer. The words and concepts of spring and autumn were introduced through contact with the Romans.

In Western countries it is widely agreed that the seasons begin in March (spring), June (summer), September (autumn) and December (winter). But in Ireland, for example, the seasons are considered to begin a month earlier, tying in with ancient festivals, most notably Bealtaine on 1 May and Samhain on 1 November – still celebrated with gusto by pagans in Ireland today.

Computus

Computus is the calculation of the date of Easter used by the Roman Catholic Church, since the Middle Ages. In principle, Easter is determined to follow the full moon that chases the Spring Equinox (on 21 March). The earliest possible date for Easter is 22 March, the latest is 25 April.

Months, weeks and days

Months

As previously noted, the time division of 'month' has its origin in the cycle of the Moon, with 29.5 days between full moons. It was only when the notion of the year came into play that the 29.5 number became inconvenient, as it does not tally with the time it takes for the Earth to orbit the Sun (365.25 days) – thus a little extra time had to be added and subtracted to months to make twelve in a year, which is the easiest division.

The names we have for months come from the Romans and all but two date from the eighth century BCE. The New Year then began in March and the first few months were named after gods, for example Mars (now March, god of war), Aprilis (goddess of love), Maia (May, goddess of growth), Juno (June, wife of Jupiter). But then it would seem the calendar inventors changed their minds about this convention towards the end of the year and started using numeric references instead. So the last four months of the first Roman calendar were: Septem (seven), Octo (eight), Novem (nine) and Decem (ten), which we have retained but have skewed the

44

numbers so that their original meaning has been lost (i.e. September is now the ninth month, etc).

January and February were added slightly later at the end of the year, as the Romans thought of winter as a monthless period, and relate to the god Janus (the god of the doorway) and 'februum', meaning purification and linked to a ritual in the old lunar Roman calendar. January came to be seen as the first month of the year in the fifth century BCE.

The names for July and August came later still. The first is for Julius Caesar, who oversaw the implementation of the Julian calendar in the first century BCE, and the second was named after his successor Augustus.

Janus, the Roman god of beginnings, transitions and doorways

Days

The time unit 'day' describes the length of time the Earth takes to rotate on its own axis (around 86,400 seconds or 24 hours). The world's official, 'civil' day runs from midnight to midnight. It is used to determine international time zones and Coordinated Universal Time (the standard we use to set clocks across the globe).

But before we were able to do this fancy counting, days were defined either as the time between sunsets (Ancient Greeks and Babylonians) or sunrises (Ancient Egyptians). In Jewish and Muslim traditions to this day, the day is counted from sunset to sunset.

What a difference a day makes . . .

While a day on Earth is 24 hours, it is considerably longer on our neighbouring planet Venus, where a solar day lasts 116.75 of our Earth days. Mars takes just a little longer than the Earth to rotate at 25 hours, while large planets rotate faster – Saturn and Jupiter's days are just 10 hours long, Uranus's is 18 and Neptune's 19.

Seven-day week

Aggregating days into seven-day weeks is yet another inheritance from the Babylonians and early Jewish civilizations by way of Rome. The days of the week were named for the seven 'classical planets' – those that were visible to early astronomers. They were the Sun (Sunday) and Moon (Monday), and five other planets: Mercury (Wednesday), Venus (Friday), Mars (Tuesday), Jupiter (Thursday) and Saturn (Saturday).

As well as the planet connection, the seven-day week is related to Babylonian and Jewish traditions which endow the seventh day with religious significance. In the Old Testament it was the day God rested after six days creating the Earth, and so Jewish peoples began celebrating a holy day of rest every seventh day. The Babylonians celebrated every seventh day to coincide with the new moon, a quarter of a lunar orbit or 'lunation' (but the timing is a little off so synchronization soon suffered but the seven-day week remained). The ten-day week was favoured by the ancient Chinese and Egyptians as well as in Peru, whereas the Mayans and Aztecs had thirteen days in a week.

Over the years, various nations have tried to tinker with the seven-day-week structure. Between 1929 and 1940, the Soviet Union adopted a five-day week. In 1793 in revolutionary France a whole new calendar system was briefly introduced based on the number ten – with ten newly named days per week (more on this later).

In English, our days of the week have been named for a mixture of seven Norse, Anglo-Saxon and Roman 'gods' – which tells the story of various conquerors of Britain over time. The Norse gods are roughly equivalent to the Roman gods (see below). Our neighbours on mainland Europe (e.g. France, Spain, Italy) retain the full suite of Roman gods/planets for their day names.

DAY	GOD	ROMAN GOD
Monday	Moon	Luna (moon)
Tuesday	Tyr (or Tiw in Old English) – Norse god of law, justice, and the sky among other things, including war. He is portrayed as a one-handed man.	Mars – the god of war and all things military.

Wednesday	Woden (Anglo-Saxon equivalent of the Norse god Odin) – the god of war and victory, as well as poets, musicians and seers.	Mercury – the messenger with wings on his sandals. He is also the god of trade, merchants, and travel. He too has a connection with poetry and music.
Thursday	Thor – the Norse god associated with thunder, lightning, storms, oak trees and strength. And famous for his large hammer.	Jove – also known as Jupiter, the king of the gods – and the sky and thunder too.
Friday	Frige – Anglo-Saxon goddess about whom little is known, but it is assumed she is associated with sexuality and fertility.	Venus – the goddess of love, sexuality and fertility whose Greek counterpart is Aphrodite.
Saturday	Saturn – the Roman god associated with wealth, agriculture, liberation, and time, rather than the planet also named after him.	Saturn
Sunday	Sun	Sol (sun)

Calendars

Different cultures devised their own calendars at different times and using diverse markers and measurements, but broadly speaking these calendars fall into two categories: lunar and solar.

The Moon takes 29.53 days to orbit the Earth, so the lunar year runs to just 354.36 days to complete twelve orbits or 'lunations'. Meanwhile, the solar year, based on the Earth's orbit of the Sun, is 365.25 days long.

The Moon is the easier marker of the two, with full moons shining in the sky with reassuring regularity every month. It is therefore likely that lunar calendars were long in use before anyone thought to count a whole year.

Ancient bones

An artefact considered by some to be the earliest physical calendar was found in a cave in the Dordogne Valley in France and is dated as being some 30,000 years old. It is a fragment of bone from an eagle's wing upon which is etched a pattern of notches – the notches appear in groups of 14 or 15 and rows of 29 or 30.

An eagle's bone, found in Abri Blanchard, Dordogne

Could this be a Palaeolithic lunar calendar? Some archaeologists have suggested that the bone might have been used by women to keep track of their menstrual cycles and thus their fertility (though the menstrual cycle is shorter than a lunar month at twenty-eight days). It's an interesting thought. Perhaps this artefact is both a calendar and a contraceptive of sorts. Or neither, of course . . .

West of Kiev in the Ukraine, 20,000-year-old mammoth bones were found with notches that indicated lunar months in periods of four. This has been interpreted as a 'season'.

Time markers

The Neolithic structures at Stonehenge and Newgrange can be considered to be calendars in that they demark and capture time – specifically the exact time of year at the Summer and Winter Solstices. Similar sites in the British Isles that serve as annual markers include Maeshowe on Orkney Island in Scotland and Castlerigg near Keswick in northern England. Such structures are not unique to Europe though. In China, midwinter is captured at Taosi in the Shanxi Province. And in Egypt the temple of Queen Hatshepsut is designed to welcome the midwinter sun.

Another useful annual marker in ancient Egypt was the Nile, which flooded around the same time each year (mid-June, close to the Spring Equinox)

Hatshepsut's Temple, found on the west bank of the Nile

and was used to mark 'New Year'. The flood was considered as one of three seasons that divided the year. The others were growth and harvest. And soon it was calculated that a year from flood to flood was 360 days, subdivided into twelve months of thirty days. Egyptian astronomers noticed that the time of the flood also coincided closely with the day that the sky's brightest star, Sirius, also known as the 'Dog Star', rose in the dawn sky just before the Sun. Using this marker the Egyptians started counting 365 days in the year instead. The resulting calendar became the 'official' calendar of the country used by priests and rulers.

Floods of tears

Ancient Egyptians believed that the Nile flooded every year because of Isis's tears for her dead husband, Osiris.

In Egypt today, the flood event is still celebrated as a two-week annual holiday starting 15 August, known as Wafaa El-Nil. The Coptic Church marks the flood by throwing a martyr's relic into the river in an event known as Esba al-shahid ('The Martyr's Finger').

The Julian calendar

Gaius Julius Caesar observed the usefulness of having an 'official' calendar in Egypt and decided to adopt one for the Roman Empire in the middle of the first century BCE.

The Romans had been counting years and months for quite some time – starting in 735 BCE when the city of Rome was founded by the legendary Romulus (of Romulus and Remus). As previously mentioned, the first Roman calendar had just ten months in it. Then around 700 BCE, another two months were added to the end of the year: January and February.

To bring this old calendar in line with the solar year Caesar employed mathematicians and philosophers to find the most logical system. Through their efforts the Julian calendar was born, naming 25 December as the Winter Solstice (rather than 21 or 22 December – and later co-opted as Christmas Day), but the new calendar was two months behind the solar year – and so for the first year of its existence two months were added to balance things out. This year became known as the 'year of confusion'. Adding to this confusion, Caesar also announced that the year would start in January, rather than March.

The calendar had many teething problems but was soon adopted throughout the Empire – and provided the template for the modern 'Gregorian' calendar (see overleaf). The calendar has twelve months and a leap year every four years (giving February twenty-nine days as it does today).

Sun's day versus Saturn's day

When Constantine the Great became Emperor of Rome at the start of the fourth century CE, he set about adopting Christianity as a way of unifying his crumbling Empire. As part of this project he re-invented the seven-day week. In the Bible it says that while making the Earth, God rested on the seventh day. Constantine therefore decreed that Sunday should be the 'official' day of rest instead of Saturday (Saturn's day). This decision would have meant a fundamental change to the way people lived at the time. Some cultures have never quite adopted the change – with Jews still celebrating the Sabbath on Saturday. Though thanks to the five-day working week we can now pick and choose which day, if either, we decide to practise our faiths on.

The Gregorian calendar

The Julian calendar remained in situ for some 1,600 years before Pope Gregory XIII decided to upgrade it as a rather ambitious pet-project. The main issue with the Julian calendar was that it had wrongly assumed the length of a year was 365.25 days, which is actually 10 minutes and three-quarters too long. Over time this discrepancy pushed the Julian calendar ten days out of sync with the solar year. Gregory's mission was to align the two in a long-lasting way.

First they had to lose ten days. There was much hemming and hawing about how best to do this – not having a leap year for forty years was one popular option. But in the end it was decided to get the pain over with all at once and so the day after Thursday 4 October 1582 was Friday 15 October. While getting people all over Europe to implement this change was an amazing feat, it was not without its problems. People in different countries reputedly felt that they had been robbed of ten days and they wanted them back.

As the edict for change came from the Pope, countries like Protestant Britain were slower to implement the change to the more logical system. In fact, they did not do so until 1752, at which stage eleven days had to be skipped over to align the Gregorian year with the solar year.

Leap year

Occurring once every four years in the Gregorian calendar, leap years are years that have an additional day to help keep the calendar year in sync with the solar year. In a leap year an extra day is added to the month of February, causing a shift or 'leap' in the days. So, in a 'common year' Friday 28 February would have been followed by Sunday 1 March, but in a leap year the first day of March is pushed one day along as 29 February 'leaps' into its place. Leap years are required because the solar year is a little over 365.24 days long.

A person born on 29 February is called a 'leapling' or a 'leaper' and in common years usually celebrate their birthdays on 28 February, though in some places, like Hong Kong for example, a 'leapling's' birthday is legally regarded as 1 March.

What year is it?

While years on the standard Gregorian calendar are measured in relation to the presumed birth year of Jesus, non-Christian communities often benchmark theirs against the birth, death or particularly significant episode in the lives of their own religious leaders. Taking the millennium (2000) as a baseline, here is how some non-Western cultures determine what year it is:

1379: IRAN AND AFGHANISTAN

✳ The Solar Hijri is the official calendar in these two countries – and in many ways is considered more accurate than the Gregorian, though it requires consultation of astronomical charts. To determine the Solar Hijri, you subtract 621 or 622 from the Gregorian year (622 CE was the year the Prophet Muhammad migrated from Mecca to Medina). So the year 2000 equals 1379 in the Solar Hijri.

1421: SAUDI ARABIA AND OTHER
ISLAMIC COUNTRIES

✳ The Islamic calendar is a lunar calendar consisting of either 354 or 355 days (lunar cycles are slightly shorter than the Gregorian month: 29.5 days versus an average of 30.4 days). The calendar is used for religious purposes, for example to determine the appropriate start date for Ramadan. Because of this disparity in the number of days, calculations are a little trickier than for the Solar Hijri, even though both calendars choose 622 CE as their 'Year One'. According to the Islamic calendar, the year 2000 is 1421.

Setting his country back years

Upon seizing control of Libya in 1978, Colonel Muammar Gaddafi reportedly declared that the Islamic calendar should start with the death of the prophet Mohammed in 632 CE, rather than the traditional 622 CE, putting Libya's calendar ten years behind other Muslim countries.

12: JAPAN

✽ While Japan uses the Gregorian calendar for all its official, day-to-day dealings, its year system is rather different and is based on the reign of the country's emperors. So Japan's Emperor Akihito acceded to the throne in 1989, making 2000 CE 'Year 12'.

5760 OR 5761: ISRAEL

✽ The Hebrew calendar used to determine religious days and festivals takes 3761 BCE in the Gregorian calendar system as its start date, one year *before* scriptures say the Earth was created (that happened on Monday 7 October the following year to be precise). To calculate the year 2000 in the Hebrew calendar, one adds either 3760 before Rosh Hashanah (Jewish New Year, usually falling in September or October) or 3761 after Rosh Hashanah. So while the West welcomed the millennium on 1 January 2000 it was 5760 in the Hebrew calendar, and as it prepared to usher in 2001 it was 5761.

Many Christian groups like Creationists and Jehovah's Witnesses still embrace the idea that God created the world in the thirty-eighth century BCE – making our Earth around 6,000 years old.

4637 OR 4697: CHINA

✳ Tradition holds that the Chinese calendar was invented by Emperor Huang-di in the sixty-first year of his reign (2637 BCE). But this is a date with a rather wide margin of error, with others using 2697 BCE, some 60 years later, as a baseline. So depending on what you fancy, it was either 4637 or 4697 in 2000.

5102: INDIA

✳ The Hindu calendar kicks off in 3102 BCE – the year that Krishna is said to have returned to his 'eternal abode'. As the calendar follows the same 365-day and leap-year pattern as the Gregorian, we simply add 2000 to determine that the West's millennium fell in the Hindu year 5102.

1992: ETHIOPIA

✳ Based on ancient Egyptian calendars but similar enough to the Gregorian calendar to allow easy calculation, the Ethiopian calendar celebrates New Year on 29 or 30 August. In terms of its Year One, it is pretty close to the Gregorian with just a seven- to eight-year gap due to a difference of opinion on the year date of the Annunciation of Jesus (when the Angel Gabriel told Mary that she would conceive God's son). The Ethiopians place this event slightly later than the powers-that-be in Rome, making the year 2000 equivalent to 1992 at New Year in Ethiopia and neighbouring Eritrea, and giving them some breathing space before their own Y2K panic kicked in.

Time-Travel Tip
Check out the stars!

On a clear night, take some time to look up at the stars. You won't be looking at them as they are 'now' but how they were when the light left them. That could be millions and millions of years ago. To get the full effect of the night sky, it's best to be in the countryside away from major sources of light pollution like big towns or cities that can block out all but the brightest stars from the sky.

The Sun is around 150 million kilometres away, though this varies, and it takes 8 minutes for its light to reach us. So when you see the Sun, you're seeing it 8 minutes in the past.

3
Keeping Time

Counting the hours

Like many things mathematics and astronomy-related, our time divisions came from ancient Mesopotamia, via the Babylonians and Sumerians, in the third millennium BCE. And also like the number of days in a week – or indeed the existence of weeks at all – these divisions are arbitrary, but exert considerable power over our lives nonetheless.

Why 12 and 60?

The 'sexagesimal' system, which uses 60 as its core number, is used not only for measuring time but for measuring angles and geographic coordinates too, though systems using multiples of ten are used for most other forms of counting and general calculation.

Sixty is a highly composite number – that is one with a useful number of divisors. It has 12 'factors' or ways of dividing into it (1, 2, 3, 4, 5, 6, 10, 12,15, 20, 30, 60), which helps to make fractions involving 60 or multiples of 60 simpler. It is also the smallest number that can be divided by every number from 1 to 6.

Basically, 60 is a great number.

The use of the number 12 as a core number in time and mathematics is thought to come from people counting on their fingers. Specifically, counting the three joint bones in each of their fingers using their thumb as a pointer. There are of course other reasons why 12 has caught on in a big way. There are 12 lunar cycles within a solar year for example, though counting years came long after counting on fingers. The use of 12 as a base for counting is known as the 'duodecimal' system – which was widely used in the earliest civilizations in ancient Egypt, Sumer, India and China.

Hours

Dividing the day by the magic number 12 is largely grounded in the counting preferences of our forebears rather than anything more scientific. Saying that, the ancient Egyptians divided the day according to the rising of 36 'decan' stars, constellations that rise one after the other on the horizon throughout each rotation of the Earth. The rising of each decan signified an hour division (consisting of 40 minutes) and by the 'Middle Kingdom' period (sixteenth to eleventh century BCE) this system had been refined to count 24 decan hours in a day, with 12 for the daytime and 12 for night. But to define the actual length of one of these divisions, a measuring device was required. Enter the very first clocks . . .

Sunlight and shadows

As previously discussed, the Sun is the most useful of nature's clocks. Apart from sunrise and sunset, its easiest point to read is noon, when it is highest in the sky, casting the shortest shadows on the ground. And so this became the most popular point in the day from which to count. It is not known when humans began to use the Sun to calculate the time of day. Basic markers could have been used millennia ago – we just don't know. Nor do we know whether shadows or points of sunlight were first used to tell time, though the earliest sundials we know of indicate that measuring the time of day using shadows was the more common (shadows are longest in the early morning, getting shorter to noon, then longer again towards dusk). The earliest known sundials are from around 1500 BCE, used in ancient Egyptian and Babylonian astronomy.

At its most basic, a sundial is a horizontal or vertical base with a 'gnomon', a thin rod or upright sharp edge that casts shadows onto a surface marked to indicate different times of the day. To give an accurate reading, the sundial must be aligned with the axis of the Earth's rotation and the gnomon must point towards 'true celestial north'. In the northern hemisphere this is indicated by the pole star, Polaris.

A sundial, made up of a horizontal base with a gnomon

The duodecimal markers on sundials were used to measure the length of an hour. This time measurement could then be applied to other time devices such as water clocks, candle clocks and hourglasses – inventions that helped solve the problem of telling the time on a cloudy day and at night.

Water clocks

Water clocks may have been in use as early as 4000 BCE in China, though the only hard evidence we have for them is considerably later, around 1500 BCE in Egypt and Babylon again. Time is measured by the regulated flow of water either into or out of a vessel whose size and flow rate is approximate to a specific time frame.

Examples of basic water clocks include half-coconut shells called *ghati* or *kapala* in India. A small but precise hole was drilled into this simple device that was then placed in a bowl of water. The *ghati* was sized to take 24 minutes to fill with water and sink – with each minute itself being equivalent to 60 seconds apiece. A day was therefore comprised of 60 of these 24-minute hours. The *fenjaan* clocks used in Persia in the fourth century BCE applied the same principle though not the same time measurement.

In Greece, the *clepsydra* or 'water thief' was a water clock constructed from a jar with a hole in the end. When the water ran out, the prescribed amount of time had been measured. To ensure fairness in Athenian courts, a *clepsydra* was used in court cases to fix the amount of time both plaintiffs and defendants were allotted. They are also thought to have been used by prostitutes to measure the time spent with their clients.

To measure time over a longer period required constant maintenance and counting so water clocks became increasingly sophisticated. By the third century BCE, a clock had been invented in

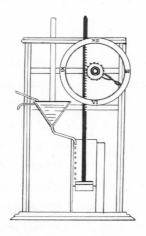

A basic water clock

Greece that used a continuous supply of water and an overflow system – allowing longer periods of time to be measured. Further innovations and mechanisation were slow to develop, though there was a particularly productive period in the Middle East and China between the eighth and eleventh centuries.

Chinese Clock inventor Su Song (1020–1101 CE) created an astronomical water-powered clock, housed in a tower of some 9 metres. The clock featured a celestial globe and panels at the front that opened to display figures holding plaques announcing the time of day.

Another clock, described in an early thirteenth-century text and located in the Umayyad Mosque in the Syrian capital Damascus, split time into 12 equal hours. The clock had dials that indicated the time during the day and night respectively – and copper balls were released to ring the hour.

The hourglass

It is thought that hourglasses or sandglasses were first invented and utilized in Europe in the eighth century. The first evidence of their use is from the fourteenth century, captured in the 1338

fresco *Allegory of Good Government* by Italian artist Ambrogio Lorenzetti. And frequent reference to them is found in ship logbooks from the same time.

An hourglass consists of two connected glass bulbs that allow a regulated trickle of material from the top to the bottom. Once the top bulb is empty, it can be turned and timing begins afresh. They were particularly useful on board ships as they were unaffected by the motion of the sea and the granular material used in hourglass – sand, powdered eggshell or powdered marble – was less susceptible to temperature changes than water-powered clocks. In fact, hourglasses were used to measure time, speed and distance on ships until the eighteenth century.

In the next chapter we'll find out about the first reliable sea clocks or 'marine chronometers' as they're known in the time business – and the extraordinary life of the man who perfected them.

71

Log lines

Another device employed by sailors to measure speed was a 'log line'. This was basically a long piece of rope with a series of evenly spaced knots in it, weighted down at one end with a piece of wood. The wood weight would be cast overboard and sailors would then count the knots in the rope as it was pulled from its coil behind the ship. The counting would happen during a fixed time (usually measured using a small sandglass) and speed would then be calculated in 'knots'.

Burning the candle . . .

Another early 'clock' that was popular across Asia, the Middle East and Europe was the candle clock. In use from at least the early sixth century, but likely earlier than that, the principle was simple – the rate at which the candle burned was used to measure the passage of time.

The candle wax was marked at regular intervals to indicate time periods. Alternatively, the candle could be placed against a marked reflective background and the height of the flame used to indicate the time where the flame lit a marking. Other candles – created to burn within a specified time period – had a nail inside them, which would fall with a clatter once the candle had burned away, announcing the end of the time being measured.

Minutes and seconds

As we have already seen, hours were initially calculated using sundials with divisions of the day based on the duodecimal system (multiples of 12). And we've also learned about the penchant for the number 60 among our forebears from ancient Mesopotamia, from whom we have inherited so much mathematical and astronomical knowledge. So it seems inevitable that the hour as a 1/24 portion of a day would be subdivided by 60 minutes and in turn those 60 minutes each divided into a further 60 short units: seconds.

Before mechanical clocks, measuring how long a second took would have been far from scientific. We can only surmise as to how or if it was done – and it was likely to be as accurate as a child counting in a game of hide and seek. Perhaps they were indicated by steady finger clicks or heartbeats. Coincidentally, the rate of a healthy man's heart comes in around 60 beats per minute throughout his adult life, a woman's just a little over.

Some of the more sophisticated water clocks designed in the High Middle Ages (eleventh, twelfth and thirteenth centuries) were capable of measuring smaller units of time. The early thirteenth-century clock at the Umayyad Mosque in Damascus, for example, also indicated time periods of 5 minutes, as well as its hours. And smaller sandglasses where used to measure shorter periods for a variety of functions.

Fixing seconds

Up to 1960, the second was defined as 1/86,400 of a mean solar day, despite late-nineteenth-century astronomical findings that showed that the mean day is ever-so-slowly lengthening. With the invention of atomic clocks in the 1950s, seconds were captured and defined in exact terms. To give you a sense of the accuracy of these time-devices, there is one in Switzerland, in operation since 2004, that has an uncertainty of 1 second in 30 million years! (More on these on page 138)

But it was with the advent of the first non-water-powered mechanical clocks that minutes and seconds came into their own, and formed the fundamental building blocks for time as we now know it.

The mechanics of clocks

As we've seen, ingenious water clocks with intricate moving parts were in use from at least the eleventh century (though there is anecdotal evidence to suggest they may have been in use over a thousand years earlier in ancient Greece). The breakthrough technology that made them possible is the 'escapement' – an invention that is still used in watches and clocks to this day.

An escapement is a device that transfers energy to the timekeeping element, also known as the 'impulse action', allowing the number of its oscillations to be counted (the 'locking action'). Think of the inner workings of a clock or watch you've seen, with its indented wheels ticking ever onward – it's the escapement that drives this motion and which causes the clock's ticking sound, as the mechanism moves forward and locks, moves forward and locks.

The energy that sets the escapement in continuous motion comes from a coiled spring or suspended weight.

In water clocks, the escapement was designed to tip a container of water over each time it filled up, advancing the clock's wheels with every occurrence. The development of a truly mechanical clock however, required an escapement that could drive the clock's movement using an oscillating weight.

Clocks using this technology began to appear in Europe in the thirteenth and fourteenth centuries. They were necessarily very large and had to be positioned high on a wall or tower because of the sizeable hanging weights required to facilitate continuous motion. Royalty and the ultra-wealthy were alone in being able to afford such devices, and so the majority were commissioned and used by the Church – and housed in monasteries and cathedrals. Their chief function was to call people to prayer.

Medieval timekeepers

The fourteenth century saw the construction of impressive large-scale clocks throughout Europe, chiefly attached to and maintained by cathedrals. These clocks would have required constant

Earliest clock escapement?

Escapements were developed and used as early as the third century BCE by the ancient Greeks to control the flow of water in washstands. There is anecdotal evidence from this time to suggest that this complex technology had already been applied to water clocks. The Greek engineer Philo of Byzantium, creator and user of escapements and author of a treatise on pneumatics, comments that the technology he is using in his washstand is 'similar to that of clocks'.

maintenance and probably resetting due to inaccuracies – but represented incredible strides in timekeeping nonetheless.

Among the many masterpieces produced were Richard of Wallingford's clock at St Albans (1336) and Giovanni de Dondi's in Padua (1348). Though neither clock still exists, we know from detailed descriptions that both had multiple functions. Wallingford's clock had a large dial with astrolabe detailing (a dial device used to locate and predict the positions of heavenly bodies), and an indicator of the level of the tide at London Bridge. Its bells rang on the hour, their number announcing the time. The Paduan clock featured dials showing the time of day, including minutes, the movements of the planets, a calendar of feast days and even an eclipse-prediction hand.

Another lost but reportedly spectacular early clock was at Strasbourg Cathedral. Its most impressive feature was a gilded rooster (a symbol of Jesus) that flapped its mechanical wings and emitted a crowing sound at noon, while three mechanical kings bowed to its splendour. This clock also featured an astrolabe and calendar. Other great fourteenth-century clocks include Wells cathedral's (now at the Science Museum in London and still working), the Gros Horloge at Rouen and the Heinrich von Wick clock in Paris.

Still in operation today and drawing crowds daily is the Orloj in Prague's Old Town Square. Constructed in 1410, this beautiful device combines a mechanical clock, astronomical dial and zodiacal ring, and features many animated figures that are set in motion on the hour. These represent Vanity, Greed/Usury, Death and a Turk (representing sinful pleasure and entertainment). The Twelve Apostles also make an appearance at the doorways above the clock every hour – it's quite a show! It has been repaired and augmented many times over its 600-plus years, and was heavily damaged by German forces during the Second World War.

The Orloj in Prague

What's in a name?

The word 'clock' came into usage in the late fourteenth century, replacing the Latin *horologium* (though the practice of clock-making is still known as 'horology'). The reason for this name change relates directly to the earliest common purpose of clocks – that was to call a church's congregation to prayer through the related ringing of a bell. The word 'clock' comes from an earlier word meaning 'bell'. This word is probably Celtic (*clocca* or *clagan*, meaning 'bell') which found its way into medieval Latin, Old French (*cloque*) and Middle Dutch (*clocke*) – all with the same meaning. The use of the word is thought to have been spread throughout Europe by Irish missionaries. The modern Irish word *clog* can mean both 'bell' and 'clock'.

Alive and ticking: the oldest working clock

Older though slightly less beguiling than the Orloj is the clock at Salisbury Cathedral. This clock is thought to date from 1386, making it just six years older than the Wells Cathedral clock mentioned above, which has been dated at 1392.

Some horology conspiracy theorists (yes, they exist!) believe that the Salisbury clock is in fact from a later date, as the construction is quite advanced and similar to clocks made in the sixteenth and seventeenth centuries.

In 1993, a symposium at the Antiquarian Horological Society voted that the Salisbury clock is indeed the older of the two – but around one third of the participants voted against, expressing their belief that the clock is of a much later date. The Salisbury clock has not been in continuous use. In fact, it was only rediscovered after many years' absence in 1928, and was not restored and reinstated until 1956.

Time-Travel Tip
Ignore all clocks!

Our lives are completely dominated by the time systems discussed in this chapter – the constructs of hours, minutes and seconds – captured in devices from the primitive to the sophisticated. Ditch your watch, hide the clock, turn off your mobile and free yourself from this time prison for a few days, and experience time as your prehistoric ancestors would have done – through the movements of the Sun, demarked by dawn, noon and dusk. For the full back-in-time experience (and to safely escape time-keeping devices which are *everywhere*) you're best off taking refuge in a cabin in the woods somewhere and not seeing anybody for the duration. It will likely be a very disorientating experience. Good luck!

4
The Best of Times

Golden age

In this chapter we'll look at some of the great leaps forward in timekeeping during the periods of the Renaissance, the Enlightenment and beyond. During this 'golden age', scientific innovations came thick and fast – from the invention of new mechanisms within clocks and watches to make them ever more accurate, to the physical and philosophical contributions of the likes of Galileo and Newton. We'll journey through some of time's most momentous events, as well as some of its silliest (see 'Cuckoo clocks' on page 116).

We'll also meet some of the timekeeping titans of this golden age. These include John Harrison, inventor of the magnificent maritime measuring machines that revolutionized sea travel, and Abraham-Louis Perrelet, inventor of a self-winding mechanism for pocket watches – technology found in modern wristwatches to this day.

Spring time

The next major development in timekeeping was the invention of the 'mainspring' as the power source for clocks. Replacing weights to drive the escapement, spring-driven clocks appeared in the early fifteenth century. The mechanism works by winding – which twists the spring spiral tight and releases energy as it unwinds over a period of time. The earliest existing spring-driven clock belonged to the Duke of Burgundy (now part of modern France) and dates from 1430.

Later in the fifteenth century, clocks which indicated minutes and seconds began to appear – though none indicating seconds have survived (the earliest example is from 1560). Before that, most clocks had just one hand, with the face split into four sections of 15 minutes.

The advent of the mainspring led to a boom in clock and watchmaking, especially in the German cities of Nuremberg and Augsburg. As the technology became more affordable, demand soared.

Small timekeepers were very fashionable in the mid-sixteenth century and would have been worn ornamentally on a chain around the neck or fastened to clothing. They would have required regular winding – twice or more times a day.

The well heeled of Nuremberg who wanted to stand out from the crowd commissioned all manner of unusual and eye-catchingly shaped watches – representing animal forms, flowers, insects and skulls. The face of watches was exposed, though many had lids to protect the hands. Glass over the face only began to be used as standard in the early seventeenth century.

In 1510, the German master clockmaker Peter Henlein (1485–1542) created the 'Nuremberg Egg', one of the first-known watches. Henlein is often credited with 'inventing' the watch, though the Nuremberg of his time was bursting with talented clockmakers dead set on turning out ever-smaller and more intricate timekeepers for their fashionable clientele.

Indeed, the business was so competitive that it turned violent. In September 1504, Henlein

The Nuremberg Egg

was involved in a brawl with fellow locksmith/ clockmaker George Glaser, in which his rival was killed. The details are sketchy but we do know that Henlein fled to a local Franciscan monastery were he sought sanctuary for four years. By 1509 he was back in favour and was appointed the master of Nuremberg's locksmith guild.

King Phillip and the clockwork monk

When King Phillip II (1527–1598) of Spain's son and heir Charles suffered a serious brain injury his father was naturally distraught. And when Charles miraculously recovered, the king believed it could only be the work of God favouring his family and answering their prayers. Phillip vowed that he would thereafter honour God with continuous prayers. But being king is a busy job. So, instead of doing the praying himself, Phillip commissioned an automaton (aka robot) to be made to do his praying for him.

Using the latest in clockwork technology, the automaton was made of wood and iron, standing at 15 inches tall. It was driven by a key-wound spring and could walk in a square, strike its chest with one hand, and raise and lower a wooden cross and rosary with the other. When operated, its head nodded, turned, rolled its eyes and opened and closed its mouth in rickety 'prayer'.

Four hundred years later, this perpetual prayer machine is still in good working order and lives in the Smithsonian Institution in Washington, DC.

Huguenot horologists

The centre of European clockmaking activity moved from Germany to Switzerland in the early sixteenth century – following a highly skilled group called the Huguenots. Originally from France, the Huguenots were followers of John Calvin and members of the Protestant Reformed Church during the sixteenth and seventeenth centuries. Highly critical of the Catholic Church, they were victims of intense persecution. During the St Bartholomew's Day massacre in 1572, up to 30,000 Huguenots were slaughtered by Catholics in Paris, sparking similar attacks in provincial towns and cities in the weeks that followed. This brutality was officially sanctioned – the perpetrators were pardoned for their actions against the Huguenots.

It is estimated that as many as 500,000 Huguenots fled to Protestant countries including England, Denmark, the Netherlands and North America. But it was in Switzerland that they established themselves as master clockmakers and gave that country the leading edge, which it is still famous for to this day. King Henry VIII welcomed the Huguenots into England. In fact, he personally brought a group of clockmakers over from France to attend to the clocks in his palaces.

Big swing

The horological innovations continued apace, though the one I'm about to describe took quite some time to get from idea to practical application.

The story goes that the Italian polymath Galileo Galilei (1564–1642), known variously as the 'father of observational astronomy', the 'father of modern physics', and the 'father of modern science', was in the Cathedral or Duomo in Pisa in 1582. The young student was reportedly wiling away the service observing the swinging motion of a large bronze lamp in a draught. Galileo timed the swings against the beats of his pulse and found that regardless of how wide the swings of the lamp, the time between them was always the same – nine or ten pulses. He got home and tried a number of experiments and found that the length of the rope used to create the pendulum motion affected the swing rate – the longer the rope, the longer the swing time.

Galileo applied his findings to the creation of a portable pulse meter, which he used in his medical work. The usefulness of the device was soon recognized by the medical establishment. Later in life, Galileo discovered that the pendulum could be applied to clocks and drew up plans for the first pendulum clock in 1637, but he never built it. His son Vincenzio started work on the clock in 1649, but died before he completed it.

It was another polymath, Christiaan Huygens from the Netherlands, who finally brought Galileo's vision to life in 1656 when he constructed the very first pendulum clock – which was accurate to less than 1 minute per day, highly accurate at the time. In 1675, Huygens also invented the spiral balance spring for the balance wheel of pocket watches, making them significantly more accurate.

While Huygens's pendulum clock was certainly revolutionary, the type of escapement it used, known as 'verge', gave too wide a pendulum swing

A basic pendulum clock

and its accuracy was compromised. The invention of the 'anchor' escapement around 1670 reduced the pendulum's swing significantly, and the shorter the swing the greater the accuracy of the clock. The anchor quickly became the standard escapement used in pendulum clocks, though who actually invented it is unknown. Clockmakers Joseph Knibb and William Clement, as well as the scientist Robert Hooke, are variously credited with its creation.

Grandfather clocks

The preferred swing range of pendulums was narrowed further still and soon the seconds pendulum came to be favoured, swinging once per second. The long narrow clocks built around these pendulums were first crafted by Englishman William Clement around 1680 – and became known as grandfather clocks. Minute hands were also introduced as standard around 1690.

The name 'grandfather clock' is thought to have come from a popular song from the 1870s called 'My Grandfather's Clock', written by abolitionist Henry Clay Work. The eponymous clock resided in the George Hotel in Yorkshire, England, and was renowned as a very accurate timekeeper, that is until one of its two owners passed away and it began to mysteriously lose time. When the second owner died, it reportedly stopped working altogether.

The metronome

The invention of the pendulum led to the creation of the first prototype metronome in 1696. Designed by French musical theorist Etienne Loulié, the device had an adjustable pendulum that could be set to different speeds, but it did not make a sound nor have an escapement to keep the pendulum in motion.

Another hundred years-plus would pass before the metronome proper was invented, this time in the Netherlands in 1814 by Dietrich Nikolaus Winkel. Though Winkel invented it, another man called Johann Maelzel developed, patented and started manufacturing metronomes in 1816 under the name 'Maelzel's Metronome' lest there be any confusion. It was designed as a tool for musicians to keep a steady tempo – at various speeds. The tempo is measured in beats per minute (bpm) ranging from 40 to 208 bpm.

Five rather interesting facts about Galileo

So as well as coming up with the pendulum, Galileo Galilei made significant contributions to the fields of physics, maths, astronomy and philosophy.

1. As a medical student and practitioner he invented not only a pendulum-based pulse meter but a 'thermoscope', a forerunner to the thermometer.

2. He was an instructor at the art school Accademia delle Arti del Disegno in Florence where he taught perspective and *chiaroscuro* (the lighting effect used by Caravaggio and Rembrandt).

3. He made improvements to the technology of the telescope, equipping himself to confirm the phases of Venus and to discover the four largest lunar satellites of Jupiter, named the Galilean moons in his honour. He also studied sunspots and the Milky Way, which had previously been largely dismissed.

4. He championed the Copernican theory that the Sun rather than the Earth was at the centre of the 'universe'. This met with opposition from both his astronomical peers and the Church. He was accused of heresy, tried and forced to spend the last fifteen years of his life under house arrest for daring to challenge the establishment. In 1939, Pope Pius XII described him as among the 'most audacious heroes of research' and eventually, in 1992, Pope John Paul II issued an official apology for how Galileo was treated, on behalf of the Roman Catholic Church.

5. Among his other achievements, he invented a military compass that allowed greater accuracy in cannon use, created a compound microscope, described an experiment for measuring the speed of light, and put forward a principle of relativity that provided the basics for Newton's laws of motion and Einstein's special theory of relativity!

Pocket watches

Outside of church clock towers, time and timekeepers were very much the preserve of the moneyed – and their practical uses were often secondary to their material expression of wealth and fashion. This was especially true of the pocket watch. In fact, it is thought that the pocket watch evolved to complement a burgeoning fashion of the late seventeenth century – the waistcoat.

Actually, it's not entirely true to call the waistcoat a 'fashion'. The generously bewigged King Charles II of England, Scotland and Ireland introduced the waistcoat as a part of 'correct' dress during the Restoration of the British monarchy (his father was executed by the government of Oliver Cromwell in 1649). The diarist Samuel Pepys wrote in October 1666 that 'the King hath yesterday in council declared his resolution of setting a fashion for clothes which he will never alter. It will be a vest, I know not well how.'

The pocket watch evolved, with its close-fitting lid and rounded edges, to slip neatly into the pockets of such a vest or waistcoat.

Sir Isaac Newton

It's hard to know where to place Sir Isaac – so great was his contribution across so many of the areas featured in this book. His book *Philosophiae Naturalis Principia Mathematica* (Mathematical Principles of Natural Philosophy, first published in 1687), set out Newton's laws of motion and universal gravitation – paving the way for the study of physics thereafter.

Among his other achievements were his astronomical calculations, which cemented the belief that the Sun is the centre of our 'universe' rather than the Earth (which went without the punishment meted out to Galileo for the same). He built a reflecting telescope, studied the speed of light and contributed to the development of calculus.

Newton distinguished between 'absolute' time and 'relative' time. In his conception, time was 'not liable to any change' – it exists without us, is independent and absolute, and it progresses at a consistent pace throughout the universe. According to Newton, people can only perceive 'relative' time, which we measure through perceivable objects in motion like the Moon or Sun – or indeed clocks. Through these movements we create our sense of the passage of time.

But despite his apparent scientific rationalism, in later life Newton dedicated a great deal of his time to alchemy (trying to turn base metal into gold) and the study of biblical chronology. In fact, through his work on the latter, Newton estimated that the world would end no earlier than 2060 – though he would give no firm prediction as to when it would actually end. Instead, he stated: 'This I mention not to assert when the time of the end shall be, but to put a stop to the rash conjectures of fanciful men who are frequently predicting the time of the end, and by doing so bring the sacred prophesies into discredit as often as their predictions fail.'

The end of time

Most world religions, the Abrahamic (Judaism, Christianity and Islam) and non-Abrahamic, have specific teachings on the 'end time'. Across belief systems, the end time is usually characterized by a period of tribulation, redemption and/or rebirth, ushering in a new era where life is eternal.

Renowned theologian Hippolytus of Rome and others predicted that Jesus would return in the year 500 CE and usher in the end time with his second coming. Following this non-event, others including

Pope Sylvester II (946–1003) predicted the end on 1 January 1000. The anticipation of this millennial apocalypse brought thousands of pilgrims to Jerusalem, as the ground zero of the Christian end time.

When this too failed to occur, other Christians decided the end would happen on the 1,000-year anniversary of the death, rather than the birth, of Jesus – 1033. Determined to keep the anniversary theme alive, 2000 was the next obvious year to focus on. The possibility of Jesus reappearing to do battle with the Antichrist tended to be overshadowed by grim apocalyptic visions of nuclear holocausts, asteroid strikes – and of course the much anticipated technological disaster of Y2K.

Recent years have seen a glut of predictions. Fear of the Large Hadron Collider brought apocalyptic visions of the planet being devoured by black holes. The 'Rapture' was due to happen on 21 May 2011 according to US Christian radio host Harold Camping. He predicted that on that date around three per cent of the world's population would ascend into heaven and the rest of us would die horribly with the Earth five months later on 21 October. Camping had previously stated that the Rapture would occur in September 1994. Rather than throw his rather battered hat in the ring a third time, Camping announced that his attempt to date the end of time was 'sinful' and that his predicting days were numbered.

Many people got stirred up with talk of the Mayan apocalypse – based on a very subjective reading of a stone inscription. The world was due to end on 21 December 2012 and again defied predictors.

Undiminished, apocalyptic predictions for our third millennium CE abound among Christian, Muslim and Jewish theologians. Scientists are a little more generous with the end date though, giving planet Earth at least another 5 billion years or so – at which point it will likely be swallowed by the Sun. Though before that, as the Sun grows hotter, life on the planet may become impossible in a mere 1 billion years. In turn, the 'Big Rip' theory suggests that the entire universe will eventually be torn apart by its continuous expansion in around 22 billion years' time.

Setting the time

Up until the 1670s, nobody outside of the maritime world really cared about a fixed concept of time – and that remained the case until quite a few years later. Time was localized not synchronized. In the absence of mass communications or basic infrastructure, it really didn't matter what time it was in the next town or city – only the ringing of your own church bell counted.

But for mariners, knowing the time was essential. It gave them control over navigation (more to follow on this), and also of the tides – knowing when the tide would be high or low according to their tide tables was vital for organizing sailing times. In London, the hub of maritime life in Stuart England, Greenwich on the River Thames was selected as the place where clocks would be set before voyages.

The Royal Observatory, Greenwich

In 1675, the restored King Charles II of England (he of the waistcoats decree) established the Observatory at Greenwich as the place where his Astronomer Royal would 'apply himself with the most exact care and diligence to the rectifying of the tables of the motions of the heavens, and the places of the fixed stars, so as to find out the so much desired longitude of places for the perfecting of the art of navigation'.

The Observatory was designed and built by Sir Christopher Wren, the man who rebuilt St Paul's

Cathedral and countless churches destroyed in the Great Fire of London, as well as designing the massive Royal Greenwich Hospital for Seamen at the bottom of the hill upon which the observatory stands. The Observatory has the further distinction of being the first purpose-built scientific research facility in Britain, housing the finest equipment and telescopes in the land.

But while this worthy work of mapping the heavens for the benefit of English seafaring was going on, the Observatory's foremost use was a time collection point for mariners disembarking from the docks of Deptford and Greenwich. In the 20-foot-high Octagon room were two clocks created by Thomas Tompion (see 'Timekeeping titans', on page

112), each with an enormous pendulum measuring 3.96 metres and giving time to an unparalleled accuracy of 2 seconds per day. Before setting sail, clocks and watches would be set at Greenwich. But despite careful maintenance, accuracy could not be safeguarded for long at sea – and we'll soon see how one master clockmaker, John Harrison, dedicated his life to creating the perfect marine timekeeper.

In 1833, to save mariners trudging up the steep hill, a time ball was installed on top of the Observatory. This bright red orb was, and indeed still is, raised just before 1 p.m. every day and drops exactly on the hour, so sailors in situ on the Thames could set their marine chronometers accordingly. A few years later in 1855, the Shepherd Gate clock was mounted on the wall outside the Observatory. It has a 24-hour dial and is an early electric slave clock – driven by electric pulses transmitted from the master clock inside the main building. It is thought that this clock was the first to display 'Greenwich Mean Time' to the public.

From 5 February 1924, the British Broadcasting Corporation began transmitting a time signal direct from Greenwich. The 'pips' as they were known, were intended to help people to set their watches

Flower clock

How well the skilful gardener drew
Of flow'rs and herbs this dial new;
Where from above the milder sun
Does through a fragrant zodiac run;
And, as it works, th' industrous bee
Computes its time as well as we.
How could such sweet and wholesome hours
Be reckoned but with herbs and flow'rs!

Andrew Marvell, The Garden, 1678

Many years after Andrew Marvell wrote the above lines, botanist Carolus Linnaeus wrote about the idea of a flower clock in the 1751 publication *Philosophia Botanica*. Subsequently a number of botanic gardens attempted to plant flowers as he suggested – that is, so flowers bloomed and closed in sequence, demarking different times of the day. Sow thistle for example, typically opens at 5 a.m. and closes at 12 p.m. Hawkweed opens at 1 a.m. and closes at 3 p.m. The latest closing flower recommended by Linnaeus was the Day-lily at 7 to 8 p.m. Seasonal and weather changes make this a rather tricky clock to maintain.

and clocks to the correct time. There were six pips in total, the last one longer than the others and announcing the exact moment of the start of the next hour. Because radio waves travel at the speed of light, the pips could be transmitted to the far side of the world and still give a time reading accurate to around a tenth of a second.

The pips are no longer broadcast from Greenwich, but from the National Physical Laboratory in Teddington, Surrey, which uses Coordinated Universal Time (UTC) – the successor of GMT – for its reading.

Maritime time and the longitude debacle

The 'Age of Sail' between the sixteenth and nineteenth centuries saw a worldwide revolution in trade and human movement around the planet. But as we've read, sailing was a precarious adventure, not least because of the difficulties in determining longitude – the location of a place on Earth east or west of a north-south prime meridian line.

Seafarers used calculations based on astronomical maps and live readings of the stars to try to determine their location at sea – but with the result that they often missed their end destinations by a considerable margin, or in worst cases experienced shipwrecks and lost lives. So great was the problem that in 1714 a competition was announced to find the best solution to the longitude problem, with the British Parliament offering a considerable prize of £20,000 (approximately £2.9 million in today's money).

Self-educated carpenter and watchmaker John Harrison from Yorkshire took up the challenge to invent a sea clock capable of keeping time in the harshest conditions and thus aiding a simpler, time-based calculation of longitude. In the process he pitted himself against the astronomical establishment. His chief competitor was Nevil Maskelyne, an astronomer with strong support on the Board of Longitude working on a 'Method of Lunar Distances' for calculating longitude.

Harrison invented five masterpieces of maritime timekeeping over a 40-year period – each one breaking new ground in horology. He started with the large and beautifully ornate H1 and finished with the deceptively simple H4 and H5 (oversized pocket watches which could withstand the shocks of sea travel). When H4 was tested on a transatlantic journey to Jamaica, it was just 5 seconds slow.

When the ship returned, Harrison expected to be awarded his £20,000. He was wrong. The Board of Longitude stated that this accuracy could be luck and requested further trials.

On H4's second journey, this time to Barbados, it was accurate to within just 39 seconds. Also on this second voyage was Nevil Maskelyne, testing his Method of Lunar Distances for measuring longitude, which was accurate to within 30 miles – an impressive result, but still not as strong a performance as Harrison's H4. Plus Maskelyne's calculations required considerable time and effort, unlike the sea clock.

Harrison's H4

Again the Board of Longitude said that H4's accuracy was a matter of luck and required that it undergo further testing by the Astronomer Royal, the newly appointed Nevil Maskelyne. Maskelyne unsurprisingly returned a very negative report on the sea clocks' performance and scuppered Harrison's chance of claiming the prize.

Though he felt 'extremely ill used' by the establishment, the dogged Harrison began work on H5 and enlisted the support of King George III – who himself tested the clock, reported on its incredible accuracy and advised Harrison to petition parliament for the full prize. At the age of 80, Harrison eventually received £8,750 of the longitude prize money but he never received the official award, nor did anyone else for that matter. He died three years later in 1776 at the age of eighty-three – bucking another time trend of the era by living so long. By the early nineteenth century, the use of sea clocks was the norm for establishing longitude in maritime travel.

Prime meridian

For the purpose of global navigation, the prime meridian is the agreed point of 0° longitude which encircles the Earth. This notional line divides the planet into eastern and western hemispheres, just as the equator divides it north and south. However, unlike the equator, the position of the prime meridian is arbitrary. As a consequence, many countries have tried to claim that the invisible 0° line should pass through their little patch.

The first recorded meridian line is found on Ptolemy's 'world' map of 150 CE, though the idea of a prime line of longitude dates to the third century BCE. Ptolemy's map consists of about a quarter of our globe – stretching west to east from the Canary Islands in the Atlantic off Spain as far as China. And under the Arctic circle in the north to the top half of Africa in the south.

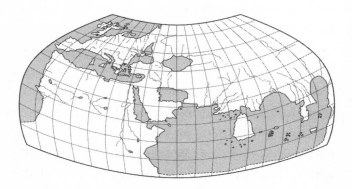

Ptolemy's world map, 150 CE

The meridian line on this map passes through El Hierro, one of the Canary Islands, as it was the westernmost body of land known at the time. This map and location of the prime meridian were influential in cartography right up to the late fifteenth century, until explorers such as Christopher Columbus started to rapidly increase the size of the known world.

The focal point of the line moved a little south and west to Cape Verde off the coast of Africa on the advice of Columbus, becoming known as the Tordesillas line, after a treaty between Spain and Portugal to settle territorial disputes over newly discovered land. The line fluctuated between Cape Verde and the Canaries for another 200 years until the early eighteenth century, when the British went hell-for-leather trying to solve the longitude problem and assigned Greenwich as the point the prime meridian passes through. With so much nautical information and guidance pouring forth from Britain – the Greenwich meridian soon became the norm. In 1884, an International Meridian Convention held in Washington, DC officially agreed that Greenwich was indeed the site of the prime meridian, though the French continued to use Paris until 1911. Greenwich Mean Time was also established as the standard time from which the rest of the world should measure its time of day.

The site of the prime meridian in Greenwich is a major tourist draw, with lines of people queuing to get their picture taken straddling the eastern and western hemispheres. At night the observatory shines a green laser beam into the sky to proudly demark the line that determines the degrees and measurements on every contemporary map of the world.

The revolutionary power of ten

Not a country to be told to fall in with either standard time or a standard calendar, France attempted to break with both during the years following its revolution. The French Republican Calendar was used for about twelve years from 1793 and was adopted as part of France's bid to embrace decimalization (using 10 instead of 12 as a fundamental unit), as well as to divorce the calendar from religious associations.

The government abandoned the Christian system for years, dating the new calendar from the birth of the Republic (Year One being 1792), and though

110

it continued to split the year into twelve months, these were divided into three ten-day weeks called *décades*. Keeping the decimal theme going, these days were split into 10 hours, each made up of 100 decimal minutes of 100 decimal seconds. So the new hour was more than twice as long as the old one of 60 minutes of 60 seconds. Even the minutes got longer – they were equivalent to 86.4 seconds rather than 60, though the seconds themselves were shorter at 0.864 of a conventional second.

Clocks were created to report decimal time, but their makers were not inundated with orders. Decimal time was only mandatory for two years and abandoned completely in 1805, as ironically it proved a complete waste of time.

The names for the 'new' months were vivid and evocative, relating to nature and the weather. The autumn months, for example, were Vendémiaire (Grape Harvest), Brumaire (Fog) and Frimaire (Frost).

The ten days of the week were somewhat more functional: Primidi (first day), Duodi (second day), Tridi (third day) . . . ending with Décadi (tenth day) which was a day of rest equivalent to Sunday.

Rather than have saints' days like the once-dominant Catholic Church, the French adopted a system of assigning an animal, plant/food, mineral or tool to each day of the year. The twenty-eighth day of Vendémiaire (22 September to 21 October), for example, is the day of the tomato, and the fifth day of Frimaire (21 November to 20 December) is the day of the pig.

Timekeeping titans

The seventeenth and eighteenth centuries saw so many great innovations in timekeeping and the creation of such a vast array of intricate, beautiful and sometimes just plain weird timekeepers that doing them justice would require another book. However, there are a few heroes of horology who must be mentioned.

Thomas Tompion (1639–1713)

Referred to as the 'Father of English Clockmaking', Thomas Tompion created the first two 'regulator' clocks for the Observatory at Greenwich, used by the very first Astronomer Royal, Sir John Flamsteed. Accurate to within two seconds a day (the most accurate in the world at the time), these clocks could run for a full year without rewinding – and they continued to run while being rewound. They were used to literally 'keep' time at the observatory – providing the time for all other clocks and watches in use there and for seafarers.

Year Zero

Inspired by the French Republican Calendar, the Cambodian despot and head of the Khmer Rouge, Pol Pot, declared 1975 to be Year Zero to mark the occasion he took control of Phnom Penh, the largest city in the country.

But Pol Pot was very literal-minded with his changes to time in the country – and he was determined to alter not only the calendar but the epoch in which Cambodians lived. He sought to de-industrialize the country, levelling the societal playing field by effectively making everyone a member of an uneducated, peasant class. The country's history was to be erased – and so intellectuals, teachers and artists, who might keep the cultural memory alive, were targeted for persecution.

During the four years of Pol Pot's rule, approximately 2 million people lost their lives as a consequence of political executions and forced labour.

Tompion employed a number of skilled French and Dutch Huguenots (who we know were reputed for their horological talents) in his workshop, which may account for the consistently high quality of the timekeepers he produced. Tompion's workshop built about 5,500 watches and 650 clocks during his career. He also created a serial numbering system for his spring and long-case clocks, perhaps the first for manufactured goods.

George Graham was Tompion's most famous protégée and ultimately his business partner. Graham invented the 'Graham dead-beat escapement' in around 1715, which developed on the escapement first made by Tompion in 1675 for the Greenwich clocks. His support for John Harrison was also invaluable – he loaned him £200 so he could start work on his first marine chronometer, H1.

Julien Le Roy (1686–1759)

This master craftsman belonged to the fifth generation of a family of clockmakers and made his first clock at the age of just thirteen. He moved to Paris from his hometown of Tours a year later and rose through the ranks of guilds, the Société des Arts, and ultimately became the official clockmaker or *Horloger Ordinaire du Roi* to King Louis XV in 1739.

Le Roy made many mechanical innovations, including a special repeating mechanism that greatly improved the precision of watches and clocks. He made one for Louis XV that is thought to be the first to allow the owner to remove the clock face to see the intricate inner workings.

During his professional life, Le Roy and his workshop produced some 3,500 watches – around 100 per year – while other workshops would have produced somewhere in the region of thirty to fifty timepieces per year. Examples of his work are housed in the Louvre in Paris and the Victoria and Albert Museum in London.

Continuing the dominance of this clockmaking dynasty, Le Roy's son Pierre (1717–1785) is responsible for three major innovations in horology that paved the way for the modern precision clock and marine chronometer, the latter inspired by the work of Englishman John Harrison. These are the detent escapement, the temperature-compensated balance and the isochronous balance spring.

Cuckoo clocks

For a pretty daft invention, the cuckoo clock has some impressive forebears. The Greek mathematician Ctesibius fashioned a water-driven automaton of an owl for his second-century BCE clock. It whistled and moved at certain times. Then in 797 CE, Harun al-Rashid of Bagdad gave Charlemagne a clock from which sprang a mechanical bird to sound the hours. And the renowned fourteenth-century clock in Strasbourg Cathedral featured a gilded rooster, which flapped its mechanical wings and emitted a crowing sound at noon each day.

There were a few clocks featuring mechanical cuckoos in the seventeenth century, but the eighteenth saw a veritable flurry of them coming out of the Black Forest region of south-west

116

Germany — but we don't know who started the trend or why. They became increasingly more elaborate and intricate with time. So much so that the *Guinness Book of Records* has a category for the World's Largest Cuckoo Clock, which at the time of writing resides in Sugarcreek, Ohio, and is 23 feet tall and 24 feet wide, featuring a five-piece band, a couple dancing a polka and, of course, a large cuckoo singing in the half-hours.

Cuckoo clocks have a metaphorical association with madness — and there are a remarkable number of them which are said to be haunted. Yes, haunted. I've come across accounts of one that supposedly starts by itself and goes straight to the right time unaided, and another that produces a ghostly apparition when it chimes midnight. Some of the mechanical birds are thought to have wicked intentions — with the spirit of a real bird trapped within. Given that cuckoos are such nasty nest-stealers by nature, it's scarcely surprising.

Abraham-Louis Perrelet (1729–1826)

In the 1770s, this ingenious Swiss horologist invented a self-winding mechanism for pocket watches. The mechanism works using the oscillating up-and-down motion of a weight as its owner walks – operating on the same 'automatic' principle as the modern wristwatch. A test conducted by the Geneva Society of Arts concluded in 1777 that 15 minutes walking would keep a Perrelet watch ticking for eight full days. Another of his inventions was the 'pedometer' – a device that measured steps and distance while walking, and now a rather popular, though usually digital, item for avid walkers and runners.

The Perrelet brand is still producing luxury timepieces in Switzerland, and claiming in its promotional tagline to be the 'Inventor of the Automatic Watch'.

Time-Travel Tip
Past-life regression

Put your scepticism aside and book yourself an appointment with a hypnotist. As they lull you into a trance you may have the potential to travel back in time from the comfort of their leather couch.

Practitioners of past-life regression believe that you can recover and relive memories from your own past – forgotten or repressed – or go even further back into previous incarnations, lived in different physical bodies long deceased.

Even if you don't believe what you find yourself saying, you'll learn something of the vividness of your imagination and the gems you have stored in the recesses of your wonderful, complex mind.

5
Modern Times

Standard time

We saw in the previous chapter how Greenwich became the centre of timekeeping and the site of 0° longitude. But despite these advances it would take another 150 years for the notion of 'standard' time to take hold – and that was down to the arrival of the railway.

A brief history of rail travel

The idea of rail travel, that is pulling goods along a purpose-built surface, goes right back to ancient Greece in the sixth century BCE. Spanning 6 kilometres of grooves cut into limestone, the Diolkos 'wagonway' was used to transport goods (in trucks pushed by slaves) for over 600 years. Railways using tracks or grooves appeared from the fourteenth century and by the sixteenth century narrow-gauge railways with wooden rails were common in European mines.

Britain led the way in the development of more ambitious railway lines. By the seventeenth century, wooden wagonways were in common use for transporting coal from mines to canals, and horse-drawn railways sprang up throughout the eighteenth century. The Industrial Revolution saw the invention of the steam engine and in 1825 an engineer called George Stephenson built the 'Locomotion' for the Stockton and Darlington Railway, north-east England, which was the first public steam railway in the world. He followed this with the intercity railway line from Liverpool to Manchester, which opened in 1830.

The steam locomotives built by Stephenson were soon in use throughout Britain, the US and Europe. By the early 1850s, Britain had over 7,000 miles of rail track.

In America, building railways was a much more laborious undertaking, given the sheer scale of the country, but they were critical to pioneering

An early steam locomotive

businessmen who wanted to open up access to the west. Keeping a keen eye on developments in Britain, America opened its first small-scale railways in the 1830s and 1840s, but it was the period between 1850 and 1890 that saw rapid expansion of the railroads and America becoming home to one third of the total track mileage on the planet. The first transcontinental railroad was aptly completed in 1869 following the civil war, connecting the country together for the first time.

Train time

With the surge in railway building across Europe and America, it became pretty obvious that a standard time was needed for services to run efficiently.

Greenwich Mean Time was first officially used by the railway system in Britain in 11 December 1847 – with every train having its own portable chronometer set to GMT. And to facilitate the precision of 'railway time', as it became known, the Royal Observatory in Greenwich began to transmit time signals by telegraph in August 1852.

However, it took another thirty years-plus for standard time to replace local time on the US railway system. The different railway companies in America set their own time standards. The leading standards were New York time, Pennsylvania time, Chicago time, Jefferson City (Missouri) time and San Francisco time – and with so many competing 'local' times in use, things got rather confusing.

In October 1883, the heads of all the US and Canadian railway companies met in Chicago and agreed to adopt a four-time-zone standard (five time zones are now in use). On 18 November 1883, all the railways readjusted their clocks as per their relevant time zones, though Standard Time was not enacted into law in the US until 1918.

The railways literally carried standard time around these countries and in just a few years all time was set to match it – except the time kept by the British Post Office that is, which continued to be 'London time' rather than GMT until 1872. GMT became the legal time in Britain in 1880.

Time zones

There are twenty-four time zones in use across the world, which use the notional lines of longitude to define their boundaries, with each one taking Greenwich Mean Time (GMT) as its reference or 'offset' time. Every 15 degrees of longitude adds or subtracts an hour to/from GMT depending on whether it's going west (minus) or east (plus) – with 360° of longitude ultimately adding up to 24 hours.

Some nations and territories are more flexible in terms of how they interpret time zones and longitudinal boundaries. Our two most populous countries in the world, India and China, apply a single time zone to their vast expanses (more on time in China shortly). India also uses half-hour deviations, along with Newfoundland, Iran, Afghanistan, Venezuela, Burma, the Marquesas, and parts of Australia. Other nations and provinces, including Nepal and the Chatham Islands, use quarter-hour time deviations.

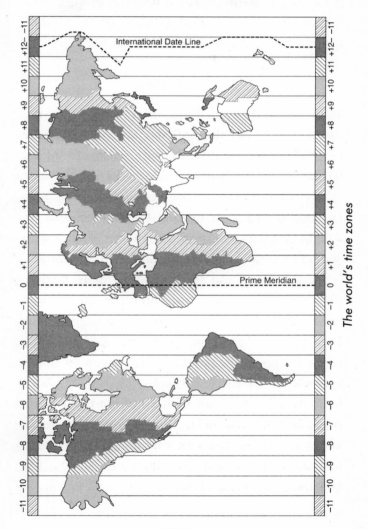

The world's time zones

125

Coordinated Universal Time

Commonly known as UTC, this system is largely a continuation of Greenwich Mean Time, with the terms GMT and UTC being used interchangeably with much the same meaning – to laymen at least. The introduction of UTC was led by the International Astronomical Union, which called for a more stable and accurate time standard that took into consideration the Earth's natural 'wobble' – and the fact that the Earth's rotation is slowing ever so slightly due to the drag of the tides.

The abbreviation of Coordinated Universal Time to UTC rather than CUT may seem a little odd. In French it would be *Temps Universel Coordonné*, or TUC, so as a compromise with France it was agreed that Universal Time Coordinated or *Universel Temps Coordonné* would be used and abbreviated to UTC, even though it is most commonly referred to as Coordinated Universal Time.

Many would be unaware of this, but GMT ceased to be the world's 'official' time standard in 1972. UTC is held by a number of atomic clocks, some 260 in total, in forty-nine different locations around the world (more on atomic clocks soon). The master of all these clocks is at the US Naval Observatory in

126

Washington, DC. Though it's unlikely to captivate the imagination as the centre of time quite like leafy, lovely historic Greenwich (I've lived there – I'm rather biased).

All the time in China

Technically, the colossal country that is modern China straddles five time zones, but it uses only one. Officially the entire country is 8 hours ahead of GMT (or UTC). The decision to have one time zone instead of five came in 1949 when the Chinese Civil War saw the end of the Republic of China and the start of the People's Republic of China. With this new communist era, the country was unified under one time, known as Beijing Time, though out of necessity local time continued to be unofficially used in western parts of the country that are up to two and a half hours behind Beijing Time.

Mecca Time

While Greenwich is the largely agreed upon site of the prime meridian for secular, administrative purposes, there are a number of other meridians dotted around the world – the most interesting among them relating to holy sites.

The Great Pyramid of Giza, the largest and oldest of the mighty pyramids of Egypt, for example, was an obvious and popular choice for the line to pass through up until the latter part of the nineteenth century. The Church of the Holy Sepulchre in Jerusalem was a popular meridian point for devout Christians but again it didn't catch on globally. But much more recently Mecca, which is the centre of the Muslim world, has been proposed as a new and appropriate site for the prime meridian. Time at the Mecca meridian is UTC+02:39:18.2.

The idea that Mecca should become the focal point of the prime meridian came in 2008, when Muslim clerics met in Doha, Qatar, at a special conference titled: 'Mecca: the Centre of the Earth, Theory and Practice'. Then the world's largest clock (more on this later) ticked into life in Mecca at the start of Ramadan in August 2010 – displaying Mecca Time – well sort of. In fact, it was ultimately set to display Arabia Standard Time, which takes its lead from the meridian at Greenwich rather than leading with its own.

Daylight saving time

Daylight saving time is observed largely in the northern hemisphere: Europe, Canada and America, along with a couple of African and Latin American countries, New Zealand and part of south-east Australia – though many more countries observed it in the past, including Russia, China and India. The basic principle is adding an hour in spring and subtracting that hour back in autumn to make our days a little bit longer and brighter in the evening – in summer at least.

Daylight saving time was first introduced in the early twentieth century during the First World War by Germany and its allies as a way of saving coal and other energy sources. Their enemies – Britain, France, et al – decided this was a good idea and followed suit, as did many of the neutral countries on the peripheries of the war. By 1918, Russia and the US had adopted daylight saving time too.

Many countries abandoned daylight saving time in the years following the war with the exception of the UK, France, Ireland and Canada – though other countries dipped in and out – and with the coming of the Second World War it was widely adopted once more. The 1970s energy crisis saw a spike in popularity for pushing clocks forward in springtime to reduce the amount of fuel used for electric lighting.

From pocket to wrist

In the last chapter we saw how the trend in portable pocket watches sprang from the seventeenth-century fashion for waistcoats – and in popular culture the image of the well-heeled gent, with a gold chain across his midriff, is familiar from that time right up to the early twentieth century. But with ever-increasing numbers of watches being produced, and continuing advances in timekeeping technology, the pocket watch went from being an item sported only by the wealthy to a much more ubiquitous one. Functional as well as fashionable, the pocket watch had to evolve to keep the market fresh and so, in the early twentieth century, along came the latest must-have item: the wristwatch.

A clock of birds

The Kaluli people of Papua New Guinea still live their lives by the 'bird clock'. The early morning calls of certain birds tell the people to get up and the afternoon calls of others tell them to go home, ensuring that people are safely back in their villages while visibility is still good.

Of course, the crowing of cocks still heralds the start of the working day in rural areas in the West, though they are likely supplemented with an alarm clock just in case. Like humans, chickens have a 'circadian' cycle – with biological processes relating closely to the 24-hour day. Light cycles exert influence over their heart, brain and liver functions and, in male chickens, testosterone, which relates to their crowing behaviour.

Chickens have been known to shift their roosting and crowing patterns in response to changes in light intensity caused by the changing of the seasons or living on higher ground. In a mountainous area of northern India it was found that cocks started 2 to 3 hours before sunrise. The intervals between their crows increased the closer it came to sunrise, despite the fact that the Sun was not visible to them.

Wristwatch No. 1

The story goes that in 1904 the aviator Alberto Santos-Dumont asked his friend, the French watchmaker Louis Cartier, to design a watch for him that he could easily refer to while flying – the pocket watch being an inconvenient item to consult mid-air. And so Cartier developed the first wristwatch. Well, technically it wasn't the first – the Swiss watchmaker Patek Philippe developed the 'lady's bracelet watch' in the 1860s as a stylish piece of timekeeping jewellery for the woman about town – but Cartier's wristwatch design caught on in a way that PP and others could only dream of. And the main advantage it had was war.

As well as seeing the first widespread use of daylight saving hours, the First World War also saw a surge in popularity for the wristwatch – a much more convenient item for an officer to wear on the battlefield.

Luxury brands

Like the pocket watch before it, the wristwatch started life as an exclusive item, worn by middle- and upper-class men because of its initial expense. The 'inventor' of the men's wristwatch Louis Cartier marketed his first 'Santos' watch to the great and good in 1911. He followed that in 1912 with two models that are still on sale today – the 'Baignoire' and 'Tortue' – and because the war created such demand, he also released the rather macho-sounding and still popular 'Tank' in 1917.

Cartier remains a luxury brand to this day – selling high-end watches and jewellery. Visit the Cartier website and you'll find the least expensive watch on for a tidy £1,600, while the price of the most expensive is undisclosed – you have to request it. But the uppermost price on display is an impressive £50,000 for a diamond-encrusted, white-gold affair.

A browse through many of the online catalogues of the most luxurious of the luxury watch brands yields the same silence on price. Most of the most exclusive companies are Swiss and pretty old – TAG Heuer, Vacheron Constantin, Breitling, IWC, Zenith, Audemars Piguet, Girard Perregaux, Blancpain, Patek Philippe, Piaget, etc. It would clearly be vulgar to put a price on watches so special.

Steel and plain old gold are the cheapest materials relatively speaking. But white, yellow and pink gold see the prices soar, and they go rather stellar when you throw in some precious stones, platinum, titanium or palladium.

The most expensive timepieces

At the time of writing, the Chopard 201-Carat Watch is the most expensive watch on the market, coming in at a cool $25 million. And it is also one of the most hideous-looking things around. A blur of gaudy precious stones, with a tiny watch face tucked away in there somewhere, it's impossible to know how you'd even wear the thing. Amusingly, the second most expensive is a pocket watch made by Patek Phillipe in 1933, priced at $11 million. Indeed, vintage Patek Phillipe watches tend to fetch millions at auction without fail – take that, Mr Cartier!

Back in 1999, a Thomas Tompion clock from 1705 fetched over $2 million at Sotheby's and would likely make much more than that if re-auctioned today. But the current clock record is held by a French design by Abraham-Louis Bréguet. Built in 1795, this rare Sympathique clock is currently valued at $6.8 million.

Clever clocks

Advances in physics in the twentieth century revolutionized timekeeping and clocks became very, very clever indeed. It's all a bit much for my unscientific mind, but in the following pages I've done my best to outline the chief advances that have changed the way we tell time for ever.

Piezoelectricity

Some solid materials – crystals, ceramics, biological materials like bone – accumulate and store an electric charge. Known as piezoelectricity (from the Greek 'to squeeze' – as squeezing releases the energy), it was first discovered and demonstrated in 1880 by brothers Jacques and Pierre Curie (husband of Marie). They revealed how an electrical charge could be generated when mechanical force was applied to crystals (including quartz), sugar cane and Rochelle salt.

Piezoelectricity was subsequently used in sonar devices developed during the First World War, including an ultrasonic submarine detector, phonograph cartridges, telephony devices and aviation radios, among other innovative new technologies.

But more importantly for us, piezoelectricity powers the quartz crystal oscillator that is the driving force in most modern wristwatches.

Quartz timekeepers

Quartz crystals have been used in both clocks and watches since the 1960s. When electric pulses are applied to the crystal it vibrates – and these vibrations can be fine-tuned to any desired frequency. For clocks and watches, the crystal is cut into the shape of a tiny tuning fork and manipulated until it vibrates to a frequently of 32,768Hz – equivalent to a 1-second pulse. This is all terribly precise and revolutionized timekeeping.

The first quartz clock was developed in 1927 and the National Bureau of Standards in the US used quartz time as the time standard for the whole country from 1929 until the 1960s. The first quartz wristwatch came onto the market in time for Christmas in 1969 and cost the same as a small car. Despite the high price, Seiko's Astron model sold well and, with research and development, quartz watches were soon affordable for the majority.

Omega Speedmaster and NASA

In 2013, the popular men's body-spray brand Lynx unveiled a new advertising campaign during the coveted US Super Bowl ad break spot. The ad features a statuesque and fearless lifeguard undertaking a daring rescue of a damsel being distressed by a shark. After he's beaten up the shark and returned the young lady to land, the pair share a tender moment until she spies a man approaching wearing an astronaut suit. She abandons the lifeguard and races into the arms of the astronaut as the tagline 'Nothing Beats an Astronaut' appears on screen.

But the truth is nothing beats the extraordinary advertising coup of the Omega Speedmaster watch back in the late 1960s. First, it was endorsed by NASA as spaceflight-ready, then it was worn during the first American 'spacewalk' on the Gemini 4 mission in 1965 (when astronaut Edward H White floated around in space outside his ship for 20 minutes), and *then* it was worn by none other than Neil Armstrong when he took those first steps on the Moon.

Atomic clocks

While quartz oscillators still proliferate in clocks and wristwatches, such devices are no longer used as the source of standard time. Earlier in the chapter I mentioned that Coordinated Universal Time is held and maintained by a number of atomic clocks, some 260 in total, in forty-nine different locations around the world, with the master of all these located at the US Naval Observatory in Washington DC. But what is an atomic clock?

These clocks are accurate to within 1 second every 30 million years. Born out of particle physics in the 1930s and 1940s, atomic clocks use minute vibrations emitted by electrons in atoms to calculate time. There are 9,192,631,770 atomic vibrations in every second. The first accurate atomic clock was invented in 1949 by the American physicist Isidor Rabi (1898–1988).

Atomic clocks are used to control the wave frequency of television broadcasts, and in global navigation satellite systems – from which the GPS in your car or mobile phone draws its data.

Quantum clocks

A close relation of the atomic clocks, quantum clocks bring aluminium and beryllium ions together in an electromagnetic trap and cool them to near absolute zero temperatures. Now, I can't pretend to know what that does, except that vibrations are involved, but I do know that it makes quantum clocks even more accurate than the atomic clocks which are the current keepers of standard time – more than thirty-seven times more accurate apparently. The most accurate of these ultra accurate clocks was built in February 2010 by the clever people at the US National Institute of Standards and Technology. It uses a single aluminium atom and is expected to lose just 1 second in 3.7 billion years. Though how this will be tracked is another issue entirely.

Why-oh-why-2K?

Reading about an invention as complex and precise as the atomic clock, accurate to within 1 second in 30 million years, it's hard to grasp the relative silliness of Y2K. Also known as 'the millennium bug', Y2K was going to be the end of us all – because we hadn't programmed our computer technology to cope with a change of date from 31 December 1999 to 1 January 2000, from the twentieth into the twenty-first century. With most computers using a two-numeral system to represent the year date i.e. 99 rather than 1999, it was thought that the change to 00 would bring about confusion and chaos in our global systems. So systems were upgraded in a hurry toward the end of the 1990s, but that didn't stop a media frenzy predicting the end of modern civilization.

People started stockpiling food and saying prayers to protect themselves against this impending technological apocalypse. But when the date came, the apocalypse was nowhere to be seen. Though there were some computer failures, the exact number isn't known, because, well, it's a rather embarrassing thing to admit. Saying that, there were a couple of scary occurrences as a result of the 'bug'. In Japan, radiation monitoring equipment failed and at a nuclear plant an alarm sounded just after midnight causing panic. A significantly less scary thing happened in Australia, where ticket validation machines on buses failed in two states. And in America some slot machines in Delaware gave up the ghost.

Bearing in mind my initial comment about atomic clocks, the US Naval Observatory that runs the master atomic clock for UTC gave the wrong date on its website on 1 January 2000 – posting the year as 19100 instead – as did France's national weather forecasting service. Proofing against Y2K cost over $300 billion worldwide.

For the record

So far this book has sought to capture the history of time and timekeeping, and to report on some of the phenomenal advances in technologies and some of the silliest too. But before we take a leap into the future in the next chapter, it's time to take stock of where we are now and take a peak at some mind-boggling records of the day.

The shortest time ever measured

Back in 2004, scientists claimed to have measured the shortest interval of time ever: 100 attoseconds. An attosecond is one quintillionth of a second. One attosecond is to a second what a second is to around 31.71 billion years – more than twice the commonly held age of the universe. The 100 that have been measured, if stretched so that they lasted 1 second, would last 300 million years on the same scale. It boggles the mind!

We're unlikely to hear much about attoseconds in our day-to-day lives, but milliseconds, microseconds and nanoseconds are already here and will be increasingly important in the future.

First off, let's consider the second itself. In Chapter 3 we touched on the ancient origins of the duodecimal (12) and sexagesimal (60) counting systems and how the idea of a second was born of that (24 hours of 60 minutes, each subdivided into smaller units of 60 – aka seconds). Up to 1960 the second was defined as 1/86,400 of a mean solar day, but now it is measured by atomic clocks and defined by atomic vibrations, so 1 second equals 9,192,631,770 vibrations.

When you're dealing with numbers that big, there is plenty of scope to drill down into smaller and smaller parts. A millisecond is a mere one-thousandth of a second, or one beat of a midge's wings (a housefly's takes about 3 milliseconds). Milliseconds are handy for measuring computer activities, which tend to operate much faster than the human mind. For example, computer monitor response times tend to be between 2 and 5 milliseconds.

A microsecond is one millionth of a second, or a thousandth of a millisecond. It takes the human eye around 350,000 microseconds to blink. These and nanoseconds (a mind-boggling one billionth of a second) are used to measure light speeds and sound frequencies. There are also picoseconds (one trillionth of a second) and femtoseconds (one quadrillionth of a second) which are used to measure things like the vibrations of atoms in molecules.

The longest-running clock

The longest-running clock, that we know of at least, is the 'Beverly Clock', which lives in the reception of the Department of Physics at the University of Otago, New Zealand. Constructed in 1864 by

Arthur Beverly, the clock has never been manually wound, ever. Instead, its mechanism is driven by perpetual motion caused by variations in atmospheric pressure and changes in daily temperatures. The temperature variations either

cause the air in a 1-cubic-foot airtight box to expand or contract, pushing on the clock's internal diaphragm. A variation of 6°C over the course of a day will create enough pressure to lift a one-pound weight by one inch and drive the clock's mechanism onward.

Now, the clock may never have been wound, but it has actually stopped a few times. On occasion the mechanism has needed to be cleaned or it has failed and needed to be repaired, or at other times the temperature variations have not been sufficient enough to power the clock.

At the University of Oxford in England lives the Oxford Electric Bell, or 'Clarendon Dry Pile', which is an experimental electric bell that has been continuously ringing since 1840 – well, almost continuously. Thankfully for the other occupants of the building that houses the bell, its ringing is inaudible behind two layers of glass.

The biggest clocks

The biggest clock in the world, in terms of the size of its visible workings, is the same clock discussed earlier as the keeper of 'Mecca Time'. This gargantuan clock sits atop the Abraj Al Bait Towers in Mecca, Saudi Arabia. Its face has a diameter of 43 metres. The clock tower that houses it is the tallest in the world (and the second tallest building in the world), and the building that houses the tower has the world's largest floor space. It'll be a while until anyone trumps this place.

Other notably enormous clock faces are the Cevahir Mall clock in Istanbul (36 metres) and the Duquesne Brewing Company Clock in Pittsburgh (18 metres). The famous Big Ben in London is a mere 6.9 metres in diameter (you could fit six of them on the Mecca clock face with room to spare).

The littlest clock

What qualifies as a clock these days is up for discussion. Clocks are embedded in most of our technological devices and invisible apart from that digital display in the lower right-hand corner of our computer monitor or the screen of our mobile phone.

The current record holder for the 'smallest atomic clock' was constructed at the National Institute for Standards and Technology (NIST) in Colorado in the US. It was unveiled in 2004 and is the size of a grain of rice and is accurate to 1 second in 3,000 years – so considerably less accurate than the most accurate atomic clock in Switzerland, which is accurate to 1 second in every 30 million years. But still, a clock the size of a grain of rice and that accurate is pretty impressive.

The longest-running time experiment

Back in 1927, Thomas Parnell of the University of Queensland, Australia, commenced what is now the longest-running time test: the pitch drop funnel experiment.

Pitch is a petroleum product, an elastic polymer, with a tough rocklike appearance. When heated up pitch becomes highly malleable and is used for waterproofing boats. At room temperature pitch feels solid – even brittle – and can easily be shattered with a blow from a hammer. If heated and left to its own devices it takes years for it to change and move.

Parnell was curious about this material and wanted to demonstrate the fluidity and high viscosity of pitch, so he heated a batch of it and poured it into a funnel. He sealed off the funnel, allowed the pitch three years to settle, trimmed off the end of the funnel and waited for it to drip. Eight years passed. And then the first drip fell from the pitch, in a blink of an eye, in December 1938 – eleven years after the experiment commenced.

Since that time the pitch has slowly dripped out of the funnel. At the time of writing, over eighty years since the experiment began, the ninth drop is only just forming for its all-too-brief journey out of the funnel. The time it takes for the drips to come out is inconsistent. For example, the sixth drop fell in April 1979, 8.7 years after the previous one, but it then took 9.3 years for the seventh to come out in July 1988 and then 12.3 for the next one in November 2000.

Images of the funnel can show a large droplet of pitch hanging tantalizingly from its mouth – looking ready to drop at any moment – but still with years to go. When it does drop, it takes just an eighth of a second. The experiment's current custodian is John Maidstone. He's been watching it since January 1961 – and he has never seen it happen. He has missed this grand event five times. In 1988, he missed it while making a cup of tea. In November 2000, he set up a camera to monitor it as he was away in London, only to find that the camera had failed and the drop was not captured. Maidstone described it as one of the saddest moments of his life.

The fact is nobody has ever seen it drip. But next time they definitely will – whether in real time or captured on camera. Not willing to risk missing it again, Maidstone now has three cameras continually focussed on the pitch to capture the moment it drops. And, rather sadly, people across the world are watching it live online. You can too at the University of Queenland's School of Mathematics and Physics website.

If you find you develop a taste for such things as a consequence, I recommend www.watching-grass-grow.com – the web address tells its own story.

The longest and shortest lives

Relative to other creatures with which we share the world, humans live a long time, though life expectancy varies widely depending on where you are born (see page 206).

According to botanist and ecologist Ghillean Prance, 'The shortest biography is said to be that of the mayfly: Born. Eat. Sex. Die. Pausing neither to eat nor to court, mayflies emerge from the nymph stage with all the food they need for their adult life, and mate in flight. Typically they live only one or two days.' It is worth noting that the immature part of the mayfly's life, the 'naiad' or 'nymph' stage, can last up to a year, before its all too brief adulthood.

The brief stages of a mayfly's life

Insects tend to dominate the 'shortest living' category. Among mammals, the house mouse probably has the shortest innings, with those living to four years being in the geriatric class. Among fish the mosquitofish is an OAP by two, and among birds hummingbirds are way over the hill if they make it to seven or eight.

In the animal kingdom, the Asian elephant has been observed to live as long as eighty-six years, while the oldest living bird is the macaw, which can live up to 100 years in captivity. The lizard-like tuatara reptile of New Zealand can live up to 200 years, while the Japanese koi fish can live more than 200 years in the right conditions. One such fish, called Hanako (meaning 'flower maid') was reportedly 226 years old upon her death in 1977. Greenland sharks, native to the North Atlantic, are believed to live to around 200, and the slow-moving Galápagos tortoise can keep going till around 190 according to current data – and there are many examples of tortoises living in excess of 150 years. The Bowhead whale is also thought to live to around 200 if life is relatively incident free.

The longest-living known creatures are molluscs in the bivalvia category (whose bodies live in shells of two hinged parts). One quahog clam, affectionately known as Ming (comparing its great age to that of the Chinese Ming Dynasty), was believed to be 405 to 410 years old when discovered (and killed) off the Icelandic coast in 2007. Its age was judged by the annual growth rings on its shell – it is unknown how long this creature may have continued to live on the ocean floor had it not been 'discovered'.

There are sponges near Antarctica which are thought to be at least 10,000 years old and black coral in the ocean off New Zealand that may be 4,000-plus years old.

We should consider the speed at which life is lived and experienced by these different creatures. The tortoise lives its long life with a glacial slowness that befits its age, while the tiny hummingbird can beat its wings as often as 90 times per second when hovering, while some short-lived flies like midges can beat theirs more than 1,000 times per second. So another way of looking at it is that hummingbirds and flies pack as much into their little existences as tortoises do – just a hell of a lot faster.

The oldest old folks

According to the Guinness Book of Records, Jeanne Calment of France lived the longest life on record – dying in 1997 at the tender age of 122 years, 164 days. Prior to Calment the record was held by Japanese centenarian Shigechiyo Izumi – though it turned out that Mr Izumi's record could not be verified and he may have been a mere 105 at death rather than 120. Typically, Izumi's longevity was not hampered by the fact that he put away a daily dose of booze and took up smoking at 70. Japanese woman Misao Okawa who is 115 at the time of writing, took possession of the Guinness World Record as the oldest living person in June 2013, when her Japanese compatriot Jiroemon Kimura expired at the tender age of 116.

Time-Travel Tip
Dash across the
International Date Line

This imaginary line around the Earth passes through the middle of the Pacific Ocean, following the similarly imaginary 180° longitude line. Well, it doesn't so much follow it as zigzag in proximity to it as it journeys from the North to the South Pole. On either side of this imaginary line it is a different calendar day. A traveller crossing the International Date Line going east has to subtract a day or 24 hours, heading west they add a day. So criss-crossing the International Date Line allows us to travel back and forward in time by 24 hours!

In Jules Verne's *Around the World in Eighty Days* (1873), Phileas Fogg believes that he has lost his famous wager to complete his eighty-day journey by the evening of Saturday 21 December 1872. Disappointed, a little humiliated and believing it to be Sunday 22 December, Fogg realizes, just in the nick of time, that he forgot the Date Line in his calculations and that he did in fact complete the journey in seventy-nine days, and dashes to claim his prize. Good old-fashioned time travel in action.

6
Future Time

Real time

In August 2011, I was living in Greenwich, London, the home of time. Between the 6th and 11th of that month, multiple riots broke out all over London and elsewhere in England. Out the window of my flat on Blackheath Hill I could see a helicopter hovering over nearby Lewisham, where clashes with the police and looting were taking place. Meanwhile I had the television tuned to the live news on the BBC where the images captured by the aforementioned helicopter were being broadcast, and in my hand I held a smartphone upon which I was following live reports on Twitter from the ground in Lewisham.

154

The events were happening, being reported, accessed and processed in 'real time'. In real time, events are captured and transmitted at the same rate that the audience experiences them. And for a generation of young technology users, real time is, well, real time. Information is instantaneous, as is our interaction with it. This is the new normal for now. But real time is set to get a whole lot faster.

Instant messaging

The biggest change in mass communications since the advent of postal systems was the invention of the telegraph. The first electrical telegraphs were sent in Germany in the 1830s and could travel a distance of around 1 kilometre. The subsequent flurry of activity on both sides of the Atlantic in developing the technology and laying the requisite cable meant speedy advances in telegraphy in the 1830s and '40s, most notably by Sir William Fothergill Cooke and Charles Wheatstone in the UK, and Samuel F. B. Morse, of Morse code fame, in the US.

By the 1850s the first commercial telegrams had been sent the 750 miles between New York and Chicago – taking a mere quarter of a second to travel that distance (that's 11 million miles per hour).

The first people to use it could barely fathom that such a thing was possible. By the 1860s a transatlantic telegraph cable was in operation, and by the 1870s Britain was wired to its faraway colony India. In 1902, the telegraph system spanning the Pacific was complete and the world was fully encircled by wires, relaying and receiving information over vast distances at previously inconceivable speeds. And then it went wireless.

Using radio technology, pioneer Albert Turpain sent and received his first Morse code radio signal in France in 1895. It only travelled 25 metres, but was a considerable achievement. The following year an Italian called Guglielmo Marconi sent his first radio signal a full 6 kilometres. Marconi took his technology to Britain and the rest is history. In 1901, the first wireless transmission, the letter *S*, was sent across the Atlantic.

Concurrent with these developments, other inventors were working on transmitting not just signals, but human voices through wires. The electric telephone was invented in the 1870s and the first commercial services were established in New Haven, Connecticut, and London in 1878 and 1879 respectively. Telephone exchanges were established

in every major city in the US by the middle of the 1880s, but it wasn't until 1915 that the first US coast-to-coast, long-distance telephone call was placed – from New York to San Francisco. And it would be another twelve years before human speech could be carried across the Atlantic, when in 1927 radio was used to transmit voices back and forth.

It's hard to imagine how profound an impact these new forms of mass communications had on everyday life and people's perceptions of the world they lived in – and of speed and time. Where once a letter would take weeks and even months to bring news of its writer across the world, messages could now be relayed in moments. But once these things became the 'new normal' people came to expect them, and to expect faster, better ways of sending and receiving information at that.

The innovations continued thick and fast. In the UK, the BBC put out its first radio transmissions in 1922, and by 1925 some 80 per cent of the country was being reached through regional and relay stations. Also in 1925, the Scottish inventor John Logie Baird demonstrated the transmission of moving pictures (just silhouettes at that time) at Selfridges department store in London. Two years later the cathode ray tube was invented and the BBC started its first experimental broadcasts in 1932, with an expanded service launching from Alexandra Palace

The transmitter at Alexandra Palace

on a high hill in North London in 1936 – a world first.

Flash forward to today, through the innovations and inventions of colour television, videotelephony, satellite phones, radio and television and all the advances in computer technology. On a single device we can now access full-colour, high-definition television or listen to radio in 'real time', play games, read the newspaper, receive video calls, send email, and communicate with friends, family and the wider world instantly through myriad social channels, take photos or video footage – and tell the time – all while walking down the street. And it's only been possible to do all of these things together since the late 2000s. Now that's time speeding up.

If we want to slow it down again, we can always watch the pitch drop experiment livestreamed from Australia on this same device. It's due to drop any day now . . .

The speed of money

The average person's electronic interaction with their money is a speedy affair. Banks communicate with each other instantly, relaying the information necessary for us to make a quick financial transaction almost anywhere in the world, or to complete multiple transactions from the comfort of our desks through online banking. But this speed and ease is laughable next to the lightening-fast activity on today's stock markets.

On the stock market, where countless goods and financial products are traded – the tangible and intangible – 50 to 70 per cent of all the trades are executed by an algorithm with no human input. And buying and selling is conducted in milliseconds.

A 'high-frequency' electronic trader might do 1,000 trades in a minute, but for every trade conducted there are numerous uncompleted transactions that disappear into the ether. These high-high speed computers test the market, sending out buy-and-sell orders and when another computer connects with an order, all the others that weren't taken up are cancelled.

Further computer programs have been designed to identify and defy other similar trading algorithms. These jump into the market, push the price up and sell to other algorithms, making huge sums in seconds.

In the New York Stock Exchange there is a room that is 20,000 square feet (about three football fields) filled with row upon row of servers, around 10,000, owned by various financial institutions and each analysing 'the market' and trading. This is all done without any human involvement and significantly faster than any human can think, let alone act.

Information wars

In the highly competitive world of stocks and shares, the speed at which information travels from, say, the commodities market (basic goods) in Chicago to the equities market (stocks in companies) in New York is critical to closing deals faster than the other guy. Every millisecond counts. Fibre-optic cables allow information to travel between these markets in 15 milliseconds. But traders want that information even faster. This demand started a race to get the straightest and therefore fastest fibre-optic line from Chicago to New York to shave a millisecond or two off the speed at which information travelled, providing much-valued time to the ultra-fast trading computers.

The speed of light through air is even faster than fibre optics. So to capitalize on this, towers are now being constructed to beam information between the trading centres in an estimated 8 milliseconds. One day soon these transmissions may be conducted in microseconds, or possibly even nanoseconds.

Speed dating

So I hope we've established that the way we live and the way we interact with each other is accelerating. And as a consequence time is becoming ever more precious. In this fast, frenetic, multi-tasking world we're streamlining everything, including how we find our partners. Enter speed dating. Rather than spending all that time trying to meet 'the one', you can now go to one place and meet a number of 'ones', talk to them for short intervals of between 3 and 8 minutes, and if a connection is made before the bell rings, note it, pass it on to the organizers and let them tell you whether your potential beloved returns your affections. Cue wedding bells.

Faster and faster and faster

Information travels far faster than humans can. But humans can travel pretty fast. The fastest footspeed record currently belongs to the appropriately named Usain Bolt, who made it up to 27.79 mph (44.72 kph) during a 100-metre sprint in 2009. Bolt completed the 100m race in 9.58 seconds, beating his own previous world record of 9.69 seconds. Humans are still considerably slower than other animals. Cheetahs are the fastest creatures on Earth and, in 2012, a Cheetah called Sarah created a new world record by running 100 metres in 5.95 seconds, reaching a top speed of 61 mph (98 kph). Saying that, even a domestic cat could outrun Usain Bolt – reaching recorded speeds of 30 mph (48 kph).

Travelling faster and reducing the time spent getting from A to B has been a key human endeavour. Next, we'll look at some of the fastest modes of transport ever invented and consider the future of how we travel at ever greater speeds.

Planes, trains and automobiles

The Wright brothers' first successful engine-powered flight in 1903 reached a whopping 6.8 mph (10.9 kph) speed. By 1905 their speed record was up to 37.85 mph (60.23 kph). Today's airspeed record for a manned flight was set by the Lockheed SR-71 Blackbird in July 1976. This bird got up to 2,193.2 mph (3,529.6 kph).

The fastest commercially available car is the Bugatti Veyron Super Sport, which can go from zero to 60 mph in 2.4 seconds and reach a top speed of 267 mph (431.07 kph). You can get your own for just $2.4 million. There are, however, no roads upon Earth on which you can legally drive at that speed – the highest legal speed limit is a mere 150 kph in Italy (followed by 140 kph in Poland, Bulgaria and the United Arab Emirates). There is no speed limit on the German autobahn, though 130 kph is recommended. Travelling 300 kph faster in a Bugatti would likely not go down too well.

To give a sense of just how fast we've speeded up over time, the first commercial automobile powered by petrol, designed by German Karl Benz (of Mercedes-Benz), hit the road in 1888 with a maximum speed of just 16 kph. The fastest train on the planet is currently the CRH380A in China, which has a top speed of 302 mph – making it the fastest legal way to travel by land.

Breaking the sound barrier

The speed of sound is 343.2 metres per second (or around 768 mph). The sound barrier was first encountered during the Second World War when aircraft started to see the effects of compressibility – an aerodynamic effect that struck their crafts, impeding further acceleration. Hitting the sound barrier in an unsuitable craft creates loud cracks or 'sonic booms'. Design changes to aircraft, making them more aerodynamic, allowed them to break through this barrier and increase acceleration. The sound barrier was officially broken by American Chuck Yeager in 1947 flying an XP-86 Sabre.

The first time a land vehicle broke the sound barrier was just one year later in 1948, when an unmanned rocket sled reached 1,019 mph (1,640 kph) before jumping off its rails. The first manned vehicle was driven by Briton Andy Green in 1997, when his vehicle, the Thrust SSC (supersonic car), achieved a top speed of 763 mph (1,228 kph).

In October 2012, Austrian Felix Baumgarter became the first skydiver to travel faster than the speed of sound, reaching a maximum velocity of 833.9 mph (1,342 kph). To achieve this he jumped from a balloon floating 24 miles (39,045 metres) above New Mexico (and way above the stratosphere) – and in doing so also broke the record for the highest-ever freefall. To put that in perspective, your average Boeing 747 reaches a maximum height of 13,000 metres and Mount Everest peaks at just 8,848 metres. Baumgarter's fall to Earth took just over 9 minutes, with only the last 2,526 metres negotiated by parachute.

Rocket speed

In May 1969, the *Apollo 10* space rocket set off on a dry-run mission, testing all the procedures required for landing on the Moon – without actually landing on the Moon. That was done by *Apollo 11* in July of the same year. During that mission, *Apollo 10* is thought to have reached the highest speeds ever attained by a manned vehicle – 24,791 mph (39,897 kph).

In 2004, NASA tested a hypersonic aircraft, which used a rocket booster to launch and ultimately reached speeds of 7,000 mph (10,461 kph). If this technology could successfully be applied to manned passenger flights, it would utterly change the way we move around our planet and how we experience time and distance.

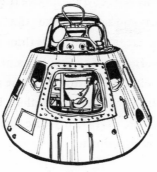

Apollo 10

Future travel

✻ Flying cars: We've all seen the sci-fi movies in which sleek, aerodynamic automobiles glide through impossibly high cityscapes. But the flying cars we may drive in the future will more likely draw on microlight technology and look a bit like two-person, enclosed gliders with detachable wings. Such vehicles will allow us to fly to nearby countries with ease. With fuel-efficient engines and being able to fly at around 150 mph without having to navigate roads, flying cars will be an attractive, environmentally friendly option. And they won't cost the Earth either – perhaps the same as a new high-end family car.

✳ Rubbish-powered autos: The film *Back to the Future* was made in 1985 and its closing scene featured the futuristically dressed character 'Doc' feeding waste matter into a fuel converter on this time machine/car. Back in 1985 this seemed like a pretty far-fetched idea, but today it is already a reality. Waste-to-energy plants are mushrooming across Europe, turning our unrecyclable rubbish into electricity. This electricity could soon be used to power road vehicles. While there are only a few electric cars currently on our roads, one day they'll be the norm, if hydrogen-powered cars don't beat them to it. These cars of the future will not only be greener, but considerably safer too. Traffic may even be controlled by satellite technology with vehicles talking to each other, and traffic jams could be a thing of the past.

✳ Magnetic trains: Elevated train tracks and monorails are nothing new. But magnetically levitated trains, which travel at average speeds of 260 mph, are. The first 'Maglev' train line is already in operation between the city centre in Shanghai and Pudong airport. The downside is that this new style of train transport is expensive to put in place, requiring new track. However, other train technology is catching up – and can travel nearly as fast as the Maglevs on standard tracks. Soon it'll be possible to zip from city to city in new record speeds and, as it cuts out the faff of checking in, may be even be faster than air travel in some cases.

* Slow travel: While the emphasis so far has been on speeding up, environmentalists are urging us to slow down. Largely a reaction to low-cost air travel, many in the green movement look on travelling, not just as a process of being transported from one place to another, but of experiencing the journey – preferably by taking the greener options of a train or boat. We are asked to pause and question whether we really travel any more, or do we just arrive . . . This is an entirely different approach to time – valuing the journey as much as the destination – experiencing it in real time, if you will. But as we know, real time isn't really real time – but already faster-than-human time. And it doesn't look likely to slow down any time soon.

Time travel

Humans have been fascinated by time travel for millennia. The first known story of time travel (and indeed space or inter-dimensional travel) goes back as far as the eighth century BCE in Hindu mythology. A story in the Sanskrit epic Mahabharata sees King Revaita (or Raivata) travel to a different world to meet Brahma, the god of creation, and find that many ages have passed when he returns to Earth.

Einstein's work on relativity has exerted the profoundest influence over modern thinking about time and time travel. He said that time beats at different rates depending on how fast you move. If you go fast, time slows down and this has been proven true. One experiment synchronizes two clocks, then places one in an airplane that takes off, travels around at high speed, decelerates and lands. It will be a little behind the clock that stayed on land, as the clock on the plane will operate more slowly when travelling. The difference will be small, but it will be there nonetheless. According to Einstein, both times are equally true.

Cosmonaut Sergei Krikalev holds the current record for the longest time spent in space – totalling 803 days (2.2 years) over three expeditions, the longest of which lasted 438 days. Because of the incredible speeds he was travelling (around 17,000 mph), Krikalev actually travelled into the future. In fact, he also holds the record for time travel into the future – a whopping 20 milliseconds.

These days physicists talk with considerably more confidence about the possibility of time travel – though the conditions are rather difficult to create and capture. Options include travelling at the speed of light, using cosmic strings or black holes, or prizing open tiny fissures in the space-time continuum (wormholes) and jumping into them.

Back to the beginning: finding the 'God Particle'

What is going on in the massive collider in Switzerland is way over the head of most of us mere mortals. The variable names for things and language used to describe the experiments doesn't help much either – with the terms Higgs boson, the Large Hadron Collider, CERN and the God Particle all used seemingly interchangeably. To clarify: the Large Hadron Collider (aka supercollider) at CERN (the European Laboratory for Particle Physics in

Geneva) is looking to confirm the existence of the Higgs boson (aka the God Particle).

Physicists hypothesize that the complex universe we currently know and the laws of physics that govern it evolved as the universe cooled in the first moments after the super-hot Big Bang. Now, by crashing together subatomic particles at mind-bending speed in the 17-mile circuit of the Large Hadron Collider, physicists hope to recreate and revisit the super-hot conditions of these pre-universe times to see what might have gone on back then. It is ultimately a search for original simplicity, before everything got so terribly complicated.

On the wishlist of things to find are particles, which could constitute clouds of dark matter

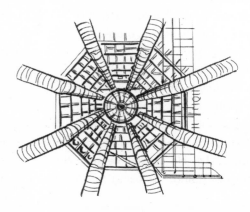

(the stuff believed to produce gravity and hold everything together and in place) and, of course, the Higgs boson – a particle which creates a sort of cosmic molasses and imbues other particles with mass. To do this, physicists are recreating the conditions of less than a billionth of a second after the universe was created, and they're doing this up to 600 million times a second. In July 2012, a new particle was found that is 'consistent with' Higgs boson but at the time of writing physicists are still reticent about giving it a firm thumbs up.

Living in the past, literally

David McDermott is an American artist who refuses to acknowledge or live in the 'present day'. He lives in mod-con-free nineteenth-century house in Dublin, Ireland, surrounded by articles of a bygone era and dressed like a country gent crossed with something out of a gothic novel, top hat and all. He refitted his house with older fixtures, fittings and furniture (though he does have a phone – an old Bakelite obviously). He says, 'I've seen the future, and I'm not going.' Refusing to use the Internet or credit, David has to physically withdraw money from the bank when he needs it.

His long-standing collaborative relationship with fellow artist Peter McGough has produced a body of painting, photography, sculpture and film that uses historical rather than modern processes in its production – as well as mixing historical eras to 'destroy the linear time system'. My personal favourite is a large painting showing a Victorian garden party against a primeval backdrop of dinosaurs and smouldering volcanoes.

Freezing time

The owner of the biggest railroad company in the US and racehorse enthusiast Leland Stanford was curious about how horses trot and wanted to know if all four feet leave the ground during the action. To find out, he recruited the photographer Eadweard Muybridge to try to capture the horse's motion in a brand-new way. In 1878, Muybridge set up twenty-four trip wires across a racetrack – capturing the motions of a galloping horse. His photographs did indeed show the horse with all four feet off the ground. He took many such series of pictures, freezing time to demonstrate the minutiae of movement. And when shown in rapid succession through a projector, we had our first 'movie'.

Leaping forward to today and experiments in freezing time have become rather more sophisticated. Harvard physicist Lene Vestergaard Hau has been conducting experiments that may pave the way for a new form of time travel – a non-human kind anyway.

Hau heats room-temperature sodium so that its atoms vibrate faster and faster. At around 350°C the atoms form a vapour. Then she forces the atoms through a pinhole and hits them with a laser beam which slows them down. This traps the atoms in an 'optical molasses' – slowing them down until they are ultimately frozen using an electromagnet. At this point, 5 to 10 million atoms are suspended in a tiny cloud, colder than any known temperature and creating a totally new state of matter. Vestergaard Hau then shoots a laser beam of light into this cold atom cloud. Consequently the light is slowed down from 186,000 miles per second to just 15 miles per hour. Once the light passes through the atom cloud it speeds up again.

Light can be slowed further and can even be stopped as if frozen in a block of ice. Not only that but Dr Hau can stop the light in one part of space and revive it in a totally different location. All the information about the light is imprinted in the atoms, creating a physical matter copy. This light can be stored indefinitely for later reactivation, thus the moment of the light is frozen in time.

Time travellers

After all that science it's time for a little science fiction. Below are my top-ten time travellers from popular culture.

10. BILL AND TED

These two guitar-playing, Californian flakes are visited by a man from a future utopia (where they are worshipped as gods) in order to help them pass a critical history test by travelling to different eras.

9. BUCK ROGERS

He started off in the 1920s and first made it onto TV in the 1950s, but the late '70s Buck Rogers is one of the most memorable time travellers around – for his ultra-tight catsuits if nothing else. An air force pilot in the year 1987, unconscious and set adrift in space for 504 years, Buck Rogers wakes up in the twenty-fifth century where he finds himself helping to defend Earth from the evil planet Draconia, with the assistance of comedy robot Twiki, and computer brain Dr Theopolis. Vintage.

8. SUPERMAN

In the first of the *Superman* films, starring Christopher Reeve (1978), we see Superman turn back time (literally) to save the woman he loves. Apparently this can be done by flying around the Earth backwards at high speed until you reverse its rotation and, therefore, time. FYI.

7. EBENEZER SCROOGE

In at seven we have everyone's favourite miser from everyone's favourite seasonal tale, *A Christmas Carol* by Charles Dickens. Scrooge leaps between past, present and future with the help of some Christmas 'ghosts' to learn lessons about generosity and love.

6. SAM BECKETT

Physicist builds time machine. Physicist tests out time machine and experiment goes pear-shaped. Physicist ends up inhabiting the bodies of men and women who lived during his lifetime to help 'put right what once went wrong' – before leaping into the next body. Physicist has holographic friend who provides him with historical data about the situations he's in. I give you Sam Beckett, lead of the gloriously implausible *Quantum Leap* (1989–93).

5. GEORGE TAYLOR

Played by Charlton Heston in the first of the *Planet of the Apes* (1968) films, George Taylor is an astronaut who takes a wrong turn and ends up propelled into the future – to find that Earth is now inhabited by intelligent, if rather bloody-minded, talking apes.

4. MARTY MCFLY

The hero of a generation, skate-boarding teenager Marty McFly of *Back to the Future* (1985) is propelled back to 1955 when trying to escape from Libyan terrorists in a time-travelling car (as you do). There he accidentally ruins the moment when his parents first meet, jeopardizing his very existence – and has to get them together in a race against the clock to get back to his own reality in 1985. In the second and third films of the franchise, Marty finds himself coming face-to-face with his future self, in a dystopic present of his own creation, and back in the Wild West.

3. THE TERMINATOR

When Arnold Schwarzenegger said 'I'll be back', he really meant it – starring in the first three films of the franchise about a cyborg killer sent from the future to the past/present to variously do away with or protect the mother of future rebel leader John Connor, then John Connor himself. Crucially, all time travel is conducted nude.

2. DOCTOR WHO

Not just a time traveller, but a Time Lord, the Doctor has been travelling through time and space in his blue police box getting into all manner of adventures since 1963. One of the longest-running TV franchises, *Doctor Who* has enchanted generations and is considered to be the most successful sci-fi series of all time.

1. THE TIME TRAVELLER

This gentleman inventor from Richmond in Surrey, England, is the central character of H. G. Wells' groundbreaking science-fiction novella *The Time Machine* (1895). The book is considered to have popularized the concept of time travel and the very term 'time machine' was coined in its pages. Testing out his new invention, the Time Traveller journeys to 802,701 CE where he encounters a race of people called the Eloi, whose conquering of technology has made them lazy, undisciplined and ultimately apathetic. Perhaps with time H. G. Wells will be seen as something of a prophet, the comparisons between the futuristic Eloi and our modern couch-potato culture are uncanny.

Time-Travel Tip
Open up a wormhole using negative energy . . . and see where it takes you

OK – so this is a little more demanding than my other tips. And chances are, if you're reading this book you're not an experimental physicist. So my advice to you is seek one out and make them your new best friend. Preferably one researching the possibility of opening wormholes using negative energy.

This area is very much in the theoretical phase – a wormhole has never been found – but who knows what might happen in the next few years? Physicists including Stephen Hawking certainly believe that they are real.

As you'll read in the next chapter, wormholes are thought to be 'shortcuts' through space and time, potentially transporting us, well, who knows where? That's if they don't close and crush us first, of course. To avoid being crushed you'd need a really fast vehicle. So far the fastest manned vehicle in history was *Apollo 10* at 25,000 mph. To travel in time through a wormhole, you'll need one that goes 2,000 times faster than that. Easy-peasy.

7
Space–time

Warping time

In the last chapter we touched on wormholes, tiny invisible tears in time and space, which could be portals or shortcuts to other ages and places. At their most basic, wormholes are thought to be bridges between two points in space–time. According to Stephen Hawking they are plentiful, but so small that we cannot detect them. Yet.

Wormholes crop up a lot in science fiction as they potentially allow interstellar travel within human time scales. Entering a wormhole can shave millennia off your journey time. The much-revered astrophysicist, astronomer and author Carl

Sagan (1934–1996) used wormholes as a travelling device in his novel *Contact* – in which a crew of humans make a journey to the centre of the Milky Way. Arthur C. Clarke and Stephen Baxter used wormholes for faster-than-light communication in their co-authored 2000 novel *The Light of Other Days*. And, of course, the latter-day crews of the *Star Trek* franchise frequently plunge into wormholes.

Warp speed, Mr Sulu

Wormholes aside, hyperdrives, warp drives and other such cunning inventions are the preferred methods of faster-than-light travel in science fiction. Though in a fantastical instance of life imitating art, some physicists are now saying that the warp drive idea may not be that far-fetched.

In 1994, Mexican physicist Miguel Alcubierre suggested that a real-life warp drive might be possible, though subsequent calculations have found that such a device would require prohibitive amounts of energy. Now physicists say that adjustments can be made to the proposed warp drive that would allow it to run on significantly less energy. And NASA is reportedly starting to look at the idea seriously and is conducting experiments with a mini warp drive in their laboratory at the Johnson Space Center, where they are trying to 'perturb space–time by one part in 10 million', according to Harold White who is leading the research.

A large-scale, functioning warp drive would involve a football-shaped spacecraft with a large ring encircling it. This ring would cause space–time to warp around the craft, creating a region of contracted space in front of it and expanded space behind. Meanwhile, the craft would stay inside a 'bubble' of space–time that wasn't being warped.

If humans are ever to travel truly great distances, we need to pursue such outlandish ideas in order to beat the speed of light (see below). The biggest stumbling block to exploring the wider universe is time – and the short amount of it we have to live.

Light and dark

Light travels at around 186,000 miles per second, or 671 million mph. If you cast your mind back to the section about instant messaging in the previous chapter, you'll recall that the first telegraphs travelled at around 11 million mph, taking about a quarter of a second. Well, light travels sixty-one times faster than that. The light from the Moon takes 1.3 seconds to reach us, and 8 seconds from the Sun, and four years from our next nearest star Proxima Centauri – so the light we see from it is already four years old. While we can travel faster than the speed of sound, travelling at the speed of light, let alone faster than it, is a distant dream. Unless NASA invents that warp drive, that is.

As previously mentioned, time slows down when it travels – so if we could get close to travelling at the speed of light we would age at a slower rate than the journey takes in time measured outside of the travelling craft. It is estimated that someone travelling at 99 per cent of the speed of light will age just one year in a seven-year-long journey.

Black holes

Black holes are places where gravity is so extreme that it overwhelms all other forces. Once inside, nothing can escape a black hole's gravity, not even light. Black holes are not theoretical entities. We know they exist.

Black holes are created when an object, such as a star, becomes unable to withstand the compressing force of its gravity – and the bigger the object the more gravity it has. When massive stars collapse, it is expected that they become black holes. Our Earth and Sun are too small to become black holes, but the wider universe is littered with billions of them. There is a 'supermassive' black hole at the core of our Milky Way galaxy.

Black holes do not emit any detectable light. However, astronomers can still find them. They do this by measuring visible light, X-rays and radio waves that are emitted by materials in proximity to a black hole. One way of identifying the location of black holes is by observing gas in space. If it is orbiting a black hole it tends to get very hot because of friction and then starts to emit X-rays and radio waves making the gas exceptionally bright, which can be seen using X-ray or radio telescopes. We can also detect material falling into black holes or being attracted by them.

A white hole is a hypothetical region of space–time, which is the opposite of a black hole. A white hole cannot be entered from the outside, and instead of pulling matter inside it pushes it out – matter and light.

Light years away . . .

We've all heard the expression and we know that a light year involves a very great distance indeed. But just how long is it? And how much time (as we know it) does it take to travel one?

Well, the 'simple' definition is that a light year is the distance that light travels in a vacuum during one Julian year (that's 365.25 days of 86,400 seconds each). That distance is calculated at 10 trillion kilometres (or 6 trillion miles).

This is obviously rather hard to get into perspective. If our Earth's circumference at the equator is just 24,901 miles (40,075 km), then a light year is equivalent to circumnavigating the equator 249.5 million times in a year. Or think about the distance between the Earth and Mars. At their most recent closest point in 2003, the planets were 56 million km from each other (the closest they've been in 50,000 years). That distance is only a small fraction of a light year, but in August 2012 when the Mars Science Laboratory named *Curiosity* was launched, the distance was around 100 million km and it took seven and a half months to reach the planet, yet it only takes light from Mars a few seconds to reach Earth. Is this helping with perspective?

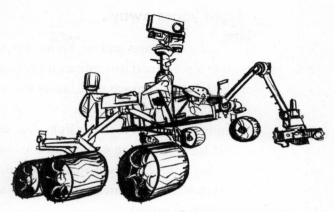

The Mars Science Laboratory, aka Curiosity

We measure in light years because we need a massive unit to make vast interstellar distances comprehensible. Our Milky Way galaxy is approximately 100,000 to 120,000 light years in diameter and contains between 200 and 400 billion stars.

The more we learn about the wider universe the larger the units of measurement we require. A trip to Mars seems like a walk in the park compared to travelling the breadth of a light year. Never mind the distances involved in parsecs (3.26 light years) or kilolight years (307 parsecs) or megalight years (307 kiloparsecs) or gigalight years (about 307 megaparsecs).

189

The ever-expanding universe

Now we're into the big numbers it's time to cast your mind back to the opening pages of this book. There we cast a cursory glance at the origins of our universe – the so-called Big Bang, when the universe started expanding from a tiny, dense and hot state. This event has been dated to between 13.5 and 13.75 billion years ago and the universe's expansion continues apace.

Recent data from NASA's Spitzer Space Telescope's observations of distant supernovae shows that the universe is expanding at a rate of 74.3 km per second per megaparsec (around 3 million light years) and it's speeding up.

We don't know why it's speeding up but whatever is causing it is currently being called 'dark energy'. Things we don't understand tend to be referred to as 'dark'. Dark matter is what scientists think makes up the bulk of the universe – but it can neither be seen nor detected directly with our current technologies. Over 80 per cent of our universe is believed to be comprised of this mystery material.

It is hypothesized that the continued expansion of the universe will lead to a 'big rip' – when the matter of the universe will be torn apart. Life on Earth, however, will be long over by then. It is thought that we have around 5 billion years before the Sun swallows our Earth up and burns it to a crisp.

The multiverse

The term 'multiverse' was coined by the American philosopher and psychologist William James in 1895 and refers to the hypothetical set of multiple possible universes (parallel universes/dimensions). Within the multiverse is everything that exists and everything that can exist. As appealing (or appalling) as this notion might sound, there is absolutely no proof for it and no way of testing it either.

Writing in the *New York Times* in 2003, cosmologist Paul Davies slings the worst kind of mud at the hypothesis, comparing it to religion: '. . . all cosmologists accept that there are some regions of the universe that lie beyond the reach of our telescopes, but somewhere on the slippery slope between that and the idea that there are an infinite number of universes, credibility reaches a limit. As one slips down that slope, more and more must be accepted on faith, and less and less is open to scientific verification. Extreme multiverse explanations are therefore reminiscent of theological discussions. Indeed, invoking an infinite number of unseen universes to explain the unusual features of the one we do see is just as ad hoc as invoking an unseen Creator. The multiverse theory may be dressed up in scientific language, but in essence it requires the same leap of faith.'

Parallel dimensions in popular culture

Fiction writers have been very willing to take the leap of faith required to incorporate parallel dimensions into their stories – and all the lovely paradoxes they open up. Indeed, the idea of another world parallel to our own is found in ancient tales, too – heaven and hell and their variations are parallel places. And mythic creatures tend not to roam our material world but to have access to another underworld.

Famous literary examples include *The Chronicles of Narnia* series (1950–6) by C. S. Lewis and *His Dark Materials* (1995–2000) by Philip Pullman, in which two children wander through multiple worlds, opening and closing windows between them.

Probably the most famous alternate universe portrayed on screen is Oz in the 1939 film *The Wizard of Oz*. But my personal favourite alternate-reality tale is not a science-fiction fable but rather the homely Christmas story *It's a Wonderful Life* (1946), in which the protagonist George Bailey gets to visit the hometown he has come to bitterly resent as it would have been had he never been born. He finds it a bleak and dangerous place, full of people whose lives have been stunted by his absence.

Time-Travel Tip
Get suspended

Suspended animation is still the stuff of science fiction – slowing the body's system right down into a deep stasis from which it can be reawakened unaffected by the ageing process. The best option available right now is cryonic freezing – that is, preserving your deceased, rather than live, body on ice in the hope that with advances in science it'll be possible for you to be raised from the dead to live in a hyper-advanced future.

You'll be in rather interesting company on resurrection day. There'll be James Bedford (1893–1967), a psychology professor at the University of California, who was the first man to be cryonically preserved by the Life Extension Society. There'll also be the mathematician Thomas K. Donaldson (1944–2006), computer-game designer Gregory Yob (1945–2005) and FM-2030 (1930–2000), an Iranian 'transhumanist' philosopher and writer, who'll definitely have the right kind of name in the future. Contrary to popular myth, Walt Disney will not be there: he was in fact cremated, not frozen.

8
Thinking Time

The time of our lives

Our bodies have their own internal clocks that keep them running within their own time frame – and we all experience time differently, at different times.

Subjective time

'When a man sits with a pretty woman for an hour it seems like a minute. But let him sit on a hot stove for a minute and it's longer than any hour. That's relativity.' – Albert Einstein (1879–1955).

As the Einstein quote suggests, time *feels* different depending on how we're spending it. A basic rule of thumb is that enjoyable experiences seem to pass quickly, unpleasant ones more slowly. In that way our experience of time is subjective – and determined by our life experiences and expectations of past, present and future (though expert on all things spiritual, Eckhard Tolle, says nothing ever happened in the past, nor will it happen in the future – everything is now).

For some, tasks performed in their first few days at work will feel laborious and long, and then feel shorter when they have grown accustomed to them. For other people the reverse is true – even if the speed at which the tasks have been performed has been consistent.

The older one gets, one can feel that time passes more quickly – this is because many of our experiences are familiar and repeated. But cast your mind back to the long summers of your childhood – when six weeks could feel like an eternity as everything was new and exciting. In extreme or dangerous situations it can feel like time slows down, indeed, that it plays out in slow motion. And for people in prison, days drag and merge into each other because there is so little to differentiate between them.

The pace or speed at which we live depends of a great number of factors – where we live: village, town, city, country; what job we do; what hobbies we have; who our friends are, etc., etc., etc. The pace at which a trader on the New York Stock Exchange lives is rather different to that of a smallholder farmer in Kansas – though they may well keep similar hours (as we've seen in Chapter 6, money moves pretty fast these days).

The pace of life in the northern hemisphere is generally considered to be much faster than in the global South – with Switzerland and Germany singled out as the countries where the pace of life is fastest.

Biological clocks and circadian rhythms

A healthy man's heart beats around 60 times per minute throughout his adult life, and a woman's just a little faster. We breathe at pretty consistent rates too, slowing down the older we get: a newborn baby can take up to 60 breaths per minute, but an adult at rest will likely take no more than 14 to 18.

Our digestive processes and energy requirements ensure we feel hungry and need to eat at regular intervals. These are the most obviously regulated processes in our average day – but many other processes – intricate and time-dependent – are going on, collectively known as 'circadian rhythms'.

Most plants and animals in the world live to their own circadian rhythms, which largely follow a pattern dictated by hours light and dark – connecting us with our Sun. The circadian rhythm in humans is controlled by the tiny 'suprachiasmatic nucleus' in our brains. Situated on the brain's midline, behind the bridge of your nose, this nucleus is the master clock of our body. There are other 'peripheral oscillators' in our bodies too, which operate independently of the master clock and are found in the lungs, liver, pancreas and skin, and other systems.

Humans are monophasic sleepers – that is, we sleep by night and wake by day. Polyphasic sleepers indulge in multiple rest-activity cycles during a 24-hour period. It is believed that our earlier forebears were polyphasic sleepers, becoming monophasic around 70,000 to 40,000 BCE. Our circadian clocks follow this monophasic pattern.

Humans keeping regular hours will be most alert around 10 a.m. At around 2.30 p.m. our coordination is at its optimum, at 3 p.m. our reaction time is fastest. At 5 p.m. we experience our best cardiovascular efficiency and muscle strength.

At 6.30 p.m. our blood pressure is highest and at 7 p.m. our body temperature at its highest. By 9 p.m. we begin to secrete melatonin (which causes drowsiness and lowers the body temperature). Melatonin secretion decreases with age, which is why adults require less sleep than children. At 10.30 p.m. our bowel movements are suppressed. We are in our deepest slumber at 2 a.m. and lowest body temperature at 4.30 a.m., and melatonin

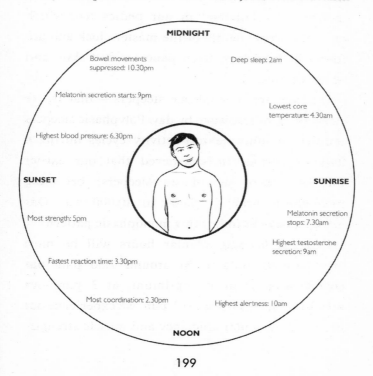

MIDNIGHT

Bowel movements
suppressed: 10.30pm

Deep sleep: 2am

Melatonin secretion starts: 9pm

Lowest core
temperature: 4.30am

Highest blood pressure: 6.30pm

SUNSET

SUNRISE

Most strength: 5pm

Melatonin secretion
stops: 7.30am

Highest testosterone
secretion: 9am

Fastest reaction time: 3.30pm

Most coordination: 2.30pm

Highest alertness: 10am

NOON

secretion stops around 7.30 a.m. as wakefulness approaches. Bowel movements commence from 8.30 a.m., with testosterone secretion reaching its highest levels at 9 a.m., and highest alertness returning again at approximately 10 a.m.

These rhythms can vary depending on the hours we keep and exposure to the Sun depending on where we live, or indeed the time of year. If we travel into different time zones and upset our internal circadian clocks, we can experience jet lag – and we need to sleep to compensate for the time difference experienced by our bodies. Sleeping on a long journey is one way of fooling your body that it has had its expected night's sleep when it arrives in a new time zone. Many people who work through the night and sleep in the day can never fully adjust to this pattern – especially as melatonin tends to be secreted at night regardless of the hours we sleep and wake.

Women have an additional 'clock' in the menstrual cycle – which comes once every twenty-eight days between a woman's teenage years and the midlife menopause.

The 28-hour day

In the 1930s, sleep researcher Nathaniel Kleitman conducted an elaborate experiment with his colleague Bruce Richardson. For thirty-two days the two lived in the Mammoth Cave in Kentucky, disrupting their circadian clocks by depriving themselves of sunlight. In addition to that, they adjusted the length of their day – living as though it was 28 rather than 24 hours long – creating a new week of six rather than seven days. They lived in a regimented way – eating, exercising and sleeping at regular times. They slept for 9 hours and were awake for 19. At forty-three years of age, Kleitman struggled to adapt to the new 28-hour, six-day week, but the younger Richardson fared better – but their results were ultimately inconclusive. Kleitman is also credited with 'discovering' Rapid Eye Movement (REM) linking dreaming and brain activity.

Accelerated ageing

Progeroid syndromes (PS) are rare genetic disorders that produce symptoms that mimic ageing. People suffering these syndromes can appear older than their actual, chronological age – and are likely to have a reduced lifespan. Werner syndrome and Hutchinson-Gilford progeria syndrome are the two most widely studied of these disorders as their effects most resemble natural ageing. The global incidence rate of Werner syndrome is one in 100,000.

People with the disorder grow normally until puberty but do not experience the expected adolescent growth spurt. Instead they exhibit a combination of growth retardation and premature ageing. They remain short, their hair grays prematurely or falls out, and their skin wrinkles. They can also experience skin atrophy, lesions, cataracts and severe ulcerations among other extreme and difficult symptoms. People afflicted with this disorder seldom live past 50 and die chiefly of cardiovascular disease or cancers.

Mating, migrating and hibernating

The behaviour of many mammals, fish and birds is inextricably linked to the seasons. Mating, migration and patterns of hibernation are all governed by the time of year and changes in the weather. Many species of birds fly south for the winter and fish such as the Atlantic salmon traverse vast distances from river to sea and back again to spawn in the streams they were born in.

To hibernate, bodies slow right down – body temperatures plummet, breathing slows to bare necessity, and heart and metabolic rates go to minimum-required function. In cold temperatures, when food is scarce, hibernators conserve energy until they can feed again. Hibernation can last days, weeks or months depending on the species. Rodents such as ground squirrels, marmots and dormice, the European hedgehog and some marsupials and primates are 'obligate' hibernators – that is, they enter hibernation annually regardless of the temperature or access to food.

Bears are among the most efficient hibernators. They rely on metabolic suppression rather than decreased body temperature to save energy during the coldest winter months and are able to recycle

their proteins and urine. They can go without
'going' for months.

Humans are one of the few creatures on the
planet whose mating patterns are not dictated by
the seasons. Similarly we do not hibernate, but back
in our hunter-gatherer days we certainly migrated,
following the patterns of our prey at different
seasons. And there are still some nomadic tribal
people on the planet, living their lives along ancient
routes to an annual cycle.

Literary clocks

The clock has been used as a sinister plot device and metaphor in many classic tales.

'It was when I stood before her . . . that I took note of the surrounding objects in detail, and saw that her watch had stopped at 20 minutes to 9, and that a clock in the room had stopped at 20 minutes to 9.' In Charles Dickens' *Great Expectations*, the stopped clock represented the life of the eery Miss Havisham, frozen at the point that she learned that her fiancé had betrayed her on the morning of their wedding. The great clock outside the house was stopped at the same time too — as the lady herself sat in darkness, still in her wedding dress, and determined to punish the male sex for the wrongs done to her.

In her mystery novel, *The Clocks*, author Agatha Christie uses timekeepers as an elaborate plot device. When typist Sheila Webb arrives for an appointment at a house belonging to a blind lady, she finds a man lying dead in a room containing six clocks, four of which have been stopped at 4:13. Investigator extraordinaire Hercule Poirot must solve the mystery of the clocks to identify the man's killer.

In James Thurber's fantasy novel, *The Thirteen Clocks*, the eponymous timekeepers of the creepily named Coffin Castle have all been stopped at ten to five and as a consequence the megalomaniac Duke of the castle is convinced that he has conquered time. But when Prince Zorn arrives to win the hand of the Duke's niece Saralinda, their love and her great beauty make the clocks tick back to life and chime the hour of five. The couple flee and the wicked Duke gets his comeuppance. A cautionary tale for anyone who believes they can beat time's passage.

How long have we got?

For humans, how long you live depends very much on where you were born and your socio-economic circumstances. In countries generally defined as 'Western', Japan has the longest life expectancy (around 82 to 83), followed closely by Switzerland and Hong Kong (around 81 to 82). Canada, Australia, Israel and various affluent European countries including the UK, are clustered close together around the 80 bracket, while the US, where the most money is spent on individual healthcare, scores a relatively low 77.97. It is worth noting that these figures are from the UN, and considerably more generous than the World Health Organization, which scores US life expectancy from birth at 75.9 for example, while the *CIA World Factbook* gives it a generous 78.37.

According to the UN, the global average life expectancy at birth is 67.2 years (65.71 years for males and 70.14 years for females), which is pretty good considering it hovered around the 30 mark from the Bronze Age to the early twentieth century for the man in the street – and a huge number of children never made it past infancy.

Consider again this global average of 67.2 years against the poorest-performing Western countries at 76 to 78 years. There's a pretty grim reason for that ten-year disparity – and most of the countries with the lowest life expectancy are on the continent of Africa (between early 40s and late 50s), with the notable exception of Afghanistan which currently has an average life expectancy in the mid-40s.

We have a lot more time in the West. So when you're feeling stressed and musing on how little time there is to get the things you want to do done, just think of those fifty years you have on the unfortunate man from Swaziland, whom the CIA suggests might not see his thirty-second birthday.

Expressing time

In the course of writing this book I've become acutely conscious of how many expressions and phrases relate to time, as well as just how often we use the word 'time' in simple, everyday speech.

Time heals all wounds, it flies when you're having fun, it runs out on us, there's no time like the present, unless what you're doing constitutes bad timing. When things are running smoothly they're like clockwork, though it's best not to wait till the last minute or the eleventh hour or to just keep things ticking over. Saying that, it's better late than never or at the very least in the nick of time. Prisoners 'do time' and have time on their hands. Time and again, and time after time, a stitch in time saves nine.

Time to philosophize

Time and space have long fascinated our greatest thinkers. For example, do they exist independently of our minds, and do time, space and the mind exist independently of each other? Do times other than now exist concurrently with the now?

Saint Augustine of Hippo (354–430 CE) summed up the difficulty in defining and expressing time in his *Confessions*: 'If no one asks me, I know; if I seek to explain, I do not.' To him, time could only be explained by what it is not; saying what it is was another issue entirely.

How long we, and our planet, have been in existence influences our understanding of time. This book, for example, has a defined beginning point – somewhere between 13.5 and 13.75 billion years from the birth of our universe, and 4.54 billion years since the birth of our planet. But to ancient Greek philosophers there was no beginning, only an infinite impenetrable past. We've seen that later creation beliefs influenced our sense of the Earth's age – with Abrahamic religions dating our beginning to around 6,000 years ago. This was very welcome to believers as the infinite is so hard to grasp, as is nothingness and the absence of time.

Chronology and history are important to our sense of identity, but what about the nature of how we experience time and space?

Get real

Early realist philosophers believed that time and space existed separate from the human mind. Our minds are merely processors, interacting with and making sense of these external forces. Isaac Newton (1642–1727) believed that time was absolute – that there's a cosmic clock created by God that sits outside the universe and that space is the stage upon which everything happens. In his conception we have no control over time, we just have our subjective interpretations of its passage. His chief detractor was Gottfried Leibniz (1646–1716), who in the early eighteenth century challenged Newton, arguing that his 'absolutist' position did not take into consideration God's plan – there must be a specific reason why God invented time and space, if you will.

The hugely influential Immanuel Kant (1724–1804) said that the notions of time and space allow us to comprehend and coordinate our senses – but that neither have substance in themselves. To Kant, such notions are a framework we use to structure our experiences. For our purposes time and space are 'empirically real' (that is, observable), in that we use them to measure objects and experiences.

To Albert Einstein (1879–1955) time was not absolute. He thought of it as woven into the fabric of the universe and therein created. He also thought of it as something we can influence and control, as supported by the findings of many of today's physicists.

Perceiving time

Earlier we touched on the way we experience time as subjective, largely in relation to speed and pace of life. Now it's time to consider how we perceive and process it. American philosopher and psychologist William James (1842–1910) said that to live a normal life we needed a sense of 'pastness' and that our identities are constructed largely from memory and a sense of history. But this applies to much shorter time frames – our present is constantly influenced by the immediate past and often the future – as each action and thought builds on a past one towards a future one. According to James, we live in a 'specious present', rolling time frames each

211

lasting approximately 12 seconds, and which we experience as the flow of time.

The French philosopher René Descartes (1596–1650) spoke about time being perceived as a series of instantaneous 'nows'. Similarly the contemporary spiritual teacher Eckhard Tolle (1948–) says, 'there never was a time when your life was not now'. It sounds plausible enough, but when you stop to think about it it's nigh on impossible to capture the essence of 'now'. Is now now? Or has it just past? And we know from developments in neuroscience that we don't experience or perceive things immediately, but shortly after they have occurred. It takes time for your brain to communicate information to the relevant body part, for example. It may only be half a second – but when we're talking about 'now' it all counts.

Time superstitions

Superstitions around time often relate to clocks — and may well spring from the way in which such technology encroached upon and ultimately regulated lives over the last few hundred years.

The stopped clock is perhaps the most universally known. If a clock that has stopped suddenly starts working again or chimes, it heralds a death in the family. It is also considered bad luck to stop a clock in a room in which someone has just died. These days, with clocks present in so many devices, that's quite a task.

Dreaming of clocks is meant to be prescient of an upcoming journey, while turning the hands on a clock backwards is bad luck. This likely comes from the fact that forcing the hands of older clocks with a chiming mechanism backwards can damage their workings.

In these modern times we can now predict the date of our deaths on the Internet. It is somewhat more 'scientific' than worrying about stopped clocks and takes one's date of birth, weight and body mass index into consideration. Check yours out at www.deathclock.com. I've got till October 2050 if I don't quit smoking very soon, and July 2057 if I do. Watch this space.

Time-Travel Tip
Hang out with an Amazonian tribe

Now I'm not advocating that you contact an 'uncontacted' tribe – they're best left alone. But by journeying to the Amazon, or indeed other parts of the world where the indigenous people continue to live their lives as they have been lived for millennia, it's possible to step not so much into the past, but out of time. Or out of our time at least.

Pitch a tent with the wandering Bedouins of the Middle East, meet the Maasai of East Africa or pay a respectful visit to the Amondawa in Brazil, and you will see lives lived in a different time to your own – at a completely different pace, with different rules, and different perceptions of age, past and future.

References

Books

Bryson, Bill *A Short History of Nearly Everything* (Black Swan, 2003)

Callender, Craig & Edney, Ralph *Time: A Graphic Guide* (Icon Books, 2010)

Franks, Adam *About Time* (Oneworld, 2011)

Griffiths, Jay *A Sideways Look at Time* (Tarcher, 2004)

Hart-Davis, Adam *The Book of Time* (Mitchell Beazley, 2011)

Holford-Strevens, Leofranc *The History of Time* (Oxford University Press, 2005)

Kieran, Dan *The Idle Traveller: The Art of Slow Travel* (Automobile Association, 2012)

Wilkinson, Richard & Pickett, Kate *The Spirit Level: Why Equality is Better for Everyone* (Penguin, 2010)

Articles

Davies, Paul *A Brief History of the Multiverse* (*New York Times*, 12 April 2003)

Hawking, Stephen *How to Build a Time Machine* (*Daily Mail*, 27 April 2010)

Jeffries, Stuart *The history of sleep science* (*Guardian*, 29 January 2011)

Palmer, Jason *Amondawa tribe lacks abstract idea of time, study says* (BBC News, 20 May 2011)

Radio/Podcasts

BBC Radio 4 *In Our Time: The Age of the Universe*, broadcast March 2011

BBC Radio 4 *In Our Time: The Physics of Time*, broadcast December 2008

RadioLab.org *Speed* Season 11, Episode 4, broadcast Feb 2013

RadioLab.org *Time* Season 1, Episode 4, broadcast May 2007

RadioLab.org *Beyond time* Season 1, Episode 5, July 2007

Index